As they approached their hiding place the air was full of the sounds of screaming rats, all thirsty for the blood of the strangers. Once, Mawk looked back and almost swooned when he saw the savage faces coming up behind him.

The rats had painted their features with dye, circling the eyes, running bars down the nose and cheeks, so that their sharp-toothed mouths appeared more fierce than ever. They warbled with their tongues, setting up such a racket around the weasels it was enough to put a bear into a panic. There seemed to be thousands, *tens* of thousands of rats on the marshes. Mawk could smell their musty coats, hear them splashing through the murky, shallow waters. He was sure he was going to die.

'It was here,' he cried frantically, tearing away at the river bank. 'We left the raft here. Oh Gawd, it's gone. We're going to be killed.'

'Lucky if we do,' gasped Scirf, the dung-watcher not used to such exercise and out of breath. 'More like we'll be tortured until we *beg* to be killed.'

'Into the water,' snapped Sylver. 'Swim for it. Don't look back, Mawk. Just go.'

By the same author

GARRY KILWORTH

THUNDER OAK

Book One of
The Welkin Weasels

CORGI BOOKS

BOOK ONE OF THE WELKIN WEASELS:
THUNDER OAK
A Corgi Book : 0 552 54546 5

First publication in Great Britain

PRINTING HISTORY
Corgi edition published 1997

3 5 7 9 10 8 6 4 2

Set in 11/12pt Palatino
by Phoenix Typesetting, Ilkley, West Yorkshire

Corgi Books are published by Transworld Publishers,
61–63 Uxbridge Road, London W5 5SA,
a division of The Random House Group Ltd,
in Australia by Random House Australia (Pty) Ltd,
20 Alfred Street, Milsons Point, Sydney, NSW 2061, Australia,
in New Zealand by Random House New Zealand Ltd,
18 Poland Road, Glenfield, Auckland 10, New Zealand
and in South Africa by Random House (Pty) Ltd,
Endulini, 5a Jubilee Road, Parktown 2193, South Africa.

Printed and bound in Great Britain by
Cox & Wyman Ltd, Reading, Berkshire.

Chapter One

Thistle Hall was a low sprawling building surrounded by tangled trees. It was in this dark manor, with its higgledy-piggledy chimneys and misshapen windows, that the old stoat Lord Haukin lived. Animals who used the worn footpath to the nearby priory often glanced at this ancient dwelling. It was not unusual for them to see the bent shape of Lord Haukin moving behind one of the windows, his eyes fixed upon some document or book. The thane of Thistle Hall was renowned for his learning.

Sylver, a young woodland creature and leader of a band of outlawed weasels, now approached this great manor house situated in County Elleswhere. When he reached the massive door, originally made for humans to open and close, he found a smaller door at the bottom. This door had been cut for weasels and stoats, since they could not reach the great iron handle high above them. In any case they would not have had the strength to open the huge and heavy nail-studded oaken door.

Sylver knocked boldly and waited for an answer.

'Enter,' called a frail voice. 'Come right in.'

Sylver opened the door and stepped into a large

hall. Firelight coming from a huge inglenook flickered on steel weapons decorating the stone walls. There were swords, spears, shields and crossed daggers. None of these enormous weapons was of any use to Sylver or his kind. Weasels used darts and slingshots when it was necessary to defend themselves against stoat attack.

The weasels and stoats of Welkin had taken over all human possessions long before Sylver was born, and now regarded them as their own. The humans themselves had gone, no-one knew where, and animals ruled themselves. There was strife in Welkin, for some stoats had become greedy for power. In general most weasels were regarded as serfs, subject to the whims of feudal stoats, who used them as voleherds and labourers.

Lord Haukin was one of the kinder stoats, who recognized the injustice of the system.

On a long table whose great legs had been sawn down to twenty centimetres were dozens of books. These were man-sized books, open at various pages. Lord Haukin was bent over one of these huge volumes, peering with short-sighted eyes at the words upon the page. He looked up at last. 'Ah, young Sylver,' he said. 'Glad you could come.'

The weasel nodded respectfully. 'Lord Haukin. You have something you wish to tell me?'

'Yes, yes,' murmured the fussy old stoat, wrinkling his brow. 'Now, what was it?'

At that moment four weasel servants entered the room, carrying a book between them. They all bore the crest of Lord Haukin on silver collars around their throats. The one on the front right-paw corner spoke. 'You were going to tell him about Prince Poynt,' said this weasel.

'Ah, yes, thank you, Culver, thank you. The stoat Prince Poynt, young Sylver,' said Lord Haukin severely. 'The ruler of all Welkin is . . . what is he going to do, Culver?'

Culver put down his corner of the book and raised his eyes to heaven. 'He's sending Sheriff Falshed to arrest Sylver and his band.'

'Yes, yes – that's it. You have to leave Halfmoon Wood, Sylver,' Lord Haukin cried. 'Falshed is on his way. You're to be made an example of, young weasel, for not obeying the prince. You know you're expected to hunt for the royal household, as most weasels do? You know you're supposed to supply the prince with meat for his table?'

Sylver did of course know this. All woodland weasels were expected to hunt for the prince.

Sylver and his band of wood weasels refused to hunt, tend voles or grow crops for the prince. They did not recognize bondage and were therefore constantly in danger of arrest.

Something else was troubling Sylver though. 'Prince Poynt wouldn't send the sheriff all the way down here just because we won't hunt for him. It's got to be something more than that,' he said. 'It's expensive to send soldiers all this way.'

Lord Haukin sighed. 'Yes, yes, you're right, young weasel. It's this theory of yours which has upset the prince. He doesn't like the idea of you trying to find the humans. While there are no humans in Welkin, he reigns supreme. If you find the humans and bring them back here again, why, he'll no longer be a prince – he'll just be another stoat, won't he?'

It was true that Sylver wanted to bring back the missing humans. From what he knew of them he did not especially *like* the human race, he much preferred wild animals, but pedlars and travellers had recently reported a serious problem.

Welkin was an island, a rather large island but an island none the less. Much of it was below sea level, protected from flood by massive dykes – sea walls – that surrounded it. These sea walls had recently begun to crumble. The animals were not capable of repairing the damage. If the humans did not return and get to work on the sea walls they might collapse, causing havoc and devastation in the land.

The natural order of things had always meant that humans, with their superior brains and thumbs, were the group who *made* things. Houses, pictures, weapons, tools, roads, gates – and dykes.

'Prince Poynt refuses to believe the sea walls are crumbling,' said Sylver. 'He just won't listen.'

Lord Haukin sighed. He was about the only stoat who was prepared to accept that the danger of flooding was terribly real. Many creatures of the field and forest refused to see a problem until it happened: they had too much to lose by bringing the humans back. Especially Prince Poynt, who lived a life of luxury and had dominion over all the beasts of Welkin. Lord Haukin himself did not want the humans back, but like Sylver he realized it was a choice between losing their new-found status as rulers of Welkin and a horrible watery death.

Weasels and stoats, badgers, ferrets, otters, pine martens and polecats, were all cousins and had taken over from the humans when those two-legged creatures had disappeared. Very quickly, however, the stoats had established themselves as the rulers and quickly put down any other creature who tried to interfere with their enslavement programme. It was not that the stoats were so numerous, but they were vicious, single-minded bullies.

Badgers were bigger, of course, but they tended to keep to themselves and continued to live in their colonies. They preferred underground networks of tunnels and chambers, rather than the houses of the humans. Pine martens and polecats lived mainly in the eastern corner of the great island. Otters had their own watery world to live in and were uninterested in power.

Ferrets were used by Prince Poynt as auxiliary soldiers, mercenaries who would do anything for a morsel of roasted rabbit. Prince Poynt had a whole battalion of blood-thirsty ferrets ready to crush any ambitious stoat who tried to take his princedom. Any uprising in Welkin was quickly put down with the prince's Royal Guard of ferrets, who obeyed only him. Prince Poynt trusted no-one, not even his own fellow stoats.

Ferrets had the taint of human about them, since they had once hunted rabbits for two-legged masters.

Sylver knew, of course, that if the humans were found and returned to Welkin, the kingdom of the animals would revert to being what it once was. The weasels and stoats would have to live in the wild again, not in human houses. They would have to eat uncooked natural food as they once did. They would become wild creatures again, instead of taking on human values and ways. He had considered all this carefully, weighed it against the possibility of a flooded Welkin, and decided there was no choice – the people had to be found and reinstated.

'So,' muttered Sylver, 'Prince Poynt is worried about a little weasel like me? Well, we'll just have to give him something to be concerned *about*, won't we?'

The kindly old stoat looked down on the smaller creature and shook his head slowly. 'Oh dear, Sylver, you're not thinking of resisting, are you? You can't fight the sheriff's stoats, you know. They'll destroy your whole band of outlaws.'

'I prefer to think of *them* as the outlaws, Lord Haukin.'

'Well, that may be, young Sylver, but the way things are, I'm afraid the laws are made by Prince Poynt.'

Sylver left Thistle Hall after thanking Lord Haukin for his warning. The weasel made his way back to his home in Halfmoon Wood, where the rest of the band was waiting for him. There was Icham, his closest male friend; Bryony, who was wise in the ways of the Earth; Wodehed, the magician; Alysoun-the-fleet, who was the fastest runner amongst the band; Dredless, the very best shot with a dart; Mawk-the-doubter, who was never sure they were doing the right thing, whatever it was; Luke, the holy weasel; and finally, Miniver, the tiny finger-weasel, who was small enough to get into the narrowest cracks and holes.

This was Sylver's group, his friends, weasels who shared with him his ideals and hopes. There were other weasels of Halfmoon Wood and surrounding villages on whom Sylver could count in an emergency, but for the most part it was this small number who worked together to try to obtain justice for all.

Sylver had a belt of darts around his waist as well as a pouch of stones for his slingshot.

He slipped silently through the grasses and dead leaves under the trees. Sunlight and shadow rippled through his fur as he travelled in a kind of wave-flowing run across the ground. Over oak and elm roots, under the arches of fallen branches, along rotten logs, in amongst herbs and toadstools, Sylver made his way. Once or twice he stopped, to stand as tall as a dandelion on his hind legs, looking for danger.

If he had been a stoat he would have stood almost twice as tall, for stoats were larger creatures, taller and more sturdy than weasels.

When he reached the glade it seemed too quiet, so Sylver called out, 'Icham? Bryony? Are you there?'

They had obviously heard him coming, heard *someone* coming, for they had gone into their shallow camouflaged holes in and around the camp. Now they emerged, tumbling joyously out of the tangled greenwood, their tails flicking.

Their leader had returned to them safe and sound.

'Well?' said Wodehed the magician. 'What did the old stoat want? The last time you went he forgot what it was he wanted to tell you.'

'Same this time,' replied Sylver. 'Culver reminded him. I think Culver has become his memory. Anyway, it was to warn us that Sheriff Falshed is on his way with a troop of stoats, to take us back to Castle Rayn. Lord Haukin thinks that

Prince Poynt is getting jittery about us wanting to bring back the humans to Welkin.'

'I don't know why,' said Bryony. 'We're no closer to finding out where they are than we ever were.'

Icham asked, 'What are we going to do? Run?'

'No,' replied Sylver thoughtfully, 'I think it's time we taught Falshed a lesson. We're going to set some traps for him and his troops. I want you all to put your thinking caps on and come up with some really good tricks.'

Mawk-the-doubter shook his head. 'I don't know. Do you think this is wise? Why don't we just retreat towards the Far Weald? Falshed won't come too far north – he's afraid of the rat hordes out on the marshes.'

'Right,' said Sylver promptly, to the astonishment of the others, 'let's go north!'

Mawk's expression showed that he was just as anxious with this decision. 'Let's not be too hasty,' he said. 'Falshed might get a surge of courage and come after us anyway.'

Dredless clicked his teeth in amusement. 'It doesn't matter what anyone says, you never think it's a good idea. Even when you come up with an idea of your own, if we say it's good, you start to doubt it. You're never happy, Mawk.'

'Someone's got to be careful,' he snapped irritably. 'Someone's got to add a note of caution.'

'That may be true,' Sylver said, 'but now let's concentrate on the task in paw. We have to come up with some good traps. Has anyone any suggestions?'

Alysoun-the-fleet said, 'I have . . .' and proceeded to outline her plan.

The gathering began according to Alysoun's scheme. Small creatures were collected in great quantities. In the meantime Miniver, whose little claws were deft enough for any task, made some hollow clay balls with walls as thin as eggshell. These she left out in the sun to bake hard. The small creatures gathered by the others were encouraged to enter the clay balls through the small holes left at the top. Each of the holes was then plugged with a rolled-up sycamore leaf, dampened to make it pliable and easy to manage.

More gathering took place in the meadow outside Halfmoon Wood. The objects picked were given to Dredless, whose accuracy with dart or slingshot was superb. He removed the smooth stones from his pouch and replaced these with the new ammunition. Next some small saplings were stripped of their leaves and bent over to form catapults.

'Right,' said Sylver, satisfied with their work, 'now all we need is the enemy to come up over that hill.'

He stared out of the edge of the wood where the rolling downs spilled away into the distance. While there was sunshine on the grasslands and meadows, in the far west was a dark brooding area where it was almost always raining. This was where Prince Poynt lived in his castle. This was the direction from which the stoats would come.

Bryony came and stood by Sylver and began staring across the landscape too. 'No wonder he's such a miserable stoat,' she said of Prince Poynt, 'living on the rainy side of Welkin. I would be too. I much prefer it here on the east, where the sun shines most of the time, don't you?'

'Too right,' said Sylver. 'I can't stand too much rain. You have to have *some* of course, or things don't grow and the streams run dry, but they've got enough water falling from the sky over there to make an inland sea.'

Wodehed came to join the pair. 'When do you plan to attack, Sylver?' he said. 'We need to co-ordinate this plan so nothing goes wrong.'

Sylver stood on his hind legs. 'See that tor on top of that hill?' he said, indicating a tall thin rock which stood like a stone sentry surveying the countryside around it. 'When Sheriff Falshed's stoats reach that stone, then we'll attack them. I want Icham, Bryony and Mawk out there, as well as myself, to act as bait. We need to draw them into the wood, so they get lost. Now, is everyone sure of what they've got to do?'

Since he received no reply to this question Sylver assumed they were sure.

The rest of the day they did their various chores in the leafy glades of the greenwood. Since the humans had gone the weasel and stoat population had increased tenfold. This meant that game was scarce, especially now that stoats had become so greedy they no longer ate to live, but lived to eat. Mice, voles, rabbits, pheasants, partridges and other game had decreased rapidly in numbers. Sylver and his band had to survive on beetles, worms, termites – anything they could get, in fact – as well as mushrooms, roots, berries and nuts.

So they had to gather their dinners and cook them. For a long time now weasels and stoats had been cooking their food. Sylver had tried to break his band of the habit, but once a creature has tasted his food cooked, he rarely goes back to it raw.

Bryony, who was a very outspoken weasel, said it would take red-hot irons to make her go back to uncooked fare.

When the afternoon sun was high in the sky a shout came from Miniver, who was acting as lookout. 'Here they come!' she cried excitedly. 'Here comes Falshed and his soldiery!'

The woodland edge stirred with tall-standing weasels as the flash of helmets in the sun was seen on the far hill.

Chapter Two

The silver helmets of the stoat soldiery glinted in the clear air. The only other armour they had on was a kind of chain mail waistcoat, which jangled like a thousand keys. In their claws they carried a variety of weaponry, from spears to swords and daggers to darts.

'That's Falshed all right,' said Dredless, as if there could be any doubt. 'Look how he walks upright all the time. I think he's forgotten how to go down on all fours.'

'Quickly, weasels, to your places,' snapped Sylver. 'Icham, Bryony and Mawk with me. Alysoun, Luke, Wodehed and Miniver on the sapling catapults. Dredless, you come up behind my group – you know what to do – just you concentrate on Falshed.'

His orders given, Sylver began to make his way towards the oncoming troop of stoats. Bryony, Mawk and Icham were close on his hind paws. Dredless came up behind them. When they were several metres from Needle Rock, the vanguard four halted. Some of them took out darts fletched with sparrow feathers or dandelion seeds, the hafts fashioned from slivers of oak weighted with sharpened-flint points. Bryony, like Dredless behind them, was preparing to use her slingshot.

Just as the troop of stoat soldiers reached Needle Rock, Sylver stood as tall as he could in the waving grasses. The sheriff could be plainly recognized by a black burn mark on his white bib-front. Sylver had put that mark there once when he had thrown a lighted brand at the chest of Falshed.

'That's far enough, Falshed!' he cried. 'Any further is at your peril!'

Sheriff Falshed, almost twice as tall as Sylver, halted his troops with a wave of his paw. A strange twist sprang to the stoat's jaw, which was faintly recognizable as amusement. His tiny red eyes were cold, however, as he regarded Sylver and the three weasels half hidden by the tall meadow grass. He in turn had immediately recognized Sylver by the white streak that ran like a lightning scar from the tip of the outlaw's nose to his left eyebrow.

'You know the penalty for resisting the soldiers of Prince Poynt?' said Falshed in a gravelly voice. 'Or do I have to enlighten you?'

'Death, I believe,' said Bryony. 'It is *death*, isn't it? That, or a jolly good twist of the tail. Or is it a tweaking of the ear? I can never remember which it is.'

Falshed blew down his nostrils in disgust. 'You will not joke, female, when you are being roasted over the coals of Prince Poynt's summer fire.'

Prince Poynt, as everyone knew, always felt cold, even on the hottest summer's day. This was perhaps due to the fact that he had set his face against the natural order of things and refused to change from his winter to summer coat. He remained in ermine all the year round: a pure white pelt with a tar tip to its tail. No other stoat

19

was now allowed to change coats, even in winter. Poynt played havoc with tradition.

It was said he felt regal in his ermine fur, but chilly as well, which was most likely a trick of the mind. Winter garb harboured winter thoughts, so they said, and Prince Poynt shivered his way through the warmest of weather.

'You are wrong, stoat!' said Bryony. 'I always tell my best jokes when I'm cosy and warm before a fire.' With that remark she let fly with a pebble from her sling, which struck a sergeant stoat on the flank.

'Attack!' screamed Falshed to his troop of stoats. 'Tear out their throats. Bring me the weasel Sylver. I want him bound in cord and dragged back to Castle Rayn.'

The stoats spread out in battle formation. With grim expressions on their faces they began to advance across the meadow. Darts filled the air like seeds on a breezy day, falling all around the four weasels. The stoats might not have been accurate throwers, but what they lacked in skill they made up for in numbers. A wren could not have flown through that cloud of darts without being hit. Bryony took a dart in the rump. Icham was wounded in the shoulder. Both missiles were removed quickly and thrown back at the foe.

Suddenly, as the line of stoats closed on the four skirmishing weasels, Sylver threw up a bright silver dart which flashed in the sunlight. This was a signal for the four woodland weasels to let loose the sapling catapults with their balls of clay.

The counter-attack had been timed precisely. The saplings were sprung. Hollow cannon balls flew through the air and burst on the ground at the feet of the oncoming stoats. Out of these shattering missiles sprayed clouds of small black dots, which covered the stoats and caused them to stop in their tracks.

'Ants!' shrieked one. 'They're filled with ants.'

The ants were enraged at being imprisoned in the hollow clay balls. They swarmed over the stoats, biting them in a thousand and one places in amongst their fur. They were like an army themselves, only an army of millions, as they poured from the broken shells of clay and swiftly covered the nearest stoats.

'Help me!' cried a beleaguered soldier. 'I'm being stung to death! I'm being eaten alive! Lord Falshed, help me!'

Alysoun, on the edge of the wild wood, called in a sweet voice, 'This way to the lake. Get rid of your ants in the water of our lovely lake. No charge on this fine summer's day.'

The harried stoats ran blindly towards her voice, eager to reach water where they could wash off the ants. Their distress was evident in their terrible cries. The ants were merciless, each tiny one of them biting a dozen times in a dozen different places under the fur of the pain-racked stoats. Fear and agony drove the stoats to desert their master, who called to them to return, telling them they would be punished for cowardice.

'Any stoat who runs away,' screamed Falshed, 'will find himself hanging by his feet from a flag-pole tonight, a feast for the barn owls. I swear if you do not come back, you lily-livered loons, I'll string up every one of you.'

His voice wailed to no heed. The poor creatures who were his soldiers could not hear him through

21

the singing of pain in their ears. They would not have obeyed him if they could, for their distress was such that they were in desperate need of water to rid them of their tormentors. They ran on towards the greenwood, into which they would disappear and get lost, since they were creatures of castle, not countryside.

Sheriff Falshed whirled on Sylver and his crew now, his expression revealing his rage. 'If I cannot get my stoats back, I shall still have your pelts,' he cried. 'Am I not a full-blooded stoat, with sinews of wire and muscles of steel? I shall tear you apart, you pathetic creatures. I shall make you pay for your audacity today on this field of battle.'

And the weasels knew he was right. Falshed was a stoat and stoats were formidable creatures, which was why they ruled the world of Welkin. Only trickery had prevented Sylver and his band from being arrested before now. It was to cunning, therefore, that Sylver turned at this moment, when the terrible shape of Sheriff Falshed was bearing down on him.

'Now, Dredless!' called the weasel.

Dredless, with his accurate slingshot, let fly one missile after another, and stopped Falshed in his tracks.

The missiles were fungi – puffballs – which burst on the sheriff's body and in his face. Inside the puffballs was a dry mustard-yellow powder which coloured his head. It went into his eyes and blinded him like pepper. Falshed stopped, sneezed, clawed at his eyes, trying to rid them of the stinging puffball dust. 'I can't see!' he shrieked. 'Where are my stoats? Help me, you fools! I'm blind.'

But the troop had now scattered in the woods, searching for the non-existent lake which Alysoun had promised them lay within the leafy trees. Some might find the stream, eventually, and others Thistle Hall, where no doubt the kindly Lord Haukin would give them refuge, but most would wander the woods until nightfall, not knowing one tree from another, nursing their poor bitten bodies and swollen limbs and feeling sorry for themselves.

'Take him,' cried Sylver. 'Bind him.'

They fell upon the blind, struggling Falshed and bound him with cords until he could no longer move. Once he was secure, Bryony ran back to the wood to fetch a container of water. This she threw into Falshed's face, washing away the puffball powder. Bryony was nothing if not compassionate. She hated to see another creature in distress, even if it was the prince's stoat.

The sheriff spluttered and spat and was at last able to open his eyes, even though they felt as if they were full of grit. He glared at the weasels as the dirty-yellow water dripped from his jowl whiskers. He said nothing, however, knowing he was in the claws of his enemies and could do nought about it but wait and see what they would do.

Mawk pushed a pole through the bonds and the stoat was carried between two of them, into the forest.

Once the band of weasels had their foe in their camp within the greenwood, Sylver could not help but crow over him. 'Well, my burnt-bibbed stoat. I thought you had come to teach us a lesson? It seems to me you will learn something, rather than teach it. I wonder what we're going to do with you? Roast you, perhaps? Or leave you tied upside down to a tree, so that the owls think you're an offering on the gallows? Or perhaps bury you up to your chin in soft earth, next to a termites' nest? What do you think? Have you a preference?'

'Drat you, Sylver,' growled the sheriff, struggling against the restraining cords, 'I'll see you roasted first.'

'Oh, I don't think so, Falshed. I give you full merit for your courage, but unfortunately you're a bit tied up at the moment, aren't you?'

'A bit short of grey matter in the head, if you ask me,' said the slim-shouldered Icham. 'Long on boldness, short on brains.'

'By heaven, you'll pay for insulting the prince's sheriff,' cried Falshed.

'Insulting or assaulting?' asked Icham. 'Are you an ass to be so ass-aulted?'

They left the hapless sheriff tied to a tree. Wodehed built a fire, for it would be cooler in the coming evening, and they would have to cook their food. While the faggots were burning, a lost stoat stumbled into the glade, still pleading for directions to the lake, and was sent on his way again, deep into the heart of the wood.

Once the band were gathered around the fire, Luke offered up prayers for their safe deliverance. 'Thank you, lord of the forest, lord of the field, for our victory today,' he intoned. 'It was a good one, if not unexpected considering how brilliant we weasels are and all that. Our leader, Sylver, would like thy blessings to fall upon him like sweet gentle rain from above, and if possible send down rocks and stones upon the heads of our enemies, Prince

Poynt and evil Flaggatis – that barbaric sorcerer exiled to the kingdom of the rats. May they feel thy wrath, O Lord, in the form of hard things falling from heaven. Amen.'

'You'll feel my teeth in your throat if I ever get out of this,' snarled Falshed from his tree.

'The point is,' said Luke, '*will* you ever get free?'

The weasels ate and sang weasel songs around the fire, recalling the good old days when they hunted through the world of humans. They drank cool water from cuckoo pints, and told stories about famous weasels of the past. They recited poetry in the old tongue, which was better for verse, being darker and richer in its tones. They made up a new poem about the battle they had fought on this day, rhyming 'gungy Falshed' with 'dunderhead'. They became cheerful, they became sad, they vowed eternal friendship with one another and swore on the blood of their grand-fathers to remain true friends.

Bryony and Icham had their wounds tended by Wodehed, who used the white flowers of the herb yarrow in a poultice to prevent infection.

Then they all fell asleep around the ashes of the fire, mellow and warm by its glowing embers.

Dawn came many hours later, creeping in a pink skin up the sky. Long after the creatures of the field were awake and busy at their daily tasks it sent its glow into the woodland, down through the leaves, onto the forest floor.

The band of outlaws woke, stumbled to the stream, drank their fill. Alysoun brought some water for the sheriff, who drank it down greedily without offering any thanks. Luke and Icham chewed on the remains of last night's stew, while

25

Mawk and Miniver went out into the fields to taste fresh green grass as an animal often will to clarify its digestive system.

Later, Dredless called for cord and staves.

'What do you want those for?' asked Falshed suspiciously, knowing they were going to make something for him. 'Are you building a cage?'

'Not a cage,' said Dredless. 'Guess again.'

'A stretcher, then, to carry me on,' said Falshed, noticing that the way they lashed the staves together made the object into a flat platform. 'Something to bear me on?'

'Something to bear you on, yes, but we ain't going to carry you,' said Icham. 'Perish the thought. If we were going to take you across land, we'd roll you all the way, have no doubts about that, my stoaty friend.'

'I am not your friend,' Falshed snarled, 'I am the prince's sheriff and you would do well to remember it.'

'We never forget it,' snapped Sylver. 'No, what we're going to do is put you on a raft and say goodbye.'

Falshed jerked his bonds. He did not like the sound of this. He hated water, almost as much as he hated Sylver. He was *terrified* of water. For one thing, he did not think he could swim. Never having tried, he was not sure, of course, but there was a firm idea in his mind that he would sink like a brick if ever out of his depth. He had no wish to test this theory. He would rather live out his life without getting even so much as the tips of his toes wet, if he could manage it.

'What are you doing to me?' he hissed. 'I *refuse* to go on a raft. I – I forbid you to put me on a raft.'

26

'Refuse? Forbid? Oh, I don't think you can attack us with evil intentions and start making demands, giving orders, old stoat,' said Sylver. 'I'm afraid we're just going to have to tie you to a post in the middle of this excellent seaworthy vessel and set you adrift down our little stream. How about that, eh?'

'You pig's orphan!' cried Falshed. 'You monster!'

'You should have thought of that, before you attacked us yesterday,' Bryony told him. 'Now you'll float down the stream and into the river. The river's quite fast at that point. It will carry you swiftly – provided you don't crash on rocks or overturn in the rapids – down to the sea. There you will be gently wafted by the current over the salt marshes to the kingdom of the rats. I'm sure they'll love to have you.'

'The rats?' groaned Falshed. 'Not the rats.'

'Only if you don't sink and drown before you reach them,' reminded Mawk-the-doubter. 'I personally doubt you'll get further than the first bend in the river.'

'I hate you all,' Falshed snarled, struggling again. 'I'll – I'll see you in green hell.'

'I'm sure you'll be there first, to greet us as we come in,' replied Wodehed.

The raft finished, the staves lashed tightly together, they fixed a pole in its centre. To this mast they securely tied the unfortunate stoat. Then the raft was carried on their many sturdy backs down to the small stream which wound its way through the greenwood.

The mossy banks of this brook were covered in primroses and forget-me-nots, with wild herbs tucked away in peaty nooks, and daisies dripping into its cool flowing waters. Rainbow trout could be seen, gliding amongst the smooth stones on the beck's bed, on their way to the river. Sticklebacks and shrimps darted from rock to rock. The roots of willows burst through the bank here and there, curving down into the stream to get at the refreshing water. Dragonflies and damselflies danced over its surface, where pond skaters boated amongst chickweed.

This enchanting scene did not interest Falshed, as he was pushed out into the current. 'I'll have your pelts flayed from your backbones,' he shrieked. 'I'll lay your ribcages bare of flesh.'

Sylver shook his head as the sheriff was swept around the first bend. 'He does go on a bit, doesn't he?' said the weasel. 'I'm not sure he's good company, even for himself.'

On this merry note, Sylver and the other weasels made their way towards Thistle Hall, to see Lord Haukin.

Chapter Three

Sheriff Falshed was terrified as the swiftly flowing stream took his raft swiftly onwards like a matchbox along a gutter full of rainwater. The raft spun round, hit snags and jammed for a few seconds, bumped into logs and did everything short of actually turning over. The stoat began feeling terribly motion-sick after only a few minutes.

There was a badger on the bank ahead, munching something unrecognizable.

'Help!' cried Falshed, with a quiver to his tone. 'Help me!'

The badger paused in his munching, screwed up his face in disgust at being interrupted in his meal, and watched the raft go swishing by with a calm expression. 'What do you want me to do?' he called as Falshed was swept further downstream. 'Jump in after you?'

'What can you expect from *badgers*,' groaned the unhappy Falshed. 'They're only interested in themselves.'

The trees rushed by on the banks of the stream as the water became frothing and white. Rapids were all around the craft. Falshed then came to a sudden halt, rattling his teeth, as the raft went aground on a shallow bed. Then another rush of

29

water from upstream lifted the raft again, re-floating it.

Around him, the forest became denser and darker, with the sunlight stabbing as spears of light. Through these penetrating beams flew startlingly blue dragonflies. A kingfisher came zipping by, its wicked beak intent on piercing a fish. Drinking deer, wary of wolves, twitched and rippled as the raft went by, wondering whether to stand or run. Falshed was certainly seeing the world, but failed to enjoy the experience.

The raft came to a dead stop again as it hit a jam of twigs and branches which completely blocked its path. The water was able to flow through the network of sticks, but the raft was well and truly held. Falshed began yelling for help again, hoping another stoat would hear him.

Instead, a fox came out of the undergrowth to see what all the fuss was about.

As the fox peered through the gloom, Falshed shut up immediately. He knew if he kept still the fox would not be able to see him, for foxes can only see moving creatures. He held his breath, his heart thumping in his chest. 'Go away,' he murmured to himself. 'Go away, you stupid creature . . .'

The coat of the fox struck red when he crossed through a sunbeam. The rest of the time he looked like a grey ghost moving through the brambles. His bright eyes searched for movement but, finding none, he slipped back into the forest again and left Falshed feeling alone but relieved.

'Thank the devil those creatures are half-blind,' said Falshed. 'Thank the devil too he didn't wander close enough to smell me—'

At that moment a head popped above the water.

'Talking to ourselves, are we?' said the head. 'Having a little chat? Must be pretty boring, since you know what you're going to say even before you say it. The last person I want to speak to is *me*. Still, perhaps you like being bored.'

Falshed had jumped when the head appeared, but now he could see it belonged to a female otter. Other otters began to appear around him. There were at least a dozen of them, in and around the dam of twigs. Their sleek muscular bodies were visible through the clear water of the stream.

'Ah,' snapped the sheriff, 'you can bite through these cords for me, can't you? I need to get away quickly so that I can catch those weasels. Come on then, get chewing.'

The female otter who had first spoken looked at one of her companions. 'I don't think I like being ordered about, do you?' she said.

'Not on your life,' replied the companion.

Falshed realized he was in a very delicate position. He had no troops to back him up, and in any case otters were notoriously disobedient. They had their own watery world to live in and they did not care very much for stoats.

'Look,' said Falshed silkily, 'I'll see you're all well rewarded – er, what would you like? Some delicious rabbit? A few voles? Just name it and I'll see you get it.'

'How about a nice salmon?'

Falshed shook his head. 'Can't give you any fish, I'm afraid. Stoats and weasels are not very good at catching fish.'

The otter shook her head, spraying him with water. 'In that case, we can't help you. Sorry.'

The sheriff began to panic. He was not above

promising things he could not deliver to the otters, if it meant getting his own way with them. He thought very carefully for a moment, while the glossy, elegant otters climbed out of the water onto the bank, and then spoke again. 'Listen, I think I can guarantee to supply you with as much fish as you require, once I've had a talk with Prince Poynt. So if you'll just nip through these cords . . .'

'You're lying,' said one of the otters. 'You said a moment ago that stoats were not good at fishing. I believed you then. I don't believe you now.'

'Well, we've – we've got our own otters at Castle Rayn, who are quite willing to do our bidding. Not *slaves*, you understand, but otters willing to work for the common good of the animals in the castle. I – I could get them to dive in the moat and get some salmon for you.'

The same otter said, 'Salmon don't live in moats.'

Falshed could not help but get angry. 'Well, carp then, or pike – any old fish you like.'

The female otter said, 'Oooo, doesn't he get huffy? I don't think we want to waste any more time on this one, do we?' She began to remove sticks from the dam with her claws and teeth. The other otters started to help her.

'I'll get you for this, you bunch of mealy-mouthed wetbacks,' snarled Falshed, shedding his smarmy act. 'I'll come back through here with a blasted army and hunt you down like – like rats. I'll make your lives hell for this.'

An otter nipped his nose, making his eyes water. 'Better be quiet, stoat,' he warned in a friendly tone. 'You're not exactly in a position to issue threats at the moment. At least wait until you're out on the current and we can't catch you.

Otherwise we might have to pull out a few patches of fur, while we're in the mood. Wouldn't like that, would you?'

Falshed ground his teeth in frustration but said nothing further while the otters were destroying the dam.

Finally, the log-jam of sticks was breached and the raft was swept over the small waterfall into the fast current again.

'You stinking, oily fish-gobbling toads!' Falshed yelled back, taking the last otter's advice. 'May your offspring be legless frogs. May your pelts dry up and wrinkle in the sun. May ragworms eat your babies live. I despise you . . .'

But it was not a satisfying set of taunts, for it meant nothing really, and the otters were soon out of earshot. The miserable sheriff was soon shooting downstream again, his fate uncertain, his heart full of hate for the otters. He had never felt so helpless in his life. It was certain now that he would reach the river without being rescued. Then what?

The raft was flushed through open meadows now, as the stream left the Halfmoon Wood behind. There were holes where coypus lived on the bank, but none of these rodents was visible. Suddenly, Falshed saw something striding across the meadow, coming down towards the stream. It gleamed dully in the light of the day. It left deep footprints in the soft turf of the good bottom land as it strode through wild flowers.

It was a live bronze statue, one of those which stoats and weasels called a 'gong'. There were other living statues: blocks (statues made of solid stone), puddings (plaster), stumpers (wood) and chunks, which were just busts and heads. Gongs, blocks, puddings, stumpers and chunks wandered the island of Welkin, the chunks often carried by one of the statues with legs. Few stoats or weasels could hold a sensible conversation with these creatures. They had taken on life when the humans left, though no-one had any idea why. One or two wizards and sorcerers spent time conversing with them, but that was all.

Certainly the sheriff had never held a conversation with a statue. Normally Falshed was quite wary of them, but today he needed help. He was not too proud to ask a statue for its assistance. The bronze gong reached the water's edge before the raft passed the spot where it was standing. It put out a foot and halted the raft. This was promising and Falshed began to feel hopeful.

'Ooouuuuooo,' wailed the statue, whose open mouth was in the wind. 'Oooouuuooo.'

'Untie me,' cried Falshed. 'You have fingers, even if they are going green. Use them to get me free of these cords.'

The metal statue came squeaking and creaking to its knees. It was as if every joint in its body needed oiling. In form it was a soldier of some kind, with a spear and shield slung over its shoulder. It had probably formed part of a monument, when the humans were around. Like all statues it was probably looking for its First and Last Resting Place – the place where it was first extracted from the ground in the form of metal ore, and to which it wished to return.

The soldier's statue seemed to know what was being asked of it. Its fingers sought the knots to the cords behind the pole. However, its efforts were in vain – much to Falshed's frustration – for the fact

34

that it was fashioned of bronze made its fingers awkward. They would not bend very much at the joints. The statue was trying to do the job with half-clenched hands, the way a human might with frozen ones, and not doing very well. In the end it simply gave up and let the raft float on.

'Thanks very much, ball bonce,' yelled Falshed. 'I hope your joints rust and seize up!'

The raft was carried through the fields down to the river Bronn, where it bobbed about on a much wider stretch of water. Falshed was almost hysterical with fear. Whereas before he had been able to see and almost touch the banks of the stream, the river was different. It had vast volumes of water flowing seawards. There were other objects in the water now – pieces of wood, large logs, masses of weed – which threatened to overturn the raft and send the luckless stoat to his death.

'I don't want to drown,' he cried into the wind. 'I hate water.'

Finally the river opened to a vast wide mouth. There were reeds growing like a beard through its surface. In places the reeds were so thick they became a piece of solid land. Falshed was taken down through a muddy creek, into a basin, where the raft finally came to rest against an island of poa grass sprinkled with sea lavender and bladderwort. The tide then went out slowly leaving him stranded on the mud.

Falshed hung from his mast while the seagulls whirled about him making insulting sounds.

After a while there came a rustling from the grass on the small island. A pointed face suddenly poked through the reeds. There were whiskers on the face. Small eyes stared at Falshed. It was a rat.

The creature spoke in a harsh, guttural almost-language, but not in any tongue the stoat could understand. '*Maarashika grubba krikklina Hkellosh,*' said the rat. '*Culmnaggarrisha hgorsh?*'

'Speak Welkin, you barbarian,' Falshed snarled.

Unlike all the other animals outside the family of stoats and weasels, the rats had developed a strange and savage intellect, under the evil guidance of the sorcerer, Flaggatis.

The rat obviously knew he was being spoken to abruptly. He could see that the sheriff was securely bound. This gave him courage. He flew at Falshed, his jaws snapping fiercely. The weight of the brute hitting the sheriff in the chest caused the mast to snap. Rat and stoat went sprawling together on the raft, the rat's pointed yellow teeth clashing together just a fraction of a centimetre from Falshed's throat.

Falshed's bonds were now loose and unravelled themselves. The stoat was soon free. Having escaped from his ties the stoat sheriff was more than a match for a single rat and the rodent knew this. He ran across the mud to the river, slipped into the water and began swimming away from the raft, his pointed head just above the surface.

Falshed picked up the broken piece of mast and hurled it after the rat in rage. It skimmed past the creature like a javelin. Then the rat dived under the surface, and Falshed saw him no more.

There would be other rats coming for him though, if he did not quickly get away from the marshes. There were thousands, tens of thousands of the creatures in this wasteland. He got off the raft and immediately sank waist-deep in foul-smelling mud. He found a piece of driftwood from an orange box which he could use as a paddle.

There was now nothing for it but to drag the raft back along the creek to the river, where he launched it again. This time he was free to row the raft back up the river, which he knew would pass near to Castle Rayn at some point. Falshed was exhausted and very upset, but there was a feeling of elation in his breast at having thwarted the outlaw's plan. 'I'll find that weasely Sylver,' he promised himself with a catch in his voice, 'and tear him from teeth to tail.'

With this pleasant thought in mind, the stoat paddled himself against the current, finally reaching a place where the rain came down in torrents. Then he knew himself to be in stoat country once again and could breathe more easily. Another hour of tiring paddling finally brought him within sight of Castle Rayn, which stood on a miserable little rise. It appeared out of the drizzle like a warm welcome cottage on a winter's night.

'At last,' he said with a savage sob, his eyes resting gratefully on the cold, wet, grey stones of the castle walls. 'Home. Home again. I never want to leave it – unless it's to go out and destroy that pathetic little weasel band.'

Then he remembered that he had failed Prince Poynt, had lost his troop of soldiers, and had to face his master with the news that Sylver and his band were still at large. 'Oh, my,' he said in despair. 'Oh, my, my . . .'

Chapter Four

Prince Poynt was enraged with his sheriff for failing to bring to justice the weasels of County Elleswhere.

The monarch strutted the halls and corridors of the castle, shouting at courtiers, bellowing at servants and screaming at Falshed. The capture of Sylver and his band had become important to him. It was just possible that the weasel outlaws might find a clue to the whereabouts of the humans and bring them back – and Poynt would lose all that he now owned.

He had expected his orders to be carried out quickly and efficiently – and, above all, successfully. 'What are you thinking of?' he wailed at the trembling sheriff. 'A whole regiment of my finest stoats. It's a good job I didn't send the Royal Guard with you. I'd have lost my ferrets as well, wouldn't I? Now I've had to send them on their own, with one of my secret weapons.'

Falshed saw a way to blame someone else. 'Actually, the ferrets will do a *much* better job, my prince. You can see I could do nothing on my own, once deserted by my troops. The Royal Guard would never have fled the battlefield and I would have been victorious.'

Prince Poynt's white fur quivered. He whirled

on the unfortunate sheriff. 'You must have done something wrong for them to *want* to desert you. A good commander is revered by his troops, as I am adored by my Royal Guard. They must have seen something in you which spelled defeat, or they would never have run.'

Falshed knew he was not going to win this argument, so he shut up and let the prince rail at him. He knew it would not be long before the shouting was over, so he suffered it in silence. In the meantime, stragglers began to arrive at the castle from Halfmoon Wood. Remnants of the regiment of stoats, having found their way out of the trees, had begun drifting back to the castle, hoping not to be punished. In this they were too optimistic, for if Prince Poynt did not discipline them, Sheriff Falshed intended to do so, once he himself was back in the prince's good favour.

When most of the regiment was back in the castle (some would never return, lost for ever in the wild forest) a noblestoat, a tall lean creature by the name of Jessex, went to tell Prince Poynt. 'The soldiers are back,' he said. 'Do you wish them punished, my lord.'

'Yes,' snarled Falshed, answering for the prince, 'hang them by their heels upside down from the battlements.'

'Quite right,' Prince Poynt agreed. 'And hang their leader with them.'

So Sheriff Falshed ended up studying the countryside upside down from the battlements, hanging by his hind legs alongside the troops who had failed him in battle. He could see the fields, *very* green after all the rain, and the river down which his raft had come. When evening arrived he saw the shadows creep into the hollows of the hills and slowly become darkness. The moon came out, and with it the fear of barn owls out hunting on the wing, but late in the warm evening Falshed was hauled up and cut loose. He had at last been forgiven by the prince.

Since it had been drizzling the whole time he had hung from the walls, his fur was soaked through. Once back inside the castle walls, however, it did not take long to dry. Prince Poynt had fires roaring in every room, and torches blazing in the corridors, trying to keep the coldness out of his bones. Still he shivered though, while everyone else sweltered.

'Ah, Falshed,' he said, as if greeting a long-lost friend without whom he had been very lonely, 'come up here, old fellow, and keep me company amongst these brash noblestoats.'

The prince was seated at a long table, cut down in height, and along each side were his courtiers.

In the corner of the vast hall, on a platform of straw, was a group of weasels playing thin piping music on reed flutes. To any human ears the sound would have been strange and eerie, resembling the wuthering of a low, narrow wind blowing across the necks of slender bottles. Weasels and stoats had always had these ancient tunes in their heads, even when they had been wild animals, but their new intelligence had allowed them to release the weird sounds and hear them played for the first time.

A female weasel was doing a sinewy dance in the middle of the room. No-one was paying much attention to her. The prince shivered and clutched a rabbit bone in his paw, gnawing on it occasionally. 'Come up and sit by my side, my good sheriff. I am in need of powerful company.'

So Falshed went to the head of the table, nudged a noblestoat out of the way, and sat next to his prince. A jester weasel went out onto the stone flags of the floor and began to copy the dancer, mimicking her actions to make the prince click his teeth. The prince thought his jester, Pompom, quite funny and clicked at his antics as the jester exaggerated the jill's movements. The poor dancer had to continue her act with another weasel making snaky movements behind her, mocking her art.

'What entertainment can you devise for us this evening?' said Prince Poynt, turning to Falshed. 'Have you some ideas in that head of yours? Something must have trickled down into it, while you were hanging over my tower windows today.'

'His brains more likely,' shouted Pompom, 'since he normally carries them in his feet!'

Prince Poynt clacked his teeth in appreciation of this jest, his pure white body shaking with mirth, while Falshed simmered and stared with narrowed eyes at the jester weasel.

'How about pinning Pompom to a wheel and spinning it, while the rest of us throw darts between his legs?' said Falshed nastily.

'What a good idea!' cried the prince.

'No, no!' quailed Pompom. 'You've all been drinking honey dew. You're drunk. You might miss.'

Prince Poynt slapped a paw on the table, his white fangs gleaming in the torchlight. 'He's right. I don't want to lose my jester to some bad shot from one of you pieces of pond weed. Wail not, little

41

Pompom, your prince shall not sacrifice you tonight. Perhaps we'll do it when I'm in a bad mood.'

Pompom shot a wicked look at Falshed, who felt he was getting a little of his own back on Sylver's lot, since the jester was after all a weasel like them.

'Come on, come on,' growled Prince Poynt. 'Let's have another idea, Falshed.'

'Skittles then,' snapped the sheriff, 'but not with bottles, with servants.'

Once again the prince's paw smashed down on the table. 'Grand idea, sheriff. Send down to the kitchens. Get some scullery jacks and jills up here. What do you say, you rumbustious lot? What shall we use for balls?'

'Turnips!' growled a noblestoat. 'Good, hard turnips!'

So nine of the kitchen staff, all weasels of course, were brought up from the castle depths and made to stand tall on their hind legs at the end of the hall in a hexagonal skittle group. Their little white bibs shimmered in the torchlight. Some of them looked quite terrified at their coming ordeal.

'No swaying!' yelled the prince as he took aim from the other end of the hall with a topped-and-tailed turnip. 'If you can't bear to see the ball coming, then close your eyes.'

Most of the weasels did this, making the expectation of being struck by a hard rolling turnip that much more frightening.

The prince bowled, the turnip thundered over the stone flags, and missed the right side of the group by six centimetres. 'Drat,' he said. 'They moved, didn't they? They skipped out of the way.'

Although the kitchen staff had stayed perfectly still, Jessex agreed with the prince. 'Your ball was straight and true, my lord. It was those cowardly weasels who spoiled a good strike for you. Otherwise you'd have felled the lot.'

'That's what I thought,' said Prince Poynt petulantly. 'We'll call it a strike then – nine skittles down. That means I get another go, doesn't it?'

He aimed and rolled the second ball. This time his turnip skimmed the washing-up jack, on the extreme right of the skittle group. This weasel had learned his lesson now. Although the turnip had hardly touched him, he fell violently sideways, knocking the two weasels next to him. 'Fall over,' he hissed. 'All of you fall over.'

In twos and ones the kitchen weasels fell rigidly to the floor as if struck by one of their fellows, until they all lay in a heap, before the turnip had come to rest against the wall behind them.

'Oh, well done, sir,' cried Falshed, clicking his teeth in appreciation of the shot. 'Quite brilliant. I'm sure none of us will be able to match two strikes in a row. Superb bowls-stoat-ship. Magnificent aiming!'

'Hear, hear,' cried all the courtiers, while Pompom, standing behind the prince, suddenly went down like a stick of chopped celery, crying, 'A hit, a hit. I've been felled by the wind of your majesty's fine bowling.'

'Ha!' Prince Poynt cried. 'The ermine does it again. Let's see if any of you newts'-tails equal *that*!'

Falshed stepped up next. He picked up a heavy-looking trimmed turnip. Then, after a long run, he took careful aim and let fly. It was not that he wanted to beat the prince. In fact he knew if he did so he would be in for a long night on the battlements. But he hated weasels so much he needed to see them scattered over the floor, preferably with broken bones.

His accurate turnip sped down the alley of courtiers towards the kitchen servants. They knew if Falshed beat the prince *they* would also be in trouble. So when the turnip reached them they executed marvellous serpentine movements, twisting their bodies almost into loops, to avoid being hit by the ball. Only the last weasel, right at the back, suffered any hurt as the turnip took him off his feet and carried him into a bale of straw right at the back of the hall.

'Oh, well done, Falshed,' said the prince. 'One down. Good shot. Pity it wasn't more.'

'They moved!' cried the sheriff. 'They sort of wiggled out of the way. I saw it go through the middle.'

'No, no, you're mistaken, sheriff,' murmured the prince. 'None of them moved – they wouldn't dare. They all stood their ground. Unfortunately your turnip was ju-u-u-s-s-st a lit-t-t-tle too much to one side. Never mind, better luck next time.'

'I want another go,' said Falshed, through gritted teeth.

'No, it's the turn of Jessex now,' said the prince. 'You didn't score a strike, so you're out. You can have another go later. Jessex? Next!'

One by one the courtiers and noblestoats bowled down the alley at the weasels, each one failing to hit more than one or two skittles. Yet when the prince tried again, all the skittles fell to the floor, even though the turnip might have been expected to take only two or three at the most from the left side of the group of kitchen paws.

'It's all in the wrist, Falshed,' said Prince Poynt, willing to give advice and tutoring to his sheriff. 'You notice how I barely touched the left side of the skittles, but if you hit them right they go crashing into one another. The correct spin on the turnip makes them go shooting sideways. I suspect you don't have the skill or the eye for this game, but do your best.'

Once again Falshed sent down a fast, unerring ball which miraculously failed to hit any skittles at all. The prince was joyous. The courtiers clacked their teeth in applause of their prince's prowess. Poynt went down to the skittles and told them all they might take a morsel of food when they got back to their kitchens. 'You can scrape the crusty bits off the cooking pot,' he said generously, 'where the stew's boiled over. You've been a *fine* set of skittles.'

'Thank you, my lord,' they chorused, one of them limping as he left the great hall.

Pompom fell in behind this one and copied his limp, stopping and looking innocent every time the creature looked round to find the cause of the uproarious clicking and clacking amongst the noblestoats.

'Pompom,' cried the prince, 'you're an out-rageous fellow. I ought to have you branded for my own.'

'You already have, my lord,' replied Pompom with some pique, showing the prince the mark on the rear of his flank. 'You did it last spring with a red-hot embroidery needle.'

This was the cause of much merriment amongst the courtiers, and indeed clacking rang out from the prince himself. 'Outrageous,' he screamed in delight. 'You are such a card, Pompom.'

'Yes,' said Pompom, in a tone that sounded suspiciously like a snarl to Falshed. 'Aren't I just?'

At that moment a stoat came running into the hall and fell full length at Prince Poynt's feet. No-one was quite sure whether or not it was an act of subservience, or whether the stoat had actually tripped. He lay there face down crying, 'My lord, the serfs have revolted. Some weasels ran from the fields tonight, instead of returning to their villages. They say they have gone to live in the woodlands like that outlaw Sylver.'

'Did you leave the door open?' asked the prince, shivering.

'What?' said the messenger, looking up.

'Did – you – leave – the – door – open?'

The messenger was perplexed. 'The door, my lord? Yes, I came straight in. I thought you would want to hear the news immediately . . . I – I didn't think.'

'Next time, make sure you think. You know I hate draughts, especially in July. It's so cold at this time of year. Do you want me to catch a chill? Do you? Is that what you're trying to do? Kill me off, so you can take over my throne, is that it?'

'N-n-n-n-no, my prince.'

'Then go back out and close the door, so we can all get warm again, there's a fine fellow.'

'But – but what about the rebels, my lord?'

'Falshed,' said the prince, 'see if you can get it right this time – round up the runaways.'

'Yes, prince,' snapped Falshed, eager to put things right again. 'I shall have them back in the morning.'

Chapter Five

Dredless had built a huge repeating catapult, similar to those used to fire the ant bombs, but with an elaborate catch-and-trigger device. 'You fill this pocket here,' he said, pointing to a bird's nest where the ammunition was to go, 'then flick back on this forked twig. The branch springs forward, fires the missile, then on the recoil it clicks back into place. That way it's always ready to fire. You just have to keep feeding ammunition to the bird's nest and pulling the trigger.'

Bryony flowed around the device, peering into the mechanism and shaking her head in doubt. 'What are you going to use for missiles?' she asked Dredless.

'Well, I was thinking of dried newts,' replied Dredless, with not a flicker of humour on his face.

Miniver drew in her breath sharply. 'Newts?' she said. 'You mean you're going to catch poor little newts and fire them at stoats?'

'No, no,' said Dredless, 'I was thinking of dead ones.'

'You're going to catch newts and kill them, just to supply your catapult with ammunition?' cried Bryony incredulously.

Dredless felt he was swimming against the tide here. He realized he had not explained himself well enough. It was due to the fact that whenever he came up with an idea, he got too enthusiastic about it. What he knew he should do was remain calm and objective. Instead, he was getting over-excited, not explaining things well enough, and having to repeat himself.

'You keep getting it wrong,' he argued with Bryony. 'I don't want to *kill* any newts. I'm thinking about gathering newts that are already dead. You know, newts who've died of natural causes. You find them drying all stiff and sharp in the sun? They would make good missiles because their pointy bits would stick into stoats' fur and make it difficult to remove them. Now do you understand?'

They gave up on him in disgust and left him to fiddle with the trigger mechanism while they went back to the hollow tree where the pair of them slept every night.

Sylver was down by the big hornbeam with Icham and Wodehed. He was planning an expedition for the band. This had come about because of a recent discovery by Culver.

Not too long ago Culver had found a child's diary hidden behind a shelf of large dusty books in the library. On reading this diary Lord Haukin had decided that the human child, a young girl named Alice, had been reluctant to leave Welkin. It seemed that her father had owned Thistle Hall and she had not wanted to abandon the house and its gardens for ever.

On close study Lord Haukin had detected a code in the diary, revealing the existence of cryptic clues which in turn pointed to the whereabouts of the Welkin humans. These clues had been hidden throughout Welkin by other children, as concerned as Alice that one day the missing people should be reunited with their homeland. For some reason Alice had not been able to leave a message in plain language.

Perhaps, Lord Haukin had suggested to Sylver, the Welkin humans had not left by choice but had been *taken* away by others. Perhaps this Alice child had feared discovery by those who were responsible for removing the humans from Welkin.

Whatever the reason, she had left behind her the coded diary, in the hope that it would be found by some person or creature who cared enough to find out where the Welkin humans had gone. On first reading the diary had seemed quite innocent and ordinary with phrases such as, 'This morning the sun was shining brightly and the meadows were full of wild flowers.'

Lord Haukin, cleverest stoat that ever lived, was fond of puzzles, however, and had seen little repetitions and strange uses of verbs and twisted clauses in the text. On delving further he had discovered the code and within that code the suggestion of clues. It was all very elaborate but no doubt there was a strong reason. Perhaps Alice and her friends would have been killed had they been discovered leaving directions.

The first clue was apparently hidden in a place called Thunder Oak. Neither Culver nor Sylver had heard of it, but Sylver wanted to know more. 'Where is this Thunder Oak?' he had asked. 'Can you show it to us on the map?'

'Thunder Oak does not appear on any chart or map in the library,' Lord Haukin had answered.

'I've studied them all, but can find no mention of it. These maps are not perfect. There's only one perfect map in the world, and that lies on the highest of the Yellow Mountains.'

Wodehed, when questioned by Sylver, told him he had heard that in the Yellow Mountains of the east was the nest of the great sea eagle which, it was said in magic circles, laid a marvellous egg. Wodehed said the band needed to obtain this egg.

'What's so marvellous about it?' asked Icham of Wodehed. 'And how are we going to wrest it away from a great sea eagle? I'm not sure that's a good thing to do in any case. I mean, the egg is her future offspring . . .'

'No, you misunderstand me,' said Wodehed, who felt like Dredless had done when being questioned by Miniver and Bryony, 'I don't intend us to steal the egg while the bird is in occupation. Spring has come and gone. It's high summer now. The chick that was in the egg has since hatched and flown.'

'So,' Sylver interrupted, 'we're looking for *pieces* of eggshell, right?'

'Correct,' replied Wodehed, who was the oldest of the weasels in the group. 'Two main pieces, I hope. A great sea eagle doesn't usually shatter its shell into a dozen pieces but breaks it in two, often leaving both halves complete.'

'You still haven't said why it's so special,' grumbled Icham, scratching himself in impatience.

'No, I haven't. Well, the reason is this. A great sea eagle flies over the whole world – over oceans, over continents, over islands – and the landscape below becomes imprinted on the shells of her eggs.

We've studied the maps in the books in Lord Haukin's library, but I feel there are places missing from those maps.'

'Why do you think that?' asked Sylver.

'For one thing, those charts are made by human seafarers, who can easily sail by an island in the fog and miss it completely. The great sea eagle's shell is the only *true* map in the universe, because the eagle flies high above the earth and sees *everything*. The contours she sees with her eyes go into her brain and eventually the patterns are reproduced on the shells of her eggs, when she gives birth. Perhaps she is passing on those patterns to her young, so they have maps to guide them on their travels through the skies above our planet.'

'Who knows?' said Sylver, wonderingly. 'But you're right, Wodehed, we could do with one of those maps to help us find the lost humans. We'll set out to find the nest in the Yellow Mountains at dawn tomorrow.'

Icham asked, 'Why do they call them the Yellow Mountains?'

Wodehed shook his head. 'We'll have to ask Lord Haukin.'

So the three outlaws went once more to Thistle Hall, carefully avoiding the animal highways where they might be liable to meet gangs of stoats. It did not matter that Prince Poynt's soldiers were not in the region at the moment. There were plenty of ruffian stoats who were not in the army, out looking for trouble. Some of them just liked to bully the country weasels, steal from their stores, make themselves at home in their hovels, generally knock them about.

Of course, Sylver would not take this sort of

treatment lying down, and he and his band were a match for any group of thugs they were likely to meet on the highway. But there were more important things for them to be doing than battling with boneheaded stoats. If they wanted, their whole time might be taken up getting in and out of fights with such rogues.

Nevertheless, the inevitable happened. When they crossed a small stream and were approaching Lord Haukin's lands, a gang of stoat scoundrels came along a narrow winding friar's path. They had been drinking honey dew and were in the mood for a fight. On seeing Wodehed, Icham and Sylver, the stoats let out a joyous roar and picked up some heavy sticks and stones.

'Look what we've got here,' said a big rascally stoat with a swollen bruise over one eye. 'Some weasels.'

'P-please, sir,' said Sylver in a quavering voice, 'we're not looking for any trouble.'

The stoats stopped in their tracks and clacked their teeth at this remark.

'Not looking for any trouble?' growled the big one again. 'Well, that's not a thing you have to *search* for, weasel-brain. You can find it without looking. It just so happens you've stumbled across some trouble by accident. Now isn't that interesting, eh?'

The other ruffian stoats thought this was a great joke and clicked their teeth by way of applause.

'I hear tell,' Icham said, looking around him as if he were nervous, 'that the feared outlaw Sylver and his band live near by. If he hears you've attacked some weasels in his territory, he might come looking for you.'

The big jack pushed out his chest. 'Then he'll find me, won't he?'

'He already has,' said Sylver quietly, fitting a stone into his sling.

'What?' cried the stoat, as the other two weasels also loaded their slingshots. 'What's this?'

'Retribution, stripling,' Wodehed told him. 'We are the weasels you hoped never to meet.'

The three stalwart weasels then whirled their slings around their heads and let fly at the half dozen brutish oafs who blocked their paths. Before the first three pebbles had even struck their targets, the slings were reloaded and whirled again. Again, before the stoats even realized what was happening they found themselves in a hailstorm of smooth stream-pebbles, battering them back along the path towards the village from whence they had come.

One or two of them tried to throw their rocks, and a single stoat braver than the rest rushed forward, wielding his cudgel, but to no avail. The shower of stones from the deadly accurate sling-shots forced the stoats into retreat. The bullying braggarts ran away, yelling threats about getting Sheriff Falshed's troops to hunt down Sylver and his band, saying they would see Sylver's skin stretched on a gallows-frame and drying in the sun before the red days of autumn struck the forest.

'He's tried that,' cried Icham after the cowardly crew had scuttled away. 'We sent them packing too!'

'Well done, you two,' said Sylver. 'They were an ugly lot, weren't they? I pity the poor weasel household who has to put up with *them* tonight. But we can't be everywhere at once. I just hope they get so drunk on honey dew they fall into a ditch and sleep away the dark hours until the morning light.'

When they arrived at Thistle Hall, Icham banged on the knocker fixed to the small door set in the large door. Eventually a harassed-looking Culver opened it from the inside and let them in. 'As if I haven't got enough to do,' he said, 'without answering doors.'

'Why?' said Icham. 'What have they been asking you?'

Culver was not in the mood for Icham's pale humour and a glower from him informed that weasel of such.

The band were shown into the library, where Lord Haukin was as usual buried up to his bib in books. Besides books there were around the room hundreds of bottles of different sizes, shapes and shades of coloured glass. Lord Haukin loved bottles as well as books. He said they had beauty in their slender necks, their bulbous bodies, their dimpled depths. He loved to see them polished, some of them so clear they sparkled, and if you did not find him poring over a book, he would be peering into blue or green glass and stroking his bottles.

He looked up as they entered and muttered, 'Ah, it's so-and-so and what's-your-name, isn't it? And, of course, your companion, who's-it?'

Sylver said, 'Your memory never fails to astound me, Lord Haukin. We are indeed those of whom you speak.'

'I thought so,' said Lord Haukin. 'I never forget a face. What brings you to my mansion at this hour? Do you want food from my kitchens? Go and see the cook.'

'No, we require advice,' replied Sylver. 'We're planning an expedition to the Yellow Mountains and want to know how they got their name. Is there anything in particular we need know about them before we set off?'

'The Yellow Mountains?' murmured the old stoat, shuffling through some documents. 'I was reading about them only the other day for someone just like you . . .'

'Looks like you were reading about *everything* the other day,' remarked Icham, staring round the room at the piles of books and papers. 'I expect if we'd asked you where a coot's feathers went after that pond bird left this life, you'd have probably been reading about it the other day.'

'They become waterlogged and sink down to settle in the mud,' murmured Lord Haukin, still reading. 'Now, where were we? The Yellow Mountains. I wish you wouldn't keep distracting me, young weasel, it makes me all of a twitter.'

'Sorry,' said Icham.

Eventually, Lord Haukin found what he was looking for amongst the debris. 'Here it is,' he said, squinting at the paper. 'Yes, the Yellow Mountains. They're yellow because of the sulphur, you know, which covers the slopes like snow on colder mountains. It's a volcanic range of mountains, so there's a lot of underground activity – bubbling lava, hot mud, that sort of thing. I shouldn't go there, if I were you.'

'But we've got to,' cried Wodehed, 'if we want to find the first clue to where the humans have gone.'

'In that case,' replied Lord Haukin, lowering the document before his eyes and looking over the top at Wodehed, 'may I say it has been a pleasure to have known you, sir, whatever your name is, and may your passing bells be merry.'

'Passing bells?'

'The bells they toll for the dead. Priory bells, chapel bells, cathedral bells. They say those mountains have swallowed lives like a river swallows bricks. Indeed, the mountains themselves are merely giant tombstones, huge monuments to those who have lost their souls on the yellow slopes.' Lord Haukin stared at his guests. 'Oh dear, I hope I'm not frightening you, my dear weasels. That's not the intention. You've all gone dreadfully pale. I'm trying to warn you, you see.'

'We appreciate that, Lord Haukin. No, Wodehed is right, we can't let the fact that many have died trying to scale those yellow walls put us off. We've got to go and that's that. We have to find the great sea eagle's egg.'

'Ah,' nodded Lord Haukin, gravely, 'in that case the Yellow Mountains are the only place to go. You won't find any great sea eagles around *here*, that's certain. Those sort of creatures don't like woodlands. The trees get in the way of their wings, you know, and there're not many fish left in the ponds of Halfmoon Wood, are there? Whereas, beyond the Yellow Mountains lies the Cobalt Sea.'

'Exactly,' said Icham.

Lord Haukin looked at the outlaw weasels through narrowed eyes. 'Just what do you hope to achieve by this expedition?' he asked.

Sylver said, 'We hope to find the great sea eagle's egg, which is a map of the world.'

'For what purpose do you require such a map?'

'To help us find Thunder Oak,' sighed Icham,

rolling his eyes to heaven. 'You know we have to find the Welkin humans.'

Lord Haukin wrinkled his brow. 'Is that so? Is that so?' he murmured. Then his face brightened. 'Yes, of course, the Welkin humans. Alice and her friends, eh? Naturally, the dykes need to be repaired, don't they? Well, good luck to you all – good luck, good luck,' and with that he disappeared into the depths of his library.

They heard him trying to take down a book, which almost crushed him before they quickly went to his aid. When the book was open on the floor, Lord Haukin pored over its pages. His eyesight was so bad that his nose brushed the print as he squinted at it. 'Yes, you're quite right – Thunder Oak is where the first clue lies. Do you know where to find Thunder Oak?'

'No,' said Sylver patiently, 'that's why we need the map.'

'Please be careful, my little friends,' said the old stoat with genuine affection. 'I've come to like you, even if your heritage is somewhat lowly. I'm not one of your snobbish stoats, you know, and the under-classes are quite as dear to me as any highborn noble family such as my own. It matters not to me whether your ancestry begins and ends in the greasy scullery of some dirty hovel. The great unwashed are my brothers and sisters, just as much as those regal and stately figures of my own family line. Farewell. Try to return.'

Icham raised his eyebrows at Sylver during this speech from the old stoat, which clearly showed him to be a snob deep down into his soul, almost as far as his toes.

Sylver said, 'Goodbye for now, Lord Haukin.

We'll call in the minute we get back. Don't wait up for us though.'

'Oh, I never wait up,' said the kindly old stoat. 'I need my sleep, you see. It's important to me.'

'Yes, I'm sure it is,' replied Wodehed. 'It helps refresh your brain, doesn't it?'

'Precisely, er, what-d'you-call-yourself? Precisely.'

Once they had left Thistle Hall, Sylver summarized what they had learned for the benefit of the less clever weasels amongst them, such as Mawk. 'Basically,' he said, 'it comes down to this. Someone or something has forced the Welkin humans to leave this island home. Where they have gone is supposed to be kept a secret from anyone else. The children, perhaps because they were not under such close scrutiny as the adults, managed to leave behind a complex set of clues. They couldn't be plain and open because if the clues had been recognized for what they were every clue would have been destroyed and the children punished.

'We have to find and follow the clues if we want the people from Welkin back again – and we do, because the sea walls are crumbling and we'll all be drowned if they *don't* come home and repair them. Now, are there any questions?'

'Yes,' cried Mawk firmly. Then, as the others sighed in exasperation, he said unhappily, 'Could you go through all that again, please . . . ?'

Chapter Six

'That old stoat must have a million empty bottles in his house,' said Icham. 'I wonder what he does with them all?'

Sylver replied, 'They're like pictures to him. Pictures by famous artists. I can see why he likes them. All those deep colours – the rich blues, the pond greens, the earthy browns – you should see his face when he holds one up to the light. You would swear he could see a smoky genie inside.'

'Well, I think it's all a waste of time and space,' snapped Alysoun. 'They're just empty containers to me. You should either throw them away, or fill them up again.'

'You have no romance in your soul,' said Sylver. 'You should use your imagination. Personally I find anything made of glass fascinating. Especially bottles.'

'I like bottles, too – full ones,' said Mawk-the-doubter.

The monk Luke grunted, 'Full of honey dew, no doubt, you poor sinner.'

The band were on their way through the Lightless Forest on the far side of Halfmoon Wood. Trees in this part of the wood were conifers: pines and firs. No birds lived here, no animals in the branches. There were no badger setts, no woodpecker hollows, no owl perches. Rabbits did not live here, nor mice, nor voles, nor any kind of creature larger than a beetle. It was a silent forest, thick and brown with needles underneath, dark and gloomy in the lifeless branches above.

Suddenly, out into the narrow aisle through the trees stepped a huge and formidable shape. It moved stiffly and awkwardly, as if its joints had seized. First it faced away from the band, but after whispering to itself in an annoyed fashion, it eventually turned round ponderously, until it was bestriding the path and looking directly at them. It swayed there for a moment, a little drunkenly, then seemed to gather itself together more tightly and compactly.

'Go no further,' said the figure. 'This path is forbidden to weasels of all denominations.'

Denominations? thought Sylver. 'I think it means you, Luke,' he said. 'You're the only holy weasel here.'

'Me?' said Luke indignantly. 'A monastic person of *my* standing? The very idea.'

'You especially,' cried the figure. 'No-one shall pass me without he lose his head.'

Sylver stared at the monstrous shape before him as it stepped forward into a ray of light. It was a knight in black armour, wielding a two-handed sword. The metal gleamed under the errant beam which filtered through the trees. A flying black plume of feathers topped the helmet, which had a pointed face and metal grids for the eyes and mouth. The knight seemed to rustle from within, as if the creature inside were too small for the suit and continually fidgeted.

'Is it a statue?' murmured Bryony. 'I should

61

think it must be, for there are no humans left on Welkin to fill such a suit of armour.'

Wodehed said, 'I've never heard a statue speak in such clear and precise tones before. You remember you normally have to get me to interpret what they say, and then I have to concentrate very hard. This is not a statue.'

'Then it *must* be a human,' Sylver said. 'It stands to reason. I'm inclined to speak with this knight.' He paused, then called, 'What is your name, knight of the forest?'

The knight swung the double-handed sword from side to side and almost overbalanced in the effort. He really was a giant when compared to the weasels, even when they stood tall on their hind legs. He towered over Sylver, Icham, Alysoun-the-fleet, Luke, Wodehed, Dredless and Mawk-the-doubter. To little Miniver, the finger-weasel, he was like a mountain. The metal creature rattled itself before replying, 'Malach – no, Riach – no, Silach . . .'

'Strange,' said Dredless. 'Doesn't he know his own name? Why would he have *three* different names?'

'And all of them ferret names,' murmured Sylver. 'That really is strange. Why would a human call itself after a ferret in the first place? It doesn't make sense.'

'Are you lot going to push off, or do I have to chop you to pieces with this battle-axe?' cried the knight in quite a different tone to the one he had used before.

'Battle-axe? It's a two-handed sword, you lune!' yelled Bryony.

'Whatever it is, it's jolly sharp,' grunted the

knight, clearly embarrassed. 'I shouldn't be surprised if it could split a weasel whisker down the middle. Now push off home, before I have to use my fearsome weapon on you.'

The giant metal man gave the sword another swing, got it stuck in the fork of an overhead branch, and had to tug hard to release it again. On pulling it out of the fork, however, he swung it too hard in the opposite direction, and got the point caught in a mossy bank. Once again the knight pulled on the weapon awkwardly, almost falling over with the effort.

Alysoun said, 'He's a bit awkward, isn't he? He's not very deft with that weapon of his. I've never seen a knight before, but I'm sure he's supposed to be more skilful than that, especially if he's guarding an important pathway.'

'He is a bit lacking in dexterity,' said Icham.

Sylver said, 'Dredless, give him a taste of the treasures of the stream bottom.'

Dredless unhooked his slingshot from his girdle and then took a smooth pebble from his ammunition pouch. He fitted the stone into the leather saddle on the sling. Then he whirled the weapon around his head and let fly. The stone zinged through the air and struck the knight's helmet like a gong with a loud *clang*, causing a dent to appear in the metal.

The knight seemed to shudder from head to toe. His great pointed-faced helmet almost spun round back-to-front. A step was taken to the fore, another step was taken to the rear, both with the same leg. The other leg remained perfectly still, as if it were nailed to the floor. To balance himself, the knight's torso spun right round in a full circle and back again, like an owl's head on its shoulders. It sent shivers down the spines of the outlaws. It seemed that what they were up against was a demon of some kind.

'Hey!' cried the knight in a squeaky voice. 'I can't hear now. I've gone completely deaf.'

One of the arms swivelled at the elbow joint, so that the sword twisted like a mincing blade.

'That made my ears ring,' complained the knight from one of his knees. 'I heard it all the way down here.'

'None may pass this place,' said the knight resonantly from deep in his chest. 'We – I mean – *I* stand firm!'

'Not likely,' cried the helmet in the squeaky voice. 'You come up here and say that!'

'Stop arguing,' cried the knight in a third, soupy sort of voice from one of the elbows. 'Do as you're told.'

Wodehed shook his head. 'This is very strange,' he said. 'We've got a knight who throws his voice in several different ways. The fellow talks to himself. He must be some sort of mad ventriloquist. No wonder he doesn't know who he is. I wouldn't know my own name either, if I was in such a state.'

'I think I know what's going on,' said Sylver. 'Look, everyone fill their slingshots, and when I say "now" I want you all to let loose at the same time. Icham, go for the right arm, Bryony for the left, Alysoun for the right leg, Wodehed for the left, Luke for the head, Dredless for the body, Mawk for the right shoulder, Miniver for the left. I'm going to aim for the belly. Now, are you ready? One, two, three . . . NOW!'

They let fly a shower of pebbles, which all struck their marks, some harder than others. The suit of armour rang out like a timepiece suddenly striking nine o'clock, with its notes bunched together. Dents appeared all over the surface of the black armour and there were yells and shouts to follow.

Suddenly, the armour began to come apart at the joints. The arms fell from the shoulders, then parted at the elbows. The legs dropped away from the thighs, then split open at the knees. The head rolled to the ground. The torso fell like a great metal drum, to break in twain at the waist on impact.

Out of each one of these separate parts came a ferret. One out of the forearm, one out of the upper arm, one out of the head, one out of the chest, and so on. These creatures slunk away into the darkness on either side of the pathway, flowing into the forest, some shaking their skulls as if they had flies in their ears. The last one to leave came staggering out of the helmet. He tottered giddily this way and that, seemingly unsure of which direction to take, before finally following the ferrets who had vacated the armoured legs. He was muttering: 'It's all right for them. I was all the way at the top. You get a sort of *donging* at the top which nearly blows your brains out. You can't expect a ferret to put up with that kind of sound for long. It isn't right . . .'

'So there's the mystery solved,' said Sylver. 'The suit of armour was full of ferrets, probably a forward patrol from Prince Poynt's Royal Guard. No wonder the knight had so many different names. No wonder he had such a variety of voices. And no wonder he couldn't work his sword arm very well.'

The band of outlaws inspected the bits of armour and decided they had indeed come from Castle Rayn. Icham said it looked like it had belonged to a knight with very little couth. One of those rough fellows who always ignored the code of chivalry and stabbed his enemies in the back when he got the chance. 'What can you expect from Castle Rayn?' he went on. 'It's a breeding ground for rogues and scoundrels. I expect this lot was sent along by Prince Poynt to delay us, while the main force came up behind. We'd better get out of here quickly – no doubt the whole Royal Guard will soon be here.'

The band were now able to continue to the other side of the forest, where they found themselves in a field of tall grass. It was here that Sylver said they would make camp for the night. They made bivouacs from sticks and grass, mainly to camouflage themselves. Sylver had no doubt that Prince Poynt would send stoat patrols out from the castle to try to harry the band. Such expeditions as theirs did not remain secret for very long. There were spies everywhere, willing to pass on their movements to the prince in return for favours.

The band passed a peaceful night and woke to the sound of birds singing. A skylark on the far side of the meadow was climbing up to the heavens as Sylver woke. He wondered why it was making so much fuss. Skylarks did not normally get upset unless they thought someone was about to find their nest. 'I can smell stoat troops in the air,' he said to the others. 'Icham, go back to the edge of the forest and climb a tree – see if you can see anything ahead.'

Icham did as he was bid and returned some time

later. 'A thousand stoats at least,' he said breath-lessly. 'They're hiding in a ditch on the other side of this meadow. I don't see how we're going to get past them.'

Sylver nodded thoughtfully. 'It's not going to be easy, is it? Let me think for a minute . . . wait, look at those mounds all over the meadow!'

'Moles,' said Bryony. 'You know what they're like – show them a meadow with nice soft loam underneath and they'll soon turn it into hummocky land.'

'That's it,' Sylver said, his eyes shining brightly. 'We'll go underground. We'll use the network of mole tunnels to take us past the stoats. There's no reason why they shouldn't extend into the next field, is there? That way we'll go *beneath* the stoats.'

Alysoun shuddered. 'It's *dark* down there – and you know what moles can be like – rough characters.'

Dredless professed he was none too keen on going subterranean either. 'How will we find our way in the darkness?' he asked.

'You have a point there,' muttered Sylver. 'Can you work some magic, Wodehed? Someone must have some idea how to get round this problem? Luke? Bryony? How about you, Mawk? Miniver? Icham? Come on, someone.'

Chapter Seven

'I have in here,' said Wodehed, the magician, 'a small needle which should assist us in finding the way.'

'A *needle*?' scoffed Luke. 'What do you expect to do with that?'

Wodehed looked haughty. 'I am about to tell you, if you will be so patient as to wait. This needle has been magnetized by me. You can do that to certain metal – that is, metal with iron, cobalt or nickel in it – and it turns the needle itself into a magnet.'

'So far, so good,' growled the sceptical Luke. 'We have a long magnet with a sharp point. What do we do with this object?'

Wodehed took out a thread of cotton from his pouch and tied it to the centre of the needle. 'We turn it into a pointer,' he said, dangling the needle from the thread. 'You see how it spins? It's lining itself up with the lodestone mountains of the north. Once it settles we'll know which way north is and be able to work out the direction of the Yellow Mountains, which as you all know are to the east of Welkin.'

'Brilliant,' said Sylver.

'Thank you,' replied Wodehed modestly. 'I didn't invent it, of course – I merely *discovered* it.'

Luke snorted in a jealous fashion. As the two learned members of the band they were often in competition with one another. Their rivalry was brisk.

'So much for the direction, but how do you think we're going to be able to see a needle in pitch blackness?' said Luke. 'If we take flaming torches down there we'll suffocate on the smoke.'

'I think you'll find,' said Wodehed in a superior tone, 'that it will not always be pitch black down in the tunnels. There will be times when we shall get close to the surface – where those mounds appear, for instance – and we will be so used to the darkness by that time we'll be able to see the needle in the light which filters down through the loosened soil.'

'You hope,' said the huffy Luke.

'Right then,' Sylver said, 'down we go. I think it's best we go in single file. I'll go first. If we meet any moles I don't want a scrap. That would only slow us up. We'll have to change direction or hope that the mole turns and runs.'

They dug away at a mound and found the entrance to the mole network. Sylver went first with Wodehed close behind him carrying the magic needle. Luke had been right, though – it was as dark as the inside of a tree. Tunnels went off in all directions. It really was a maze of corridors and passageways, punctuated by the occasional large chamber.

It was also hot and sweltering down under the ground, as Sylver found his way along a narrow tunnel, hoping not to bump into a mole, or perhaps even a badger, whose tunnels might interconnect with those of the moles. Or indeed, *any* creature who lived below the surface of the world in this subterranean darkness.

Finally, it happened, as Sylver rounded a corner and immediately scented a mole ahead of him. He stopped suddenly, only to have Wodehed bump into him, and Icham into Wodehed, and so on to the end of the line. No-one spoke though. They all knew instinctively that Sylver had stopped for a very good reason. It was best to keep silent until they knew what that reason might be.

Each one of them heard the slow chomping of a mole eating what sounded like a rather juicy worm.

Sylver decided to brazen it through. 'Out of the way, mole,' he called. 'Fierce weasels coming down the tunnel!'

The chomping sound stopped, then there was a scuttling, and soon the scent of the mole was merely a lingering odour in the tunnel ahead, which had now been vacated.

'Huh, that was easy enough,' said Sylver over his shoulder. 'It looks like we're not going to get any trouble from the moles, if they're all like that one.'

And so it turned out. This appeared to be a peaceful colony. The moles scuttled ahead of the band, not wishing to tangle with weasels, whose scent was now filling the tunnels where they lived. There were certain moles, brigands and thieves, who could be savage creatures. These gangs were to be found mainly in the east. Here it seemed they did not go looking for fights, but happily avoided them.

Every so often the band would come upon an air shaft, down which the light filtered through the loose soil above. Here Wodehed would check his magnetic needle to find which way north lay, and then if there was a fork in the tunnels they could take the nearest to an easterly direction.

Sylver was travelling down one tunnel, confident all was going to plan so far, when he came across two evil-looking eyes, staring directly into his face from a metre away. 'Out of the way, mole,' he growled. 'The weasels of Halfmoon Wood are impatient to be travelling on.'

The yellowy eyes with narrow black pupils did not move. They continued to stare at Sylver with burning hostility. When he came to think of it, they did not look like mole's eyes at all. They certainly did not belong to a rabbit. No rabbit's eyes could be that sinister, nor any rabbit bold enough to stand and outstare a weasel. He tried to recall what badger's eyes were like, but not having had much to do with those unsociable creatures he failed to remember.

Sylver turned to the other weasels waiting nervously in a line behind him and asked, 'What *other* creatures are we likely to get under the ground?'

'Wildcats?' suggested Mawk, helpfully. 'Wolves? Wild dogs?'

'Don't be silly,' said Bryony. 'Your imagination's running away with you. It couldn't possibly be any of those large carnivores. It's probably only a fox.'

'A fox!' yelled Luke. 'If that's a fox we're done for! It might be the dreaded Magellan.'

'I can't *smell* fox, can you?' said Sylver. 'In fact it doesn't smell very much at all. I simply don't recognize the faint scent it puts out at all. Foxes can get pretty rank, you know – they would be especially so in a hot place like this. We'd smell a fox a mile off.'

'Can we turn round and go somewhere else?' suggested Miniver. 'It's not moving. It's just staring at us.'

'This is the direction we want to go,' said Sylver. 'We'll just have to face it out. I'm going to go forward. You lot stay here until I see what it is we're up against.'

'Could be a giant toad,' said Mawk, helpfully. 'Or a shrunken deer.'

'Thank you, Mawk,' muttered Sylver, 'I'm sure we'll find out soon enough.'

And Sylver did. He had only taken a few more tiny steps forward when the creature hissed violently into his face. A forked tongue flicked out only a few centimetres from Sylver's nose. Sylver retreated rapidly. 'Snake,' he said, his heart beating fast. 'I shouldn't be at all surprised if it isn't an adder. Grass snakes are not usually so aggressive, are they? No, what we're dealing with here is a rotten old adder, who won't get out of the way.'

'Back!' cried Miniver. 'Let's go back!'

'Wait a bit – let's see if we can think of something else first,' said Sylver. 'It would waste too much time retracing our passage here. Anyone got any ideas? Wodehed? Luke?'

'Not me,' said Wodehed. 'I don't like snakes.'

'Who does?' Luke said, scornfully. 'Listen, I read in one of Lord Haukin's books that snakes are dreadfully afraid of mongooses – that is, mongeese – no, correction, I think it is mongooses. Anyway, they're scared of them.'

'What's a mongoose?' asked Sylver.

'Well, it's a creature a bit like us, really, only they

72

don't live in Welkin, obviously, or we'd all have heard of them. No, they live in some land across the seas. They jump on a snake's neck and they bite it. I read that they're quicker than lightning dipped in lard . . .'

'*Greased* lightning,' muttered Wodehed.

'Yes,' said Luke, not at all put out now that he had centre stage and all the other weasels were looking to him to find a way out of their present problem. 'That sort of lightning.'

'So what's the plan?' asked Sylver.

'The plan is,' replied Luke, 'you pretend to be a mongoose.'

'And how do I do that?'

'Search me,' snapped Luke. 'I can't be expected to solve all the world's problems in one go, can I?'

Sylver said he was quite right, he could not be expected to do that. It was up to the leader of the band to come up with an answer. 'You try and think a bit more about what you read, Luke, while I have a go at this adder.'

Then he turned and yelled, 'I'm a mongoose. I'm coming through, snake. If you don't get out of the way I'll bite the back of your neck!'

The adder's head shot forward a few centimetres. It hissed fiercely into Sylver's face. The bright, burning eyes bore into him with unerring hatred in them. The snake's jaws opened and in the weak light coming from an air shaft ahead, Sylver could see two long white fangs glinting wetly. The snake's nostrils flared. It did not seem as if this ploy of Luke's was going to be at all successful.

'Any more ideas?' croaked Sylver, with the snake's nose almost touching his. 'We need a few ideas *very* quickly.'

'I could try my slingshot,' Dredless cried. 'I might be able to bean him one, but the space is a bit tight.'

'You'd probably hit me,' said Sylver, 'even though you're the best shot in the band.'

Luke suddenly let out a little cry. 'Wait, I've remembered what sort of sound mongooses – mongeese – no, mongooses make. They make a sort of *tikki-tikki-tikki* noise when they face up to a snake. Shall I try that?'

'Please,' Sylver whispered as the eyes came even closer. 'As quickly as possible.'

Luke made the noises which he thought were right, clicking with his tongue on his upper palate. The adder's eyes changed on hearing this sound. Gradually it began to withdraw. Sylver could sense fear in the snake.

Probably something deep within the ancestral memory of the snake told it that this sound was associated with a killer of snakes. Perhaps back in prehistoric times, even in Welkin, there were mongooses – mongeese – no, mongooses who terrified snakes with that sound. Perhaps the reason a mongoose made that sound was *because* it alarmed snakes. Whatever, it seemed to work, and soon the tunnel was clear again.

'Well done, Luke,' said Bryony. 'You see – all that reading you do doesn't go to waste.'

'I never said it did,' replied Luke testily. 'It's dunderheads like Mawk who say things like that.'

'Who's a dunderhead?' cried Mawk.

'Stop that quarrelling back there,' whispered Sylver. 'Listen!'

They all ceased making a noise and listened hard. Above them they could hear the harsh tones

74

of stoats, talking to each other. The weasel band was obviously now directly below the ditch where the enemy forces were gathered.

'Can you see them?' said a voice from above. 'Where are those weasels? They seem to have disappeared.'

'Probably cowering in the grasses,' cried another stoat voice. 'You know what lily-livered loons those weasels are – we'll have to go looking for them, I expect.'

A third clacked raucously. 'They're probably running all the way back to Halfmoon Wood, their knees knocking together. I've never met a weasel yet who could face a stoat on equal terms . . .'

'Equal terms,' growled Sylver. 'There's at least a thousand of them up there!'

'Forget it,' whispered Bryony. 'You know what braggarts they are – you know what they're like – just let them get on with it. We'll have the last click of teeth, when they realize we've tricked them. Prince Poynt will have them hanging from the battlements by their heels before evening.'

'You're right,' Sylver replied. 'Come on, let's get to the end of this tunnel. I'm fed up of having worms and spiders for company. I need some fresh air.'

The group finally emerged in the middle of the next field. When they looked behind them they could see the stoats all lying along the ditch, looking in the opposite direction. Sylver was tempted to shout, 'Oi, you lot! Over here!' but knew that would be foolish and managed to restrain himself.

When they were well away from the stoats they found a stream and washed the dirt off their coats.

Icham made a fire with some flints and they dried themselves. Their escapade under the ground had taken the best part of a day and the evening was coming on now. A big red ball of a sun was descending slowly behind the forest they had left behind.

'Well, I hope we don't have to do that again,' said Alysoun. 'I hated it down there. I'm definitely a weasel who likes the light and open air.'

'Once upon a time we used to make our nests in holes under the ground,' Bryony remarked.

'Well, yes,' admitted Alysoun, 'but in hollow stumps and places like that as well. I suppose I'm a hollow stump sort of a weasel. I don't like the smell of earth. Give me ivy and fungus any time.'

Now that the second day of their expedition was over they were almost at the border of County Elleswhere, the shire where they held sway. Tomorrow and after the weasel band would be in unfamiliar territory, where animals would not know them too well. Lord Haukin's county was now behind them, and Lord Ragnar's county, Fearsomeshire, was before them.

'Get a good night's sleep, everyone,' said Sylver. 'We need to be up bright and early with the dawn.'

Chapter Eight

Sylver felt responsible for the decision to make a journey to the Yellow Mountains, even if the others had agreed to it. He knew it to be a dangerous expedition, because they were going into un-known country. There might be weasels there, who would help them, but equally there might be rogue polecats, or pine martens with a grudge against ground animals, or even strange danger-ous misfits. There was still magic and mystery on Welkin, in small pockets, caught like marsh gas in the peat hags. Sylver felt it was up to him to make sure that the expedition did not fall foul of some accidental catastrophe.

'The wolves are howling tonight,' said Bryony, hunched up by the small fire. 'They must be going out for a hunt.'

'Perhaps they're just singing because they like it,' Sylver suggested. 'I mean, I've always envied the wolves because they can sing. Weasels *try* to sing sometimes, but what always comes out is a thin whine rather than a full-throated note. Listen to that sound. It's as mellow as a full moon.'

Mawk-the-doubter shivered. 'I just find it creepy. I don't like the sound at all. It's like the hooting of owls. You know it's coming from the throat of a creature who could tear you open just like that, with fangs and claws. Creatures of the night.'

'Some animals think the same about us,' said Luke.

They listened to the baying wolves, far off in the distant hills, for a while longer. Sylver thought he could detect a sad note in their calling. Perhaps, he thought, they're mourning a wolf who has passed on. Or an infant lost in the high snowy mountain peaks. Or some remembered great ancestor, who had left behind him or her a power which was good. Sylver did envy the wolves their sense of togetherness. The pack worked, played and slept as a single family, and the pack was more important than any solitary wolf which belonged to it.

Sylver's band was a little like that, but with the wolves it came naturally, whereas the outlaws had been thrown together by necessity, because they had been tyrannized by Prince Poynt and the stoats of Welkin.

When they awoke next morning they were mindful of the fact that they were in Fearsomeshire, the county ruled by the stoat warlord known as Ragnar-the-warrior-chieftain. Although Sylver had never had a lot to do with Lord Ragnar, one of Lord Haukin's cousins, that stoat's reputation was not a good one. Sylver had heard stories of weasels being tied to the horns of sleeping stags, so that when the timid deer awoke they went charging over the grasslands, the weasels fighting for breath in the wind.

Also, being in Fearsomeshire was no protection against the prince's troops, who could enter any county in search of outlaws.

'Let's stick to the ditches today,' said Sylver, 'and if you scent a stoat, hide straight away. We don't want to rouse the whole county against us.'

'Won't Prince Poynt have sent a messenger to Lord Ragnar, telling him we're coming this way?' said Miniver.

Sylver replied, 'I expect so, but I've heard that Lord Ragnar is not fond of Prince Poynt – he's rather jealous of the prince – he might not put himself out much to catch a few weasels in order to send them to Castle Rayn.'

So the band proceeded cautiously through the countryside, moving through the dry, dusty weeds of the ditches. There had been little rain in this part of the country for so long that the ground was hard and parched, cracked in places where the clay had shrunk and parted.

Some ditches had seen so little water that they had been abandoned as places of habitation. Normally a ditch bank was covered in homes: holes for mice, shrews, rabbits, voles, ducks and various amphibians. Now the trenches crackled with sun-burnt docks and wind-burnt thistles, as if they were passing blue electric sparks between their fronds.

'Not many weasels know,' said Wodehed, who was showing off his knowledge again, 'that there are four different types of mice and three different types of vole which live in the countryside of Welkin. There's house, wood, harvest and yellow-necked mice and water, bank and field voles—'

'What about dormice?' interrupted Luke, who hated it when Wodehed got all the attention. 'There's the hazel dormouse and the grey dormouse.'

'True,' said Wodehed, 'but I was going to get around to them, after I'd told you about proper mice.'

'What about the field mouse?' cried Icham triumphantly. 'You forgot about the *field* mouse.'

'No we didn't,' said Luke and Wodehed, banding together against the common enemy.

'A field mouse . . .' began Luke.

'. . . is a *wood* mouse,' finished Wodehed. 'They're the same thing.'

'The wood mouse is also known as the long-tailed mouse, as well as the field mouse,' added Luke.

'So there,' finished Wodehed.

Icham very wisely kept his peace, knowing that he would have trouble arguing with just one of the learned weasels, let alone two of them together.

Towards evening the band came to a gloomy stretch of open country which could only be described as a wasteland. It was bleak and wide, with a troubled sky resting heavily on its shoulders. Shadows chased each other like flattened snakes across the rocky, scarred ground. There were hills, but these were stunted and bald. Here and there were the gnarled remains of trees, which now jutted from earth like rotten teeth.

'I don't like the appearance of this place,' said Sylver. 'It looks like a forgotten corner of the kingdom.'

The band of weasels stood on their hind legs and stared over the darkening landscape, hoping to find some oasis in this lifeless plain. A copse of trees, perhaps? Or a live pool, instead of the stagnant, smelly ponds that gleamed as dull as lead? But there was nothing which gave any sign of hope out there. Sylver wondered whether they ought to camp on the edge of this vast dead land, and go on in the morning. Despite the fact that it was high summer, this place seemed cold and forbidding.

Suddenly Bryony pointed. 'Look!' she said.

Sylver and the other weasels stared in the direction of her raised paw. A light had appeared, out on the wasteland, in the shape of a cross. It seemed to hover there, above the ground, like some miraculous sign. But as they stared, they gradually came to see a solid shape around that light. It was a building of some kind and the cross was a window. Behind that window someone had lit a lamp.

'What do you think?' asked Sylver. 'The wind's getting up. It's going to be a bit cold and blustery here, without any shelter. Shall we risk calling at that place?'

Alysoun shivered. 'Let's give it a try,' she said. 'At least there's light and warmth there.'

'What if it's a garrison of stoats?' muttered Icham. 'Or some hideout for bandit polecats?'

'I suppose we'll have to take a chance on that,' Sylver decided. 'I'm not happy about staying out here without any protection. Foxes, wolves, wildcats – you name it – they're probably all in the vicinity. There's no wood around to start a fire to keep them off. Come on, let's go.'

They hurried across the stretch of open country and came to the stone building. It seemed to be fashioned of round towers, which all locked into one another. The towers were of different heights and girths, making it appear as if the structure was formed of tubes. Each tower had a door to the outside world, which made Sylver feel better. If they did go into this place, there were lots of ways to escape from it. 'Knock on the door,' he said to Luke.

'There's a bell,' said Luke. 'See what's written on it? "Milkstone Monastery." This is a holy place.'

There was no small door for weasels and their kind. Whoever lived here was as large as a human, or close to it. Sylver felt a tingle of apprehension on realizing this, but he was too late to stop Luke ringing the bell.

They waited.

After some time, just when Luke felt he ought to ring again, they heard the hard sound of footsteps approaching the door. Instinctively Luke stepped back, to be with the others, as the great mahogany door swung open to reveal a figure dressed in a long dark-grey robe. It carried a lamp on a short pole, the end of which disappeared up the figure's right sleeve.

The figure was tall alongside the weasels and towered above them. It was also hooded so that they could not see its face. The robe, which was a monk's habit, was too large for it. It flowed around the creature in a pool, completely covering legs and feet. The sleeves were also too long, and hung loosely and limply after they had passed the point where the upper limbs ended.

'Yes?' said the monk gruffly. 'What can I do to help you, friends?'

The deep, gravelly voice seemed to come from the depths of the robe. Sylver stared into the hood, trying to see the creature's face. However, there was not enough light coming from the oil lamp to assist his vision and the shadow inside the hood was quite deep. Sylver thought he caught a glimpse of whiteness in there, but could not be sure what he had seen. Perhaps the creature was an albino of some kind and shy about the fact that it had no pigment to its pelt.

'We're on our way across this wasteland,' said Sylver, 'and we wondered if you could put us up for the night. We have no money or goods to offer you, but we're hard workers and could pay for our fare by doing some chores.'

'Weasels?' said the figure as if noticing what they were for the first time. 'Weasels with fine hides.'

This seemed a rather strange thing to say, but then the band remembered that they were out in the wilderness, where hard lives and lonely days were lived. Creatures in these cloistered places were driven to unusual contemplations by their secluded environment. They were different from woodland animals, had different thoughts, said different things.

The huge monk stepped forward quickly, alarming some members of the band. But then he halted just as suddenly on the dark-grey slate threshold of the doorway, whose shade seemed to become part of his robe. Sylver saw that white gleam again below the hood – like a long curved streak – then it was gone.

'Come in, come in,' said the monk eagerly. 'Welcome. Welcome.'

The figure retreated again and stepped aside, allowing the band to enter the abbey. They went inside and looked around them. In the pale light of the lamp they viewed their surroundings.

They were in a dim dusty hallway, with cobwebs filling almost every space above them.

Spiders chased each other through the vaulted ceiling above. A musty smell was coming from somewhere below the floor, perhaps from a crypt. It was, when all was said and done, a most unpleasant atmosphere. Sylver wondered whether it might not have been better for them to stay on the wasteland.

Instead of suggesting this, he said, 'This is most kind of you – er – sir. Could I ask what this place is?'

'It is an ancient abbey,' grunted the creature lost in the depths of the robe. 'It is a holy place. I sense one of you is a compatriot of mine.' The hood turned towards Luke.

'Yes,' said Luke, 'I am a monk – like yourself, though I do not wear robes. We weasels consider our pelts enough covering to keep us warm. You obviously feel the need to wear a garment and the reason for that would be ... ?'

'You're not one of the Silent Order, obviously,' murmured the figure with what sounded like a chuckle. 'Or we should not be speaking.'

'I am of the High Order of Weaselhood,' said Luke proudly. 'And you? What is your Order?'

'We call ourselves the Friars of the Drum,' the figure replied. 'The drum is our symbol of the Lord's voice. He speaks to us through the medium of the drum.'

Luke opened his eyes wide. 'Well, that certainly is an unusual Order. How many are there of you?'

'Just me,' murmured the figure. 'The others – have all gone – all gone.'

'How sad,' Bryony said. 'Did they die?'

'No, they gave themselves to the Lord,' replied the figure with some mystery. 'But come – you must be tired. Let me show you to your cells—'

'Cells?' cried Icham sharply. 'I'm not going into any dungeon.'

'No, no,' said the figure, 'you misunderstand me – *monk's* cells. It's where we friars sleep and pray. Our living chambers are called cells.'

'Is that right, Luke?' asked Icham suspiciously, turning to that weasel.

Luke said, 'Yes, it is. Don't worry, Icham.'

So they followed the figure out of the hall and into curved passages. As they walked Sylver had the sensation that the floor was moving, ever so gradually, and he could hear a grinding sound like two great boulders being rubbed together. He spoke to the monk about this.

'Oh, that noise? That's just our old boiler, down in the cellars. You'll hear it from time to time.'

Wodehed, now that he was inside the monastery and becoming bolder, decided to ask the question which had been on all their lips since the monk had first opened the door. 'Excuse me,' said the magician, 'but might I enquire what kind of creature you are? You can't be human, since there are no humans left on Welkin. And you're not a statue, because your speech is so clear. Perhaps . . .'

The monk had stopped and had drawn himself up to his full height of just over a metre and a half. He towered over the small weasels, a very imposing figure. 'It is forbidden,' he said to them. 'Our Order forbids it.'

'Forbids what?' asked Sylver.

'We are not permitted to divulge the nature of our earthly forms. We are what is known as Gnostics, you see. Gnostics believe that all things of the world and the flesh are the Devil's works. So

85

we make no reference to the shape or form of our bodies – we are only allowed to talk of our *souls*. The spirit is the important thing, not the blood and bone.'

'Oh, I quite agree,' said Luke. 'The spirit is the important thing – but you can't ignore the fact that we do *have* earthly forms.'

'Oh, but we *must*,' replied the monk. 'We must ignore it, otherwise we acknowledge it. If I ever knew what I was, I have forgotten it, for I have not thought of it for so long now. It is unimportant. Our Order tells us to wipe from our minds what we are in this life and to concentrate on what we might be in the next . . .'

'How devout,' said Bryony.

'How pious,' said Icham.

'How *convenient*,' murmured Sylver, but not loud enough for the monk to hear him.

'And here,' cried the monk dramatically, as they came to a row of stone rooms with wooden beds and straw mattresses, 'are your cells. I shall let you rest before you eat. Sleep well, friends. Sleep *deeply*.'

Chapter Nine

Sylver, once in his cell, did not sleep at *all*, let alone deeply. Something about this place did not feel quite right to him. He could not imagine why the monastery did not recruit new monks, to fill its chapel, its kitchen, its manuscript rooms. That a single monk, no matter how large he was, should run a whole monastery on his own seemed ludicrous.

Who did the hunting? Who worked in the fields? Who transcribed parchments?

Thus, Sylver remained on the alert, not letting his guard down for an instant. Indeed, not long after they had been shown to the cells, a silent shape appeared in the doorway. It seemed it had a long gleaming instrument strapped to its fore-limb – a knife or a sword. Sylver sat up quickly in his cot and said, 'Yes?'

The implement instantly disappeared within the folds of the monk's sleeve, which dropped suddenly to cover it. 'Just making sure you were comfortable,' murmured the monk. 'Get some rest now.' The creature then went away again, muttering something to himself.

Later Sylver and the others went down to the dining hall, where food and drink were laid out on a long table. There were benches down either side.

The monk sat at the head of the table, but despite the candlelight, no-one could see his face under his hood. The outlaws talked amongst themselves as they ate, while the monk simply sat there quietly feeding food into the dark cavern that was his hood. This was done with a forked twig sharpened on its two points.

Finally, Sylver said to him, 'You mentioned you were of the Order of the Drum?' he said.

The monk's head came up quickly and Sylver could feel two sharp eyes boring into him from inside the hood. 'Yes?' said the monk in a spiky voice. 'What of it?'

Sylver was surprised that his question had obviously shaken the monk. 'Nothing really – I just thought, if you're the Order of the Drum, you must have some drums.'

'Of course,' replied the monk, this time a little less aggressively. 'A whole room full of them.'

'I'd very much like to see them,' Sylver said. 'Would that be possible?'

There was a general murmuring of agreement amongst the other outlaws. Yes, they said, they would all like to see the drums. Could they see the drums after supper?

'I – I think they're away being cleaned,' the monk faltered. 'Yes, I'm sure they are.'

Icham asked innocently, 'Who's cleaning them?'

'Why, the people in the village, of course. Who else would be cleaning them?'

Bryony said, 'I wasn't aware that drums needed cleaning.'

The blade of a long curved knife appeared from inside the monk's left sleeve, and he used it to cut the meat before him. Sylver could not be sure, but he thought he had seen that kind of instrument before. It was a skinning knife, used by humans to strip the hides from the flesh of cattle.

'What do you know about drums, jill?' said the monk, with a kind of quiet threat to his tone. 'Or any of you jacks? Drums are very special instruments. These drums are even more special. They have to be cleaned, and that's that. Would you call me a liar?'

This outburst surprised the outlaws even more. Clearly there was some secret attached to the drums, some mystery which was not yet ready to reveal itself. Sylver determined to look around once the meal was over and try to find out what it was all about. 'I think I'll have a stroll outside,' he said after the meal was over. 'It was a clear sky at sunset. I'd like to see the stars—'

'That's not possible,' said the monk.

'What? Why not? All I have to do is open the door and walk outside. Are you saying we're prisoners here?'

'No, no. But – but it's dark outside. And probably raining too. Yes, I do believe it's raining. You would get wet. I strongly advise you to stay within the monastery. In fact, I *insist* upon it. I'll have no weasels sick with colds and flu under my roof. You will all go to your cells immediately. In the morning you can do what you like.'

With that the monk hurried out of the room, the gown trailing on the floor behind him picking up crumbs and bits of meat in its hem. It was actually a filthy garment around the bottom, which swished after its owner like a ratty dog chasing a pair of sticks. Just as the monk swept through the doorway the gown caught on a nail and lifted slightly. Sylver's keen eyes caught sight of what looked like a cloven hoof.

He said nothing about this discovery, however, as the others crowded round him.

'What are we to do?' asked Alysoun. 'I'm worried about staying here the night. I'm not sure the monk is as holy as he pretends to be. And even if he is, he has some very peculiar ways about him.'

'We'll all go back to our cells, otherwise he'll get suspicious,' Sylver told his band. 'When he thinks we're all settled, I'll go for a prowl.'

'I'll come with you,' Icham said.

'No, it's best I do it on my own. If the monk comes to check on the cells, which I'm sure he will, I want you all to shuffle around so he thinks the cells are all full. Once he's checked on one end, that weasel can creep past the monk while he's in another cell and get into my cot, with his face to the wall, so the monk doesn't suspect anyone's missing.'

'Good,' Wodehed said. 'Once you've found out what's going on here, Sylver, you can let us all in on it.'

So they pretended to go quietly back to their cells, all chattering about how tired they felt and how good it would be to get a full night's sleep in a proper bed. 'The forest floor's all right,' said Dredless loudly, 'but you get twigs and things amongst the dead leaves and they always stick into your back . . .'

Sylver gave it a short while before he crept from his cell once more. He went immediately through the dim passageways to the front door and opened it. He was astonished to find himself in the dining room on the other side.

'Must have had the wrong door,' he said to himself. 'I'll try another . . .'

Every door he tried, however, led to the dining room. Now that he came to think of it, there had been an enormous array of doors around the dining room, which he had noticed while eating his supper, but had not considered important. He thought that perhaps they led to store rooms and cellars. The only open doorway from the room led up the winding stone staircase to the cells above.

There was only one other door at the end of the row of monks' cells, which the monk himself had taken. This presumably led to his own quarters. It was possible to squeeze through an arrowloop window facing the cells, but judging from the number of steps they had had to climb to reach that part of the monastery, Sylver was sure there would be an enormous drop to the ground on the outside.

'Somehow the monk has locked us inside,' he murmured. 'For some reason no door leads to the outside world. Every passage, every corridor, every door ends up in the dining room. It's as if he's turned the monastery inside-out, while we have been within its walls. How did he manage that, I wonder?'

Finally, Sylver found a door which did not lead to the dining room, but which opened onto a set of stone steps, going downwards. He suspected this was the way to the cellars or a crypt – or perhaps even dungeons of some kind – but not to the outside world.

Since it was black down below he found a candle on the dining-room mantelpiece and lit it from the embers still glowing in the inglenook fireplace. With the light in his paw he began to descend the stone stairs, which wound downwards around a central point.

The air was still on the stairway, there being no windows below ground. Sylver took each step carefully, since he was not used to the rough stone stairs. When he was part way down, but still could not see the bottom, a big black beetle ran across his path. The weasel outlaw leader stopped instinctively, wondering where the beetle was going, and saw the creature disappear over the edge of the next step – into darkness.

Sylver stretched forth the paw bearing the candle.

He saw to his horror that there was no 'next step' – only a drop into nothingness. Now that he had almost been killed by it, he remembered hearing about such staircases. They ended in a pit, sometimes filled with water, in which victims unfamiliar with the building would fall and break their necks, or drown. He saw the beetle far below, scrambling over the vertical brickwork above a pool of cold black liquid.

'Thank you, my friend,' Sylver whispered to the beetle which had unwittingly saved his life. 'I owe you one for that.'

Sylver shone the light of the candle on the side of the stairway and found that a sharp turn to the right would lead him further down. Those who knew of the trap could count the stairs down to this point, then step smartly to the right, where the stairs continued safely. This Sylver did, and finally found his way to a chamber at the bottom.

Once in the chamber he discovered it was full of drums of all shapes and sizes. The monk had not been lying when he said the monastery was interested in such instruments. Perhaps there really was a holy Order of the Drum. Sylver went into the chamber and began to inspect the drums.

As he did so a chill ran down his spine. He suddenly realized why the monk had been so keen for the weasels to stay the night. He remembered too that strange remark first made by the monk: 'Weasels with fine hides.' Sylver, like others of his band, had found that statement most peculiar. Now, to his great dread, he knew why the comment had been made. It had slipped out accidentally and no doubt the monk had instantly regretted it.

Searching further, he found in another corner of the chamber a pile of bones. There were skulls, leg bones, backbones, ribs, pelvis bones – all jumbled together where they had been tossed in a heap. Like the hides on the drums, he recognized the skeletons instantly.

Sylver made his way up the stairs again, remembering to step sideways at the right point. Eventually he found his way back to the dining room. He blew out the candle and put it on the mantelpiece above the fire. As he was crossing the floor one of the doors opened and the monk entered carrying a torch.

'Hello!' cried the monk. 'What's this? Out of your cell? Trying to rob a gullible holy creature of his treasures, eh? What? Attempting to steal my gold and silver, no doubt. I should have you locked in my dungeon for this, you blackguard!'

'You'll do nothing of the sort, monk, or you'll find my band of outlaws hunting you through this strange monastery and filling your body full of darts! I was thirsty. I merely came looking for a glass of water.'

The monk boomed indignantly, 'Did you find any?'

'Yes,' replied Sylver, 'down those stairs behind that door – there's a large pool of it at the bottom.'

With that, Sylver left the monk and went back up to his cell. The others came crowding in once he was back. He told them briefly what he had discovered and promised to fill in the details the next morning. 'When I'm not so tired,' he said. 'In the meantime we're going to have to sleep in shifts. Icham and Bryony can take the first watch. We'll all remain in this one cell, while they watch the door. I'll take the second shift with Mawk . . .'

When he had detailed the watches for the night, Sylver lay on some straw on the flags and fell instantly asleep, exhausted by his night roamings.

When morning came they trooped down to the dining hall, where the monk was sitting in his chair waiting.

'Time for some answers,' said Sylver, standing in front of the monk. 'I know about the drums. You make them of weasel skin, don't you?' the outlaw leader accused the holy animal. 'That's why you invited us into your monastery. So you could kill us and skin us. You were going to use our hides to make more drums!'

The monk got up as if to attack the weasels, but slingshots and darts appeared in their paws in a twinkling.

'I wouldn't if I were you, monk,' said Bryony. 'I think you'd better show us the way out.'

'The doors are there,' growled the monk. 'Use them.' His voice changed to a whine. 'But don't go, dear weasels. It's raining something terrible outside. You'll all get wet and catch your death of cold. Why not stay here with me a little longer, eh? Perhaps you'll get to like it. I promise I won't do anything to you . . .'

'Listen, goat,' said Sylver. 'Somehow you've managed to turn this place inside out. All the doors which should be on the outside of the monastery now face into the dining room. I suspect it's got something to do with the round towers. This whole structure is built of round towers.'

It seemed that the monk was glowering underneath his hood, but finally he stood up. 'Yes, weasel, you're right. There's a secret switch just inside the main doors, which I pulled after you entered the monastery. The towers then revolved, very slowly, until all the doors faced inwards . . .'

'So that's what the grinding sound was,' said Sylver. 'I thought as much.'

'. . . but I'm not a goat,' finished the monk.

'So, what are you?' Sylver asked. 'I know I saw a flash of something long, white and pointed under your hood, like the horn of a billy goat. And more recently I saw a cloven hoof. If you're not a goat, what are you?'

The monk dramatically whipped off his habit and stood before the group on his hind legs.

There was a gasp from the outlaw band. What stood before them was a wild boar, with great white tusks that swept out of the sides of his mouth and up towards each hairy ear. His feet were indeed cloven. He was a monstrous fellow, dark-haired, shaggy and red-snouted, with small pinkish eyes. There were but a few wild boars left in the forests of Welkin and this one had vacated his home amongst the trees to take up residence in the monastery.

'You're no monk,' said Sylver. 'What do you actually do with those drums?'

'Why,' said the boar, smiling, his long tusks adding a touch of evil to the grin, 'I sell 'em to stoat thanes, who use 'em in weasel hunts. They beat the stretched hides and drive the weasels before them into catch nets, then sell 'em as slaves. You must know the slave markets of Prince Poynt. Well, weasels get this instinctive fear in 'em when they hear a paw beating on the skin of a dead brother or sister weasel – it's like beating on their own hearts – and their brain tells them to run in blind panic to get away from the sound – into stoat nets.'

'You swine!' whispered Alysoun in a voice of dread.

'Well, that's no insult,' said the boar. 'After all, I am a pig, you know.'

Chapter Ten

'You'd better let us go, boar, or we'll have to kill you where you stand,' said Sylver.

'Well now,' said the boar, whose eyes were flashing with spite, 'that wouldn't do you much good, now would it? If you killed me you would *never* find the way out of here. You'll just have to wait until I'm ready to let you go.'

Sylver was stunned by this answer. He felt sure that now the boar's secret had been uncovered, he would do what they demanded of him. But it seemed he had no intention of letting them out of their prison.

'We'll find the secret switch,' Bryony said. 'That won't take long.'

The boar sneered, his great tusks gleaming in the light streaming through the arrowloop windows. 'You could be here a million years and you wouldn't find the way out. Believe me, others have tried. I've got you where I want you.' He scratched one of his great hairy ears with a hoof, then spat on the floor at their feet. 'Don't have to keep up my manners now, do I?'

'You have to go out sometime,' cried Dredless, 'and when you do, we'll be right behind you.'

'Do I? Do I?' cried the boar shrilly, standing tall on his hind legs, his great belly sticking out, taut as a drumskin. 'Oh no, I don't. You see, there are secret recesses all over this monastery – hidden niches, cryptic cupboards, sealed rooms – full of turnips and parsnips and all the other delicious fare of a hungry boar like myself. I tell you now, weasels, as long as my name is Karnac-the-boar, you will remain my prisoners.'

With that the grotesque hog turned on his hoof and left them standing by the stairs.

'Right,' said Sylver. 'Search party. Split up into twos, search the whole monastery. There has to be a way out of here. Be careful, though. There may be more dangerous traps like the one I found on the stairs. You can't trust that old hog in the slightest. He has no shame. And watch your backs. One of you guard the other. Keep your slingshots and darts handy, or he might try to attack you . . .'

The weasels quickly organized themselves and set out in pursuit of an escape route from the monastery. All day they looked diligently in every nook and cranny of the monastery, finally meeting together in the evening to report. No-one had found a way out of the place. It was most depressing.

'Let's get some rest now. We'll try again tomorrow,' said Sylver.

'Ha! Ha!' came a booming triumphant clacking from the depths of the monastery. 'Failed, have you? There's nothing you can do, you weasels, but submit to the knife. Come to me now and I'll make it quick and easy. Strip the skin from you in one go, just like peeling a potato. If you don't, you'll slowly starve to death, while I wallow in sweet pigswill.

'Believe me, when you next see the outside

world, it will be as a bass drum or timpano or tambour bound for the paws of a skilled stoat drummer. Sticks will bounce from your backs. A *rat-a-tat-tat* will be the only cry in your throats! Oh, you poor silly creatures. Your destiny is a marching tune! A military two-step!'

'I could kill that hog now,' growled Dredless. 'Wodehed, can't you do something with him? Can't you turn him into something small and scared?'

To be quite honest, the weasel band did not have a great deal of faith in Wodehed's magic. He had never yet managed to do a spell completely successfully. Something always seemed to go wrong at the last minute.

'I've been working on it,' confided Wodehed in great excitement, riffling his fur with his claws. 'I'm just about ready. The very next time he shows his ugly snout—'

'You were saying?' interrupted a loud voice above him and the startled Wodehed jumped backwards. The boar had returned suddenly on hearing the raised, enthusiastic voice of Wodehed.

Wodehed decided it was time to assert himself. His magic, he felt, was at last ready to be put to the test. The would-be weasel sorcerer fixed Karnac with an intense stare and began to chant, while at the same time producing a small bulbous wineskin from a pouch on his belt.

> *'Swine, swine, drink my wine.*
> *Pig, pig – have a swig!'*

As if in a trance Karnac reached forward and took the skinful of wine, uncorking it. He swallowed the contents of the leathery bag in one go. Then he let the flaccid, empty wineskin fall to the stone-flagged floor with a *splat*. He stood for a moment as if transfixed, his face screwed into a look of intense concentration.

Wodehed continued his chant in excited tones while the other weasels watched with great interest as he made his magic.

> *'Boar, boar not any more,*
> *Hog, hog, thou art a FROG!'*

Karnac blinked and then let out what seemed to the weasels to be an almighty croak – which on later reflection they decided must have been a common belch – before wiping his mouth on the sleeve of his habit.

'Nice drop of claret that,' the false monk grunted. 'Pity there wasn't much of it.' With these words he turned on his hoof and left the room.

There was silence among the weasels for a moment, then Wodehed wailed, 'What happened?'

'It didn't work *again*,' complained Icham disgustedly, 'that's what happened. When is one of your spells actually going to come out right, Wodehed? You've been practising long enough, yet you always get it wrong.'

'But I *felt* it working that time,' groaned Wodehed. 'I felt the tingle going through to the tip of my tail. Whichever animal's lips that magic wine touched first should have changed into a frog. I'm absolutely *sure* I got it all right.'

'LOOK!' cried Miniver, pointing at the floor.

They all stared at the empty wineskin on the

floor. It was beginning to swell like a small balloon of its own accord. Soon it began to develop folds and twists. Finally it squatted there on a stone flag looking very much like an ugly brown frog. Two small stains which were its eyes regarded the group of weasels, before the wineskin decided to jump-jump-jump away, towards a gutter running along the foot of the battlements. It croaked as it hopped out of sight.

Icham said, with more disgust, 'The wine was touching the wineskin before Karnac swallowed it. You didn't think of that, did you, you puttock? The wineskin was made of leather – it was an animal at one time.'

'Now what are we to do?' asked Sylver practically. 'We can't blame Wodehed. He did his best. We have to do something to get out of the clutches of this fiendish boar.'

'Let me go and try to reason with him,' said Mawk-the-doubter, hurrying away towards the sound of the clacking. 'Let me see if I can persuade him to change his mind.'

There was a tremor in Mawk's voice as he said these words. Sylver knew that the frailest of his outlaws was going to woo the enemy in order to get better terms for himself. Unfortunately Mawk had a weak character. He thought of his own safety before that of the band. His own survival was his main concern.

'Come back, coward!' cried Alysoun. They all knew what he was up to. 'Come back here!'

'Must reason with him,' cried Mawk. 'Must pretend to get friendly with him – to – to help us *all*.' With that the irresolute weasel disappeared into the shadows leading to the great hall.

'Let him go,' said Sylver. 'His fawning will take the boar's mind off us and he's far too skinny to be in any danger at present. We still have to think of a way to get out of here. Has anyone any ideas?'

'We could try to squeeze through one of these arrowloop windows,' Luke suggested. 'At least, perhaps one of us could – I'm too fat, I know.'

'We're all too big to get through one of those slits,' Bryony said, 'except perhaps . . .'

All eyes turned to Miniver, the finger-weasel, diminutive creature that she was. She was little-finger-thin, with tiny proportions, and able to get into most small places without too much trouble. Sylver realized that Miniver was their only hope of getting out of the monastery quickly. 'These windows are too high off the ground for Miniver to jump, but we could try making something which will break her fall. How do you feel about that, Miniver?'

'I'm not scared of heights,' she lied. 'Can you let me down by rope?'

'That might be possible,' said Sylver, 'but where are we going to find a piece of cord that long?'

There was silence amongst the outlaw band for a while, then suddenly Icham clicked his teeth. 'Got it!' he said. 'This place is a haven for spiders, right? There are cobwebs in every corner of the room. A spider's thread is one of the strongest materials in nature. Let's unravel a few webs, plait the threads together, and we'll have our lowering rope. Eh? How about that?'

'Brilliant,' Wodehed replied. 'Icham's right – the silken thread of the spider is immensely strong.'

'We hope,' muttered Sylver. 'Right then, let's get to it.'

They worked all night, finding webs, unravelling them, then plaiting three or four thicknesses of thread together and rolling it all into a ball. Once or twice Sylver left the group to spy on the boar. Each time he could hear Mawk's voice coming from near to where the boar sat on his great beechwood chair, flattering the hog with praise, telling him he needed a friend, someone from the other side, who could advise him.

'. . . I could tell you which weasels would make the best drums,' Mawk was saying. 'I could lead more weasels to you. If you let me go *now*, I could be out and back in a jiffy, leading whole squadrons of weasels. You could slaughter them as they came in through the doorway, after I've put them at their ease, and slit them open, skin them there and then . . .'

The boar, whose face Sylver could not see, since he could only approach from the back of the great chair, was sipping honey dew noisily, listening to the chatter of the terrified Mawk. Occasionally the hog let out a great ripe belch and smacked his lips together loudly. Sometimes he broke wind against the chair, filling the room with a foul smell. On other occasions he cleared his snout into a filthy old rag, into which he blew with rubbery vibrating nostrils.

'. . . you are such a handsome fellow, Karnac,' Mawk lied in a quietly hysterical voice to the vain creature, 'and I expect you'd like a looking-glass to see just *how* lovely you are. I could get you one very easily. I have heaps of mirrors back in the forest . . .'

Karnac grunted with approval on being told he was good looking, but made no comment about letting Mawk go. He really was the most disgusting creature. He soaked up the flattery like a sponge soaks up water. Sylver left the pair, revolted by both creatures.

In the early morning they had a length of thread long enough to reach the ground from the lowest window in one of the tall towers.

'Get help in the best way you can,' said Sylver. 'Don't panic – we're all right for the time being. We'll get a bit hungry, but we can stand that for a while. Don't go and get yourself captured by Falshed and his troops. You can't help us from inside another prison! Do your best.'

'I'll get help, don't you worry,' Miniver replied.

With that the finger-weasel squeezed through the arrowloop window and scrambled down the plaited rope to the ground, where she slipped off into the tall grasses. Miniver knew there was a village near by, which would be full of weasels. There she hoped to recruit someone to her cause.

Miniver approached the village with caution, in case there were any stoat troops in the vicinity. Prince Poynt's stoats were often billeted with weasel serfs and their families, to save him the expense of building camps.

Sounds of activity were coming from the village. Like most weasel – or for that matter any animal – villages, the main street was made of hard-packed earth. This tended to be like brick and rutted in the summer, and covered in thick sludgy mud in the winter. Along the street on either side were wooden shacks and wattle-and-daub houses.

Built originally for humans the dwellings were mostly one-roomed hovels with a hole in the roof for the smoke from a central fire. Straw was strewn over the floors and this served as both seats and beds. They were miserable little abodes – but to someone they were homes.

Sure enough, as Miniver went down the street, keeping close to the shadows of the buildings, she saw evidence of a stoat presence in the village. Two soldiers were lounging around outside an inn, their bullet-shaped helmets resting on posts. In their paws were jugs of honey dew, which they frequently quaffed.

Miniver slipped into the first hovel she came to.

There was a jill weasel in the corner, cowering away from the light. She stared at Miniver with round eyes. On the earthen floor were strewn various cooking utensils, all thick with black grease. A weasel kitten was playing in the ashes of the cold fireplace with a piece of filthy string. She looked open-mouthed at the intruder. The jill herself, a fairly elderly weasel, was smudged with black – dirty and unkempt.

'What do you want?' she said. 'You'll be for it when my jack comes home.'

'I don't mean any harm,' whispered Miniver. 'I just came to see if you could help me. You see, my friends are trapped in the monastery—'

'The one with the old pig in it?' interrupted the peasant jill.

'Yes,' said Miniver, 'and I wondered—'

'You don't want to go near there,' said the jill, interrupting again. 'You got to be careful with that old pig. He'll skin you alive.'

'I'm aware of that, but I was wondering if the villagers would help me get my friends away. I can't do it on my own. This must have happened before. What did you do last time an innocent traveller stopped at the monastery?'

'You mean,' said the jill, getting the gist more quickly than Miniver had expected, 'you want crowds of villagers to go out there with flaming torches and force the pig to release his prisoners?'

'Something like that.'

'You must be mad as a loon. Who would want to do a thing like that? We've got enough to put up with here, without having to rescue weasels from the clutches of Karnac.'

'Well, that's a bit mean-spirited,' said Miniver. 'After all, Sylver is trying to get everything put to rights here, so that we can all return to our rightful places in the woods and fields.'

'Sylver, eh?' said the jill, snatching the grimy string from the infant, which immediately let out a howl of dismay. 'Nothing to do with me. I don't want to go back to living in holes in the ground. I like my house, I do.'

Miniver took a look around her, at the damp dull interior of the hovel, with its one poky little window. 'After this place,' she said, 'I would think a hole in a dung pile would be a palace.'

The jill's eyes opened wide. She clutched at a broomstick with her paws. 'You get out of here,' she cried, 'before I call the stoats! Insulting my little home. Well I never did. I expect you've got no home to go to, that's why you're jealous of the likes of me. You ought to be ashamed of yourself, coming in here, taking advantage . . .'

The youngster was letting out a shrill whine now and grabbing feebly at the piece of string which dangled from its mother's paw. Miniver backed out of the dwelling and went on to the next one, then the next, then the next, each time trying to rouse the occupants of the village to some kind of action.

Finally, she came to the smith, whose furnace was glowing red-hot in his forge. He was wearing a leather apron to protect his fur against sparks. In his right paw he held a pair of pincers which gripped a glowing piece of metal. In his left paw was a hammer with which he struck the white-hot ingot, flattening it against a huge iron anvil. Showers of sparks like feckless stars danced from the blows in a fascinating display.

When the smith paused in his work to hear what Miniver had to say, he shook his head sadly. 'You'll not find anyone here to help you, jill. This village is full of fear. The stoats would burn our houses to the ground if they knew we'd helped Sylver and his band. Don't you know we're under constant watch?'

'Everyone is,' said Miniver sadly. 'That's the trouble.'

'Well, there's leather-workers here, who sew vole skins into furry bedsheets for Prince Poynt, and weapon-makers, and a paper mill where parchments are made for the monks who record the victories and triumphs of Prince Poynt. You see, there's a whole industry in this village. We send all our goods by mouse wagon to Castle Rayn – six mice to a wagon team – and if we don't live very well by it, we survive. No-one will want to put our village at risk, just to save some swash-buckling weasels.'

Miniver saw what the smith meant and sadly left his forge to slip down between two dwellings. There were some ferrets entering the village who had been on a long march, a vicious-looking mink at their head. Though there were fewer minks than ferrets in the auxiliary forces of Prince Poynt, their rise through the ranks tended to be rapid.

Miniver crept away into the fields beyond the village to find a stream from which to drink. She had been parched when she began her search, but the heat in the smith's forge had made her thirstier still. She found a small brook and began lapping up the water, when she sensed a presence behind her. 'Who's that?' she cried, whirling on the intruder. 'What's your name?'

Confronting her was a weasel bigger than herself – which was no strange thing since she was one of the smallest weasels around – but this was a very filthy animal. There were patches of fur missing from his coat. His face was smeared with dung, around which hovered a constant cluster of flies. His limbs were scabby and his tail mangy. In truth, he looked a very poor specimen of a creature. He grinned at her with yellowed teeth and then flicked his own nose with a lean red tongue.

'Scirf,' said the intruder.

'What?' asked Miniver. 'What was that?'

'Me name. It's Scirf. And I've come to give you assistance, like, to get your comrades out of jail. You can rely on me, jill. I can get the business done. It all depends on what it's worth, don't it? Eh? What say?'

Chapter Eleven

'I don't see how one weasel can help us,' Miniver said. 'We need a thousand weasels, armed to the teeth with terrible weapons, to make that boar see sense.'

Scirf touched his nose with his tongue. 'Ah, yes, but you doesn't know the ways of pigs, does you? I knows 'em, see. I'm wise to the ways of pigs. I can sort out that old swine quicker'n hog can bite its own tail.'

Wondering why a hog would *want* to bite its own tail, but not wishing to open another line of conversation which would only waste time, Miniver said, 'You mentioned some sort of fee – for helping us. We're not very well off. We don't have much use for money in Halfmoon Wood, though I dare say we could scrape together a few groats.' She was certain the weasel Scirf could not give them assistance, but since he was all they had, she was duty bound to listen to any ideas he might propose.

'My reward would be to join the outlaw band, see. Always fancied meself as an outlaw. Sounds sort of exciting. Better'n looking after the rhubarb dung.'

'The what?' asked Miniver.

'Dung what goes on the rhubarb patches. That's

me job in the village at the moment. Dung-watcher and part-time flycatcher. You might have noticed a bit of the stuff about me person. 'S'difficult to guard manure without getting a little dab of it on your pelt.' In fact he was covered in dung, but particularly around his facial whiskers.

'You – you seem to have a certain amount of – of organic fertilizer on your nostrils,' she admitted.

Scirf grinned and licked his nose quickly with that long slim tongue. 'No need to get fussy, is there?' he said. 'It's only straw and whatnot.'

It was the *whatnot* that worried her. 'But how do you manage to get it on your face?'

'Why, I got to eat, haven't I? It's the beetles what live in the nice soft warm dung. They're the main dish of an evenin', so to speak. Nice crunchy black beetles with oily shells.' He began to look wistful. 'They gets a sort of *sweet* taste when they lives in the manure. Your non-dung beetle is tangy, but your dung beetle is sort of sugary . . .'

'Listen,' said Miniver, wanting to change the subject quickly, 'I'm afraid I can't speak for the rest of the band in allowing you to join us, but I'm sure they'd all be very grateful for your help. Please, what ideas do you have?'

Scirf shook his head in a determined fashion. 'No, no – you got to promise to let me join the band. I want to see a bit of the world. I want to see Welkin. I'm fed up with looking after a pile of steaming—'

'Yes, so you said, but the authority does not rest with me,' explained Miniver carefully. 'Sylver is the leader of our band – he's the one who makes the ultimate decision.'

'Jills got no say, eh?' said Scirf, a little contemptuously. 'Jacks run the place, do they?'

'Certainly not,' replied Miniver, her feminist instincts rushing to the fore. 'Bryony has a lot of influence in the band – so does Alysoun – and myself. But we elected a leader and that leader is Sylver. He listens to advice, much of it from us jills, but he makes the final decision.'

'Well, that's it then, isn't it? Can't talk to this Sylver bod, so I can't help you, can I? Stands to reason. You can't give me a promise, I can't get 'em out.'

This put Miniver in an agony of concern. Scirf, for all his scruffy appearance, did seem quite confident of being able to free the band. But Miniver wondered just how long the band would put up with this filthy creature covered in rhubarb manure. It did seem, however, that she had taken over temporary leadership of the outlaws in the absence of Sylver. She *was* the whole band at the moment, since the others were in jail and unable to take part in any decision-making. 'All right,' she said at last, 'I promise you a place in the band – now, what have you got for me?'

Scirf shook his head. 'Nah, nah – you got to take me to where they are, and I'll get 'em out.'

'I've told you – they're trapped in Milkstone Monastery.'

'Where's that?'

Miniver was aghast. 'You mean you've never been there – met the boar monk?'

'Well I've heard of him, of course, and this monastery, but I've never been out of the village before. Just know pigs, that's all. Our family has

111

had dealings with pigs all our lives. We know how they think' – he moved closer to Miniver's ear and whispered like a conspirator – 'we knows the ways of 'em, see.'

'He's more than just a pig. He's a wild boar, with great sweeping tusks that fly out of the corners of his mouth, the points of which almost touch the tips of his bristly ears. He's big-boned and nasty – *huge* – with a girth like an old oak. He's rough and ill-mannered, thick-headed and ugly.'

'A pig's a pig,' stated Scirf, picking a dried crusty bit of dung from his coat and studying it closely, 'no matter how he's painted. He don't scare me none. I knows the ways of him, see.'

'Yes, yes, so you said,' Miniver replied, moving hastily away from the source of the smell. 'All right, I'll take you to the monastery. Er, wouldn't you like to wash in the stream before we go? It won't take but a moment to get clean.'

Scirf looked offended. 'Certainly not. I wouldn't know myself, if I was clean. I'd feel sort of, well, a sissy. Nothing wrong with a good bit of honest earth. Weasel of the land, that's me. Son of the soil.'

'Is it?' she murmured. 'Well, far be it from me to rob you of your identity. Come on, then.'

She led the way back to the monastery. Scirf followed jauntily behind, taking note of the countryside as he went. He was accompanied by horse flies and other airborne insects which hovered around his caked nose. This did not seem to bother him at all. Even a couple of speckled wood butterflies seemed interested in the load he carried in his matted fur.

Miniver kept upwind of the rustic weasel, whose job it had been to watch over the village dung pile, the smell of him offending her delicate sense of nature. She enjoyed the fragrance of wild flowers – forget-me-nots, campion, herb robert, wood anemones – not the odour of manure fresh from the yard.

On their way they met a weasel pedlar laden about his person with pots and pans. He clanked and clattered as he walked, whistling a merry tune. Pedlars seem to have the secret of life, at least when the sun is shining. Who knows where pedlars go when it's raining? This one, who had often visited Scirf's village in the past, stopped Scirf with a curt nod. 'Someone lookin' for you,' he said.

'Who?' asked Scirf.

'Statue – woodcutter – used to stand in your village square.'

'What's it want?'

'Don't know. Been asking for you all over.'

Scirf narrowed his eyes and scoured the countryside. On seeing it bare of statues he said, 'You haven't seen me, right?'

'If you say so,' said the pedlar, 'but it might want to give you a thousand gold pieces.'

'Doubtful,' replied Scirf. 'More like a bash about the head. I ain't done nuffink to no statue, but you know how thick they are – it might think I have.'

'Mum's the word then,' said the jaunty pedlar, going on his way.

'What was all that about?' asked Miniver afterwards.

'Blamed if I know,' replied Scirf. 'Some rotten statue wantin' to 'ave a word with me. I ain't interested. They get flies in their heads, these statues. Best to avoid 'em.'

When they reached Milkstone Monastery it was

113

evening. The cross which had guided the weasels to the place was not visible – no light shone behind it to attract wayward wanderers to the monastery doors. It was also very silent. Miniver wondered whether she was in time to save the weasel band from the boar's knife. 'Well, what do we do now?' she whispered to Scirf.

'Do?' cried the scruffy weasel loudly. 'Why we goes up and rings the bell, that's what we does!'

With these words he stepped up and pulled the rope on the end of which was the bell. It clanged loudly somewhere within the stonework. Miniver was terrified. She might have run, except that it was too late. The boar would surely catch her easily.

The great door swung open and the boar in his monk's habit stood there. 'Yes?' he said silkily. Then he noticed Miniver. 'Ahhh!' he roared. 'The one that got away. Come home again, have you? Inside with you!'

Miniver skipped over the threshold, followed by Scirf.

'Where d'you think you're going?' asked the boar from within the folds of his robe. 'Who asked you inside?'

'The coat may look a bit tatty,' said Scirf, 'but it's got a good solid rind underneath. Me old mum used to say to me, "You'd make a good drum, you would, Scirfy-me-little-kitty. You've got a leathery look about you, you have. Your father was the same, Gawd bless his hide. Even when he was hanging on a gibbet out in Long Meadow, he was prime pelt, he was."'

The boar stood for a moment, still holding open the door, then he shut it with a bang. Immediately the tower began to revolve slowly, changing the position of the outside world to the outer door. 'On your own head be it,' he growled. 'I might need something for a corner bit if I run out. Otherwise you'll do for patching, I suppose, though I can't imagine why you want to lose your skin and be made into a drum.'

Scirf rounded on Karnac. 'Why, what more glorious use could we be put to after we have to leave this world? A drum. Why, there's *majesty* in that word. There's a regal sound to it. Drums goes with everything, don't they? Bugles and drums, *fife* and drum, hautboys and drums. I shan't be sorry to be a *drum*, oh no, don't you worry about that, monkie-my-lad.'

'Monk,' murmured Karnac. 'Monk, not *monkey*.'

'Sorry,' replied Scirf. 'Just a sort of affectionate saying, like. Monk it is then, pigface.'

The boar took off his hood and blinked rapidly. 'Although I belong to the hog family, I do not like to be referred to as "pigface".'

'Oh?' said Scirf, looking surprised. 'Why's that, then? You've got the face of a pig, haven't you?'

Miniver was looking from one to the other of the two animals, wondering why Scirf was playing these games of words, annoying the boar intensely.

'Yes,' replied Karnac through gritted tusks, 'I *do* have the face of a pig, because I *am* a pig. But the term "pigface" is used as one of abuse. It's offensive. How would you like it if I called you "weaselface"? I don't suppose you'd like it.'

'But then I'm not a pig, I'm a weasel, an' I don't mind if you call me weaselface,' said Scirf, looking round as if searching for a door. 'Now then, where's the dining room?'

'What?' asked Karnac.

Scirf turned to face him again. 'The dining room, where we eats. You surely got to give us food before you cut our throats. A bad diet ruins the skin, don'tcha know. Lack of good nourishment can shrink a weasel quicker than a hog can bite its own tail. Why would you want to starve your weasels when, if you feed them up fat, you'll get twice as much material for your drumskins, won'tcha?'

Karnac suddenly saw the logic in this. Of course, he thought to himself, if I let them grow skinny there'll be a smaller hide on their backs. Whereas, if I feed them up like this weasel with the big mouth suggests, their hides will stretch even further across the drum tops!

'I was going to feed them all,' said Karnac, 'just before you came. You, little weasel – go and fetch your comrades. I guarantee your safety during the meal. Lord knows I don't want you all to starve to death.' He shuddered dramatically before adding, 'I'm not a *monster*.'

Miniver went off to the cells, where she found Sylver and the band had barricaded themselves in behind the doors. They were surprised to see her and had many questions to ask her.

'Are you here to set us free?' asked Bryony eagerly. 'Oh, I knew you'd do it, Miniver. Did you bring all the weasels from the village with their pitchforks and sickles? Has the countryside risen against the false monk? How many are out there – a thousand, a hundred, two dozen?'

Miniver coughed. 'One – and he's *inside*.'

'One?' said Sylver. 'You mean, one *village*?'

'One weasel.'

116

'A single weasel?' cried Icham. 'And you let him get himself caught?'

Miniver replied, 'I didn't actually – he gave himself up. He said he could handle the boar easily. Said his family had been doing it for generations.'

Alysoun said, 'And you believed him?'

'I had no choice. The villagers wouldn't come. They sent me away with a flea in my ear.'

'So we're left with this *single* weasel,' said Luke.

'Who's *inside* the monastery,' added Wodehed.

'I'm afraid so. Look, he's persuaded the boar that you all need feeding. He's sort of rough and ready, is Scirf, but he's got a way with words. We're to go down now, to the dining hall, where the boar will feed us.'

'Scirf?' repeated Sylver in a disappointed tone. 'That's the name of this saviour you brought?'

'Yes.'

'Not the White Knight, or Mighty Giant, or even Great Ogre, but *Scirf*?'

'Yes.'

'Not exactly the name of a hero, is it?' said Bryony.

'No,' said Miniver, feeling smaller now than she had done in her whole life. 'Are you coming to the table?'

'Rather than go hungry, I suppose we've got no choice,' said Sylver. 'Come on then, let's go and meet this *Scirf*.'

He led the band down to the dining hall and entered cautiously. At the table Mawk was already tucking into what looked like rabbit stew. The boar was munching quietly on a turnip. The other creature at the table, a shabby-looking weasel with a threadbare pelt, gestured heartily to him. 'Come on, you lot, there'll be nothing left. Not after guts here' – he nudged Mawk in the ribs, making him splutter and cough – 'has been at it. You must be Sylver, eh? What – I've heard a lot about you, haven't I, eh? Leader of the most ferocious band of outlaws since the hog bit its own tail, eh?'

'This is *him*?' whispered Sylver to Miniver, appalled at the creature before him. 'This is the one who's going to rescue the outlaw band from the wild boar?'

'Yes,' squeaked Miniver in an unsteady voice.

The outlaws were too hungry to hold back any longer. They took their places at the great table and began to scoff the food which was spread before them. The boar kept telling them to eat heartily, make themselves nice and fat, get a bit of weight under their belts, spread their waistlines a little.

'We know what you're up to, so forget it,' said Bryony. 'We'll eat just as much as we need and no more.'

'Oh really?' replied the boar, trying to look as if he were puzzled by her meaning. 'We'll see about that.'

Chapter Twelve

Under the light of flaming torches in iron-cage holders on the dining-hall walls, the outlaws ate a hearty meal, conscious of the fact that the boar was watching them with mean pink eyes. He seemed delighted that they should be expanding their skins by indulging in the feast he had laid out. His long shadow was cast over the length of the table, the tusks and ears standing out above the rest of the silhouette.

'A fine repast, is it not?' he murmured. 'Worthy of a set of creatures such as yourselves?'

'Speaking of creatures,' Scirf said, addressing Sylver with his mouth full, 'I understand you lot want the humans back.'

'That's true,' Sylver said, wondering when this Scirf fellow was going to make his bid for the freedom of all the weasels in the room. 'We have strong reasons for wanting them to return – to do with the sea walls around Welkin.'

'Ridiculous,' muttered the boar. 'Utterly preposterous.'

'In any case, villages and towns are no place for animals like us,' continued Sylver. 'We belong in the greenwood, in the fields, the mountains, the valleys . . .'

'So, the humans will be back in their houses, eh?'

said Scirf, reaching quickly for a piece of voles'-milk cheese before Mawk could get his grubby paws on it. 'Eating what humans eat.'

Sylver looked thoughtfully at the new weasel. 'I suppose so – whatever it is they *do* eat.'

'Ah, as to that,' Scirf said, 'I understand what they really enjoyed was a nice piece of fried . . .' He swung round quickly to look the boar directly in the eyes. '. . . PORK!' he yelled.

Karnac started backwards and instantly went pale under his dark bristles. He stared at the scruffy weasel in horror. It was all he could do to find a quavering voice in his throat. 'Don't – don't say that word,' he whispered hoarsely. 'That's an ugly, *horrible*, word.'

'Oh, fine,' agreed Scirf. 'In that case I have to tell you that a human's next favourite meal is sizzling – BACON!' He yelled the last word.

The boar put his trotters over his ears. 'Stop it! Stop it! Somebody stop him saying those words.'

'. . . failing that,' continued Scirf, 'a nice piece of succulent – HAM!'

The boar stood up, his eyes wild with fear, his jaw hanging open in terror. 'Arrrhhhhhhggg!' he yelled, pressing his hooves to his ears. 'I can't stand it!'

'TROTTERS!' shouted Scirf, standing on the table and bellowing into the hog's ear. 'CHITTERLINGS! SWEETBREADS!'

'AAAARRRGGGGGGGGHHHHHHHHHH!'

The others stood up now, tall on the table, and began to chant in high voices. 'RASHERS! PIG'S FRY! CHOPS!'

Karnac could stand no more. He ran from the room, pursued by the yelling mob, until he reached the tower with the outer door. Feeling with his trotters, he found a stone switch on the floor and pressed it. The tower ground round. Then the great door flew open and the boar rushed out into the night. With his robe flowing behind him he ran towards the distant forest, the outlaw band still yelling: 'GAMMON! KNUCKLE! CRACKLING!'

When Karnac-the-boar was safely out of sight the band gave a huge sigh of relief and clicked their teeth.

'That showed him,' said Miniver. 'That got rid of the mad monk.'

They all clicked again, then went back inside to where Mawk and Scirf were fighting over the last scrap of stew.

'Mawk, leave the stew. We're not done with you yet. Just because we've ignored you up until now doesn't mean you've got away free.'

Mawk's mouth dropped open and he allowed Scirf to wrest the stew bowl from his claws.

Sylver then addressed the dirty new weasel. 'Well done, Scirf. We owe you a great deal. And you, Miniver, for doing your part. I would never have guessed we could get rid of the boar that way.'

'I knows the ways of pigs, I do,' Scirf said, nodding hard. 'I was brung up knowing 'em. Well, do I have to go through some sort of initiation rite? What about it, eh? Do I have to stick me head in a bucket and recite *The Battle of Maldon*? Or do a complete circle of me body holding a broomstick with both paws? What's it to be, ladies and knights, nights and days, daze and clearheads? Eh? Give me your best shot.'

Sylver shook his head under this barrage of

words. He turned to Miniver. 'What's he talking about?' he asked.

Miniver cleared her throat before replying, 'I think he's referring to the fact that I promised him that if he set us free, he could join – join – join our band, sir.'

'WHAT?'

'That was the transaction,' said Scirf, greens hanging from his teeth like a moustache as he chewed. 'And a promise is a promise. You've been set free, I get to join.'

Icham said, 'You didn't have the authority, Miniver.'

'Pardon me, chief, but she did,' interrupted Scirf. 'Listen, you lot, all of you. Did you not send her out in the dangerous wide world to get help? What was she supposed to offer people to get that help? Old beans? Seems to me, Sylvie, you gave over your authority to this weasel once you sent her on her errand. Am I correct or am I right? Feel free to put me in my place.'

'Be quiet for a moment,' said Sylver. 'I can hardly hear myself think while you chatter on. I'll talk to you in a minute. Miniver, this Scirf creature's right about one thing, we owe you a great deal. Despite what Icham said, you did what you could under the circumstances. Everyone, including Icham, is grateful, so please accept a general thank-you.'

'You're welcome,' said Miniver, looking down shyly. 'I did my best.'

'And a good best it was,' Mawk said, clicking his teeth in appreciation of her efforts. 'I say we sing "For she's a jolly good fellow . . ."'

Sylver and the rest of the band turned and

looked coldly at Mawk, who suddenly realized he was not going to get back in favour that easily.

Sylver said, 'Mawk, it'll be a long time before you're forgiven for what you've done. I'm seriously thinking of sending you away. Banishing you – for ever.'

Mawk went very pale. 'You wouldn't do that, would you? Please, Sylver?'

Sylver stared at the errant Mawk for a long time. Finally he said, 'If you ever do anything like that again, you're out, do you hear me? You acted in a cowardly and devious fashion, while brave Miniver went out and found someone who could help us . . .'

'Me,' Scirf said, smirking. 'I'm the help.'

Sylver rounded on Scirf again. 'We're all very grateful. At the present time I'm speaking with one of my band, if you don't mind.'

'Don't mind in the least, squire. Your band's your own – but I will say this – I heard you'd got *honour*. You know, that stuff which makes you do things you don't want to? Got it coming out of your ears, so they said. And what's more, they tell me you accuse Prince Poynt of having *none* of the stuff. But, take your time, talk with the little one here, just let me know when you're ready to speak to me.'

Sylver ground his teeth. It looked as if the band were stuck with this talkative weasel with the foul coat. He could not send the creature away, now that Scirf had saved them. However, there was one thing he could do. 'Right, the initiation ceremony . . .' he said.

'Yes?' Scirf said, jumping to the floor. 'Want me to daub meself with mud and twigs and run around the block twice?'

'No, every member of the band, on joining, has to immerse him- or herself in *water*. It's our way of saying "Welcome". A sort of baptism, you might say. A symbolic cleansing of the body and soul.'

Now the weasel Scirf had gone pale under his fur. 'Doesn't sound very symbolic to me,' he said. 'Sounds more like your *actual*.'

They took Scirf to the kitchen, where he stood and trembled while they drew water from the well. To give the weasel his due he stood firm as the buckets were filled and their contents sloshed over him, though it was obviously painful to him. Finally they announced him ready.

'A-m-m-m I a m-m-member of the band yet?' he said, shivering.

'Looks like it,' said Miniver. 'Welcome to the ranks of the enemies of Prince Poynt.'

One by one the other weasels welcomed Scirf into the band. Wodehed said privately to Sylver that he wondered about the wisdom of bringing another weasel into the group, but Sylver had no choice. Scirf had been right. It was a question of honouring promises made by Miniver as his deputy. Whether they liked it or not, the moth-eaten Scirf was now an outlaw.

Cleaning up the creature had done little to improve his general appearance, of course. His tail was still like a rat's tail; there were bald patches on his pelt; his nails were far too long and he still talked nineteen to the dozen.

'We'll have to get those nails sorted out,' said Miniver, who had taken him under her wing. 'Soon as we come across a piece of sandstone I'll do them for you.'

"S very nice of you, titch. Very nice. Did I ever

tell you about the time when I let 'em grow as long as harvest mice tails? It was to get at the beetles what hide *deep* in the dung, don'tcha know . . .'

The band left Milkstone Monastery and went out into the night. There was no sign of Karnac, though they guessed he would be back. However, with the mechanism of the doors exposed they managed to find the switch and sabotage it, so that the towers remained jammed with the doors facing the outside.

In the meantime, Sylver had ordered everyone to bring a drum and some bones with them from the cellar, and these were buried with due ceremony in the first good piece of bottom land they came to after leaving the house. The graves of those poor unfortunate creatures who were now nothing more than skin and bone were left unmarked, as was the custom with the outlaws. They did not believe in showing scavengers where bodies were buried, just so they could be dug up and devoured.

'. . . as mould turns to tree food, blossoms to dirt, may these skins enrich soils and these bones become earth.'

They stood there for a moment in the silence, still in the pools of moonlight, each privately watching for any barn owls that might be on the wing. Then they set forth again for a copse near Scirf's old village. There they spent the night in safety, tucked up in roots and holes. In the morning, when the sun splashed its yellow warmth on the leaves and woodland floor, they rose and set forth again.

They came at last to a long and mighty dyke on one side of which was a deep trench. Both the dyke and the trench had been built by the humans, to act as a border between two rival parts of Welkin, a sort of fortification which crossed the whole country. Now both these human-made defences were covered in turf and formed a pleasant grassy walk. Sylver decided they ought to travel along the trench to avoid being seen by stoat troops.

About noon they came across a strange *thing* lying in the dyke. It seemed they had to pass this shapeless object or risk being seen on top of the dyke. A quick run up the bank and survey of the surrounding countryside revealed it was crawling with stoat soldiers. The troops with their helmets glinting in the sunlight seemed to be avoiding the very spot where the outlaws were hiding.

'Is this a good sign, or a bad one?' murmured Sylver. 'Difficult to tell until we go by that *thing*.'

Sure enough, as they got closer, the *thing* stirred, sat up – if it could be called *sitting* – and stared at them – with many dozens of eyes.

'What do you want?'

'Where are you going?'

'Who's that with you?'

'What's your name?'

'How do they call you?'

'Speak up now.'

'Don't be slow.'

Then those dreaded but expected words. 'You may *not* pass.'

These comments and more came from the many heads of the being, which appeared to be made from dozens of arms, legs, bodies and heads of different statues, though none of them appeared to match. It was as if the *thing* had been made from a junk pile of discarded statue parts, but stuck together willy-nilly.

Arms came out of the sides of heads, heads were stuck on knees, thighs and even bottoms. Hands were attached to hips, legs to shoulders, torsos to each other. Bronze, granite, marble and plaster were welded together by some unknown force. There were cracks and fissures running the length and breadth of the *thing*. In places these had been filled with dirt and grime and were now growing moss, lichen and even small plants. It was a sort of walking ruin, a grotesque mass of waving arms and legs, hands and feet – and, of course, talking heads.

'Come closer to Odds-and-Ends at your peril!'

'Take no further steps!'

'Keep your distance.'

'Watch yourself, stranger.'

'Hello, hello, has anyone got the time?'

The last remark came from a head on the other side of the monster, as it rose from the ground and towered over the band. It was standing not on feet, but on a dozen or so hands, at the ends of arms and legs. It was like a giant metal-and-stone spider, but tall as a tower with many projections. Wavering and waving on all points, sprouting green fronds and moss like an old garden statue, it mesmerized the group of weasels.

At least they had got its name now. *Odds-and-Ends*. When you had someone's name it meant you could talk to them, gradually growing more familiar, until you had their sympathy – hopefully.

'Ah, Odds-and-Ends, is it?' said Sylver, staring up at the multiplicity of arms and legs and heads. 'I wonder if you have some sort of *toll* for letting weasels past.'

'Toll?' cried a dozen heads together. 'What's a toll?'

'Well, it means we have to give you some sort of payment in order that you step aside and let us continue on our journey.'

The statue of bits and bobs swayed before them, silent now as each of its heads absorbed what had been said to them. No statue was very bright, but this one seemed particularly stupid, being made up of discarded parts. Since statues were looking for their First and Last Resting Places, this one must have been particularly confused. It had many, many first and last resting places, which would be great distances apart. It was probably going through a great torment of indecision, not knowing which way to go, which path to take.

Chapter Thirteen

The monstrous statue with its grotesque appendages did not think very much of a toll.

'Can't use it,' said one head.

'No need for it,' said another.

Icham said, 'We could give you a live weasel for
your very own slave,' and standing behind Scirf he
pointed down at the ex-dung-watcher.

'Hey!' said Scirf. 'You watch it.'

'You're so full of ideas,' Icham said. 'How about
coming up with one now we need it?'

Scirf glowered. 'Oh, yes, I know how to deal
with pigs all right, but statues is another thing,
ain't they?'

It seemed that there was no way the group were
going to get past the giant. Bryony climbed the
bank of the trench carefully and looked out from
the edge of the dyke. In the distance she could see
a regiment of stoats. They seemed to have some
kind of war engine with them, but quite what it
was she could not make out. Some sort of catapult,
she guessed.

It was certain, however, that if the band tried to
go around Odds-and-Ends they would be seen by
the stoats.

She slid back down the bank and reported her
observations to the rest of the outlaws.

All the while, in front of them, the stone-and-metal monstrosity grumbled with its many mouths, creaked and groaned, ground and grated whenever it moved. Bits of foliage and soil dropped from it as it moved. A small hawthorn tree, growing from a crack in a shoulder high above, became dislodged when the giant turned. It seemed the statue had caught sight of the stoat regiment.

At that moment a huge boulder came flying through the air and struck Odds-and-Ends in the chest, scattering a few loose arms and legs.

'Hey!' cried several heads.

'What?' called one or two others.

'We're being attacked, we're being attacked,' said the topmost head of all.

Two dozen hands reached down into the trench and picked up stones. These were hurled back at the stoats, but with less force than the boulders coming back at the giant. The outlaws found they had to retreat back along the trench to avoid being struck themselves. They watched in amazement as the battle proceeded, with stones filling the air like hail.

Great rocks smashed into Odds-and-Ends, gradually breaking it apart and reducing it to a pile of rubble. It was horrible to watch. The outlaws stared in amazement and revulsion as the giant gradually fell to bits, its garden areas dropping to the ground. Arms and legs were strewn over the dyke and trench, torsos dropped as dead weights to the ground, heads rolled over the turf.

No sooner was Odds-and-Ends in pieces, however, than it began to put itself together again. Two arms soon became attached to a head. Thus, with eyes and something with which to walk, the gathering process began. Yellow clay from the dyke was used to stick the appendages and extremities together again, until Odds-and-Ends was once more itself, except in a different shape. All the bits were in different places, but essentially it was Odds-and-Ends fully formed again.

'Uh-oh,' said Bryony. 'Now we'll see some fun.'

In the distance the stoats were desperately searching for more rocks for their huge siege catapult, having used all the surface stones in the vicinity. They found one, which took off a single Odds-and-Ends head, but the giant stone statue had many more. It was a positive junk pile of heads. It had more arms than a regiment and more legs, too. It was rich in torsos.

It picked up its severed stone head, which had at one time been that of a great general of some human tribe, and bowled it swiftly towards the terrified stoats. The rolling head shrieked, 'Charge!' as it trundled speedily towards the soldiers. Its wicked-looking helmet was like half a horse chestnut, covered in spikes, and looked extremely dangerous.

'Run!' cried a stoat captain. 'Run for your lives!'

The head smashed into the siege catapult as the stoats were scattering this way and that. It knocked the war engine over on its side. Odds-and-Ends plucked another head from its shoulders, this time the bonce of a learned man – some cleric or other – and pitched it fully at the catapult.

'Awake!' cried the head on its journey through the air. 'Awake, ye sons of Satan, for a messenger of the Lord is about to strike ye down where ye stand!'

The full force of the head's wonderful hooked nose struck the main crossbeam of the war engine and it cracked in two halves with a thunderclap sound.

Odds-and-Ends was beginning to enjoy itself, smashing the siege catapult apart. It plucked two more heads from its many-headed form and sent them flying towards two main groups of stoats who were running for their lives.

'Tally-ho!' cried one bronze pate, as it whistled through the atmosphere. 'Give 'em hell, Cecil!'

This remark was addressed to the other head, which looked as if it belonged to the great god Pan rather than anyone called Cecil. It had horns, goat's eyes and a funny little beard, all wrought in black iron. When it struck the earth, it pinned a kicking, screaming stoat to the ground, one horn on either side of the creature. The stoat struggled like mad, yelling for his comrades to assist him, while the head tried unsuccessfully to bite his flicking tail.

The bronze head, that of a favourite horse of some warrior king, landed on its neck and stuck fast. It whinnied shrilly into the nearby ear of a stoat sergeant, causing that poor creature's eyes to start from his head. He staggered away into the undergrowth of a copse, looking as if he had been rolled into a ball and used for catapult ammunition.

After that heads began raining down on the stoats, plucked like berries from the body of Odds-and-Ends, until finally the giant statue had none left to throw.

At this point in the battle Sylver thought it wise for the group to move on, and they slipped quietly down the trench to continue their journey.

That night they camped in the ruins of an abbey, whose stone walls were almost as close to nature as the rocks and stones which sprang from the rolling downs. The weasels used the weathered ruin for shelter from the wind and to protect their fire from the sight of stoats. They sat around the flames and discussed where they were going next.

'There's a forest between us and the Yellow Mountains,' said the wizard Wodehed. We have to go through that valley if we are to reach our destination. I'm told by a reliable source that a moufflon lives in a cave there and we are to be wary of having anything to do with the creature.'

'A *moufflon*?' said Mawk. 'What's that?'

Ever since Sylver had given Mawk his dressing down after the Karnac affair, the outlaws had deliberately ignored Mawk-the-doubter. They had not trusted themselves to speak to him, even in wrath, knowing they would have lost their tempers. Time had blunted their anger, however, and although they still felt betrayed by Mawk they were ready to meet his pathetic gaze. Not that he was going to find friendship in their eyes.

They all stared at him pointedly, making him feel uncomfortable. 'Did someone speak?' asked Luke. 'Did I hear the voice of the traitor in our midst?'

Mawk's face became glum again. 'I'm no traitor,' he said. 'I was trying to help.'

'By fawning on that beast?' said Alysoun.

'I flattered him, yes,' said Mawk, 'but that was just to get on his good side. I wanted to persuade him to let me go, so I could fetch help from Thistle

133

Hall. You can't prove that wasn't my plan – a very devious scheme it was, too!'

It was true. No-one could say what had been in Mawk's mind. But most of the outlaws were sure that Mawk's reasons had been purely selfish. It was always like this. They were certain he had been out to help himself at the time, yet now he cast doubt in their minds and they were not so sure. As always, Sylver gave Mawk the benefit of the uncertainty over his motives, believing a weasel was not guilty until proved to be so.

'We'll try to forget it this time, Mawk, but you'll do something like that once too often,' said Bryony.

'You work in your way and I'll work in mine,' said Mawk sullenly. 'I'm just as entitled to do things my way, as you are to do them in yours.'

So they left it at that, but still only Miniver and Scirf remained sitting near Mawk, while the others still treated him coldly and edged away from him.

'So,' said Sylver, once this business had been settled. 'What *is* a moufflon, Wodehed?'

'It's a kind of wild mountain sheep, with long curved horns. The one we have ahead of us enjoys a reputation for witchcraft,' explained Wodehed. 'You must have heard of her, Luke. Her name's Maghatch.'

'Maghatch? Oh yes, I know of her. A godless creature if ever there was one. I'm told her victims are imprisoned for years in the foul oubliettes of her green chapel . . .'

'Oubliettes?' questioned Icham.

'Small wells with iron grids into which animals are lowered and then forgotten. They survive on insects which crawl down there – and water which runs on the damp stones. The green chapel is a huge green mound, not unlike a human grave in appearance, open at both ends. When you enter the green chapel you descend into a hell of stone-lined underground passageways, one at least of which leads to the Otherworld of witches.'

Bryony shivered. 'I take it we shall be avoiding this Maghatch.'

'If we do not,' said Wodehed, 'it will be the worse for all of us.'

With this happy thought in mind, someone stoked the fire a little higher to gain comfort from the light of the flames.

'Why is this world full of Karnacs and Maghatches?' muttered Mawk. 'Why can't it be full of *nice* animals.'

'Where's your spirit of adventure?' cried Scirf, his eyes shining at the news. 'Where's your flambeau, young Mawk? How can we strive to be better weasels wivout barin' our teeth in the face of evil? This is a chance to make good, see? This is a golden opportunity to show what we're made of, comrade!'

'You show the world what *you're* made of,' muttered Mawk. 'I prefer to hide my flambeau under a bushel.'

No-one said very much after that. Those that were not on watch lay down their heads and got some sleep. Each of the two sentries for the night went to one end of the group, taking a quiet stand on the dyke, staring out in opposite directions. The night was a dark one, with few stars and no moon. The sentries had little to stare at except blackness.

They were relieved twice during the night. The

135

last pair, Dredless and Alysoun, had the misfortune to watch the dawn creep in over the land. Grey twilight is a strange time, when shadows are light and sinister and seem to flit around like bats looking for a cave in which to hang.

You see things in the dawn that are not really there. The light plays games with your eyes. The shades play tricks with your brain. You think you see something out of the corner of your eye, but when you turn your head quickly to look, it is gone. It seems to have hidden itself in some outcrop of rocks, or to have run into a tangled thicket to lurk there. You have the feeling that something, many things, are watching you from cracks in the world. Their sinister eyes stare out at you, waiting for the time when you relax and are off your guard, before they swiftly change position again – moving closer.

Alysoun was never so glad as when the time came to wake Sylver and the others. Dredless, too, was a lot happier when the band was awake and chattering, driving away those dark fears from his head. Both these two sentries would have been happier if there had been no talk of witches the night before.

In the bright light of the new day, however, all that seemed quite silly now.

Chapter Fourteen

The outlaw band came to a forest where the trees swept up the slopes like a giant sea wave. Inside the tree line the forest was dark and musty. Like the Lightless Forest, here were only fir and pine trees in which no living creature dwelt, unless it were unspeakably menacing. Under foot was a soft thick bed of pine needles; overhead a dark-green canopy which blocked out the sky.

Here Silence reigned alone over an empty kingdom, queen only of herself.

'We shall need Wodehed's magic needle in here,' said Sylver. 'One fir tree looks much like another and the darkness makes it difficult to see our way.'

Wodehed removed the needle from his pouch. As he dangled it on its thread it swung towards the lodestone mountains of the north.

Thus equipped, the Welkin weasels entered the gloomy forest, where lurked those unknown dangers for which one can never fully prepare. They kept their slingshots and darts at the ready, just in case they were wrong about the place being empty. Such a thickly wooded area could hide an army of savage creatures, ready to spring out from behind the uniform trunks.

'Did I say I wanted to join your band?'

whispered Scirf, as if to talk in a normal voice would be to invite the wrath of the forest gods. 'Bit hasty of me, weren't it? Maybe I might change me mind in a minute.'

'It may be too late now,' Mawk said in a quivering tone. 'But if you do want to go, let me know, I might come with you.'

Under the canopy of firs strange mosses grew, which glowed in the darkness. Occasionally one of the outlaws would cry out and point at what looked like a figure, only to find on closer inspection that it was a moss shaped like an animal or a bird, or not like any living shape at all, but still scary.

There were also roughly hewn rocks, some cut in the semblance of a man. Certain standing-stones were placed throughout the forest, probably old signposts meant for human travellers when they made their way through the gloom. But they seemed not to be on any kind of track or path. And if they had ever had symbols on them, these were now worn away.

At one point Scirf was at the end of the line and he suddenly disappeared into the darkness. A few moments later, as the group was approaching a weird standing-stone, Scirf leapt out from behind it to confront them.

'YAAAAHHH! DIE!' he yelled, breaking the silence with this terrible ferocious yell.

Mawk almost fainted where he stood. 'Oh Gawd!' he cried.

The others naturally jumped, but when they saw it was only Scirf, they were annoyed.

'What's the matter with you?' snapped Sylver. 'Are you motley-minded, or what?'

'I think I must be a what, 'cause I ain't motley-minded. It was only a joke. Thought I'd liven things up a bit, see. Gets flippin' spooky in here. What's the matter, can't take a bit of fun? Come on, 's just a clack, init?'

The others had begun to back off from Scirf at this point, as a huge dark shape moved across and behind him. Scirf could not see this monstrous thing, a great mound of fur with claws and teeth. It was as tall as a man, but much bigger round the girth. Since the floor was so soft no footfalls could be heard and Scirf had no idea that something was passing behind him.

His sense of smell had long since gone. Having lived on dung heaps for most of his life, he had lost it. One of the reasons, probably, why he saw no need to wash.

The huge dark shape loomed over him, then moved on. Still he was unaware of its presence.

'What? What did I say?' he pleaded. 'Don't look at me like that. All right, come back. I won't do it again, I promise. Why are you all going backwards? You're not going to run off and leave me here . . .'

The great form, which they all now realized was a bear, vanished into the gloom behind Scirf. The outlaws all let out a sigh of relief. Sylver moved forward to take his place at the front of the line. 'You'll never know,' he said to Scirf. 'You'll just never know.'

The others all murmured in agreement with their leader.

'What?' cried Scirf, realizing he was the brunt of a joke, and wanting to know what it meant. 'What?'

'It doesn't *bear* thinking about,' replied Icham.

The group enjoyed the opportunity for a clack after such a close encounter with a giant.

'If only the *bare* facts were known,' added Wodehed.

Another clicking from the crowd – that is, from all except the unhappy Scirf.

'You *barely* made it that time,' said Dredless.

Alysoun said, 'Good job you didn't *bare* your teeth.'

'Whoa! Whoa!' cried the ex-dung-watcher. 'I've got a feeling you lot are makin' fun of me. You watch it. I can't bear being made fun of . . .'

They all clacked with merriment, leaving him feeling absolutely bewildered.

In the deepest part of the forest the trees began to thin out a little. They were not so dense here. Grass began to appear in little glades. Rocks which had not been placed there by human hands began to poke their backs above the surface of the land. Clumps of undergrowth appeared, where the light penetrated the canopy. There were pools of water.

Sylver halted his band and surveyed the area ahead. 'This looks a more dangerous region,' he told them. 'While the forest is black and lifeless, we have little to fear, but places like this can support life. Be on your guard. Watch for any sign of habitation.'

They moved forward more cautiously now, going in and out of the light, which now fell over them in ripples. Finally they came to a spot where there were dark square shapes in the upper branches of the trees. Here was a village high above ground.

'What are they?' asked Bryony. 'Rooks? Is this a rook colony?'

'Rooks still live in nests,' Wodehed said. 'You won't find rooks building huts in the trees.'

At that moment the keen-eyed Sylver noticed grey-brown shapes with dark-brown faces above white bibs, moving amongst the trees ahead. Some were wearing helmets which looked as if they might be made of tree bark. They held spears in their forefeet and had armour strapped to their breasts and backs.

Suddenly one of these creatures detached itself from the darkness of the trees and rushed forward. Sylver could see now that the helmet was like a mask, with two eyes looking through holes in the tree bark strapped around the creature's head. Two knobbly bits of root stuck up like horns from either side of the helmet. On the creature's knees, all four of them, were caps made of horse-chestnut cases, bristling with spikes.

'Haaaaaaa!' cried the creature, throwing a spear.

Even while the weapon was swishing through the air, the strange warrior had vanished to one side, into the forest again.

The spear came down with the point between the toes of Mawk's right hind leg, as he stood on tiptoe trying to see what was happening. It quivered there, stuck in the ground. The rest of the band, still startled by the suddenness of the attack, took a moment to recover, before rapidly retreating to a safer place.

'Good grief!' cried Mawk. 'What was that? I nearly lost a foot. What in the devil's name was it?'

Sylver took a dart from his belt. 'I think we've

run across a village of savage pine martens,' he said. 'Can't be sure, because of those mask-helmets and the body armour, but I saw a flash of dark brown against a lighter brown, and a cream bib.'

Icham, who had been looking around him, suddenly gave a gasp. 'Look at this,' he said. 'What are all these?'

The outlaws stared in the direction Icham was pointing and realized they had crossed a line of posts with faces carved in them. The faces were grotesque and horrible, with bulging eyes, tongues sticking out, nostrils flared. This was some kind of sacred area for the martens, over which the outlaws had stumbled.

Luke said, 'Pine martens' burial place. Look!' He indicated some platforms built out from the trunks of trees. From these rough shelves made of dried bracket fungus and twigs hung the skins and bones of tree martens. They dripped bits of pelt, scraggy tails and hanging claws. One or two sight-less skulls, still partially covered in skin, stared down between rough bars made of sticks. Sheets of flies like moving black shrouds covered the suspended corpses.

'We've trespassed on sacred marten ground,' cried Wodehed. 'They'll want to kill each and every one of us!'

As if to confirm his words, a fierce group of warriors came out from behind the trees, and rushed forward yelling and screaming, throwing their spears as they did so. The air was thick with spikes. Weasels hastily sought the protection of the tree trunks near by, just as the deadly shower descended.

'Can't we talk to them?' cried Bryony. 'Do we have to fight?'

One look at the savage warriors before her answered her question. Behind their mask-helmets with their twiggy projections the eyes were wild and barbaric. These were not creatures you sat down and talked with over a jug of honey dew. These were frenzied warriors who spoke with their weapons. Their rugged body armour testified to the nature of their souls. They were tree bark inside and out, these martens.

'Load slingshots!' yelled Sylver. 'Form a square!'

The outlaws immediately put pebbles in the saddles of their slingshots and formed what was actually a rectangle, with two weasels on each of two sides and three on each of the other two sides. Scirf, who had never done this manoeuvre before, seemed to find his place naturally.

From this position they were able to fire their slingshots, driving back the hordes of tree martens who now came at them from every part of the forest. Sylver had guessed that while they had been discussing the burial place, they had been completely encircled by the martens.

These martens had always lived in the darkness of the forest, away from the rest of the animal world, and had never become fully civilized. They still had in them the savage souls of primitive creatures. Their ferocious attacks were terrible to withstand. Icham was wounded in the shoulder. A spear clipped one of Bryony's ears. Luke was injured in the knee by a heavy stone.

'Stand fast, weasels!' cried Sylver. 'If we show them we are firm, they'll become dispirited!'

These tactics proved to work. After a while the

pine martens tired of their constant attacks. Yelling
and screaming and rushing about take their toll on
a warrior. Many of them had suffered slingshot
hits on their bodies, though most of the weasel
pebbles had struck bark armour. The martens were
also running out of spears to throw. They had a
limited arsenal on the ground and had to go up
into the trees, to their overhead huts, to fetch more
weapons.

Gradually, these brutal fighters began to fade
away into the forest, leaving the path ahead clear.

Breaking the square at last, the weasels went
forward.

Icham was given some healing moss by
Wodehed, and strapped it as a pad to his wounded
shoulder. Bryony's ear was badly torn and
required a yarrow poultice, the last of that rare
medicinal plant which Wodehed was carrying in
his pouch of dried herbs. Luke needed a leather
brace for his knee. Once the wounded had been
patched up, they took stock.

Luke found a bark helmet, with slits for eyes,
nose and mouth. He tried it on but it was too large
for his head. It was hot and stuffy inside the
helmet.

Alysoun found some body armour, dropped by
a marten struck on the leg by a stone from her
sling. 'Look at this,' she said wonderingly. 'It's
made of pine bark – really thick stuff – you
couldn't get through this with a dart or stone.'

Underneath the huts the group found razor-
edged flints, obviously the instruments with
which the martens cut their armour and sharpened
their wooden spears.

'Do you think they'll be back?' asked Mawk,

who had been absolutely terrified the whole while. 'I mean, they're out of their heads, aren't they? Do you think this dark place drives them crazy? It would drive *me* crazy. Perhaps they'll pursue us when we try to leave the forest. Maybe now we've entered forbidden ground they won't ever let us alone.'

'So what do you suggest, squire?' asked Scirf. 'Shall we give ourselves up to 'em? Let 'em hang us from saplings by our legs?'

'We could go back the way we came,' suggested Mawk. 'Maybe they'll think they've won then.'

Sylver snorted. 'If we do that they *will* have won. No, we're pressing on, right this minute. Scirf, Luke and Icham, you three go at the back and keep your eyes to the rear. Bryony and Alysoun, you watch the right side, Wodehed and Dredless, the left. Mawk, Miniver and myself will guard the front.'

In this manner, a sort of awkward tortoise formation, they left the glades behind them. They moved slowly, for fear of another attack, constantly stopping when a breeze lifted a branch, or an insect scuttled from a dead log.

After a time they found themselves back in the dense forest, where the trees were so close together an attack by a horde of savage beasts would be impossible.

'Don't let up on your vigilance,' ordered Sylver. 'You must never underestimate pine martens.'

No sooner were these words out of his mouth than the group came across another great clearing. In the middle of this glade lay a long barrow such as great chieftains built for their tombs or farmers built to store their winter root vegetables.

This barrow hid neither mouldy kings nor old potatoes, however.

It was fashioned for quite a different purpose.

'Maghatch's green chapel,' said Wodehed. 'We must avoid this place like the mange.'

Chapter Fifteen

The outlaws gave the grave-mound chapel a wide berth, slipping around the edge of the dark clearing, staying close to the trees. Once past, they again ventured into the thick of the forest. Soon the light went completely as evening came upon them, and they stopped to camp, remaining ever wary in this place which was ruled by the moufflon witch.

In the middle of the night Luke was on guard with Miniver. His wounded knee, still stiff and uncomfortable, kept him unusually alert. Suddenly the faint sound of horse's hooves came to him.

'You hear that?' he asked Miniver.

The hoofbeats got louder and Miniver said, 'Yes . . .' but before they could wake the others a mounted figure came crashing through the trees. It halted before them, the horse rearing in metallic slowness. Luke raised a burning brand and in its light beheld a bronze king on a bronze horse. The king's face was lined with anxiety, as kings' faces often are, such men being forever concerned about the worries of their position.

Both horse and rider were green with corrosion. There were splits in the metal, like long gaping wounds. Three on the flank of the charger would have revealed its ribs had there been any beneath. But of course the creature was hollow. Two long rents in the king's chest were bent outwards at the edges, as if a mighty sword had been thrust from the back and cut through him like paper.

The king's eyes were but empty holes in his head, though it seemed that the horse could see. 'Help him,' cried the king. 'Help him.'

These words startled the two guards, who looked at each other, both equally puzzled. 'Help *who*?' asked Miniver.

'The badger. Help him. Prisoner of the witch.'

With that, the bronze statue galloped away, crashing through the lower branches of the trees again. The king's crown caught on several branches and some of its points were bent backwards. The sword in his right hand slashed blindly and ineffectively at shrubs and brambles as he passed through them. A rather thick branch, broken halfway along its length, struck the king on the shoulder and left a deep dent. Soon the horse and rider were gone, disappearing into the network of trees.

Sylver, wakened by the sounds, came running from his bed of soft pine needles. 'What was that?' he cried.

'A gong,' replied Luke. 'Some king on a horse.'

'What did it want?'

Luke explained to his leader that the gong had told them of the witch and her prisoner. '. . . A badger, he said. Nothing much to worry about, from the sound of it. Not our business at all.'

By now everyone was awake and listening.

Sylver said, 'I'm not so sure it *isn't* our business – or at least, mine. There is a badger to whom I owe a great deal, in the name of my father. It might be he.'

148

Scirf said, 'So Maghatch has caught a badger and is holding him prisoner?' and shrugged. 'Who's this badger you're thinkin' of then, eh, chief?'

Looking round him, Sylver realized the others felt much the same as Scirf. They had no especial love for badgers, who were generally unsociable creatures. Yet he knew that he could not leave any beast helplessly caught in the clutches of fiends such as Maghatch. He stared thoughtfully along the avenue which the bronze king had cut with his mount and sword. 'I suppose we can't ignore it, even though it might be a trap.'

'What?' cried Mawk. 'You're not thinking of rescuing this prisoner, are you? A *badger*. We have little to do with badgers, after all.'

'Badgers are not our enemies. What if it were one of us and a badger had been asked to help?' said Sylver. 'A creature should be judged by the quality of his character, not by the thickness of his fur. This badger may be a worthy animal. We cannot leave him in the clutches of the witch without at least *trying* to help him.'

Mawk put his head in his paws. 'No, no – I don't believe this. We go out of our way to avoid meeting this powerful witch – and now we're playing into her hooves. Of *course* it's a trick. What else would it be? She sent the gong to trap us into going back. Can't you see?'

Bryony shook her head. 'Sylver's right. Someone has asked for our help. We have to do our best. Badger or no badger, we have to go back.'

Mawk let out a wail of despair. 'You fools. It's a trick. It's so obviously a trick. Well, I'm not going,' he added hotly. 'You lot can go to your doom if you wish. I'm staying right here.'

Scirf said, 'Tantrumy little beggar, ain't he?'

'I mean it!' cried Mawk. 'I'm staying here.'

Alysoun said gently. 'On your *own*, Mawk?'

Mawk stared around him at the darkness. 'Wha— what do you mean?'

'I mean with all the dangers of the forest. Once we enter her chapel she might double back, of course, and come here.'

'Why would she want to do that?' squeaked Mawk.

'Why, to get any stragglers left behind. I hear she boils animals in vegetable oil until their eyes pop. Yes, you stay here, it might create a diversion. That's a good tactic, Mawk – you draw the witch away from us while we set this badger free.'

'You do it yourself,' shouted Mawk in a strained voice. 'I'm going with Sylver. I go where my leader goes. You stay here and do your own diverting.'

They all clicked their teeth at this, much to the discomfort of the wavering weasel, whose strength of character so often failed him in moments of crisis.

So in the morning the group retraced their tracks until they came again upon the green mound. Deciding that boldness was the best approach, they went down into the greater darkness of the green chapel. The entrance was covered with cobwebs, at the corners of which lurked monstrous spiders, some of them covered in yellow-and-black hair. Inside, hanging from the ceiling, were the petrified larvae of dragonflies, which are the ugliest creatures in the universe. On the floor were scattered tattered rugs made from the skins of deceased rats.

'It stinks in here,' whispered Bryony, wrinkling her nose.

There was indeed a foul smell, a sort of musty odour, which came out of the very dirt from which the chapel had been built. They knew, of course, that the mound itself had been created from grave earth stolen from human tombs. Slabs of stone, which acted as pillars, were covered in writing and dates. These were headstones from a human burial place. Rotten chunks of coffin wood were placed as panels around the walls.

'What a terrible place,' said Dredless. 'Look, a tunnel! Where do you think it leads?'

'I don't care, I don't care, I wish I'd stayed in the forest,' moaned Mawk.

'Pull yourself together,' said Icham, his quavering voice giving his fear away. 'There's nothing to be scared of – is there, Sylver?'

Sylver did not answer. Instead he was staring at a dark shape in the corner of the chapel. It was tall – almost as tall as a man. On its head were two thick horns, which curved and twisted. Its eyes were as hard as flint.

'The witch,' said Sylver. 'Maghatch.'

'What?' cried Mawk, the fear making his fur stand on end. 'What witch?'

'He's talking about *me*,' said a deep, grating voice.

A moufflon on its hind legs stepped out of the darkness into a beam of light from one of the two doorways. It was indeed *her*, the sorceress. She sneered wickedly at the band. Mawk gave a squeal of fear and hid behind Wodehed.

'So,' said the moufflon, bringing her foreleg hooves together in a sharp *clack*, 'you believed my story about having imprisoned a badger? I knew if I had said a *weasel* you would never have come – you would have been too suspicious – but a badger, now that was a stroke of genius, was it not?'

'Do something, Wodehed,' cried Mawk. 'Use some magic on her!'

Wodehed, trembling from head to tail, stepped forward and began chanting: '*Wither, witch, wither away – droop and drop – floop and flop – wither, witch, shrivel and shrinkle – may your skin dry up and all your bones wrinkle.*'

'*Floop?*' murmured Scirf, disbelievingly. '*Shrinkle?*'

Nevertheless, these doubtful words aside, everyone waited in expectation. Even Maghatch stood as if she was wondering if the magic would work. Then one of her horns gradually sagged from the middle. It had turned into a two-day-old dead herring. Even Maghatch wrinkled her nose at the smell. One horn more or less was nothing to the witch, however, who sneered at Wodehed.

'Well, it worked a *bit*,' said Wodehed defensively. 'What do you want of us, witch?'

'I want *him*,' she said, dramatically pointing to Sylver. 'I want him for a slave. How much more powerful I would become, having the renowned outlaw leader Sylver for my hoof-servant. My status amongst witches would rocket. I will become the comet of my kind, the meteor of all witches.'

'And what about *us*?' asked Mawk. 'If you take him, will you let us go?'

'I think not. Yet' – she tapped one of her horns with a hoof – 'perhaps I might. You see, I do not wish to *force* the great Sylver into my household. He must agree to it – he must come of his own free will. Anyone can *make* a creature into a slave. To have a willing servant, why that is *power*.'

Sylver stared at this witch, whose shaggy hair hung from her chest like curtains. 'I could never agree to be your slave,' he told her.

'Well in that case, we shall have to do something about your friends,' grated the moufflon.

With that she let out a series of strange utterances, similar to the sound of choking frogs. The outlaw band – with the sole exception of Sylver – began to change shape. The witch was turning the other weasels into tall gangly creatures. Mawk, the last to begin altering, let out a strangled cry, his eyes wide with fear, as he began to grow and transform. Soon there were nine completely different beings standing before Sylver, where his faithful friends should have been.

'Humans!' he cried. 'You've changed them into humans!'

The witch screeched with delight. 'Humans, yes. Humans don't frighten me. But you'd better watch yourself, Sylver. Humans don't like *weasels*.'

The shambling figures of nine humans began blundering around in the darkness of the green chapel. They were wailing to one another, crying out in human tongue. Sylver was filled with fear and dread. Although he was working towards the time when humans could return to Welkin, he was still scared of such creatures. In the normal course of things, weasels and humans can share the world without ever crossing each other's paths. To be confronted by such big and ugly creatures made Sylver's blood run cold with terror.

To his shame he ran from the place, dashed out of one of the exits and into the forest. There he found a hole in the roots of the tree and hid himself, his heart beating wildly.

For the next few hours he remained hidden, while the humans fumbled about in the undergrowth around him. They seemed to be searching for him, hooting to each other. Such clumsy creatures they were too, smashing and crashing around as if plants and fungi were easily replaceable. They broke almost everything they touched, crushing delicate little flowers under foot, kicking toadstools, snapping branches willy-nilly.

After a long while the sounds of blundering humans ceased and Sylver crept out of his hole to find them all asleep on the ground. They had exhausted themselves. He went from one to the other, staring at their faces. The funny thing was, they still had the faint *appearance* of the creatures they used to be. He could recognize Bryony, and Icham, and Mawk, whose face was still mapped with lines of terror.

Sylver crept back into his hole, miserable and unhappy for his friends. He knew they were scared, trapped inside the bodies of humans, and he seriously considered going to Maghatch and agreeing to become her slave. It would be a terrible life. And he would have to give up his plans for bringing humans back into the world.

Would that be a bad thing, he thought, if they were such stupid creatures as these?

Yet Maghatch might have deliberately made them clumsy and awkward, just to upset the weasels.

In the early dawn Maghatch came by. She did

not know exactly where he was hiding, but she called out, knowing he would hear her. 'Sylver? When the sun rises above the trees and strikes the faces of these humans, they'll change again, into something else. That'll be nice, won't it? You should be here to see it. Your friends will expect it . . .'

When she had gone Sylver once again left his hole. He stood watching his comrades, who were still asleep on the grassy banks and moss-covered roots. Gradually the sun came up over the distant hills and penetrated the forest with its rays.

This time, he thought, I'll stay and talk with them. I won't run away, no matter what they turn into. I'll suggest we get away from here, out of that moufflon's reach. Get to somewhere where Wodehed can make some magic and turn them all back into weasels again. Yes, this time I won't run away, even if they turn into demons . . .

Sylver, who had never liked anything to do with magic, gathered his courage together. The sun's rays struck the faces of the humans lying on the grass. Suddenly they began to change. They started to shrink, grow fur, and their hands and feet turned into paws.

This is a good sign, thought Sylver hopefully.

Then their ears began to stretch, their noses to flatten; small fluffy tails appeared. They opened their eyes as they woke. Sylver stood before them. They saw him.

'Friends,' he began, but could get no more words out. The creatures before him scattered in all directions before he could talk to them. *He* had not run, but *they* had. And how could he blame them? Who could expect a bunch of *rabbits* to stand and listen while a weasel beguiled them with his lies and hypnotic eyes?

They were indeed rabbits, and as such they expected Sylver the weasel to pounce on them and kill them.

'Come back!' yelled Sylver. 'I won't harm you!'

But of course the hearts of the rabbits ruled their heads. Their blood pounded through their veins. They had panic coursing through their arteries. There was no way in heaven or on earth that they were going to stand and listen to a weasel. They found holes themselves, hid from their old leader. He had wicked sharp teeth, little red glinting eyes, a small pink tongue that liked to savour the taste of bunny.

The sound of moufflon laughter crackled through the forest like wildfire as Sylver wandered around in despair.

Chapter Sixteen

'All right,' conceded Sylver, miserably, 'I'll become your slave if you restore my friends to their rightful shapes.'

Maghatch shook her head. 'You must do my bidding for a week – then I'll let them go. If I change them back now, you might just run off and escape.'

Sylver could do nothing but agree. He took one last lingering look at the woods and fields, where the rabbits would gambol in their innocence once he had gone, and then followed the witch down into the green chapel.

'I suppose you want me to clean the place up,' he said with a heavy sigh, looking around him at the filth and dirt which decorated every wall and floor. 'Get rid of the spiders and all that.'

The moufflon turned on her hooves and stared at him in horror. '*Clean up?* Are you mad? Certainly not. This is the way I like my dark home. Dust is my closest companion. Spiders' webs make the place more attractive, like lacy curtains, don't you think? Very suitable for my craft.'

Sylver didn't think so, but he kept his peace. 'Well, what *do* you want me to do then?'

'Fetch and carry, jack! Fetch and carry. When I'm doing a spell I shall need things – toad's spawn, lizard's vomit, saliva of newt – I shall want you to rush out and get them as I call for them.'

'What if I can't find any lizard's vomit?'

'Stick your paw down a lizard's throat,' she said, smiling wickedly. 'They throw up their breakfast every time when you do that.

'If you *don't* bring me what I want, it's going to be a nasty night for your rabbit friends, because I can call foxes and owls on a whim.'

Sylver saw what she meant.

For the rest of that day Sylver did the moufflon's bidding, rushing around gathering all manner of disgusting items for her store cupboard and immediate use. Some of the things he was asked to fetch were so revolting he had to hold them at limb's length, his nose held with his other paw, and hurry them into some jar or pot.

The witch was tireless in her demands and not at all grateful. She screeched and screamed at him when she thought he was too slow and gave him no praise when he was quick. They were a series of thankless tasks. And what was more, Sylver did not believe she was going to keep her promise about letting the others go once he had been with her a whole week. He had the feeling that week was going to stretch.

'Here's a bowl of gruel,' she said, hoofing him something that looked like pond water. 'You might think it's thin but there's a lot of good meat in there.'

Sylver, exhausted by the day's work, began to lap the gruel greedily. There was not an ounce of goodness in the soup, despite the grey bits floating on the surface. It appeared to be made of nothing more than water stained with dead leaves. It tasted

158

faintly of snail slime. 'What's it made of?' he asked her, as he sat hunched in the darkness at the back of the green chapel. 'What's it called?'

'Bark gruel, made from the best tree branches,' she snapped at him, as she dug into her swede mash. 'Consider yourself lucky.'

Sylver sighed at this show of meanness. It seemed his new mistress was not only bad of character, she was stingy too. 'I thought at least I would get well fed,' he grumbled.

'You know what thought did?' she snapped back at him. 'Followed a dung cart and thought it was a wedding.'

'Very funny,' said Sylver, the tiredness coming over him so heavily that he did not care about eating anyway.

He curled up into a coil of fur and fell asleep amongst the spiders and beetles that worked busily on the floor, careless of their tickling antics.

The next day he was woken at five in the morning and the whole thing began again. He was immediately sent out into the forest to find slugs that had died in the night, and on his return had to peel them and put their skins in a jar. Peeling freshly dead slugs is not an easy task, as those of you who have tried it well know. Their skins are so loose they wrinkle under pressure and tear at the slightest mistake. Maghatch wanted only *whole* slug skins, with not a rent or hole in them.

On his trips into the forest, Sylver took the opportunity of swallowing a few mouthfuls of mushroom to keep up his strength. He also tried to call the rabbits, but as soon as they scented him, or heard his voice, they shot down their holes. He was alarmed to see that when he first went out there were about a hundred of them in the great glade. How was he to tell which were his outlaw band and which were real rabbits? The whole thing was a nightmare from which it seemed he would never wake.

At about noon a new danger presented itself. Sylver was gathering the cast-off cases of moth larvae when who should tramp wearily into the glade but Sheriff Falshed and a troop of stoats. They quickly surrounded the hapless weasel.

'GOT YOU AT LAST!' bellowed the sheriff, in great glee. 'I knew if we marched night and day we'd catch up with you.' His triumph was so heartfelt he dribbled down his burnt bib. 'At last, at last. Don't look so glum, you miserable wretch, I'm not going to hang you yet. Prince Poynt wants to do something to you with red-hot hooks first. He's been looking forward to it.'

'Can we have a go at him first?' said a corporal with an especially menacing pike. 'Can we have a go on the way back to the castle, sir?'

'I'll see,' replied Falshed. 'But no promises.'

'Thank you, sir,' snarled the corporal, his eyes glinting with anticipation. 'Me and the other jacks aren't particularly fond of marching over hill and dale.'

Sylver stared at the hard faces of the other soldiers and realized he was in for a rough time. However, the upside of things was that Maghatch, having lost him, would hopefully free his band from their bondage. Unless she was thoroughly evil she would not leave them in the shape of rabbits for ever.

Then again, perhaps she was irredeemable. Sylver, however, did not have any choice. 'Well, what are we waiting for?' he said. 'Let's get on the road.'

Falshed looked at Sylver with suspicion. 'Why are you so eager to be captured?' he asked. He looked about him fearfully for a moment. 'Where's the rest of your rogues?'

At that moment Maghatch appeared, towering over the stoats. Some of the soldiers quailed and prepared to run. Others almost fainted away on the spot. Falshed, to give him his due, remained where he was, outwardly calm, though his voice quavered a little when he spoke. 'What do *you* want, witch?'

'Keep a civil tongue in your head, unless you wish to be a toad for the rest of your life,' she snapped back. 'What are you doing with my slave?'

'Your slave?'

'Sylver the weasel belongs to me for as long as I choose to keep him. Now piddle off somewhere else, you poor excuses for gnat's leavings, I've got work to do.'

'I – I have to take Sylver back with *me*,' said Falshed. 'My prince expects it.'

Maghatch whirled on the sheriff and stood over him, at least ten times his height. Her shadow blocked out the sun. Falshed went back on his hind legs, quivering with fear under the glare from the slitty eyes of the witch. He knew he was dangerously close to becoming something low and foul in the food chain. The hairs on the nape of his neck stood on end.

'Little stoat,' said Maghatch, slowly and carefully. 'Do be careful . . .'

'Yes, yes, I'm sorry,' croaked Falshed. 'He's

161

yours for as long as you want him, of course. I'll – I'll just wait around here for a while with my troops, until you've finished with him. Then perhaps you won't mind me dragging off what's left of him in chains, to be roasted over a slow fire.'

'When I've done with him, you can do as you like,' she said, losing interest. 'Now come on, slave – let's have those items I asked for!'

'Yes, ma'am,' muttered Sylver.

Maghatch left the glade and Falshed stared hard at Sylver. 'We'll be here,' he said menacingly.

The sheriff turned to address his soldiers. 'Let's kill a few rabbits for the pot,' he suggested conversationally, 'while we're waiting.'

'NO!' cried Sylver.

Falshed swung round and stared at the weasel.

'That is,' continued Sylver quickly, 'don't you know the voles around here are so much tastier? Maghatch breeds very appetizing voles, don't you know? I would give the voles a try if I were you, Falshed.'

'I don't understand,' said the sheriff, his eyes narrowing. 'Are the voles poisoned in some way? Eat venomous toadstools, do they? Full of nasty fluids, are they?'

'No, no, that is, you can't trust the *rabbits*. Maghatch feeds them on – on twigs and fir cones. They're as tough as brick. You would not like the rabbits.'

'We'll see,' said Falshed. 'In the meantime, hadn't you better be doing your mistress's bidding? Go on, slave, get to work. Run around, gather things.'

The stoats clacked their teeth together in appreciation of their leader's joke. Then they all went off to find mossy banks to sleep on. Sylver was at last left alone to his misery.

He gathered together his bits and pieces for Maghatch, then took them back to the green chapel. The witch was busy with one of her spells and she nodded impatiently when he came in, indicating that he should put the stuff on the ground beside her and then get some rest. Sylver did so gratefully.

Later, when it was dark, he had to go out again to get those items which could not be had in the daytime. While he roamed the woods he could hear Falshed's men, getting tipsy on honey dew, shouting and bawling to one another. They found it difficult to speak in normal voices, did stoats, having been raised by loud parents with no social graces. The soldiers were happier nudging one another, bursting into raucous teeth-clicking, telling ribald jokes.

He could hear Falshed's voice above it all, wanting to be one of the jack soldiers while there was fun to be had around the camp fire, yet expecting to be instantly obeyed when he flung his orders at them during emergencies.

Eventually Sylver got to bed, but not before midnight. Even then he had to remain awake.

When Maghatch was herself fast asleep, Sylver crept wearily from his bed. He began a search of the green chapel to see if he could find clues to the spell Maghatch had used on his band of outlaws. It was true she used no books, as Lord Haukin did, but Sylver wondered whether there might not be other, more tangible artefacts, which would lead him to the restoration of his friends.

The weasel found nothing but death watch

beetles, guarding the exits to the green chapel. He spent the rest of the night wondering how he was going to keep going, if Maghatch drove him as hard as she had been doing. He was tempted to run, to go seeking elsewhere for the remedy to his troubles, but he managed to put this unworthy thought aside.

So it was that he went back to bed yet again, only to be woken two hours later to do the witch's bidding.

The stoats were, of course, up and waiting for him, to jeer and taunt him as he went about his tasks. When they got tired of this sport and went back to their sluggard's beds, the rabbits came out, keeping their distance from Sylver. He stared at them, thinking that if he could only recognize *one* of his number amongst them, he could get that one to fetch help.

Suddenly, as he was watching them, it became obvious to Sylver which one of the rabbits was *definitely* a weasel in the wrong fur coat.

At last he had something to work on.

Chapter Seventeen

Sylver crept closer to the feeding rabbits, using his old weasel skills of sneaking and skulking, until he was within earshot of one particular rabbit. This creature was nibbling the grass more enthusiastically than the others. In fact he tore at it, swallowed it in great clumps, and it seemed he would rather choke to death than forgo that extra blade of grass in his mouth. In a double word, he was a greedy-guts.

This rabbit also had fur coming out on his coat, leaving bald patches. He was dirty around the paws and jaws. His cotton-tail was more a ragged-tail, and there were creatures nestling in the fur about his ears. Sylver knew exactly who this rabbit was and hoped to capture his attention.

'Pssst. Scirf! Over here!'

The rabbit paused in his eating – reluctantly, it seemed – to look up.

Now when confronted with dangers like weasels, rabbits do one of two things. They either bolt or they freeze. Fortunately for Sylver, Scirf froze, his eyes popping – though he actually looked as if he might run at any moment and Sylver had to calm the creature with a few words. 'Don't run, it's only me, Sylver. Listen, I know you can't talk to me, but you can talk to the others. I want you to tell them something. Tell them that I've gone away to fetch help, but I've not abandoned them. If the witch comes looking for you all, hide amongst the real rabbits. Have you got that?'

Scirf made no reply. He simply sat there with his mouth in mid-chew, his eyes still starting from his head.

'I have to go,' continued Sylver, 'because you are all in real danger of ending up in a stoat stew pot in your present forms. I'm certain Maghatch has no intention of ever willingly letting us leave this place.'

Scirf shivered from bobtail to the tips of his ears.

'You'd better go now, Scirf,' whispered Sylver. 'Remember what I told you . . .'

Scirf bolted.

Sylver was not sure whether the message had got through or not. He had no experience of rabbits, who ordinarily seemed quite stupid creatures. Whether his outlaws would retain their old weasel sense in some part, even though their bodies might be rabbit, he did not know. Sylver could only hope that some of his words had sunk in.

With this accomplished, Sylver set out on a journey. He was going to see an old friend of his father's, to try to get help. Sylver's father had been a law-abiding weasel who served Lord Haukin until the soldiers of Prince Poynt had dragged him away to an unknown fate for some trumped-up trivial offence which Lord Haukin could not dispute. Sylver had never seen his father again, after that dew-bedecked morning in June. His mother had died of a broken heart the following spring.

Sylver travelled east, knowing he would be quickly missed by both the witch and the sheriff. Falshed would be bound to follow him, even if Maghatch remained in her green chapel. Over weald and through woodland he went, across streams, under roots, behind hills, into valleys. Finally he came to a sandy bank where there were a number of holes. It was here that the badgers of Gath lived. Taking his courage into both paws, Sylver entered the nearest tunnel and went down to the chambers below.

It was dark under the ground but Sylver, like most creatures, could 'see' in the dark by using feel and scent, building up a picture of his surroundings as he went.

A female badger confronted him almost before he had gone ten metres. 'A weasel!' she cried in the strange clicking old-tongue which Sylver's father had taught him. 'What do you want, weasel?'

'I've come to see a badger named Kalthas,' clicked Sylver in the same ancient language. 'He knew my father.'

The badger, whom Sylver judged was enormous, grunted in suspicion. 'How am I supposed to know you're telling the truth, weasel? Weasels are too fond of lying. I wouldn't trust a weasel as far as I could throw a bear.'

'Look,' said Sylver reasonably, 'would I come down into a badgers' sett if I was not on official business? We both know I'm taking an awful risk being down here. I do have good reason for wanting to see Kalthas. Please?'

The female badger snorted through her rubbery nostrils, blowing dust into Sylver's face. But it was not an ill-mannered act, it was simply something badgers did all the time. Then she turned and said, 'Follow me,' leading him into the bewildering system of tunnels that made up the community of badgers.

Eventually she came to a chamber which smelled strongly of slept-in hay and badger's fur. Inside the chamber was a great form, heaving slowly in sleep. The female stood outside for a moment and motioned for Sylver to go in. 'You can wake him,' she said, 'after I've gone. He's like a bear with toothache when he's woken. I shouldn't be surprised if he doesn't whack you flat with his claws. Still, that's up to you, isn't it? Personally, I'd cut and run.'

'Thank you,' murmured Sylver. 'Most kind.'

The weasel entered the chamber and stood by the warm fur mountain, watching it rise and fall. There was nothing for it – he would have to wake the badger. It was certainly something he was not looking forward to.

Sylver nudged the sleeping form gently. 'Kalthas?' he said.

Nothing. Not a stir.

'Kalthas?' he said more loudly, giving the mound a push with his fore paws.

Still nothing but regular heavy breathing with the occasional snuffle and snort.

'KALTHAS!' yelled Sylver, kicking the badger's rump.

The badger still did not move, but his eyes shot open. They were red-veined and frightening. Sylver backed away slowly from the glare of those eyes. Then the great head rose a little, as the badger regarded this weasel who had dared to interrupt his beloved sleep.

'Whaaaaat?' growled Kalthas. 'Whaaaaat, what, what, what, what, whaaaaaaaaaaaaaaaat?'

'Sorry to wake you,' said Sylver timidly, 'but it's quite important.'

The badger stretched and yawned, revealing frightful teeth and frightful claws.

Then he stared again at Sylver. 'What? Woken by a *weasel*? Do I swallow you whole or save some bits for later? Eh? Give me a hint.'

'Er, you listen to what I have to say and then you might be quite surprised at how good I make you feel.'

'I doubt it,' growled the badger. 'I sincerely doubt it. I think I'll end up killing you. I *want* to kill you now. It would help my state of mind. I think killing you is the only thing which would make me feel good.'

'You remember my father?' said Sylver hastily. 'Blackie, my father? I'm his son, Sylver.'

'That would make sense – if he was your father, then you must be his son. So? What of it? Quickly, I'm impatient to kill someone and I think it's got to be you. There's no-one else around at the moment.'

'Well, my father always told me that if I was ever in trouble, and in the region of Kalthas the badger, that Kalthas would help me.'

The badger's eyes narrowed. 'I wonder why he said that.'

'I was under the impression that he and you were good friends,' replied Sylver, now doubting his father's word for the first time in his life. 'He once told me he had saved you from death. He said you were at heart a kindly soul, who merely put up a show of aggression for effect.'

'Just shows you how wrong weasels can be, doesn't it?' the badger growled. 'So what if he did save my life? What do I care about a weasel?' There was a telling pause, during which the badger studied Sylver's looks. Then he said in an almost gentle tone, 'How is the old fool, anyway?'

'My father's dead. We believe he's dead. Prince Poynt had him arrested and threw him in the dungeons. No-one has ever seen him since.'

'I see,' said the badger. 'You were going to tell me a story about something or other. Get it over with. I haven't got for ever. I need my twenty-three hours' sleep a day. Try and be very brief, young weasel, or I might change my mind and kill you anyway, Blackie's son or not.'

'Yes, Kalthas. Well, here it is . . .' and Sylver told the badger about his mission, his band, the capture by the witch, and the need to get help. 'So there you have it. I have to have some assistance to persuade the witch to let my weasels go.'

Kalthas lay there in deep thought for a time, until Sylver actually believed the badger had gone back to sleep again, but then finally the mountainous pelt stirred. The big eyes regarded Sylver again. 'Are you scared of canines?' asked the badger. 'Do wild dogs bother you?'

'Of course they do,' cried Sylver, alarmed. 'Why wouldn't they?'

'Yes, I thought so. Well, you're going to have to conquer that fear. There's a wild dog, a huge creature named Gnaish. He doesn't know what breed he is, but I suspect if you found all the dogs which were on their way to becoming wolves and rolled them into one, that would be Gnaish.

'Now, as you know, moufflons are sheep. Sheep

170

have never been very keen on dogs either. If I were you I'd go and see Gnaish, offer him something, and ask him to accompany you back to the green chapel. That's my advice. Here's a map.'

And with that Kalthas drew a chart in the dust with his claw, showing Sylver how to reach the cave of the wild dogs, and said to say Kalthas sent him. 'Now push off and let me get my sleep,' he said. 'I'm tired of talking with weasels.'

With that he rolled over and seemed to fall instantly asleep. However, as Sylver crept from the chamber a voice behind him said, 'If you ever do see your father again – tell him Kalthas sends his warmest greetings.'

Sylver left the badgers' sett and followed the instructions Kalthas had given him. As he crossed the countryside to a distant rockface, in which was located the cave of the wild dogs, Sylver tried to think of something he could offer Gnaish for his services. He could not come up with anything, however, and was thoroughly upset by his own lack of resourcefulness.

Finally he reached the cave, to find the wild dogs lazing in the sun outside their home. They were not asleep, as the badger had been, but warily resting, one eye open, the warm sun on their backs. They saw the weasel coming and hardly moved a muscle, keeping him in their vision with a rolling of that one eye in each head. One or two flicked their tails, indicating that Sylver was proceeding at his peril.

Scattered untidily on the ground outside the cave were gnawed bones of unrecognizable animals.

With his heart beating fast, Sylver stopped at a

safe distance, and called to the dogs. 'I'm looking for Gnaish,' he said. 'I've been sent by the badger Kalthas. Is Gnaish there?'

None of the dogs on the ground outside the cave moved, but a great dark shadow stirred in the doorway. A shape which Sylver had previously decided was a large rock suddenly moved and got to its feet. It was an enormous dog, of proportions exceeding any other dog the outlaw had ever seen.

'I am Gnaish,' said the dog. 'Who calls?'

'The weasel, Sylver, of Halfmoon Wood, County Elleswhere, where Lord Haukin holds sway.'

'What do you want with *me*, weasel? You take your life into your paws coming to the cave of wild dogs.'

'I'm always taking my life into my paws,' said Sylver. 'I come to seek your assistance, to help me free my friends from the magical bondage of a moufflon witch. You are someone she would be afraid to cross, even with her magic. A wild dog is not a creature *I* would cross at any cost . . .'

'Don't try flattery, weasel,' growled the dog. 'What have you got to offer me?'

'I admit, nothing at present, dog. Nothing comes to mind. But if we once free my friends I'm sure that one of them will have a suitable reward in mind. Can you trust me?'

Gnaish shook himself, his great muscle-ridged back quivering with strength and energy. 'Trust a weasel? I'd say not. But I'll come anyway. If Kalthas sent you, that's good enough for me. I'm bored just sitting around with these jackals. Look at them, they haven't stirred a bone since you came – even while this conversation has been in progress they've done nothing but follow us with their

172

eyes.' He addressed the pack, of which he was obviously the leader. 'I'll be back,' he said. 'In the meantime, clear away these weasel skeletons littering the front of the cave. They make the place look scruffy . . .'

'Weasel skeletons?' questioned a dog, looking puzzled.

'Just joking,' said Gnaish. 'Sense of humour. Caught it from the humans when they were around. Now let's be off. Get up on my back, we'll travel quicker that way. I might as well tell you now, if your friends don't come up with a suitable reward, you *will* be decorating the ground in front of my cave, in many different pieces – you understand?'

'I understand,' said Sylver. 'I have faith in my brothers and sisters at the green chapel. By the way, don't kill any rabbits on the way. The moufflon changed my band into rabbits – into humans first – then rabbits. I don't want you murdering my weasels by accident.'

'I never murder anything by *accident*,' snarled Gnaish, making his point precisely.

With Sylver on his back they set forth.

And still the dogs around the cave had not moved, except to yawn a floppy yawn or scratch their fleas in the sun.

Chapter Eighteen

Gnaish covered the ground back to the forest in quicker time than Sylver could possibly have made it. The great hound loped and bounded, clearing hedges and ditches with ease, passing through dells and dales, over hillocks and humps, until very soon they were on the edge of the forest. Gnaish entered the forest without fear, for the only creature who might have been a threat to him was no longer around. Only the hunter with the gun would be brave or foolish enough to accost a wild dog.

As they neared the green chapel, stoats suddenly appeared from behind trees and confronted them. The stoats had made a siege catapult out of a sapling. This was drawn back with a large rock placed in the instrument's saddle. Helmeted and semi-armoured, the stoats obviously felt they were strong enough to halt the progress of a large dog.

'Stop!' cried Sheriff Falshed, stepping in front of the dog and weasel. 'Go no further.'

Gnaish opened his jaws and bared some horrific fangs. 'Out of my way, you puny creature,' he snarled. 'I'm on a mission to save this weasel's friends.'

'That weasel,' said Falshed, 'is a liar and a cheat,

a murderer and a thief. His father is a respectable ditch-digger and his mother a cabbage-stripper, but much to the sorrow of his family this one left them in penury and turned bad. He's lately escaped from an institution for the criminally insane. The halt and the lame have accused him of robbing the poor to line his own pockets. He's also wanted for stealing babies from their mothers' nests. Be so kind, dog, as to give him over.'

'You have proof of all this?' said Gnaish.

Sheriff Falshed clicked his teeth together. 'Oh, plenty – plenty. Now if you'll be so good . . .'

'Show me this proof.'

Falshed sighed and made a show of going through his armour, then he shrugged. 'I do not have it on me, unfortunately.'

'In that case,' snarled Gnaish, 'I'll ask you to step aside – and I'll only ask *once* . . .'

Falshed stared at the dog, glanced quickly at his stoats manning the catapult, and decided that he was in no shape to start a battle with a massive hound. 'You'll regret this, mongrel,' he said, stepping aside. 'You realize what that weasel is trying to do? He wants to bring back the humans to Welkin. You want to be hunted and shot to death, do you?'

Gnaish paused and narrowed his eyes. He shook Sylver from his back and stared down at him. 'Is this true, weasel?'

Falshed stood by, his face beginning to register triumph.

'Yes it is, I'm afraid,' Sylver replied. 'I know humans do a lot of damage to the countryside, and we walk in fear of them, but it's a fact that the sea walls are crumbling all around Welkin and that all of the lowlands will be drowned, unless we get the humans back to repair them . . .'

'Rubbish,' snapped Falshed.

'You think what you must, sheriff – some of us believe differently. I'm not worried about humans. I'm worried about us, the beasts of the field. What will happen to us when all the grasslands and woodlands disappear under water?'

Falshed smirked, turning to Gnaish. 'But perhaps the wild dog here has different ideas.'

Gnaish said to Sylver, 'You really think you can get the humans to return? Is that what you're trying to do?'

'I'm afraid it is,' replied Sylver, bracing himself for the worst.

'Good,' said the dog in a voice choked with emotion. 'Very good.'

Falshed cried, 'What? You approve of this mad plan? You, a wild dog?'

'My kind were not always *wild* dogs,' growled Gnaish. 'We were once the friends of men. My grandfather sat at the feet of a man in his home. There were fires then, in the grates, and bowls full of potatoes and meat. There were warm nights and dry days in the winter, and a companion to take walking.'

'You sentimental fool,' Falshed said sarcastically. 'Excuse me while I shed a wet tear.'

'I'll excuse you while I rip your head off your shoulders,' snarled Gnaish, the distant look vanishing instantly from his face. 'Just because I look to a golden time doesn't mean I'm a weak snivelling coward, stoat. I'll destroy you and your troop of bullet heads if you don't get out of the way *now*.'

Falshed did as he was asked with alacrity. Gnaish and Sylver passed through the troops.

When they were some way past, Falshed shouted after them, 'I won't forget this, dog! You'd better stay out of my way in future. Don't sleep with both eyes closed for a few weeks. You've chosen the wrong stoat to . . .' and so on, and so on, the threats finally drifting into the silence of the woods.

When the pair reached the green chapel, Sylver called out to Maghatch the moufflon. 'Witch. I'm back.'

The moufflon rushed out of the hole in the ground, her eyes blazing, only to be confronted by a wild dog.

Now a moufflon is not much more than a wild sheep, and sheep are not happy in the presence of dogs. She was a powerful sorceress, it was true, but even magicians need time to gather their magic together, form some sort of pattern of actions. Maghatch had no time. There was a wild dog not a metre away, and rather a large one at that, and her natural instinct was to go down on all fours in a submissive pose.

'What – what do you want, dog?' she bleated.

'I want you to turn this weasel's companions back into their proper forms,' he said. 'Otherwise I'll chase you over the horizon and you'll never see this glade again. You understand me? Do it – *now.*'

'The rabbits are still down their burrows . . .'

'*Now.*'

Maghatch glowered. 'I shall have to go down to my den, where the spells are made.'

'Fine,' said Sylver, 'and we'll go with you. Just in case you try to turn Gnaish here into marsh gas. You wouldn't try anything like that, would you?'

Gnaish said, 'I've left instructions at the cave that if I don't return within the day, the whole pack is to descend on this hellhole and rip it – and you – apart.'

'No tricks, no tricks,' murmured Maghatch silkily. 'Please follow me.'

Within the hour the other weasels were back at Sylver's side, examining themselves, talking about the strange time they had been through.

'It was like a dream,' said Bryony. 'I kept feeling I had to wake up – and finally I did.'

Icham said, 'I *hated* it down those burrows. Those rabbits are not such tame creatures when you're one of them. I got bullied from inside to outside and back again.'

'And all the while,' said Dredless, 'I kept thinking, They'll find out I'm a weasel in disguise and tear me limb from limb. I felt like some kind of spy in the rabbit camp. I felt I was impersonating someone.'

'Well, you're free now,' Sylver told them. 'And one animal you have to thank for it is this dog, Gnaish. We have to think of some way to reward him.'

'No reward needed, now,' said Gnaish. 'You just continue your quest – bring back the humans. That will suit me and my kind.'

'We'll do our best,' Scirf told him, scratching. 'Lord, these blasted rabbit fleas is the worst, ain't they though? I never got bit so much in me life before.'

The band said goodbye to the wild dog, after thanking him again for his assistance, and went on their way. Towards evening they made camp on the edge of the forest, before proceeding out into the foothills of the Yellow Mountains. The atmosphere was pungent with fumes from volcanic cracks, where snakes of gaseous heat danced on their tails. It was not unbearable, but it was annoying.

In the distance they could see a rambling dwelling, half hidden by tall rushes growing from the shallows of a lake. Smoke was coming from the many crooked chimneys of this single-storey building, which appeared to be made of split logs. The sun glinted on the glass in misshapen windows.

'We'll see what that place is tomorrow,' Sylver decided. 'In the meantime, we'll stay inside the tree line for the night.'

Dredless, Alysoun and Icham went out hunting to fill the stew pot, while the others fashioned defences for the night. The band of outlaws had been caught out too often now and were in a part of the land where magic was not unknown. Sylver was not familiar with the region and wanted to be prepared for any attack by hostile animals. Not only that: Sheriff Falshed was somewhere behind them with his troops. It would not take that stoat long to realize that the outlaws had once more slipped past him. No doubt Maghatch would not be reluctant to tell him.

By the time the three hunters returned, there was a fire going inside a ring of wooden stakes. Brambles and blackthorn branches had been wound into the circle of sharpened sticks, forming an effective barrier against intruders. There was only one gate, guarded by two weasels at a time, so Sylver felt they were now reasonably well prepared for any sneak attack.

'By heaven, there's a lot of game out there,' said Icham, as he threw a brace of voles onto the ground by the fire. 'The place is teeming with it.'

Sylver was a little worried by this. 'Maybe it's stocked by someone,' he suggested. 'Do you think there's some dark lord of this region who's unknown to us? I'd rather know who we were up against, if we're trespassing.'

Wodehed said, 'I've not heard of anyone living in this area. It's on the edge of the Yellow Mountains. The sulphur in the air makes your eyes water and your breathing feel tight. Why would anyone want to live here voluntarily? It doesn't make sense.'

'You'd be surprised who wants to live where,' Scirf told him. 'There's stranger things in this life than *you* can imagine, wizard.'

The game was skinned and thrown into the pot. It was Mawk's turn to cook and he grumbled about the task the whole while he did it. Soon there was a nice thick stew simmering which smelled delicious. One by one the outlaws were given wooden trenchers, which were filled with wild onions and cherries, as well as succulent chunks of meat.

'Just vegetables for me,' murmured Bryony, when it came to her turn. 'A few onions – and some wild raspberries.'

'What?' cried Sylver. 'You're usually first at the steak – what's the matter with you? Feeling ill?'

'No, not at all,' she said, a little huffily.

Bryony went apart from the others to eat her plate of fruit and vegetables. Later, once the guard had been set at the entrance to the spike-protected compound, Sylver went to sit beside her. 'You know,' he said, 'you look as if you're sickening for something.'

'I'm all right,' she said, turning away from him. Then she turned back and said, 'I'm sorry. I should explain. The only trouble is, I *can't* explain. It's – it's just a feeling I have. I've had it ever since I – I was a *rabbit*. The idea of eating meat makes me feel ill. It's like eating *myself*. There's something dark and horrible about killing and cooking other creatures like myself.'

Sylver said, 'It's perfectly natural – we're carnivores. We're intended to eat meat.'

'I know. It sounds silly, doesn't it? But I can't do it, I'm afraid. You don't know what it's like, having been a rabbit. Part of my soul is locked inside a rabbit skin, back down there in the burrows. You wouldn't understand.'

It was true: Sylver didn't understand. He looked at the others, who all seemed fine. None of them were having nightmares about eating meat. They too had undergone the same experiences as Bryony.

Yet when he thought about it, she had always been the sensitive one. There was something fine and sharp about Bryony, which was missing from the others. Indeed, missing from himself too. She felt things more deeply, was more aware of the pulse of life around them. It was she who smelled spring in the air before any other weasel after a long winter. It was Bryony who knew just where to find the penny royals in the autumn. She had this special zest for the spirit of the earth.

He shrugged and said, 'If you don't want to eat

meat, that's all right with me, jill. Anyone who argues with you, why, you just refer them to Sylver. Now, we'd better get some sleep. You and I are on guard together later in the night.'

Bryony stared at her leader. 'Thank you, Sylver.'

'What? Oh' – he felt uncomfortable – 'don't mention it – it's part of my job – to see my band happy.'

'I know,' she told him, her eyes shining. 'That's why you're such a *good* leader.'

Sylver went to a bed lined with soft hay and lay there for a while, thinking about what Bryony had said. The experience of being a rabbit had obviously affected her more intensely than the others, but she had not mentioned her time as a human. In fact none of the weasels had spoken of it. He wondered if this side of their ordeal would rear its ugly head later. It remained to be seen.

Chapter Nineteen

In the morning the outlaws rose with the smell of woodsmoke in the air. Their leader had got up early and was boiling some water for nettle soup. There was dew on the ground, a slight chill in the air, and as each furry body uncurled from sleep it shivered and stretched. Grumbling came from the direction of Scirf, who had chosen to spend the night in a hole in a tree. Mawk-the-doubter, too, was a little testy, but then he was always the same in the mornings.

'Come on, stir yourselves,' said Sylver. 'We've got to get over these foothills today.'

More grumbles, more shivering.

Once they were fully awake, however, the weasels soon got in the right frame of mind.

'We'd better collect some food to take with us,' Alysoun said, putting some nuts in the leather pouch hanging from her belt. 'Unless you want to eat sulphur for the next day or so. It doesn't make a very appetizing meal . . .'

'It'll make your whiskers turn yellow,' added Dredless.

'Apart from which,' said Wodehed, who did not like this kind of flippant banter about something which he regarded as serious, 'it's deadly poisonous.'

The other weasels followed Alysoun's example and filled their pouches with their favourite bits of forest food, travellers' fare which would keep. It was no good putting meat in the bags for that would go rotten very quickly and become more poisonous than the sulphur.

Soon they were ready to go and Sylver led his band out of the forest and into the foothills, intending to skirt that strange rambling building from which smoke was now curling into the yellow atmosphere above.

However, as the morning went on and their progress was slow, Sylver found himself strangely drawn towards this weird structure on the edge of a wide lake. He could not help himself. It was as if someone had thrown a rope around his neck and was pulling him from the path he wished to follow.

'Someone else take over,' he said, wondering if it was just him who was enthralled. 'Just follow the trail – it's easy enough.'

Icham stepped forward and took the lead, but he too found he could not resist the attraction of the dwelling. 'Luke?' he said. 'You try.'

Luke, that holy weasel whose duty towards the church was forever foremost in his mind, went up front and muttered prayers as he walked, but he too was unable to withstand the strong pull from the building.

So the weasel band approached the house and lake.

The structure itself was fashioned entirely of wood. It sprawled so widely that it covered an area large enough to enclose a castle. Yet it was a single-storey dwelling, with a hundred windows and a dozen doors. The whole place rose and fell in areas where the landscape dipped and climbed. No attempt had been made to flatten the foundations. Inside, it must have been like walking on the waves of a frozen sea.

From fifty chimney pots pale-blue smoke rose, drifting up into the heavens above. The roof was made of bark shingles, reddened and made brittle by the sun. There were birch-log paths leading from each doorway, similar to the footpaths monks made from County Elleswhere's monasteries, out into the countryside around.

Behind dark windows, thick with dust, moved shadowy shapes.

'Look at the lake,' cried Miniver, the finger-weasel, 'it's *teeming* with fish.'

And so it was. Their silver shapes flashed in the sun as they broke the surface occasionally, or leapt out of the water to catch an insect. Around the lake, in the reeds, were wildfowl. The whole area was rich with game.

This was not surprising because the landscape was beautiful meadows, scattered about with trees and shrubs, all tumbling down to this golden lake with its silver bounty.

'What *is* this place?' whispered Sylver, as they stood outside one of the doorways.

Icham replied, 'I don't know, but it looks like somewhere I wouldn't mind living. You could hunt and be happy here, that's for sure. I wonder who owns it all. Let's go in and find out.'

And before any of the others could stop him, he had squeezed through the gap in the partly opened door. Alarmed for his safety, Sylver followed. The others naturally trailed behind, until they were inside the great rambling building.

The sight which met their eyes was truly amazing.

The whole place consisted of just one room, which indeed undulated like a sea swell.

Scattered around the room, in the thick smoky gloom, were weasels, stoats, polecats, otters and pine martens, all carrying slings and darts. They were obviously wood-creatures, hunters, who made their living by tracking the spoor of prey in order to fill the pot. Rough and ready characters by their looks: their coats shaggy with catching on briars and their bibs dark with soot, stained with leaf mould.

There was little talk amongst them. They seemed strong, quiet animals, with little desire for talk.

There were fires in every part of the room, around which sat these hunters, silently repairing and cleaning their weapons. In the centre of the great room was an enormous iron pot, hanging by chains from the ceiling over a low fire. From this pot issued an aroma of mixed stew. Every so often one of the hunters in the room would rise and fill a wooden bowl from this pot, take it back to his or her place, and eat from it.

'That smells good,' whispered Scirf. 'Wonder if it's sort of everyone help theirself?'

'Just hold on a while, Scirf,' warned Sylver. 'We don't know who owns this place, or what the situation means. Let's make a few enquiries first. I must admit it looks like some sort of travellers' rest, a way station for hunters, but we'll need to ask one or two questions of these creatures.'

At that moment a mink was passing by them and he nodded at the cauldron of stew. 'Take some stew if you're hungry,' he said. 'That's what it's for.'

The outlaws needed no second telling. They picked up wooden bowls which lay around the fire and ladled stew into them. There were also wooden trenchers bearing hunks of bread. Soon they were tucking into a good meal. Bryony did not touch the stew, since she had forsaken meat, but there were plenty of vegetables to eat, baking in the ashes.

Sylver still felt uneasy, but he could not deny his band their food. He stared around the place as he swallowed the wholesome fare, telling himself that his earlier thoughts had been right – this was a way station for hunters.

After he had finished his food Sylver felt drowsy and muddle-headed, but he put this down to the warmth of the room and the heavy meal. He went in search of someone whom he could question about their situation. It might be that some payment was required for their board and lodging, if only in the way of work.

He found a polecat who was mending a sling. 'Who owns this place? We've just arrived . . .'

The polecat looked up and frowned in surprise. 'Just arrived?' He stared at the band of outlaws as if seeing them for the first time. 'What, all of you at once? Was it an accident or a war?' He stared harder through the dimness and then shook his head in a melancholy way. 'Oh, I remember. You're alive. You camped near by last night. It was a mistake, you know.'

The creature reached over and grabbed a pawful of what looked like dried herbs. He tossed them onto the fire. Around the room other creatures

187

began doing the same. Sylver thought this was slightly odd, but did not think it important enough to dwell on it.

The polecat's reply had thoroughly disconcerted the outlaw band, who were looking at each other in puzzlement.

Sylver decided to try again. 'Look, fellow,' he said, 'we don't understand. What *is* this place? It seems to be filled with creatures I would normally expect to see alone in the forest – backwood stoats, mountain polecats like yourself, weasel pioneers and frontier martens. You don't seem the type of creatures to seek each other's company – rather, you appear to me to be those who normally prefer to be alone.'

The polecat looked up and nodded. 'That's true.'

'Then where are we?'

'Why, you're in Hunter's Hall – the heaven of all good hunters, creatures who hunt only for food, never just for sport . . .'

Icham stared at his leader and shrugged. None of them had ever heard of Hunter's Hall, and they were mystified by this slow-talking, dour polecat's words. What had he meant by 'accident or war' and what was the 'mistake' he had referred to? It seemed the outlaws had stumbled on a place which did not seem to exist in Welkin, for one of them at least should have knowledge of it. Instead they all looked at each other in a baffled way, expecting answers but not getting them.

Scirf, the village weasel with access to travellers' tales, scratched his neck and shook his head.

'Well,' said Sylver, 'Hunter's Hall does indeed seem like a heaven for such creatures as yourself – leathery old fellows who are only happy when

188

stalking through the forest – but someone must own the place, surely?'

'No,' murmured the polecat, looking up, 'you don't understand – I mean, it is definitely *heaven.*'

Bryony was the first amongst the band to realize what the polecat was saying. 'You mean,' she said, looking round at all the quiet activity in the room, 'this is a place for hunters' souls? You're all dead? You're all in the afterlife?'

Now the polecat gave a show of mirth. 'This jill is the cleverest of her kind. We are indeed hunters whose lives have ended. Good hunters. Those who killed out of malice or for sport have gone to a different place, a less comfortable dwelling. We are in heaven here. We have game in plenty. The lake outside is for the otters. You must have seen the fish jumping. In the forest there are quarry for the polecats and pine martens; in the meadows, the ditches, the hedgerows – there the weasels and stoats hunt.

'This is our reward for a blameless life as a hunter.'

Wodehed blinked. He, like the rest of the outlaw band, was beginning to feel rather drowsy and dull-headed. The smoke from the many fires seemed to be making him sleepy. He asked the question, but he did not actually care very much about the answer. 'Then what are *we* doing here?' he said.

'That's why I asked you if you had been in an accident or a war. I was surprised to see so many new souls at once. However, it was the mistake you made which landed you here. You'll have to stay, of course.'

189

'Mistake?' asked Sylver, yawning. 'What mistake?'

'Three of your kind hunted and killed our game – the game intended for dead souls: now you have trapped yourselves by that action. You are part of Hunter's Hall. You cannot hunt our game and leave without punishment.'

The outlaws, of course, remembered the game which Dredless, Alysoun and Icham had brought back to their fire in the forest the previous evening.

'Now just a minute,' said Sylver, feeling more than a little alarmed by the polecat's words. 'This is not fair. We had no idea where we were. We didn't know the game was sacred. We were merely hunting to fill the pot, just as you would have done when you were – alive.'

'Too bad,' said the hunter mournfully. 'I'm sorry for you.'

The outlaws were beginning to slip into a lazy state of mind. Their bodies were still sharp, but their brains had gone blind. Sylver knew he should not be accepting everything the polecat was telling them, but for some reason he did not care very much.

The other hunters around their own particular fire had not made any further comment. Throughout the room they seemed intent on their tasks – preparing themselves for another day's hunting.

'This is beginning to turn into another nightmare,' said Luke. 'I should have heard of this place, but I haven't. I'd like to say what's going on, Sylver, but I'm as lost as you are.'

Sylver said, 'I can't deny I felt strongly attracted to this place, when we tried to pass on by. So did you, Luke, and you Icham. If we have indeed landed ourselves in a place of dead souls, through some error, we shall have to consider ways of righting any wrong we might have done.'

Mawk, whose survival instincts were stronger than the rest of the weasels, climbed to his feet. 'I'm getting out of here,' he said dully.

He began to walk towards the door.

The polecat seemed to have anticipated a move from this particular weasel. Mawk was one of those creatures who glowed with fear when it was on him.

'It's no good, you know,' said the polecat. 'You can't leave now.'

And Mawk found he was right. When he reached the doorway a terrible tiredness came over him, a lethargy which would not allow him to walk over the threshold. Instead, it was all he could do to stagger back and flop down by the fire again. The polecat grabbed one of Mawk's rear legs with his right forepaw and held the weasel fast. 'In any case,' he told Mawk, 'if you go through that doorway you become *the prey.*'

'What?' Mawk cried wildly. 'What do you mean?'

'I mean you will be hunted down, skinned, quartered and then thrown into that stew pot over there.'

Mawk stared in horror at the great, black, greasy cauldron which hung over the slow fire. 'In there?' he croaked.

'Just so,' replied the polecat.

Mawk sat down again, trembling from head to tail. Alysoun leaned over and gave him a pat and a hug. She knew how Mawk felt. She was feeling

191

some of it herself. It seemed the outlaws had once again fallen foul of something supernatural. She suspected the moufflon witch had something to do with it.

'I still don't understand,' Sylver said to the hunter. 'Just what is it we've done wrong? I mean, if you all hunt the prey, what does it matter if we did too? Even though you're all supposed to be dead . . .'

'We *are* dead.'

'Well, even so, you *eat* your quarry. You throw it into that pot over there and take from it. I've seen hunters go to the pot and take some. What harm have *we* done?'

'Let me explain,' said the polecat, carefully putting down his slingshot. 'You see, when we hunt the game, it is renewed the next day. It never really dies. It's a sort of never-ending cycle. If I kill a rabbit, it goes into the stew, but the next morning that rabbit springs to life again, out of the meadow grass, out of the field. The game *you* killed remains dead, because you are not like us.'

Wodehed blinked. 'So what we've taken has disappeared from your eternal larder – for ever.'

'That's it,' said the polecat. 'You have stolen from the game parks of heaven. Your punishment is to remain here, in Hunter's Hall, and serve the hunters. When we come in weary after the day's hunt you will have prepared the fires for us, cleared out the dirty straw from the floor and replaced it with fresh, clean straw. You will spread hay, gut fish, make reed baskets for carrying the game. You will work like ants until you have paid for your crime. I'm sorry for you.'

Sylver put his face in his paws. 'Oh no,' he groaned. 'Not again.'

'There are advantages to being here,' said the hunter. 'You will find that any old wounds you might have had in the real world will have healed.'

The outlaws inspected themselves, all having been wounded or injured at some time. Icham, Bryony and Luke, all hurt in the battle with the pine martens, found they were free of scars. However, Sylver thought this was poor payment for being indefinitely enslaved.

The leader of the weasels was aware that time was passing quickly. It was important they arrived at the eyrie, the eagle's nest, as soon as possible. The longer they left it, the more likely the two halves of eggshell would be crushed or damaged by the eaglet or its mother. They had to get to the nest while the map was still in two halves.

Chapter Twenty

Sheriff Falshed stared at the countryside around Castle Rayn, studying its contours in the drizzle. It was actually quite remarkable what you could see, when you were hanging upside down by your hind legs from high on the battlements. Everything looked quite different the other way up.

Falshed sighed. He wondered when, if ever, he was going to outwit Sylver and his band. This time they seemed to have been spirited away by the dawn light. He had searched for them, of course, but their trail ran out on the edge of a wide lake. The sheriff had gone right round the lake, which had looked foul and dreary – lifeless, in fact.

He had searched for some dwelling in which they might have taken refuge, but had found nothing. There was no habitation in the region. And so he had had to return to Prince Poynt and report another failed mission.

'I'll have you boiled in tar,' the white-furred Prince Poynt had screamed from his throne. 'I'll have you cooked to a crisp.'

When the tar had been ready, bubbling in the barrel over a red-hot fire, the prince had relented. Falshed had been allowed to live once again. He was marched up to the crenellations and hung from ropes by his heels. Sometimes he felt it might be better if Prince Poynt had him executed, there and then, and put him out of his eternal misery.

'Time to come up, sir,' called the stoat captain of the guard from above. 'Are you ready to be hauled aloft?'

'Just a little while longer,' he murmured sarcastically. 'I'm enjoying the evening *so* much. You have no idea how pretty the sun looks, climbing up behind the horizon.'

'Don't you mean dropping down behind the horizon.'

'I know what I mean – you should see it from my point of view.'

Sheriff Falshed was pulled up and untied. He was told that the prince had said he could go to his quarters. He took the stone staircase down to his room below one of the towers on unsteady legs. He felt giddy now that the blood was rushing away from his head and down towards his feet.

Reaching his chamber, he entered to find Spinfer, his stoatservant, waiting. 'Pour me a hot bath,' he ordered. 'Put in some of those nice salts I brought back from the marshes.'

'Yes, sir,' murmured the stoatservant.

'Oh, my aching legs,' said Falshed, staggering to a chair. 'I feel as if my joints have been reground.'

The stoatservant left to do as ordered.

The chamber in which Sheriff Falshed lived was furnished with precious ornaments and lavish tapestries. There was a silver cross embedded with rubies on the mantel, a silk carpet covering the mould on the west wall, a jade carving of an otter in the window niche, a golden-sheathed ram's horn. All these ornaments Sheriff Falshed would be proud to tell you he confiscated from their rightful owners.

The silver cross had been stolen from a monastery, hidden under Falshed's red cloak.

The carpet had been taken by force from an oriental caravan train drawn by coypu.

The jade had been a present from Prince Poynt to a stoat jill out in the hinterland: Falshed was supposed to have delivered it but kept it for himself. Prince Poynt often wondered out loud why he had never been thanked for his generous gift and sometimes made threats to visit the female. Since he had not been outside his castle in years, the threats were not taken all that seriously by Falshed.

The ram's horn had been filched from Lord Haukin's study.

All these fine items, and more, adorned the sheriff's room. They helped to remind him how far he had come since the days when he had been the son of a beetle-catcher.

Sheriff Falshed had not been born in the presence of royalty. His first home had been the hollow of a tree on Lord Haukin's estate. When he had grown through a hard winter and into a new summer, his mother threw his brothers and sisters out of the nest. Falshed had responded by throwing his *mother* out and remaining in the nest himself. This had not endeared him to his siblings, who told him they would never acknowledge their kinship again.

This was fine by Falshed, who thought of close relations – or any relations, in fact – as being worse than leeches. So far as he was concerned, brothers, sisters, cousins, uncles and aunts could go to the devil. He needed no blood ties of any kind and would have given his own grandmother up to the wolves if it meant promotion in the world.

It had been this action of ousting his own mother from her home which had brought Falshed to the attention of Prince Poynt, who loved evil deeds and their doers.

Prince Poynt had raised him first to a captain of the guard, then to Sheriff of all Welkin. 'As long as I remain prince,' the other had said, 'you will still be my sheriff.'

Of course, the prince's good opinion of his sheriff occasionally wavered but Falshed did not blame his lord and master for that; he blamed Sylver the outlaw, who brought it about. Prince Poynt was not responsible for his moods – he was a royal prince after all; it was those who changed them who needed punishment.

'Your tub is ready, sir,' said a quiet voice by his elbow.

Falshed said, 'What, eh? Oh, thank you, Spinfer.'

The sheriff slipped gratefully into a bath of hot water and marsh salts, allowing the ache to drain from his limbs. Spinfer took up a reed instrument and began to play soothing music on it, reminiscent of the sound of a breeze through leafy poplars. There came a sharp knock on the door.

'Come in,' murmured Falshed dreamily.

Then, as the door was opened and Falshed caught a flash of ermine, he realized the prince was entering his chamber. This was unheard of, since Prince Poynt never left the west wing. His whole body went stiff with fear. He reached out quickly and snatched the jade carving of the otter from the window niche. He plunged it under the soapy water and sat on it.

197

Prince Poynt stood in the doorway. 'I have come on a long delayed visit to your chambers.' he said, striding into the centre of the room. 'What is that you have there?'

'What? Eh? My lord? You – you wanted something?'

'Lost the soap, did we, Falshed?'

'What?' Falshed clicked his teeth together in feigned amusement and splashed the surface of the tub. 'Oh – yes – lost it – some – where – down – here . . .' He pretended to grope at the bottom of the tub, where he knew there was no bar of soap, only the incriminating jade ornament, which Prince Poynt would actually kill him for possessing, should he suspect its existence.

Prince Poynt stared down into the water, which Falshed tried to make murky by washing himself. 'Can I help you, my lord?' he asked, his breath tight in his chest. 'Did you require my presence?'

Prince Poynt looked up, his attention taken away from the tub at last. 'Of course I wanted you. I don't come here looking for companionship, Falshed. What nice things you have here,' he said, looking around the room. 'How wealthy I have made you, Falshed. I hope you're suitably grateful. I might have that silk rug for myself if I take a fancy to it.'

'Do please take it, my lord,' gulped Falshed. 'I have no use for such finery . . .'

'Well *I* don't want it, if *you* don't want it,' snapped Prince Poynt testily. 'Where's the fun in *that*? Now, where was I? Oh, yes. I have all the companions I need in my own wing of the castle. I don't need *your* company, stoat.'

'No, no, I don't suppose you do,' Falshed

murmured, the jade ornament sticking painfully into his buttocks. 'Er, what can I do for you, my prince?'

Prince Poynt shivered and went to the window, staring out at the rain beyond. 'I've come to a decision,' he said. 'You are obviously not going to be able to catch that snivelling weasel on your own. You need help. I've sent for one of the greatest trackers in the land. Magellan will be here in two days.'

Falshed jerked upright in his bath. A finger of fear poked at his racing heart. The name used by Prince Poynt was not one the sheriff ever wished to hear. Spinfer dropped his reed flute and it rolled across the floor. Both sheriff and stoatservant stared at each other.

Magellan! The dreaded bounty hunter was coming!

'Isn't he – er – a little *expensive*, my lord? Are you sure you want to pay a fox to do a stoat's duties? Myself and my stoats will work hard, night and day . . .'

'You've *been* working hard night and day,' snapped Prince Poynt, 'and all it's got you is blood rushing to your head and a thorough soaking on the battlements. Be sensible, Falshed, you're not getting anywhere. We need expert help.'

'But *Magellan*,' Falshed whined in despair. 'We'll be lucky if he doesn't steal the throne from under your tail. Wasn't it Magellan who killed your older brother in the forest?'

'A hunting accident,' said the prince quickly. 'Everyone knows that. Magellan's arrow glanced off a tree.'

'But they were alone, weren't they? You can't be

sure that Magellan did not kill your brother Redfur on purpose. There was talk amongst the weasel charcoal burners, who lived in the forest at the time . . .'

Prince Poynt's eyes seemed to take on a shade of vermilion. 'Talk? What talk?' he cried. His whole demeanour was ruffled. He looked nervous and on the edge of a breakdown.

Falshed had not quite expected this reaction and was now nervous himself. Spinfer had made himself scarce and was now in another room. 'Why, nothing, my prince,' murmured the sheriff. 'Not much, anyway. Just – just that Magellan killed him on purpose, murdered King Redfur.'

Prince Poynt stared into Falshed's eyes. 'For what reason? Why would he want to murder my brother?'

'Why, perhaps someone ordered—' Falshed stopped abruptly. He saw where his remarks were taking him. The only one who would have bene- fited from the death of King Redfur was Prince Poynt himself. The prince would inherit the kingdom of Welkin from the brother, who was only seven seconds older than him but who was much bigger and stronger. If anyone ordered the death of Redfur, it was most likely Prince Poynt.

Prince Poynt now came and placed his paw on Falshed's head and began to push him under the water in an abstracted fashion. Falshed gripped the sides of the tub, but the prince was very strong. Gradually, Falshed began to submerge.

'Perhaps you have often wondered,' said Prince Poynt, as if slightly distracted, 'why I have never been crowned king. Perhaps you thought I had an aversion to coronations. Well, my fine sheriff, the truth is there seems to be a curse on the kingship of my family. Kings, like my father and elder brother, seem to grow so high in stature that they fail to see plots forming amongst the nobility below them.

'Kingship seems to do that to one. Makes one so lofty that one thinks one is invulnerable. Kings grow too remote, too detached from the ordinary people. So I decided to remain a prince, close to my knights and the rest of the noblestoats. That way I can smell plots before they hatch. But I know what you're thinking,' said the prince, as he saw the bubbles coming up from under the soapy water. 'You're thinking, "Couldn't one be a king and still keep one's ear to the ground?" You might think that, my dear Falshed, but the very word "king" gives a prince pretensions and airs that are impossible to ignore. I prefer not to fall under the influence of my own ego and possibly die of an overdose of arrogance. Now, you were saying?' whispered the prince. 'Someone ordered what?'

He let Falshed up for a breath of oxygen, before starting to push him down again.

Falshed was extremely alarmed and struggled in the milky-coloured water, his soapy fingers slipping from the edge of the tub. He spluttered, 'Perhaps someone ordered Magellan *not* to be there, but – but Magellan disobeyed that order. Didn't you say he shouldn't go, my prince? I seem to remember you being worried about your brother, concerned for his welfare.'

The prince's paw relaxed a little. He studied Falshed through narrow eyes, before nodding slowly. 'You know me so well, Falshed,' he sighed.

'My weakness is that I am too mammalmane, too concerned for others. You know' – his voice fell to a whisper – 'there was some rumour that my brother had *himself* killed. Yes, yes, it's true. He was unable to sire young, you see. He was infertile. He believed he had magical powers of rebirth, that he would come back from the dead, but with his fertility intact.

'It was Lammas-tide, when it happened – a magical time in my brother's calendar.'

'That must be it,' cried Falshed, grasping at the one straw offered to him as he drowned in his bath. 'Your brother ordered his own death.'

Prince Poynt took his paw from Falshed's brow. 'Yes, yes, you are right, Falshed. How glad I am that you are my sheriff. I chose you, you know. You are like a brother to me . . .'

Considering the conversation which had preceded this remark, Falshed was not sure that he wanted to be a brother of a mad prince. Brothers of Prince Poynt tended to die young.

The regal tar-tipped ermine went first to the window, where he shivered uncontrollably, then swept back to a place in front of the fire. 'Your job will be to pay Magellan in full, once he has done his work. Once Magellan has caught and disposed of the outlaw band, you must get rid of him. When we no longer need him I want you to throw the fox into the dungeons or, better still, make him disappear – out on the marshes somewhere, or in some quicksands – but I don't want to see him here again. You understand?'

'*Me?*' cried Falshed in alarm. 'How am I going to get rid of Magellan? He's no fool. He'll slaughter the lot of us like cooped chickens, if he gets a whiff of betrayal. Please, my prince, rethink this scheme of yours. You must—'

'I *must*?' shrieked Prince Poynt. 'Must? Must? Must?'

'I – that is – I wish you would, my lord. I really wish you would. I don't think I can handle Magellan, really I don't. A fox – and a *bad* one at that. I mean, good foxes are tough enough, but bad ones – well, they are the pits. I'm sure we're going to regret this, my lord . . .'

'Why are you squirming?' said Prince Poynt suspiciously, coming to the edge of the tub and looking in. 'What's the matter with you? Have you got piles or something?'

Falshed flurried the water with his back legs. 'It's nothing – nothing for you to worry about. A touch of arthritis, that's all. Please don't be concerned.'

'I'm not concerned, you oaf. I couldn't care less about whether you're in pain or not. Just remember what I've told you. Magellan arrives in two days. You'd better be sorting out some plan for getting rid of him, once he's been useful to us. Now, I've had enough of this idle chatter. I'm going to find Pompom. I need cheering up.'

He strode out of the room, slamming the door behind him.

Falshed gave a hollow clack. '*He* needs cheering up? That's rich. What about *me*? I'm about to take on the most feared carnivore in the history of Welkin. Magellan. He'll pull me apart and use me for bookends. He'll use my fangs for pipe-cleaners. What am I going to do, Spinfer?'

'Short of leaving the country, sir,' said Spinfer quietly and politely, 'I suggest either poison or a long fall.'

Falshed pulled the jade figurine out from under his rump and tossed it to his stoatservant, who put it back in the window niche. 'I'm aware of your loyalty to me, Spinfer. It's not easy being sheriff. You have my permission to give me a sharp push, when I get too near the edge of the battlements next time. I'm sure you're right – to end it all quickly is the only way. Foxes have such deviant minds. They have ways of killing a stoat which would make a rogue wolf wince. It's sad to have come so far and yet have to end it all this way.'

'We must always keep hope alive, sir.'

'Why?' Falshed said hollowly.

When the water in the tub grew cold, he stepped from it into the warm towels held by his faithful stoatservant. Then he was dried briskly and put to bed. Spinfer brought him a hot drink of buttermilk laced with honey dew, which rippled gently through his body and induced an undisturbed sleep.

He slept all through the next morning, afternoon and even the next night.

Finally, he was awakened by the martial sound of a distant drum, beating a strong tattoo.

Fearing the worst, he rose from his bed and went to the window, staring out over the plains which led down to the river below. For once it was not raining, though the sky was heavily overcast and it looked as if it were about to pour at any moment. The wind was sweeping across the grasslands, making the ground look like a sea in a storm.

Marching towards the castle was a troop of stoats, with four drummers at the head. Strolling beside this uniform group, all in step, was a tall, rangy, red figure with a bushy tail. It was

Magellan. There was a bow slung over one shoulder and a wicked quiver full of black arrows at his hip.

Magellan wore an amused smirk on his face, probably because he found it ridiculous walking beside soldiers. He strolled with a lazy swagger, obviously seeing no need to keep in time with the beat of the drum, and those stoat soldiers near to him kept falling out of step as he put them off their stride. Every so often he turned his head slightly and spat a wad of grass juice over his left shoulder, after which he would nod his head sharply as if to say, 'That's what I think of the world.'

When Magellan and his escort were a little closer to the castle, the lean fox suddenly looked up, catching Falshed staring out of the window. Magellan gave a snort of derision and clicked his teeth twice, before turning his attention to the castle gateway again.

Falshed fumed in humiliation. How dare that blasted fox treat him as if he were a piece of dirt! He was so full of himself, that vulpine poser. 'I've got my orders for *you*, my friend,' snarled Falshed. 'Oh yes, don't you worry about that. And I'll carry them out to the letter if it kills me.'

'Which it probably will, sir,' murmured the voice of the faithful Spinfer at his elbow. 'But we mustn't let that worry us, must we, sir?' He paused before adding, 'Your breakfast, sir. Shall we be taking it in our room, or on the balcony overlooking the moat, which I must say is looking less stagnant than usual today, and the gnats are not *half* as bad in the morning as they are in the evening. Sir? Which shall it be . . .?'

Chapter Twenty-one

After a particularly warm day the occupants of Hunter's Hall had allowed their fires to get very low. While everyone was asleep that night many of the fires went out altogether. By the early hours of the morning the smoke from those special herbs the hunters put on the flames had become very thin. The atmosphere in the room began to clear.

Mawk woke and felt keen-witted for the first time since they had arrived. The previous evening he had felt unwell and, though ravenously hungry, had not eaten his stew. Now his head felt as if it had been thoroughly scoured on the inside and he could think straight for once.

Now that he *could* think clearly, his thoughts went immediately to escape and his own survival.

After a week of mucking out dirty straw and hay, and fetching and carrying for the hunters, Mawk-the-doubter had suffered enough. They had not been allowed to go outside – indeed, that terrible lethargy assailed them when they attempted it – but all the work within the hall was done by the outlaws. It was peculiar that whenever they thought of leaving the hall they felt exhausted, but then, when there was work to be done, they managed to tackle it from dawn to dusk.

Well, no more of that for Mawk! For the first time since entering the hall he felt able to make his escape, despite the fact that his forelegs ached from carrying buckets of water and his ankles hurt from standing on tiptoe to light the brands. He was terrified, there was no doubt about that, but the thought of slaving for the hunters for ever over-rode that terror. Mawk despised menial chores and even the fear of being hunted down was not enough to hold him to this place.

He blamed Sylver for getting the outlaws into the mess they were in and saw no reason to remain with the band.

He woke Scirf and spoke to him. 'Scirf, I'm going,' he whispered.

'Goin' where?' asked that bleary-eyed village weasel, rubbing the sleep from his face. 'What's all this?'

'I'm running away. I've had enough. Tell Sylver I'm sorry. If I'm caught it'll be too bad. I can't stand this bondage any longer. I'm not a serf.'

Scirf looked around him. The hunters, like the outlaws, were all lying in a deep sleep on their beds of straw. The smoke from the smouldering camp fires was like grey tendrils. There were pole-cats, pine martens, stoats and weasels everywhere, draped over floors and furniture like limp rolls of rag. No-one guarded the doorway. If Mawk wanted to run, there would be no-one stopping him. Only a chase at dawn, when the first hunters woke.

'Good luck,' muttered Scirf, looking bleary-eyed. 'Good mind to come with you meself, but I can't seem to summon up the energy.'

Scirf immediately fell asleep again. Mawk,

forever concerned with his own safety, was worried about venturing out into the world again alone. He decided he needed company and took up Scirf's limp form in a fireman's lift, slinging him over his shoulder.

With Scirf on his back Mawk picked his way carefully through the still bodies until he reached the nearest door. As always in this world which had first been populated by humans, it was a small door set in a much larger one. Mawk spat carefully on the hinges to lubricate them, then opened the door centimetre by slow centimetre. To his great relief it did not creak. Then he was out into the night, and walking as swiftly as the weight of Scirf would allow him towards a distant hill.

After a while the other weasel's body became too heavy for him to carry. Mawk was not used to lugging dead weights around and he let Scirf fall to the grass. Finding he still could not wake his friend, Mawk decided to continue alone after all. Hunter's Hall was still close by and he had visions of the hunters waking and raising a hue and cry. He left Scirf where he lay and scampered on, anxious to be gone from this part of the country where he was the prey of skilful pursuers.

He put some distance between himself and the hall, pausing to gasp for breath occasionally. Once he was over the first range of hills and climbing the second, Mawk heard someone chasing him, and terror rippled through his lithe body. He turned and cried, 'Don't kill me. I'll come back quietly. I – I was just looking for the toilet. I lost my way to the privy in the dark. All I want is a pee.'

'Be quiet, you nit,' said a voice Mawk recognized instantly. 'Do you wanna wake the whole flippin' countryside?'

Relief flooded through Mawk. 'Scirf? Is that you? Er, how – how did you get out here?'

'I dunno. I just found meself lying on a grassy knoll. Me head feels clear for the first time in a week. Didn't like that place, back there. I had a better time guarding the pile of dung outside me village. At least I could catch flies with me mouth when I got fed up. Nothin' but smoke in that place – and them hunters are as boring as anythink, ain't they? They don't talk about nuffink but huntin', shootin' and fishin'.'

Suddenly there was another sound in the grasses behind Scirf and the two weasels froze.

'Who's that?' whispered Mawk. 'Did anyone follow you?'

'I dunno,' replied Scirf. 'Didn't see no-one. Still, two of us should be able to handle any rotten hunter. You get over there behind that rock. I'll hide in the grasses here. When he comes past, we'll jump on him together, see?'

Mawk said, 'I'm not so sure . . .' but the rustling came closer and he had no option but to do as Scirf said. His heart was pounding in his chest. He was not a weasel given to violence. He preferred to talk his way out of trouble.

Scirf was already poised to leap on the person following them, so Mawk realized he would have to do the same. The pair of them waited as a long dark shape came looping up the hill. When the creature was close enough they both jumped out onto the figure. They struggled for a few moments.

The desperate Mawk sat on the creature's head to prevent any attack from a set of fangs. Scirf gripped the lower body hard.

'Got you, you rotten sneak,' muttered Scirf, sinking his teeth into the tail of their pursuer. 'Take that, you creep.'

'Ow!' came the voice of Alysoun from underneath Mawk. 'Stop that, you rat.'

Mawk instantly fell away from their prisoner. 'Alysoun? What are you doing here? Is everyone following everyone else?'

'More to the point,' said an angry Alysoun, getting up and feeling for her tail, 'what are *you* doing out here?'

Mawk said in a confused voice, 'Me? I – I was going to get help, of course. That is, Scirf and I thought we'd better try and find someone to come back with us and set you all free.'

'That's it,' Scirf confirmed, in a strong aggrieved tone. 'Flippin' heroes, that's what we are! Riskin' our necks to get you lot out of trouble. I'd like a bit more respect in your voice when you speaks to us, jill.'

Mawk admired the way Scirf attacked Alysoun before she could accuse him of running out on the band. He could learn a thing or two from this dung-watcher who had recently joined their ranks. Scirf did not sit down and take his medicine, he dished it out first, with great big spoons.

'Arrrggh,' muttered Alysoun, distracted for a moment, 'I think I've caught one of your fleas, Scirf.'

Once she had dealt with the offending parasite, Alysoun said, 'How did you two escape? I woke up and saw the door flapping open. Your patches of straw were empty and I guessed you'd gone outside. I tried to wake the others, but they were still deeply asleep. So then I followed you.'

She paused before adding, 'We have to go back, you know, and carry the others out into the fresh air. We could do it, between the three of us . . .'

'Go back?' squeaked Mawk. 'That's likely, isn't it? What can we do? You know how it is in there.'

Scirf frowned and said, 'I still don't understand it. How did we get out?'

Mawk, coward and doubter that he was, was no idiot. Now that his head was clear he had already been thinking things over carefully and had an inkling as to what had been going on. He turned to Alysoun. 'Did you eat the stew last night?' he asked.

Alysoun shook her head. 'Why, no. I was hungry enough, but the day's work had exhausted me so much that I fell asleep before I could put the spoon in my mouth.'

'I didn't eat it either,' said Mawk. 'And those herbs they usually put on the fires – the stock had run low. They put some on, but not as much as usual.'

'What's your point, squire?' asked Scirf.

'I think the stew had some kind of magic potion in it,' said Mawk, 'which was reinforced by the smell put out by the burning herbs. I have heard that if you eat in the land of the dead, you never get to leave. I didn't eat the stew because I was not feeling well last night. That's why we managed to escape.'

'What about me?' asked Scirf. 'I stuffed meself silly.'

'I carried you out,' replied Mawk, deciding to

come clean, 'but you got too heavy for me, so I left you on the grass. The clean air must have cleared your head after a while. I suspect their dark concoctions only work in the atmosphere of the hall, while they're burning those weeds.'

'You lef' me on the grass?' cried Scirf. 'Remind me to give you a thick ear sometime.'

'I got you out, didn't I?' Mawk said testily.

Alysoun said, 'All this aside, we have to go back for the others – we can't leave them to face the wrath of the hunters.'

'You must be mad,' Mawk said, shuddering. 'I'm not going back there – not for the world.'

Alysoun looked severe. 'Sylver and the others will be punished because of you. Sylver was telling me the hunters were almost ready to let us go, having paid for our crime . . .'

'Crime?' cried Scirf. 'What crime? 'Ow did we know we was committin' any crime? I'll give 'em crime. I know what crime is, don't you worry.'

'I'm sure you do,' said Alysoun, 'but the thing is, we have to go back. We're in their power at the moment.'

Scirf said, 'Well, we ain't, but the others is – I s'pose you're right, Alysoun.'

'No,' Mawk said firmly.

'You know if the hunters don't catch you,' Alysoun said, 'Sylver eventually will, and he'll be just as tough on you.'

'I don't care,' said Mawk. 'I'm not going.'

'You cankered gooseberry,' said Scirf in disgust. 'I thought you was a weasel, but instead you're nuffink but a frightened newt.'

'I can't help that. I'll wait here for a few minutes. If you come back soon, then I'll be ready to welcome you to join me. If not, I'm gone.'

Alysoun shook her head. 'You'll regret this, Mawk.'

She led Scirf down the slope to the lake side, towards Hunter's Hall, hoping that Mawk would change his mind and join them. When the pair got to the bottom of the slope, however, they both blinked in astonishment. Sure, it was grey dawn, but there was enough light to see by. Certainly they would have seen something as big as Hunter's Hall – if it had been there.

'Where has it gone?' cried Alysoun, staring at the space beside the lake. 'It was *there*, wasn't it?'

'Disappeared,' said Scirf with a tell-tale gasp of relief. 'Vanished.'

'Don't sound so pleased,' cried Alysoun, rounding on him. 'Your friends – *my* friends – they're still in that place. If it's disappeared, they've gone too. I don't want anything to happen to my friends.'

'Well, no, of course I don't wish 'em to come to any harm,' said Scirf uncomfortably. 'I was just – well – smell that lake,' he said, changing the subject. 'It pongs! Look at that stinkin' water. It looks all scummy. This isn't the same place at all. We're somewhere different.'

'Let's get back up to Mawk,' said Alysoun, upset. 'I've an idea what's happened.'

They trudged back up the hill to find a triumphant Mawk waiting to gloat over them. 'Ha! I knew you'd come back. Changed your minds, eh?'

'No,' replied Alysoun stiffly, 'we haven't. What's happened is this . . .' and she explained what they had seen down by the lake.

'Crikey!' Mawk exclaimed. 'You mean they've just gone and fizzled away, just like that?'

Alysoun nodded. 'You know what I think has happened? I think the hunter who told us we would be tracked down if we escaped was lying. I think that Hunter's Hall exists in some kind of Otherworld which we wandered into. A pale valley which one might be led into by the magic of a witch!

'Anyway, the polecat knew that once we got out of the hall and over the next hill we would find ourselves in the real world. That's why he told us they would hunt us down – an extra threat to discourage us from escaping. But, now we're out of it. We're back on our old Welkin.'

'What about the others?' asked Mawk.

'Well, they're still trapped there, ain't they?' Scirf said. 'And we can't get back in to tell them the truth. Somehow they'll have to discover it by accident, like what we did.'

Alysoun added, 'Unless they are indeed set free, having paid their dues to the hunters.'

Mawk said, 'I'm glad I thought of running awa— fetching help.'

Scirf said, 'Where does that leave us, jill? What do we do while we're waitin' for the cows to come home, eh?'

Alysoun wondered if there was some way of finding Hunter's Hall again, but could not think of one herself. In the far distance she saw a statue crossing the countryside, striding out purposefully. It appeared to be carrying an axe, so it was either an unhorsed knight with a battle-axe, or a woodcutter. 'We could ask that statue if it knows where the hall is,' she commented.

Scirf and Mawk stared in the direction she was indicating. Scirf shook his head. 'Statues don't *answer* questions, they just ask 'em.'

Alysoun squinted. 'I think that one's a wood-cutter – being a man of the forest, he *might* know where Hunter's Hall is.'

'Nah,' said Scirf, 'not a chance. Hello,' he added, staring at the statue, which was now disappearing over the brow of a hill, 'I wonder if that's the bod that keeps askin' for me everywhere. There was a statue of a woodcutter used to stand in our village, but he upped and left one morning. Then I heard he was looking for me for some reason. Dunno why. Don't think I want to find out really – might be for some reason I won't like.'

Alysoun did not really want to hear about Scirf's problems at that moment. What she wanted was help with a decision. If they could not find Hunter's Hall again, there was an eggshell map to be sought. 'We might try carrying on with the quest alone,' she said to the others, without conviction. 'The only trouble is, we haven't got Wodehed's magic needle with us, to show us the way to the great sea eagle's nest where the egg-map lies.'

'I've got an idea how we could find Hunter's Hall again,' Scirf cried. 'We could go back to the green chapel and try to find our way from there. I mean, if a magic path led us to Hunter's Hall from the green chapel once, it might do it again.'

'Oh Gawd, no!' cried Mawk. 'We can't go back there again – she'll fry our livers for breakfast.'

'That's worth thinking about, Scirf,' Alysoun replied, ignoring Mawk. 'We'll make up our minds when it's fully light.'

When the day was bright the three went down to the lake, just to make sure they had not made a mistake in the dawn's half-light.

It was indeed a dreary sight which greeted them when they reached the forbidden spot. The reeds and bulrushes were all brown and dead looking. An oily scum drifted around on top of the lake, which was choked in blanket weed and other growths. If there were any fish in there, they were hardy creatures, used to polluted waters.

The banks of the lake were in no better state. Where there had been magnificent grasslands, fine woods – now there were dirt trails through scrubby wastelands, broken trees. It was a place no self-respecting hunter would linger in for a moment, let alone an eternity. Where were the skylarks climbing up invisible poles? Where were the bullfrogs adding their bass voices to the evening choir of crickets? Where were the hedge-hogs snuffling through rich brown leaves?

The place was lifeless.

Alysoun shook her head. 'Well, we have to make up our minds. It's either an attempt at the eagle's nest, or the moufflon's den. What's it to be? Scirf?'

'I say we go back to the witch. She knows we've got powerful friends in the dogs. I'm sure she won't try anyfink this time.'

'Mawk?'

'Look,' he said reasonably. 'Why don't we – why don't we look for a dying weasel or stoat hunter and ask him or her to take a message to Sylver . . .'

'Don't be foolish, Mawk.'

'In that case,' snapped Mawk, 'I vote we go home to Halfmoon Wood and forget about all this business altogether. I've had enough of being pushed around, by you and everyone else. I've had it up to here.' He drew an imaginary line across his bib. 'Now what do you say to that, then?'

'You want to return along the path we've taken,' she said sweetly, 'that's up to you, Mawk. We're going back to Maghatch's green chapel. I just hope you don't get eaten by wolves, or killed by Sheriff Falshed, or carried off by rogue statues.'

'I haven't voted yet,' said Mawk in an indignant voice. 'Have I voted yet? I was just saying what I *might* do, if it came to the pinch. As a matter of fact, I vote we go on, into the mountains, to find the eagle's nest.'

'Well, I vote we go back to the green chapel,' said Alysoun. 'So it's two against one.'

'I hate you both,' cried Mawk. 'I just – I just hate you both so badly.'

Chapter Twenty-two

When Sylver woke in the morning he found to his astonishment that three of his band were missing. It seemed they had vanished in the night. He questioned the polecat, who seemed a little slippery and would not answer directly. Sylver had for a couple of days now suspected that the band were not being told the whole truth concerning their present situation.

'I've no idea where they've gone,' said that willowy hunter, polishing his throwing darts. 'Maybe they're still around somewhere.'

But Sylver, who had had just about enough of drudgery, could not find his friends anywhere within Hunter's Hall. In every corner of the great one-roomed building there were groups of hunters, making ready with their weapons while eating breakfast, trimming the feathers on their darts and arrows, splicing their slingshots. They were rough and ready characters, with scraggy pelts, but with bright, keen eyes staring out from their hard-weather-beaten faces.

'Have any of you fellows seen our weasel friends?' Sylver asked them. 'You must know them – they've been here a week.'

There were slow shakes of the head from most of the hunters, or a blink, or even nothing at all.

Some continued to hone the points of their darts with sandstone. Others shaved away with sharpened flints at bow stocks. These were not sociable creatures. They were solitary mammals, brought together by death, and they spoke only when they absolutely could not avoid it.

The hunters had their piles of pelts for company, which they used for blankets. These mounds of hides still stank, even though they had been scraped and cured. Bits of charcoal decorated the flagstones, where the ash from fires remained. Some of the hunters used worn logs as head rests and seats, and the teeth of their trophies littered the floor. Hunter's Hall was a place of deliberate activity amongst the dust of ages, enveloped by the ever present smell of leather, amber sap and waxy string.

'Well, that's that then,' said Sylver angrily, returning to Bryony and the others. 'None of these creatures with their moth-eaten hides has seen Alysoun, Mawk or Scirf. It seems the three of them have just vanished. Now if it had just been Mawk and Scirf, I would have said they'd run away. But not Alysoun. Not without good reason.'

'What shall we do then?' asked Dredless. 'I'm sick of this place . . .'

He began to fill his bowl with stew as he spoke, but the polecat who had spoken to them when they first arrived put a paw on Dredless's foreleg. 'Don't eat the stew,' he murmured. 'You've suffered enough for killing that game in the woods. We had a hunters' meeting last night. We've decided it's time you were allowed to leave.'

Sylver looked at the pot of stew. 'You mean – it's

the stew that's been keeping us here – making us drowsy whenever we thought to leave?'

The polecat explained. 'Not just the stew, but any sustenance partaken in this hall. It's the food of the dead and has magical qualities. So, too, the smoke from the burning herbs has an effect on those who are not dead themselves. The effects of the food you ate last night should be wearing off – so long as you don't eat or drink anything for breakfast you should be able to leave without being overcome by weariness.'

Sylver said, 'I suppose you're going to track down our friends today and kill them for the pot.'

'No, we've decided to let them go – we were going to free you all this morning anyway.'

'We've stayed here slaving for too long,' cried Wodehed as the angry outlaws made their way out of the doorway and down to the banks of the lake. 'I should have guessed about the food.'

'You weren't to know,' said Sylver.

All the weasels were very angry with themselves, but they recognized that their heads had never been very clear while they were in Hunter's Hall. Bryony said she had noticed hunters putting herbs on the fires and should have guessed the smoke produced by these herbs was making the group very docile.

Sylver was especially upset with himself. 'I think I failed you all this time.'

The others shook their heads and assured the weasel leader that it had not been his fault.

'How could you know we were being drugged?' said Bryony. 'It's the hunters who are to blame.'

Sylver realized it was no good wasting energy on anger and turned his head to more practical matters. 'There's not much we can do about Alysoun and the others for now. Perhaps they've gone up ahead. We must hope we run into them later on the trail. Now, according to Wodehed's lodestone needle we need to cross the lake.'

'Can't we just go round?' asked Miniver.

'I think it's best we follow the needle's direction,' replied Wodehed. 'If we start deviating from our true course we could get into all sorts of trouble.'

'In that case we should make some reed rafts,' replied the practical Dredless. 'Here, help me, Icham.'

The band cut down some rushes and wove them into two large rafts, plugging the holes with clay. When the rafts were ready they split up and set forth across the lake. As they drew away from the shoreline, the lake began to turn murky. Before they had gone even a quarter of a mile across the lake, Hunter's Hall began to disappear into the folding hills.

'Look at that, will you?' remarked Bryony. 'It's vanishing before our very eyes.'

'It seems it was just an illusion after all,' said Wodehed. 'I should have guessed.'

Soon the shoreline disappeared altogether and the two rafts drifted into mist patches.

'Keep that magic needle handy,' said Sylver to Wodehed. 'It looks as if we're heading for a fog bank.'

Sure enough, the two reed rafts entered a thick fog. The surface of the lake was becoming decidedly soupy by this time. The two punters, Icham on one raft and Bryony on the other, were having a job pulling their poles from the sticky mud.

There was lank weed hanging from the poles, too, like dark green hair. Ugly bubbles of gaseous minerals broke on the surface, causing great belches of smell to waft over the rafts. The fog became so dense that Bryony had to listen for the other raft, which occasionally disappeared from sight ahead of her. 'It's all getting a bit tacky,' she said. 'Don't punt too hard, Icham – stay with me. We could lose each other in this fog—'

Suddenly something gripped Bryony's pole, almost wrenching her overboard. 'Help! Sylver!' she cried, desperately hanging onto the pole. 'I need assistance.'

The able weasel leader sprang to her side and together they yanked on the pole, which seemed to be in the clutches of some monster's jaws. There was a surprising *snap* which threw both weasels off their feet, landing them on their backs. Bryony still had the end of the pole, but the other half remained down at the bottom of the lake somewhere.

'Now we've had it,' said Bryony. 'We can't control our raft.'

On Bryony's reed vessel were Miniver and Luke as well as Sylver. Icham, Dredless and Wodehed made up the crew of the raft ahead.

Icham, poling the lead craft, tried to slow down but the current there was too strong despite his efforts. They were carried out of sight. Luke and Miniver at first received a muffled reply to their shouts for assistance. They called again, listened, but pretty soon there was silence.

'Hellooooo?' called Sylver desperately. 'Are you there?'

Not a sound came in reply.

After a few moments of drifting around Sylver said, 'We'll have to paddle with our paws.'

Bryony looked nervously at the end of the broken pole, which seemed to have teeth marks in it. 'What about the creature who bit through that? There's probably a giant fish under there somewhere. Do you think it'll attack again?'

'It could have been the bottom of the lake which snapped the pole,' said Sylver hopefully.

'I don't think so,' replied Miniver. 'I agree with Bryony – we'd best be careful.'

Sure enough, even as she spoke, the silvery-green back of a great pike broke the surface. It was six times longer than any weasel and rigid with bone and muscle. They caught a glimpse of its cold wicked eyes and the spiky rows of teeth in its jaws, before it went down again, under the raft.

A shiver went through each of the weasels as they realized that there could be more such monsters down below the raft, gliding through the gloom of the cloudy waters, seeking the flesh of others.

'I think we'd better keep our paws to ourselves for a while,' said Sylver softly. 'Is this raft strong enough to resist an attack by one of those pike?' he asked Luke. 'It suddenly feels very flimsy to me.'

Bryony took some darts from her belt, as the raft drifted aimlessly on, following some sluggish current.

When the creature broke the surface again, this time closer to their vessel, she threw a dart accurately at its head. Instead of swerving away, as she expected, the pike leapt from the water and swallowed the oncoming dart. It seemed to go down its throat as easily as a blue dragonfly. Then the great fish dived again. No doubt the dart would make an uncomfortable meal, buried in the creature's stomach.

The pike failed to rise to the surface again, but they occasionally saw its dark shape cruising under their reed vessel. The cold-blooded killer was not going to invite a second attack, but it seemed it wanted to shadow the raft. Its warped vision could no doubt recognize four tasty forms when it saw them and it was not going to give up on a possible meal.

Eventually the vessel came out of the fog bank, into clearer waters, where coots and moorhens were quietly criss-crossing the lake. The birds looked curiously on the weasels, but continued to go about their business, not bothering the group at all. The pike finally made for deeper waters again, giving up on them at last.

'Can you see any sign of the other raft?' asked Sylver. 'They should be ahead of us, if they've kept the same course.'

'We could have drifted in any direction,' grumbled Luke. 'They could even still be behind us, if they went back to search for us. I suppose we'd better paddle now.'

They could see the bottom of the lake now, where fronds waved gently in the eddies. On the gravel bottom trout and sticklebacks were nosing innocently around. The weasels did not mind paddling with their paws. They made reasonable progress, but of course not as quick as they would have done had they still got a pole.

'I can see the bank now,' said Bryony. 'One more effort should do it.'

They paddled hard and, as they drew close to the bank, Luke reached out and grasped the branch of a tree which had fallen into the water and so died. He and Sylver managed to haul the reed raft along this log, until the weasels were able to jump onto the bank. They lay there for a moment, recovering their strength, glad to be on dry land once again.

'What now?' asked Luke. 'Wodehed's got the needle.'

'We walk along the bank to find the spot where they've landed,' explained Sylver.

'Which way?' asked Miniver.

'Well,' replied Sylver, 'we've got a fifty per cent chance of being right – we'll go north first of all. If we don't come to anything within an hour, we'll backtrack and try the other way. Don't worry, they couldn't have landed anywhere but on this shore – unless they're still out there somewhere, which I doubt.'

They set off along the grassy bank of the lake, following its gentle curves. Sure enough, within a short time they came across the other raft. It had been abandoned, though, and looked a little ravaged.

'Do you think they had pike trouble too?' asked Miniver.

'Looks like they were attacked by *something*,' replied Luke. 'What do you think, Sylver?'

'There's blood on the raft – look,' said Sylver

grimly. 'Someone's hurt – at best. We'd better try to catch up with them. They can't be that far ahead. Especially with a wounded weasel to carry. Let's go. Quickly. Luke, Miniver, Bryony – follow those tracks.'

'Follow that trail of *blood*,' said Bryony softly.

Chapter Twenty-three

The trail led them up into the Yellow Mountains to a cave beyond a ledge. There they found Icham and Dredless with a badly hurt Wodehed on a makeshift stretcher. Wodehed had a nasty wound in his thigh. He was still conscious, though he had lost a lot of blood, and was directing his own nursing care.

'Yarrow,' he murmured. 'I need the yarrow herb – I used up the supply I normally carry after the pine marten attack. It has to be pressed to the wound, bound there with a strip of bark.'

Icham explained to Sylver, 'There's no vegetation around here. We can't find any of the herbs Wodehed wants.'

Sylver nodded. 'Then we'll send a party down with Wodehed – down to the woodlands and fields, where these things can be found. Luke and Bryony will carry the stretcher. You'd better go with them, Icham. You're in charge. You can relieve Luke or Bryony when they get tired.'

'Right,' said Icham, disappointed that he was not going on to the top of the mountains with Sylver, but trying not to show how upset he was. 'We'll do as you say.'

Wodehed handed his precious needle to

Dredless. 'You take charge of this now,' he said feebly. 'Guard it with your life.'

Dredless seemed aware of the responsibility. 'I will,' said that stalwart weasel, placing the magnetic needle in a pouch on his belt. 'Don't you fear.'

'Now,' asked Sylver, when he had the attention of Dredless again, 'how did all this happen?'

Dredless said grimly, 'Magellan's on our trail.'

Sylver felt a quickening of the heart and a racing of the blood. As leader of the outlaw band he was meant to be afraid of nothing. Indeed, though he was often scared, he tried not to show any fear. But there were times when a flicker of dread showed on his features, and this was one of them. 'Magellan?' he repeated. 'That mercenary?'

'Magellan the bounty hunter,' confirmed Icham. 'During that week we spent in Hunter's Hall he's caught up with us. Sheriff Falshed is following on behind him – we saw their shiny helmets just before noon - on a ridge.

'Just a while ago Wodehed was standing at the front of the raft, taking a reading with his lodestone needle. A canoe came out of the fog. Magellan was paddling it. The fox dropped his paddle, picked up his bow, and fired an arrow at Wodehed all in one movement . . .'

'He was fast,' murmured Wodehed weakly. 'He was very, very fast.'

'The arrow hit Wodehed in the thigh.'

'How did you escape?' asked Sylver.

'Well, the fog was still very thick; we slipped back into it and disappeared from Magellan's sight. We've seen him since, climbing the hills to the south. I'm sure he's still on our trail. I think he's trying to get ahead of us.'

Sylver sighed. 'Prince Poynt must be really desperate to get us if he's allowed Magellan back into the kingdom. Wasn't the fox banished by the prince, after Magellan killed his brother in the forest?'

Wodehed nodded unhappily from his position on the stretcher. 'That was back in the Year of the Dandelion.'

Icham made ready for his departure from his leader. Wodehed's stretcher was fashioned from the same reeds which they had used to make the raft. It was light and serviceable. Wodehed, however, was not a small weasel and the stretcher would become quite heavy over the miles back to the forest.

'Goodbye,' said Icham to Sylver, Dredless and Miniver. 'See you back in Halfmoon Wood.'

Sylver said, 'Icham, you said Magellan's circling to the south? Without the needle, the mist is far too thick to risk crossing the lake. I suggest you take the track away from here to the north-west, so that you're going in the opposite direction to us. That way you'll avoid Magellan. Then cut down and across country to County Elleswhere.'

'You make sure you get there,' said Miniver.

'And you make sure you get that eggshell,' Bryony replied as she lifted the stretcher with Luke.

'We will,' Dredless told her, 'don't you worry.'

Sylver called after them as they began to descend the slope, 'If you come across Mawk, Scirf and Alysoun, take them back with you. There's no point in them running into Magellan trying to reach us. We'll get the eggshell.'

Icham waved to say he had heard and understood.

'Now,' said Sylver, 'let's be on our way, you two. Dredless, you take the right flank; Miniver, you take the left. I'll take the centre. Whoever spots Magellan first, let me know. I've an old score to settle with that fox.'

'Who hasn't?' muttered Dredless. 'Just about every weasel in the kingdom has been wronged by Magellan at some time.'

With that the group began to ascend the Yellow Mountains, towards the eagle's nest.

The air soon became hot and suffocating, the sulphur fumes making their eyes run and their throats dry. The ground around them sometimes heaved, causing great shudders to run across the landscape. There were deep chasms everywhere, belching gases, at the bottom of which was molten lava. It was a place of heat and discomfort. It was a place where balance could be destroyed at a moment's notice. It was a violent place of quickly changing moods.

'If there's a hell on Welkin,' said Dredless, the hot gases making his fur irritate him, 'this is it.'

Far away to the south Sylver could see a fountain of lava, spurting from some deep mouth in the volcanic mountain. There was a lake of white-hot running minerals and rock below this geyser. All around was smoking ash, crackling as it cooled in the sulphurous air. The atmosphere zinged with heat. Flecks of hot dust settled on them occasionally, singeing their coats. Whirlwinds were born out of the turbulence created by the molten pools which lay scattered around them.

'I think you're right, Dredless,' said Sylver. 'I'll be glad when we get above this area. Up there, amongst the white peaks, the air is cool and sweet. It's only in this midway region that the earth is in such chaos.'

The three weasels struggled on valiantly, fighting their way through the clouds of ash and choking fumes. After some time they could see grey rock ahead of them and they knew they were coming out of the dreadful volcanic band that girdled the range of Yellow Mountains.

'Not far to go now,' said Sylver. 'Tonight we'll camp in some high rushy glen, where the streams are not spoiled by the sulphur.'

'I'm looking forward to that,' said little Miniver. 'My legs are just about giving out.'

She turned and looked down the path they had taken, winding through the bubbling hills. She could see nothing through the haze of heat, though. Tendrils of air rose from the hot surface of the rock like barely visible snakes dancing on their tails. 'Do you think the others made it down all right?' she gasped, fighting for breath. 'I can't see them from here.'

'We'll just have to trust they did,' Sylver said. 'I hope they don't get too tired, carrying Wodehed. He's not one to miss a meal, that wizard.'

Miniver clicked her teeth. 'It should have been me,' she said humorously. 'They could have put me in one of their pouches and thought nothing about it.'

'I wouldn't wish an arrow wound from Magellan on you or anyone else,' said Sylver, gasping. 'He's deadly with that bow of his.'

Now, at last, they came out of the swirling storm of hot dust and tight air. There was little vegetation apart from the occasional stubby dwarf pine, or a brittle shrub growing from a crack in the rock, but the atmosphere was much cleaner. Miniver took several gulps of oxygen. Dredless sat down to clear his head. Sylver drew in air through his nostrils, still feeling the sting of the sulphur dust trapped in them.

'Well, we're through,' he said. 'Just get your strength back, you two, and we'll continue up to a place where we can camp for the night. Keep your eyes peeled for Magellan. If we come across him, leave him to me.'

'Why should you get all the glory?' Dredless said. 'Magellan killed my brother. I should get first dibs at him.'

Neither weasel really wanted to fight the fox, but they knew they would have to when he showed himself.

It was true that the mercenary fox had killed the brother of Dredless, back in the Year of the Dandelion. After a strong king's death a country often descends into chaos and anarchy. There is no law and morality breaks down. Those without consciences plunder and murder, making themselves rich, settling old scores. Even the body of the old king was stripped of its valuables by his erstwhile servants and left to rot on the floor of the forest while the kingdom ran riot.

Magellan himself had slaughtered whole communities in those terrible days. He came sweeping across Welkin leading a horde of rogue foxes, polecats and pine martens, who cared nothing for life or property. They burned as they

232

went, they ravaged, they pillaged even the poorest little hamlet, they massacred anyone and anything which got in their way.

Only the combined forces of the stoats and weasels, joined for once against a common enemy, managed to check the terrible tide of butchery to which Magellan had given birth.

The trio found a cleft in the rocks, beside a mountain pass, where they felt it would be safe to spend the night. There was a stream there, which tumbled headlong down the mountain. From this they drank, and in it they bathed, refreshing themselves.

The next morning they were up early, ready to be on their way. They followed the mountain path below which they had spent the night, knowing it would lead them to the ridges above, where they could begin searching for the eagle's nest.

At noon they came to a wide chasm, over which was slung a flimsy rope bridge. It was clear that the rope was rotten and Sylver was not sure whether it would support their weight, even if they crossed one at a time.

'What's the alternative?' asked Miniver. 'Can we go round the chasm?'

Sylver shook his head doubtfully. 'I don't think so. It would take us days, perhaps longer, to find another way across or round this gap.'

'Then we have to use this bridge, like it or not,' she said. 'I'll go first. I'm the lightest.'

'No,' said Dredless, stepping onto the unstable bridge, 'I'm going first this time . . .'

The other two weasels held their breath as Dredless made his way cautiously to the middle of the bridge. One or two rotten ropes snapped as he stood there, swaying dangerously in the winds funnelled down the chasm. Luckily these were not anchoring ropes and Dredless did not immediately go plunging down into the darkness of the crevasse. 'I'm all right,' he called shakily. 'I'll go a bit further now.'

He inched his way along the rope bridge, holding on to the crumbling nets which formed the sides. Gusts of wind made him pause every so often, as the bridge swung under their attack. When he was two-thirds across, he stopped dead and did not move a muscle. It was as if he had met an obstacle.

'What's the matter?' called Sylver. 'What's wrong?'

Then the weasel leader saw the problem. Actually, it was more than a problem: it was a disaster. A figure was now visible, having emerged from behind a crop of rocks on the other side. There was a strung bow in the creature's paws.

'Magellan,' said Sylver, his heart sinking.

'Oh no,' cried Miniver. 'Dredless is helpless out there.'

'Greetings, weasels,' called the rogue fox over the chasm, the smugness in his voice unmistakable. 'I see you've come to the same barrier as I have myself, only from the opposite side. You see, I came the long way round up here, from the south, only to find my way blocked by this excuse for a bridge.

'I did think about crossing it last night, in order that I might catch you all asleep. It's easier despatching animals in their sleep.

'However, I could see that the bridge was not

234

going to support my weight, so I remained here, waiting for you. Then I thought, Why not tarry until they're all on the bridge, before cutting it away and letting them fall down into the ravine? But of course, you're coming over one by one. I don't want it to be too much of a fair fight, so I think I'll just settle for the weasel on the bridge for now . . .'

'NO!' cried Sylver. 'Let *me* come across. I'll fight you, paw to claw. Dredless won't interfere.'

'That's where you're wrong,' Dredless called. 'Nothing would stop me having a go at *him*.'

'You see?' called the fox dramatically. 'It's hopeless, isn't it? You think you're the respected leader of a band of weasels, Sylver, yet when it comes to an important order, your outlaws refuse to obey you! I would find that a bit galling, myself.'

Then Dredless did the thing Sylver had been hoping he would avoid doing. He suddenly reached down to his belt and swiftly launched a dart at the fox. Under normal circumstances, Dredless was deadly accurate. But because he was on the fragile bridge, swaying dangerously in the wind, his aim was not as true as it would have been ordinarily. The dart struck the fox on the shoulder, sticking there.

A look of pain crossed Magellan's foxy face as he wrenched the dart from his shoulder. 'You shouldn't have done that, weasel,' he said, drawing back on his bow. 'I might have let you live a few moments longer, while I bandied words with your leader. Now I'm going to have to finish you off.'

'May you rot where you fall,' snarled Dredless. Dredless went for another dart, but his paw never reached his belt. Magellan fired his bow. The long-shafted arrow struck Dredless in the chest. He gave a little sigh, then took one last look towards Sylver and Miniver, as if to say he was sorry. The mortally wounded weasel then slipped through the rotten side netting of the bridge. His body fell swiftly down into the darkness of the chasm below.

The ravine was so deep they never heard the sound of Dredless hitting the bottom.

'Dredless!' cried Miniver, distraught.

Sylver was shocked to the core. Magellan had killed Dredless, the band's most able warrior. His friend Dredless was now lying at the bottom of the ravine, still and broken. It was a moment before Sylver could collect his wits.

'Oh, Dredless!' moaned Miniver again, going to the edge of the chasm and looking down.

'Gone, I'm afraid,' said the mocking Magellan, stringing another arrow. 'Now, who's next? Coming across, Sylver?'

Sylver felt the hot rage simmering deep inside him. He wanted to get hold of Magellan and break every bone in his body. He wanted to make the fox pay dear for killing his friend. But one of Sylver's best attributes was his ability to remain cool in emergencies.

To cross the bridge would be to invite certain death. As soon as he was within range of those arrows, Magellan would kill him, too. So he stood calmly waiting, hoping the fox would attempt the crossing himself, though this was hardly likely considering the flimsy nature of the bridge.

'What's the matter, Sylver? Afraid, are we?' jeered the rangy fox. 'Scared of a little drop? I'll let you get across the bridge. You want me to promise you a fair fight? All right, I give you my word. You have my oath I'll let you cross the bridge and face me. Or didn't you really care about that Dredless creature? Perhaps you're one of those leaders who believe their followers aren't worth worrying about.'

Sylver knew Magellan was trying to fan the rage he felt. He was trying to goad the weasel leader into rushing to his own death. You could not trust Magellan's promises. Once he had Sylver on the bridge, helpless, he would cut the weasel down without giving his promise a second thought.

Miniver rushed towards the bridge, her sling-shot in her claws. 'I'll teach you,' she cried in a choked voice. 'I'll make you pay for that cowardly act, you cur!'

Chapter Twenty-four

Fortunately, just before Miniver reached the bridge, it finally fell away from its securing posts. Dredless's fall through the side netting had caused it to break its rotten mooring ropes. It went floating down like a dark string phantom, like a cobweb cut from its mooring strands, to join Dredless at the bottom of the chasm.

'What a pity,' said the fox, his eyes narrowing. 'A few more moments and I could have added a finger-weasel to my list of victims. Sad, but there it is . . .'

Magellan then drew his bow and attempted a shot. The arrow arced over the wide ravine. Miniver saw it coming. She swiftly ran out of range. The arrow stuck in the ground just a metre or so behind her and quivered there. Sylver grabbed her and pulled her even further, in case Magellan tried again.

Although Sylver was burning with rage, he hid the fact. He did not want Magellan to have the satisfaction of knowing how angry he was. He simply stared calmly at the fox. 'We'll meet again, Magellan,' he cried. 'And you had better be ready.'

Magellan sneered. 'I'm always ready, weasel. For you, or anyone else. You can be sure we'll meet again. I have the royal commission. I'm to hunt you weasels down and kill every last one of you. I shall enjoy it. Farewell.'

With that the fox struck out southwards, disappearing amongst a set of boulders.

Miniver's head hung low. Sylver stood there for a few moments, looking at the spot where Magellan had disappeared. Then he went to the edge of the ravine and stared down into its dark depths. He could see nothing, of course. It was too deep and the light could not reach down far enough. There was a feeling of failure and despair in his heart.

He went back to where Miniver stood. 'I'm sorry,' he said. 'I should never have let it happen.'

Miniver replied with a catch in her throat, 'You're not to blame. Dredless was always rather headstrong. No-one could have stopped him from going for his darts. He hated Magellan with a venom.'

'Don't we all,' replied Sylver, 'but hate is a useless emotion. You and I must try to think calmly and rationally what our next move should be. Are we to attempt to find the others and regroup or should the two of us continue with the quest for this eggshell? What do you think, Miniver?'

Sylver wanted to involve Miniver in the decision on whether to go on or not, partly in order to take her mind off the death of Dredless.

'You're asking *me*?' said the distressed Miniver. 'You're the leader.'

'I want your advice,' replied Sylver.

Miniver thought for a few moments and then replied, 'I suggest we try to find Alysoun's party and reconsider our plans.'

Sylver was reluctantly inclined to agree with this decision – perhaps for different reasons to Miniver. Magellan was somewhere up in those mountains and the rest of the outlaw band should be warned of that fact.

There was also the question of whether Sylver and Miniver could find the eagle's nest without others to help them search. The finger-weasel looked weary and dispirited – she seemed at the end of her tether. Miniver had been badly shocked by the death of Dredless. Perhaps it would be better to regroup and make fresh plans.

'You see,' Miniver said, assuming Sylver wanted to go on. 'I knew you didn't really want my advice. You just want to make up your own mind.'

'No, I think you're right, Miniver. We'll set out for the lake and see if we can track Alysoun, Mawk and Scirf from there. My guess is that they didn't cross the water as we did, but set off in another direction overland. After all, they didn't have Wodehed's needle to guide them.'

Miniver looked relieved. 'We're going to look for them?'

'I don't think we're going to find the eggshell, not just the pair of us. And Magellan will try to thwart our every move. We know the way to this point now. I think it best we rejoin the others and make fresh plans.'

'Won't it be too late for the eggshell?'

Sylver shrugged. 'We must hope not. Not the worst of all this is the fact that Dredless was carrying Wodehed's needle – now that instrument is lost to us for ever.'

So they retraced their steps, going down through the gaseous yellow strip which gave the mountains their name. Emerging on the other side they travelled cautiously through the foothills. Finally they sighted the dull lake, gleaming listlessly in the afternoon light.

They camped where they were, staying well out of sight in an old rabbit hole in the ground. Nevertheless, they knew Magellan was a past master at following weasel scent and they slept in turns, so that one of them was always awake. Miniver was particularly exhausted, so Sylver allowed her to sleep in late.

They came out of the rabbit hole close to noon and stared down on the lake below. As they inspected it they saw the glint of armour flash down by the shores. There was another encampment down there.

'Falshed,' murmured Sylver. 'He's down there with his troops.'

'Perhaps Magellan is with him,' said Miniver.

'I doubt it. Magellan would not demean himself by hunting weasels with a lot of thick-headed stoat soldiers. My guess is he'll allow Falshed to clatter around the countryside with his company, while he skirts around the bush, keeping low.'

'So, we'll have to watch our backs, as well as our fronts.'

'Precisely,' replied Sylver. 'Probably the safest place at this moment is amongst the stoats. Falshed wouldn't allow Magellan to kill us in cold blood – even the sheriff of Welkin isn't that callous. He'll want to take us in alive to Prince Poynt and get the credit for capturing us.'

Miniver looked sideways at her leader. 'What are you suggesting? That we give ourselves up?'

'Well, not exactly. I'm not sure. But if we can stay

around their camp, keep the soldiers in sight somehow, we'll stand a better chance. They'll still want to search for the other outlaws, so we'll be around to look for Alysoun and the other two. What do you think?'

'Are you asking my advice again?' said Miniver with a definite sniff.

'Yes – yes, I am.'

'Well,' she replied in measured tones, 'this time I agree with you. It'll give the party with the stretcher a head start back to home. Wodehed needs attention for his wound and we must give them a chance. If Falshed thinks there are no weasels in this area, he'll look in another, and he might just come across their trail.'

The two weasels then crept up close to the camp and listened to what passed between the soldiers. They learned that Sheriff Falshed, who was never one to enjoy the delights of camping in the field for long, had ridden back to Castle Rayn with a small escort to relate the death of Dredless. It seemed Magellan had come down from the mountains in the night. The fox had made his report to Sheriff Falshed, who was now attempting to milk some of the credit for himself by delivering the message personally.

Apparently, according to the soldiers, Magellan had gone back up into the mountains.

'He's looking for us,' whispered Miniver. 'He must have passed by our rabbit hole in the darkness.' She was horrified to think how close the fox had been to their hiding place. 'What shall we do now?' she asked of her leader.

Sylver stared out at the stoats. The captain of the guard had obviously gone with Falshed, back to the castle. He had left his sergeant-at-arms in command of the troops. This stoat had, to Sylver's knowledge, never seen the outlaws before. It was a risk, but he felt that he and Miniver would be better amongst the stoat soldiers. It was the last place Magellan would think of looking for them.

'We'll go in,' said Sylver. 'If we're recognized, make a dash for it and I'll meet you in the glade of the green chapel.'

'Not there again?' groaned Miniver.

'She won't try anything else, now that hound has threatened her,' said Sylver, talking of the moufflon witch. 'You can be sure of that.'

The pair of them then rubbed dirt and mud into their fur, rolled in the dry grass to get bits of twig and hay sticking to them, and were finally satisfied they looked more like pedlars than outlaws. When they were ready they walked into the stoat camp, dragging their feet as if they were weary. A soldier rather belatedly raised the alarm – Prince Poynt's troops were not renowned for their alertness – and the sergeant-at-arms confronted the pair. 'How did these two get into the middle of my camp without being arrested immediately?' he roared.

None of his soldiers were inclined to answer this rather awkward question.

Getting no satisfaction there, the sergeant turned his attention to the weasels. 'What are you two doing? Who are you? Members of some outlaw band, eh?'

Miniver gave him a silky look. 'Would we come into your encampment, sergeant, if we were outlaws? Me and my friend here are pedlars. We've just been robbed of our wares by a band of no-good weasels – someone called Sliver or something . . .'

'Sylver?' said the sergeant, his eyes widening. 'Was it Sylver?'

'Sliver, Sylver, something like that,' replied Miniver. 'Anyway, they took all our pots and pans. I want you to arrest them, please. We're destitute without our wares.'

All the while Miniver was talking, Sylver kept his head low and hang-dog, as if he were so unhappy he could not bear to look at anyone.

'What's the matter with him?' asked the sergeant, pointing with a baton at Sylver. 'Lost his tongue?'

Miniver shook her head mournfully. 'He's not very bright,' she said confidentially. 'He's had a bad shock this morning. They knocked him about something awful, those outlaws, just because he's a big weasel and looks as if he might put up a fight. Actually, he's as soft as a pudding. Wouldn't hurt a fly. And anyway, he's too stupid to fight back.'

Sylver gritted his teeth and tried to look like the moron fitting the description being given by Miniver.

'Yes, he does look like a simpleton,' replied the sergeant, trying to peer under Sylver's face. 'Bit of an imbecile, eh?'

'Dreadful companion,' whispered Miniver as an aside. 'You've no idea.'

'Oh, I think I have,' replied the sergeant. 'Most of my soldiers are much the same. Now, where did you say you last saw those outlaws? Out on the trail, was it?'

'To the north,' replied Miniver, knowing that Magellan had gone east, into the Yellow Mountains, and the party with the stretcher had gone west. 'That way – that's where they were heading.'

'I'm not sure I should break camp without orders,' said the sergeant nervously. 'Perhaps I should wait until my commander gets back.'

'By that time they'll have our pots and pans over the horizon and gone,' snapped Miniver, feigning anger.

'I'm not worried about your blasted pots and pans, weasel,' replied the stoat sergeant. 'I'm worried about losing Sylver.'

'In that case, get on their trail,' replied Miniver. 'Begging your pardon, sergeant.'

'I should think so,' muttered the sergeant, looking wistfully in the direction indicated. He seemed to make a decision. 'You think you can show us where you were attacked?' he asked. 'If we come with you?'

'Most certainly,' said Miniver. 'And you can have one of our saucepans for free, if you catch them.'

'Stick your blasted saucepans,' said the sergeant, while Sylver had trouble hiding his mirth. 'Let's get on their trail then. Come on, stoats, break camp. Make it quick.'

Within an hour they were on their way north.

Chapter Twenty-five

Alysoun, Scirf and Mawk-the-doubter approached the green chapel cautiously. Having once been prisoners of the moufflon, they had no desire to repeat the experience. Alysoun led the way down one of the two entrances, below the surface, and into the dank, musty earthiness of the chapel itself. They paused to allow their eyesight to become used to the dark.

'This way,' whispered Alysoun, leading them down one of the many offshoot tunnels. 'We'll just have to try one or two of these burrows until we get the right one.'

'Wonderful,' muttered Mawk. 'We'll just get lost a few times before we die . . .'

Just at that moment they were passing a side chamber. Alysoun looked in to see the witch, Maghatch, busy mixing one of her magic potions. There was a faint green light in the cavern, coming from smoking oil lamps. Purple ooze was dripping like sap out of something black and shrivelled which the witch was dipping in her concoction on a piece of string. This item might have been an ancient fig, or a dried human ear – it was difficult to tell in the green atmosphere of the chamber.

The chamber itself was magnificent. It was huge

and cold, with icy draughts whiffling the severed bats' wings hung out on lines to dry. The roots of an oak came through the ceiling and made round looping rafters from which Maghatch had hung various implements: knives, choppers, glass vials, rats' tails, frogs' innards, herbs, packets of marigold seeds, bits of string, sealing wax, dried cabbages.

This was Maghatch's workshop, her den, and the clutter around the walls and over the floor was unbelievable. Yet it was tidy. The junk was heaped high, but in *neat* piles – everything from rags to clock ratchets.

Maghatch the witch was muttering away to herself in some strange tongue. Suddenly she stiffened and turned to see the three weasels in the doorway. For a moment they were all frozen where they stood, the weasels staring at Maghatch, and she in turn staring at the weasels. The suspense was unbearable and Mawk was having a quiet heart attack behind Scirf.

Finally the witch spoke to Alysoun. 'Your nose is running,' she said.

Alysoun automatically sniffed and put a paw to her nose, but she found it was dry. 'No it's not,' she said indignantly.

'How would you *like* it to run? Up a rabbit hole, through the woodland, far away from your face?' said the witch in quiet delight.

Mawk let out a strangled sob.

Alysoun said darkly, 'You know what happened *last* time you interfered with us!'

Maghatch wrinkled her face in annoyance. 'So? I was only teasing you. Can't you take a joke? Witches have a sense of humour too, you know.'

'She's a one, this 'un, ain't she?' said Scirf, shaking his head in admiration. 'You got to give it to her.'

The witch, noting Scirf's rather scruffy appearance, nodded to him and clicked her teeth. 'I like this weasel.' Then she changed her tone again. 'You're bothering me. I'm busy destroying the world. Come back tomorrow when it's gone.'

'We don't want to interrupt your destruction,' Alysoun said, 'but we have to find our way to a place called Hunter's Hall. Can you direct us down the right passage?'

Maghatch clicked her teeth again. Something had amused her. 'Oh, so you were taken in by Hunter's Hall, were you?'

Alysoun realized straight away that the witch had something to do with that episode. '*You* sent us there,' said the weasel. 'Or you put it in our path – one or the other.'

'Well, expeditions like yours need a few obstacles in their way, or they wouldn't be any fun, would they? Yes, I put it there. You didn't have to go in, you know. That was your own fault.' Her eyes brightened. 'I understand. Some of you are still in there. Heh! Heh! I knew you weren't a very bright lot. Only you three have escaped. Now you want to get the others out, is that it?'

'Cor, she's an evil old bag, ain't she?' said Scirf, with more admiration. 'Listen to the way she cackles!'

Alysoun turned and said, 'Scirf, I'm trying to find something out here. Will you please shut up.'

'I do like *him*,' murmured the witch. 'He's my favourite weasel at the moment. I'll tell you what, because of that one I'm going to give you a clue.

Take the tunnel under the pines – that's the one which leads to Hunter's Hall.'

'How can we trust you?' asked Alysoun.

'Who said you could trust me?' Maghatch shrugged. 'I couldn't care less whether you take it or not. Now will you leave me in peace to finish my spell?'

The three weasels looked at each other, then loped away from the entrance to the chamber. When they were around the bend a muffled explosion came from behind them. A wave of hot air smelling of silage came wafting over them. Either something had gone wrong with Maghatch's spell, or she had destroyed a little of the world she was so anxious to demolish.

Alysoun nipped outside the green chapel again to look for the line of pines. She found them. Making a note of their direction she went underground again and found the passageway which seemed to follow that line. 'I hope that witch is not sending us to our doom,' she said. 'I wouldn't put it past her.'

'I wouldn't put *anyfink* past her,' Scirf agreed. 'I wouldn't trust her as far as I could chuck a cathedral.'

'Doom, doom, doom,' muttered Mawk gloomily.

Scirf put a fore leg around Mawk's shoulders. 'You're a deep one, ain't you?' he said to Mawk. 'Always lookin' on the bright side. Tell you what you should do in situations like this. You got to think of something really *nice*, to take your mind off things. Something that fills your heart with gladness and puts your mind in a pleasant frame.

'Me, I always think of a nice pile of steamin'

dung. Dung's actually quite dignified when you come to think about it. It sort of sits there, heavy and majestic, not botherin' anyone, just being itself.

'Dung don't whine and complain about its condition. It knows it smells. It knows what it is and where it's come from. Yet it don't think any less of itself. It's got confidence, dung has. It sits and sweats a bit, lettin' its brown juices flow over the dirt floor. It communes with bluebottles and little black flies. And when it's in a quiet mood it contemplates itself, dung does. It don't brood, as such. It just sort of meditates, dreamin' of distant spires. It's solid, yet it's runny at the same time. Just sort of nice, really.'

'You don't say!' snorted Mawk. 'You must know – you watched it for long enough in your old job.'

'Oh, but I do say,' continued Scirf, merely warming to his theme. 'An' let me tell you, dung don't suffer fools gladly. Dung don't rejoice in evil. Dung ain't vain or puffed up – it don't think too much of itself. It's not *unseemly*. It keeps you warm in winter and keeps the crowds away in summer. It's a good companion, is dung. Dung's a bit like me, really.'

'You can say that again,' muttered Mawk through his teeth. 'If I have to go into danger, risk my life, why does it have to be with a creature like you? What did I ever do to upset anyone? What did I do to deserve this?'

'Don't grizzle,' Scirf said. 'Just walk.'

So the trio began to travel along the tunnel, which curved and twisted on its journey under the roots of the forest, then began a steep climb upwards. Alysoun led the way with Scirf taking up the rear. Mawk was too afraid to be in the front and too scared to be at the back, so he travelled in the middle. The only problem was that he was worried he might have to bolt and, with his way ahead and his way behind blocked, he would be trapped between them.

Although she expected some, Alysoun found no horrors in the tunnel, but it was a long wearisome journey. Eventually, many tiring hours later, they came to the end and could see light in the distance. Finally Alysoun led them out onto a mountainside ledge. They were high up, with a sheer drop falling in front of them and a steep cliff face behind.

'This is not Hunter's Hall,' said Alysoun. 'That witch has led us a merry dance.'

'Yes,' said Scirf, 'but you know where we are? We're miles up here on a mountain.'

Alysoun looked down over the edge. She could see nothing but a smouldering yellow band far below and white peaks above her. In the distance, beyond the yellowish hills, lay the plains and woodlands of Welkin.

Mawk ventured out slowly and took a quick peek over the edge, only to reel backwards in horror. However, when he tried to go back into the tunnel, he found his path blocked by a huge boulder that had rolled silently and swiftly to block the entrance. It was more witchery. Maghatch had taken them up and was not going to let them down by the same path again. The only way the trio could descend was down the sheer face.

'Oh no,' he said. 'That rotten witch has put us high up amongst the mountains deliberately.'

Alysoun suddenly clicked her teeth in delight,

making Mawk think she had at last gone mad. 'It's all right, Alysoun,' he said soothingly. 'We'll get down somehow.'

'You ninny,' she said, still clicking. 'You realize what's happened? Maghatch thought she was tricking us by giving us a false path up here. But in fact, this was where we wanted to be in the first place. Don't you see? We're up in the Yellow Mountains. We've crossed the dangerous bit, with the volcanic rock and hot lava beds. The eagle's nest! It must be very near to where we are now.'

There were seven peaks above her. She looked along three to her left and could see no eyrie. She looked along the three to their right and found them equally empty. Finally she looked straight up, on the mountain on which they stood, and could see, high above them, a dark roundish shape made of twigs.

'There it is,' she cried, pointing with her paw. 'We're directly below it. We're on the very mountain where the great sea eagle lives. This is our destination.'

Mawk ventured cautiously out onto the ledge, clutching anchored rocks, and took a look upwards. 'I think I see it,' he said nervously. 'But – but how are we going to reach it, Alysoun?'

Her answer made him feel faint. 'We're going to climb up there, of course, you ninny.'

Scirf strolled casually to the very edge, turned and gripped with his claws. He leaned right over backwards, his body inclined at a very sharp angle. Then he looked up. 'I can see it!' he cried. Alysoun, having a fit of the shakes on Scirf's behalf, could stand it no longer. She grabbed him by the bib front and pulled him back onto the ledge.

Scirf knocked her claws away. 'What's the idea?' he said.

'You were going to fall backwards,' she said, her heart racing. 'I could see you dropping a thousand feet.'

'Nah, not me,' said Scirf. 'Wrong weasel. I don't fall off silly mountains.'

'How many mountains have you been up, for goodness' sake?' asked Mawk.

'Counting this mountain? One,' said Scirf, holding up a single claw. 'But I feel I was born up here, you know? I feel this is me spiritual home. Maybe my mum was a mountain hare, or my dad a snow leopard. I sort of find it *bracing*.'

'Right,' Mawk said, clinging to the rock face so hard he was in danger of becoming part of it. 'You can go up and get the eagle's egg then. Off you go.'

'We're *all* going,' announced Alysoun. 'It's best we all help each other up that steep slope. Right, you come in the middle, Mawk. I don't want you running off somewhere when you get the frights . . .'

'Run off? Run off?' squealed Mawk, taking a quick look down the dizzying fall again. 'Where do you think I'm going to run off to? There's nowhere to go except out into thin air.'

'I'll take the lead,' said Scirf, beginning the precarious climb upwards. 'Come on, Mawk – last one to the top's a sissy!'

Alysoun groaned. She was stuck up on the side of a dangerous mountain with two idiots. One was so confident he was likely to go hurtling to his doom almost willingly. The other one was shaking so badly he was likely to send himself to oblivion by accident. She pushed Mawk in front of her, urging him up the mountain, and then climbed up behind, hoping that if either of the two jacks did fall, they did not hit her on the way down and take her with them to their death.

Scirf turned out to be an excellent climber, despite the fact that, he maintained, he had never done it before. He told Alysoun he had been climbing about on barn roofs since he was a kitten and had gathered his skills that way. She thought barn roofs were somewhat different to hundreds of metres up a mountainside, but refrained from saying so.

At one point Mawk suddenly froze, staring down at a long drop into a pit of nothingness. 'I can't move!' he screamed, his paws white with the effort of gripping the rock face. 'I'm going to fall. I'm going to die. Help me! Oh, please. I'm slipping. I'm going. Help me, somebody. I can't move.'

Bits of rock, dirt and gravel were falling into Alysoun's face from above, causing her to readjust her own grip.

The thing which Alysoun had feared the most was now happening. She did not know what to do. She could threaten Mawk with all sorts of things, but he was probably past that. She could try and persuade him to continue the climb, but she doubted he would respond. It was a nightmare.

Her problem was eventually solved by Scirf. 'You great lummock!' he cried, reaching down and grabbing Mawk by the scruff of his neck. 'Get up here!'

Scirf physically hauled up the blubbering Mawk, while dangling by one foreclaw and two hind legs from a rock overhang. The ex-dung-watcher then heaved the shivering Mawk, his eyes now closed and his mouth gibbering nonsense, over the top of the overhang. Then the hero turned and winked at Alysoun, saying, 'All right, jill. You want a bunk up too?'

'Not on your life,' said the breathless Alysoun. 'I'm fine, thank you.'

Scirf pulled himself up over the overhang, as if he were merely climbing over an orchard wall to get at some apples.

Alysoun reached the same point, looked down for an instant at the giddy drop below, then scrambled over to join him.

Chapter Twenty-six

By the time Alysoun, Mawk and Scirf had climbed up the mountain peak the day had turned to night. There was a bright moon, which helped them see their path, but Alysoun would have preferred less light. The moon would help the eagle to see them, just as it had assisted them with their path. Around them they could hear the call of the mountain birds, the ptarmigan, as a general alarm went up that there were weasels in the vicinity.

Mountain hares, too, a little lower down, were crouching in their little U-shaped tunnels, the homes they called forms, which normally protected them from eagles.

Above the three weasels was the nest of the great sea eagle. Stark in the rays of the moon, it appeared to be empty. They had a short conference.

'Right,' said Mawk, suddenly taking charge of the party, 'you two go up and look for the eggshell, while I stay here and watch for the eagle.'

'Are you sure you're brave enough to hide behind these safe rocks while we take the dangerous route up to the nest?' asked Alysoun sarcastically.

'I'll manage,' Mawk said.

'We're *all* going, Mawk,' said Scirf, 'so get that into your weasel skull!'

'I'm not, I'm not, I'm not,' muttered Mawk. 'You can't make me.'

'If you don't come, we'll leave you here when we go down,' Alysoun told him. 'You'll never get down without help, Mawk, so you'd better get used to the idea.'

Mawk gave her a look of hatred. 'I don't like you, Alysoun,' he said. 'I don't like you one bit.'

Thus the three weasels began the crawl up the slope, slinking in the way that weasels do, from stone to stone, seeking protection where they could find it. Finally they reached the nest, quite a long way below the snow line. It was, to their relief, quite empty. No eagle, nor, indeed, eaglet.

Alysoun slipped up between the twigs and into the nest itself. At first she could not find what she wanted and began to panic, turning over feathers, old leaves and bits of dried fern. Then, just as she was about to despair, she saw something half-buried in heather on one side of the nest. Lifting the dead heather she found two perfect halves of a complete shell.

On each half of shell there were patterns, markings, which Alysoun knew must be the map. The lines were faintly luminous in the moonlight, and she had to hold the eggshells at an angle to see them clearly. 'I've got it!' she cried.

They had at last found a map of the world. She picked up the two halves of the eggshell and was about to pass them down to Scirf, when Mawk cried out the words she had least wanted to hear: 'The eagle's coming!'

Looking up into the sky, Alysoun could see a large black dot against the moon. It was becoming larger by the second. Even as she watched, two huge wings became visible attached to a strong body. Below that body were two legs, on the end of which were two sets of talons which could rip a deer to pieces in moments, let alone a little weasel. Two fixed and savage eyes glared fury at her as the eagle descended, wind riffling through its feathers, indignation fanning its rage.

'Help!' cried Alysoun, scrambling down through the twigs. 'Quick, Scirf – take the eggshells.'

She tossed the shells down through the gap she had made in the twigs on entering the nest. They were neatly caught, one by Scirf, the other by Mawk. Then she herself dropped through the hole and landed on Mawk's head. He gave out a yell and let his half of the eggshell go. It rolled towards the edge of the mountain and would have gone over, if Alysoun had not quickly recovered her senses and dashed out to retrieve it.

'Thieves!' screamed the eagle. 'Little *thieves*!'

She landed on a rock near by, just as the weasels were running down the slope away from the nest. Alysoun tripped, slipped over the edge, and began falling. The wind whistled by her as she dropped like a stone, whipping her forelegs over her head. She still had the half eggshell gripped in her claws. Suddenly she jerked to a stop and then began floating down, as the eggshell acted as a parachute to break her fall.

'Hey!' cried Scirf, seeing what had happened to Alysoun. 'That's for me.'

He jumped over the edge of the mountain to join her, holding *his* half eggshell like a parachute. Together they fell close to the edge of the rock face, where the eagle could not swoop in and snatch them, for fear of striking her wings on the cliff. There were also dangerous updraughts of air, so near to the mountainside, which would disturb the eagle's flight.

Instead, the great raptor turned her attention to Mawk, who was still running down the slope.

Mawk-the-doubter glanced fearfully behind him to see the eagle's predatory eyes firmly fixed on him alone. 'Whaaaaaaaa!' he cried in terror. 'Whaaaaaaaaaaaa!'

She launched herself at Mawk, her great dark wings flapping powerfully. There was such strength in her flight that even the ptarmigan gasped and the hares quailed to see it. Surely now, the world around thought, this weasel has had his lot. He will soon be strips of flesh drying in the sun, his carcass shrivelling to a husk, his eyeballs being carried off by teams of efficient ants, his tongue being devoured by idle maggots.

The wind from the great sea eagle's wings raised dust and grit, which swirled in her wake.

Mawk's lungs were bursting as he searched frantically for a rock under which to hide. He searched on the run, at one point his more powerful back legs going faster than his front legs, so that his body arched in the middle and he was in danger of his rear overtaking his head and shoulders. His eyes were popping with terror, his tongue lolling out of his mouth with exhaustion, and his head was spinning.

At the last moment, just before the terrible talons pierced him, he saw a mountain hare's hole and dashed inside.

Like all mountain hare forms, this was a very short tunnel much like the green chapel, with an opening at both ends. A hare already occupied the form, almost filling it with her bulk. Mawk's sudden entrance knocked her out of the far end. She scrambled to get back in again, only to find her form occupied by a trembling weasel. Nevertheless, her fear of the eagle was greater than her fear of the weasel, and she forced herself back into the cramped form once again.

'Udge-up, udge-up,' cried Mawk, pushing at the solid backside of the hare. 'Give room, give room.'

The hare refused to comment or give way. They were left straining against each other, trying to get more space.

The eagle circled the form, once dropping down and trying to get her great hooked beak into one end, to drag out one of the two battling occupants. However, she could only just about touch Mawk's bottom, which she scratched.

'Arrhhhhhaaa! I'm wounded!' shrieked Mawk into the hare's ear. 'I'm bleeding.'

The hare made no move, no comment, nothing. She was merely there, a hump of fur and bone. She had her eyes closed and was no doubt praying to the god of happy hares. As far as she was concerned, she was on some distant island, running up some high mountain, in a place where eagles and weasels did not exist. She had transported herself in her mind.

The eagle stalked around the form for quite a while, then eventually flew off, presumably to look for the two parachutists who had descended to the valley below.

Mawk gave the hare an irritable thump on the rump, just for being there, and then crawled out of the hole. She herself made no comment. She was not there. She was somewhere else.

'I'm alive,' he said to himself, as if he could not quite believe it. 'I'm still alive.'

Mawk spent the rest of the night under a rock.

The next morning he began to descend the mountain on the far side, where there was a goat track to guide him down. He remained cautious, sticking close to rocks, dashing from one clump of stones to another, just in case the eagle returned. Halfway down the mountain he met three weasel voleherds, leading their flocks up the mountain. He stopped them to ask directions. 'Which way is the ground?' he asked. 'The flat bits, that is?'

'Down,' said a voleherd gruffly.

'You – you wouldn't have a drink on you, by any chance?' asked Mawk. 'I'm very thirsty. I've been attacked by an eagle, you see. It makes one's mouth dry.'

'You mean *fear* does,' said another of the vole-herds. 'I quite agree. Wait a minute and you can have a nice warm drink of vole's milk. I was going to milk them soon anyway.'

Without further ado the voleherd sat down by two of his voles and milked them one by one into a pail. The other two voleherds took their flocks and went up the slope a bit higher, there to rest in the shade of a mountain fir. They glared at Mawk from beneath their tree, their faces looking very hard and bitter in the dark shadow.

Mawk asked of the kind voleherd, 'Who are you? What are your names?'

'We're three brothers,' said the voleherd, still working away at the milking. 'I'm Watchful – the other two are Awake and Alert.'

261

'Well, I'm glad about that,' said Mawk, 'considering there's a blasted great eagle flitting around the azure blue of your mountain home, but you must have names.'

'Yes, those are our names.'

Mawk was confused. 'What?'

'Watchful, Awake and Alert.'

Mawk suddenly realized what the voleherd was talking about. 'Oh – oh, I see. Well, I'm not surprised I was a little puzzled. They're strange names.'

'Not for voleherds. They're to remind us of our duties. Our mother and father were particularly careful weasels. It was their idea to keep us always in mind of the need to be watchful, awake and alert.'

'But those are your names,' said Mawk, getting confused again. 'Why do you need reminding of who you are?'

'I was not referring to our names that time,' said the voleherd patiently. 'I was referring to the need to be ever vigilant, up here in the mountains.'

'Oh,' said Mawk. 'Quite.'

Once the milking was over and the two yielding voles had trundled on up to be with the rest of the flock, Mawk was given the pail. He drank from it gratefully, the warm liquid going down easily. He then thanked the voleherd.

'Think nothing of it,' said Watchful.

'My grateful thanks also to your brothers, er, Awake and Alert.'

'I'll pass them on, though for their money they'd have sooner pushed you off the mountain. They're not generous like me. I'm the kindest of the three.'

'In that case, *don't* thank them,' Mawk snapped.

'Oooo, that's a bit uncharitable,' said Watchful.

'Well, if they're inclined to push weary travellers off the path, then they deserve it. Is there any accommodation near by, of which a weasel on the road can partake? Some inn or way station, or other?'

'At the foot of the mountain lies the Black Hostelry. You'll find shelter and sustenance there,' said the voleherd. 'And now farewell to you, weasel. I must join my brutal brothers, who would have cut your throat for that purse on your belt, if they knew you were not going to give a few groats or ten for all the gallons of milk you've guzzled.'

'What?' said Mawk, realizing that Awake and Alert were coming down the path to join them. 'What was that?'

'The milk you swigged. You need to pay for it,' remarked Watchful cheerfully. 'That, or lose your pelt.'

Mawk eyed the stout staves in the paws of the three voleherds and nodded quickly. 'Yes, of course,' he said, reaching for the purse on his belt. 'Ten groats, you said?'

'There are three of us,' reminded Watchful, as his brothers joined him.

'Twent— no, *thirty*, then – ten each. That seems fair,' said Mawk quickly. He counted the money out into the paws of the voleherds, whose hard faces regarded him without expression of any kind.

Watchful said, 'I'm sure my uncharitable, unworthy brothers appreciate your money, even if they don't like the insults.'

'Insults?' said one brother darkly. 'What insults?'

'By whom?' asked the grammatically correct other brother. 'Not *this* weasel? The one paying us a measly ten groats each for the rich full milk of our precious voles?'

'The very same,' replied Watchful. 'It seems he did not appreciate your passing him by without pushing him off the path. Perhaps we should show him how we treat outsiders who come to our mountain, simply to take advantage of rural voleherds who don't know the value of money.'

'Value of money?' shouted Mawk. There was nothing like a punch in the purse to bring Mawk's courage to the surface. 'That bit of milk I drank wouldn't have cost two groats in a village inn! You blackguards. I've a good mind to break your heads for you – the three of you. Come on then, put 'em up, let's see who's the lily-livered loon here . . .'

After the fight Mawk stumbled down the mountain path with three great lumps on his head, almost as big as eagles' eggs. He was feeling miserable, hard done by, and deserted by his two companions, Alysoun and Scirf. He kept his spirits up by going over in his mind the words he would say to them when he met them again – words about betrayal, abandonment, cowardice in the face of the enemy – words about leaving a friend in the lurch.

As he reached the foot of the mountain it was coming on dusk, with the swallows and swifts just giving sky space to the bats. There in the distance he saw some lights, set in a stone building which appeared to be a kind of hostel. At least the three voleherd brothers had not lied about that.

He walked gratefully towards the lights, anticipating a soft warm bed. Then he suddenly remembered.

The voleherds had taken all the money from his purse.

Chapter Twenty-seven

Night slewed into Welkin on dark skids, as Mawk entered the Black Hostelry by the back door. He had searched the lining of his purse and had found a single groat which had been missed by the vole-herds. It would be enough to buy him some gruel and a biscuit. At least he would not starve.

He told himself that he was an outlaw and should be able to take what he needed, but none of Sylver's band had ever been any good at that sort of thing. They were too honest at heart. So although he would not be able to afford a bed, Mawk would be able to eat. And he was hoping to persuade the landlord to let him sleep in the back of the house on some straw.

In the middle of the hostelry was a parlour, where weasels and stoats sat down to supper. There were rustic tables there, and rickety stools to use. Hanging from the stained rafters were drying herbs and fungi. Old sausages were also dangling from old garlic strings, where they had been left to season into the tough gristly texture stoats required of their meat.

The parlour at this time of the evening was almost empty. An old stoat sat by the fireplace, which was unlit due to the season. Two female stoats were standing by the main doorway, talking. One or two weasel serfs, no doubt having been out in the fields all day, were quietly quaffing honey dew in the corner. It seemed they were trying to wash away the tiredness with a drink or two.

Mawk studied these weasels, seeing the dirt matting their fur, the grime ingrained in their paws. They led a hard life, toiling from dawn to dusk, for a few groats from their stoat overlord. They were not permitted to leave the lands on which they were born. They had to follow in their father's pawprints and work their lord's estates, tending the herds of voles, growing vegetables. They even needed permission to take a jill into their hovels, to begin a family.

'Another bowl of honey dew,' murmured one of the weasels to the landlord of the hostelry. 'Fill it up.'

'Money?' asked the stoat landlord with a face like stone.

The weasel produced a half-groat and the landlord duly fetched another frothing bowl of honey dew, which had been known to make angels out of hawks and devils out of hickory sticks. In other words, it took an animal quite out of his head. Only the desperate and the doomed should have drunk honey dew, but unfortunately ordinary working creatures said they enjoyed it too, because it made them forget what they were.

The landlord, an ex-soldier turned to fat by the look of him, with his roly-poly girth, came to Mawk's table.

'Hey, nonny-nonny-no,' said Mawk cheerfully. 'What fare do you have for a groat, landlord?'

'I'll have none of your nanny-granny-goats here,

thank you,' grumbled that unworthy stoat. 'You need a licence for that sort of thing, which I've not got. You'll get a bowl of gruel and a biscuit, as well you know. Do I bring them, or do I throw you out into the back yard by the scruff of your bib?'

'The gruel, please,' murmured Mawk, 'and the biscuit.'

He produced the groat before the landlord could ask for it and dropped it into the creature's paw.

A serving jill brought the bubbling-hot gruel, which in colour was a cross between khaki-green and mould-grey. It sported a webbed frog's foot swimming in its grease. The gruel was traditionally made from the waste meat of pummelled amphibians caught in storm ditches. The steaming bowl reeked of mildewed dock leaves and ragwort stalks.

Mawk stirred the unappetizing liquid around with a wooden spoon, only to find he was under the hard glare of the landlord. He took a reluctant slurp of the stuff, swallowed, gagged, and then clicked his teeth in mock appreciation. 'Nice gruel,' he said. 'Best I've tasted.'

The stoat landlord nodded slowly, as if this was the answer he had been expecting.

Mawk's eyes watered like fury. The gruel had actually been hot and rancid enough to scour the roof from his mouth. It deposited a layer of dripping around his tongue and caked the corners of his jaws with solid lumps of fat. He had wanted to scream blue murder at the landlord, not click his teeth.

Nevertheless he was hungry enough to have to eat the sludge. The biscuit was hard tack which almost broke his jaw, but he ate that too, washing down woody chips with the foul gruel.

Once the gruel had cooled, however, he could face no more of it, since the fat formed a thick crust over its surface.

The hostel parlour had filled up somewhat since he had first begun his meal. The place was mostly full of weasels, with one or two stoats sitting at the round tables in front of the windows with the best views. Not that there was much to see, since it was a starry night out, but the stoats felt the position gave them status amongst these weasel serfs.

Suddenly the door opened and a figure entered, tall and rangy, which made the place go quiet.

Mawk, hearing the sudden silence, looked up.

There in the doorway, bow in paw, quiver at the hip, was a frightening creature.

It was Magellan, the bounty hunter.

The landlord wiped his paws on his bib and stepped forward. 'Haven't you, er, been banished?' he said timidly. 'Weren't you exiled?'

'I was, but I'm back,' said Magellan firmly.

'Oh Gawd,' whispered Mawk to himself, trying to push himself into the table top. 'Oh lord.'

Magellan had not seen Mawk, however. But the frightened weasel was scared even to move a muscle in case he drew attention to himself. It just needed a twitch of a whisker for the fox to look his way. Magellan's eyes had already begun to roam around the room, when suddenly the door burst open again.

A pudding came stumbling into the parlour. 'Drizzle,' it moaned. 'Drizzle.'

Puddings, or plaster statues, hated the rain. They were afraid it would wash them away before they found their First and Last Resting Place. This pudding was clearly deluded, because it kept moaning, 'Drizzle, drizzle,' yet outside there was a clean sky with stars that almost crackled they were so crystal clear. Most statues were mindless things, with terrible reasoning powers, and this one was no exception.

'Out!' ordered Magellan, growling. 'Out, before I break your head from your shoulders and roll it into a pond.'

The pudding seemed to understand this all right, and groaned, before retreating back through the doorway.

This incident had been enough to distract Magellan, so that Mawk was able to dash to a table in a dark corner and face the wall, trembling, while the fox sat down and ordered rabbit stew with turnip mash on the side.

Mawk sat as still as death, pretending to sip a drink in front of him, although he had nothing in his paw but thin air. Fortunately he was left alone by the serving jill, who thought he was a little mad anyway. Later Magellan drank two bowls of honey dew before demanding a bed from the landlord. Mawk saw the landlord reach up to a board and take down one of the several numbered iron keys from its hook. On it was the figure 7. The fox left through the back doorway and Mawk almost sank into a pool of sweat, so relieved was he to escape notice.

Just when Mawk felt strong enough to stand up and walk from the hostelry, the door opened yet again and, to his horror, in walked a stoat sergeant-at-arms with several of his arrogant soldiers. Mawk could see by their armour and weapons that they were from Castle Rayn and were probably searching for the band of outlaws known as Sylver's weasels.

Mawk sat down again quickly, as the serving jill went up to the stoats and said in a simpering voice, 'Welcome to you, sirs – come to partake of the Black Hostelry's fare?'

'Honey dew,' said the sergeant, 'and be quick about it.'

Oh Gawd, thought Mawk. Honey dew? What else?

Just then he heard a familiar voice behind him. 'Sergeant, do you mind if we sit down? I could do with taking the weight off my paws.'

'Do as you like,' said the sergeant. 'What do I care?'

Mawk turned slowly to see with astonishment that the troop of soldiers was accompanied by Sylver and Miniver. The two weasels were covered in dirt, had bits of rag tied around their throats like pedlars, but it was them all right. Sylver had plastered mud over the left side of his face, so that his lightning streak of white was covered.

Mawk was so amazed to see his friends he stood up, knocking over his own chair which clattered on the floor, inviting all and sundry to swivel and stare at him in turn.

The sergeant looked with hard eyes at Mawk.

Sylver suddenly cried out, 'That's one of them, sergeant. That's an outlaw. I shouldn't be surprised if that isn't the dastardly Sylver himself! Look at the way he's staring at you, sergeant. I think he's getting ready to attack you . . .'

Three stoat soldiers leapt from their seats and threw themselves on the hapless Mawk, pinning him to the ground. The sergeant got up from his stool and came over to look down into Mawk's face. He nodded thoughtfully. 'This isn't Sylver. I'm told Sylver has a white streak running from his nose to his brow,' he said in a disappointed voice. 'You're blind, pedlar. Even so, I believe you're right about this one. We'll get his name out of him later, by torture if necessary.'

'Mawk,' said the frightened weasel. 'Mawk-the-doubter.'

'Well, a bit of torture will confirm that. In the meantime, you'd better be thinking of telling me where your leader is at this moment. You hear me, outlaw?'

Sylver went over to look down at Mawk too. 'Where are my pots and pans, you scoundrel?' he shrieked into the bemused Mawk's face, shaking his claw. 'What have you done with our fine wares, our beautiful tins, our ladles and spoons, eh? Sold them for a few groats, I'll be bound. I've a good mind to take you outside and thrash you—'

'You'll do nothing of the kind,' said the stoat sergeant. 'I want to skin this one alive. Can you bring a pot of boiling fat, landlord?' he called. 'I think our friend here is thirsty. You would like a drink, wouldn't you?'

'Mawk, the name's Mawk. And I've already had a pot of boiling fat, thank you. The landlord called it gruel.'

The landlord glowered at Mawk. 'I'll remember that,' he said darkly. Then, to his serving jill, 'Boil up some vole fat in the big cauldron!'

Mawk struggled against the three stoat soldiers, who were grinning evilly into his face, their hot breath on his whiskers. 'Don't!' he shrieked. 'Don't

272

do it! I'll tell you where he is, sergeant. I know *exactly* where the outlaw Sylver is at this moment. If you'll let me up, I can show him to you straight away. Please let me go.'

'Let him up,' said the sergeant.

'Aw,' said one of the stoat soldiers, disappointed. 'Can't we torture him anyway?'

'No, he looks as if he might have a heart attack at any second – look how he's shaking with fear. My job is to find Sylver and his henchweasels and bring them in. This one's going nowhere. You can have your fun with him later.'

Once he was on his feet, Mawk looked directly at Sylver. 'I'll show you the outlaw leader, sergeant. Come this way. Follow me.'

With that, Mawk led the way through the back door, the stoat soldiers walking close behind him. He ascended the stairs in the courtyard to the balcony above, along which there were several bedrooms. When he came to the door which had a big '7' on it, Mawk pointed and whispered, 'He's in here – asleep.'

'Stand aside,' murmured the sergeant-at-arms. 'You weasel pedlars, get below.' He spoke to the nearest soldier. 'You, guard this Mawk thing, while we capture his leader.'

Sylver and Miniver went down the stairs and waited at the bottom, wondering what on earth Mawk was up to.

Six soldiers, with the sergeant at their head, suddenly burst open the door to room seven and went thundering in, yelling and screaming at the tops of their voices.

Mawk immediately turned, and shoved the stoat soldier guarding him in the chest. The stoat gave a little cry and fell backwards over the balcony. He landed heavily in the back yard, knocking all the air out of his lungs. Sylver and Miniver pounced on him and quickly bound his four legs together before he could recover his wits.

Mawk was descending the stairs three at a time.

At that moment there came a roar from room seven above and a stoat flew through the open doorway to crash against the balcony railing. He lay there, stunned. Further sounds of fighting came from the room as Mawk finally reached the yard.

'Quickly,' he said, 'let's get out of here.'

The three weasels ran from the yard out into the night. They loped over the fields behind the Black Hostelry, into a wood of oaks. There they found a hollow tree, a beech blasted by lightning at some time, and collected themselves.

'You told on me,' gasped Mawk. 'You gave me up.'

'I had to, you oaf,' hissed Sylver. 'In another second that sergeant would have recognized you, and then he would have asked why we'd kept quiet! We needed him to think of us as his allies.'

'Who was in that room? Room seven?' asked Miniver breathlessly. 'Was it a demon?'

'Might as well have been,' wheezed Mawk delightedly, gulping down air. 'It was Magellan. I was almost caught by him earlier in the evening. I tell you, I've never been so scared.'

'Oh yes you have,' Sylver said, clicking his teeth in amusement. 'Every day of your life. But you did well this time, Mawk-the-doubter. You deserve our thanks. That was quick thinking this evening. I'll not forget it.'

Mawk was feeling good about himself for once. He felt his natural modesty and shyness did not allow him to take full advantage of Sylver's praise, but he knew he had done well.

'Now, where's Alysoun and Scirf?' asked Sylver. 'Weren't they with you?'

'They have the eggshell,' cried Mawk triumphantly. 'We found the eagle's nest and got the map of the world. It was all down to me. I'm the one who got it, but I gave half each over to them, so they could escape from the eagle. I suggested they used them to drift down from the mountain, like feathers on the wind, while I distracted the eagle. I've lost them for the moment, but I'm sure they'll turn up.'

'Too right,' said a voice from another part of the hollow oak. 'We'll turn up again, oh great and wonderful hero of the wildernesses beyond County Elleswhere.'

It was Scirf, back from his flight down the mountain.

'Awk!' muttered the doubter. 'You would hear that, wouldn't you, dung-watcher? Come on out, then. Let's see your ugly face, you gatherer-of-flies, you.'

'Don't be churlish,' said Scirf, emerging from a hole with a smirk on his face. 'Nobody likes a churl, Mawk, don't you know that yet?'

Chapter Twenty-eight

When Alysoun and Scirf reached the bottom of the cliff, strong updraughts of air carried them hither and thither like two dandelion seeds on the wind. They were blown apart and soon lost sight of each other in the moonlight. Alysoun finally landed near a thicket, hitting a bank of moss and rolling down a slope to the bottom. The eagle's eggshell rolled beside her, finishing up next to her right paw.

Fortunately it was undamaged.

She was about to pick herself up when she looked around to see dozens of pairs of eyes regarding her.

Hedgehogs! Over a hundred of them.

It seemed that she had interrupted some sort of ceremony. There were stones arranged in a circle on a grassy stretch of turf. In the centre of the stones a large hedgehog stood on her hind legs. Each of her many spines had a piece of ragged ribbon tied to it, so that she fluttered in the evening breeze, seeming to change shape with the vagaries of the wind. In her paws she held a sharpened willow stick. At her feet was an ominous lump of something. She stared at Alysoun for a moment, then looked up at the sky.

Clearly this priestess of hedgehogs believed that

Alysoun had descended from the roof of Welkin.

'Welcome to the convocation of hedgehogs,' said the priestess. 'You have been sent to us by the Great God Spike.'

It was not a question. The priestess was stating a fact. The Great Spike, whoever he or she was, had clearly made a gift of this weasel to the hedgehogs, for whatever purpose they desired.

'There must be some mistake,' said Alysoun, standing up. She was not afraid of hedgehogs. They were difficult creatures to handle, of course, but were not generally regarded as dangerous. 'I've just fallen out of an eagle's nest. Now I'm on my way to find the rest of my band – Sylver's weasels.'

'Really?' said the haughty hedgehog priestess, as there came a murmuring from amongst the multitude. 'You're on your way to meet someone? Why not stay with us for a while? We can make you comfortable. Come over here.'

'I'd rather be on my way,' said Alysoun firmly.

But two hedgehogs had come forward; they took her eggshell, carrying it to the centre of the stone circle.

'Hey!' cried Alysoun, becoming a little angry. 'That's mine!'

The priestess seemed to be amused by these words. 'Yours?' she said. 'Pardon me, but it doesn't look like a weasel's egg, does it? How is it yours?'

'I – I took it from the eagle's nest.'

'Took it? *Stole* it. You're a thief. We know how to deal with thieves, don't we, eh?' The priestess's voice became harsh. '*Take her,*' she snarled.

At this signal all the hedgehogs pulled pointed

black hoods over their heads. The hoods had slits for their eyes. Instead of moving in towards Alysoun, who was preparing herself for a fight, they formed lanes, passageways, down which slithered horrible reptiles. The eyes of the reptiles glinted in the moonlight. Their forked tongues flicked in and out of their mouths. They hissed ugly words.

'Snakes!' cried Alysoun. 'Vipers!'

It was well known that the one creature which was immune to the venom of a viper was a hedgehog. Not only did their prickles protect them, but for some reason the poison from a viper's fangs cannot harm hedgehogs. However, if Alysoun was bitten, she would become very ill and probably die without a physician to administer the antidote. There were five vipers in all, wriggling along the lanes of hedgehogs, occasionally turning to bite one of the prickly mob, but without effect.

Alysoun was driven to the centre of the stone circle, where the priestess awaited her. All around her the hedgehogs were chanting some sinister dirge, swaying in the moonlight. So long as she went towards the priestess the snakes were blocked from her, but if she tried moving away from the stone circle, the avenues opened again to reveal the hissing vipers.

When she reached the circle Alysoun was alarmed to see white skulls half buried in the turf, so that departed creatures looked up at her with sightless eyes of star moss.

There were teeth scattered like hailstones on the ground.

In the middle of the stone circle was a dead vole, seemingly pierced through the heart with the sharpened stick. Its eyes stared glassily at Alysoun as she entered the sacred area. This creature was obviously the latest sacrifice.

'A weasel,' shrieked the priestess to her followers, and there was a general moan of approval. 'We don't get many weasels,' she added quietly, for Alysoun's benefit.

'Many weasels for *what*?' asked Alysoun, staring at the dead creature on the ground. Then, looking around in alarm, she cried, 'And where's my eggshell?'

'It's been carried to the feet of Spike,' said the priestess. 'You can have it back soon, but first you must help us with a little ceremony. I'll explain it to you as we go along . . .'

The hooded hedgehogs were swaying and moaning all round the stone circle now. They seemed to have been transported into some kind of trance. Alysoun thought it best to go along with this farce until she got the chance to cut and run – with the eagle's eggshell, of course.

'Well, let's get to it then,' said Alysoun. 'And keep those snakes well away from me.'

The priestess then led Alysoun out of the stone circle, which seemed a promising step. The hedgehog nation followed on behind, their hooded forms still swaying back and forth. Finally, Alysoun found herself at the end of a long log, a felled and stripped tree which stretched along the ground. She was made to stand up on the end of this trunk.

'You will run the gauntlet,' cried the priestess, as

dozens of hooded hedgehogs stepped forward and took up positions all along the length of the log. 'My strongest followers will flail you with bulrushes as you try to run the log. If they knock you off, then you will be the next sacrifice to the Great Spike.'

'And if I stay on the log until the end?' asked Alysoun.

'You might have to go again.'

Alysoun guessed as much. Suddenly there came the sound of drumsticks beating hollow wooden logs. A general rush of excitement went through the mass of hedgehogs. They all crowded closer until the priestess screamed at them to give the beaters room.

Beaters? thought Alysoun. I'll give them *beaters*.

Then, at a push from the priestess she began her run along the top of the fallen trunk, high above the sturdy hedgehogs, who flailed her as she passed. They were trying to knock her off the perch, get her to fall, but they had reckoned without her nickname. She was Alysoun-the-fleet, the fastest runner in Elleswhere County, and they had difficulty in striking her as she passed them by, even though they were ready for her.

'Cheat!' cried the priestess. 'Too fast. Too fast.'

When she reached the end of the log Alysoun jumped down triumphantly, only to find a huge figure formed of bones in front of her. It appeared to be made solely of the ribcages of thousands of animals stuck into clay. Ten times her height, the great shape bristled with white spines, like a monstrous hedgehog from hell. Two great badgers' skulls formed its eyes, but for the rest of it there was nothing but curved white prickles.

'The Great God Spike!' screamed the priestess.

The multitude of hedgehogs fell on their faces before the idol and moaned in ecstasy.

The vipers, previously encircled by the hedgehogs, took this opportunity to slither away into the night.

Spike was the hedgehog deity, to whom they sacrificed unfortunate creatures like Alysoun. It looked a cruel god, with its snouty eyes and barbed body. It was a lustful god shrouded in death, its still breath filling its followers with dire thoughts. It was an image formed from the darkness of hedgehog minds and it stared down at Alysoun with never-satisfied greed. She knew it wanted her ribcage, to add to itself, to give it more power, to make it mighty. It wanted ALL the ribcages in the world.

High up, balanced on the god's head, was a sealed flagon full of dark liquid.

'What's that?' asked Alysoun, pointing to the object. 'Up there on Spike's head.'

The priestess half-closed her eyes. 'Do not speak of it with your barbaric unbeliever's tongue, your heretical mouth. This is the blood of a thousand Pikpiks, First Followers of Spike, in the Days of Yore – "In the beginning..."' intoned the priestess, going into a ritual chant.

'A bottle of blood?' said Alysoun. 'What good is that?'

'Why,' cried the priestess, reluctantly breaking off her chant, 'only a godless weasel would ask such a question. It is the life blood of Spike, contained not within His form, but without His form, giving Him thought, desires, energy. Without the blood of the Pikpiks the Great God Spike is but a heap of bones.'

'I see. That sealed flagon is the heart of Spike, so to speak.'

'Now you understand,' cried the priestess. She turned to the mob. 'She understands, she understands.'

There was a general moan of approval from the hooded multitude of hedgehogs.

'In that case,' murmured Alysoun, still smarting from the bulrush beating she had experienced, 'let's see how he gets on without his heart.'

Alysoun whipped out her slingshot, took a pebble from her belt pouch, and swung the weapon round her head. She let fly a brown stone, taken from a stream, at the huge flagon. It hit the target squarely in the middle, shattered the glass, and red fluid poured down the face of the god into its surprised snouty eyes.

Spike suddenly no longer looked terrifying – he appeared to be stunned, a shocked expression on his face.

The bottle had been very full. As the liquid seeped down into Spike's joints, washing away the clay, he began to crumble before the eyes of the crowd, his thousands of rib-bone spines clattering to the ground in a great heap. He literally fell apart before their eyes, into a boneyard ruin.

A great wail went up from the priestess, which was echoed throughout the mob of hedgehogs. They tore off their hoods and stared with horror at their mortally wounded god, whose life blood was draining away before their eyes. Anguish filled the night air. The hedgehogs began to roll on the ground in the dirt in their grief, collecting old leaves on their spines, covering themselves with bits of grass and twigs.

'Why did you do it?' wailed the priestess. 'Why did you destroy our god?'

'He wasn't a very pleasant character, now was he?' reasoned Alysoun, collecting her eggshell from the foot of Spike where it had been placed. 'You must admit that. You're much better off without him. He gave you nothing but fear. Find yourselves a nice god, a God of Apples or something. You'll be much better off without this one demanding its sacrifices.'

'An *apple* god?' the priestess cried. 'What are you saying?'

'A nice *harvest* deity. A god which gives you something to look forward to. Think of the unhappiness this one has spread abroad. No, no, you'd be much better off with an apple god – all rosy-cheeked and plump . . .'

With that Alysoun dashed off swiftly into the night, before the hedgehogs recovered from their shock. They had been stunned by grief but would soon remember who had caused it. Carrying her precious cargo of the eggshell, she ran like a hare. She wanted to put as much distance as she could between her and the hedgehog cult.

This had been a nasty experience for Alysoun and one she did not wish to repeat. The grey fingers of morning were clawing their way up the sky as she crossed the countryside. It would soon be light. She could take stock.

When day dawned she felt extremely tired and made ready to go to sleep under the roots of an elm. First she took her eggshell and began to push it into a hole beside the root, to keep it hidden. But to her horror she noticed something different about the object.

The map had gone!

She pulled it out of the hole again and examined it carefully. No, it was true, the map was nowhere to be seen.

Had she taken the wrong eggshell from the foot of the hedgehog god? It did not seem possible. Perhaps in some way the pattern on the egg had been wiped clean in the night. But that did not seem likely either. Alysoun had not gone into any water, or rubbed the shell against anything abrasive.

Maybe, she thought miserably, this has been done by the Great God Spike. His final deed, his revenge, while he fell apart before her eyes. Spike had reached out with his failing power and performed his final beastly act.

Was that a possibility?

Chapter Twenty-nine

Alysoun did not abandon the half eggshell, even though the map had disappeared. She felt somehow that she ought to show it to the rest of the weasels of Halfmoon Wood, since they had suffered so much in order to obtain it. Alysoun travelled quickly over the countryside, resting in holes at night, moving through ditches and in woods during the day.

Once or twice she caught sight of Falshed's troops crossing the landscape, but she managed to avoid any meeting. In order to stay alive she ate the roots of onion and garlic weeds, drank the dew from cuckoo pints, and generally avoided any contact with other creatures. Finally, she was in County Elleswhere and could see Halfmoon Wood on the horizon. It was with great happiness that she viewed the smoke from Thistle Hall, curling lazily above the treetops.

'Ah, smell that woodsmoke,' she said to herself. 'That's a good scent . . .'

As she neared the wood a shout went up. It was Icham, on guard in an oak tree, watching for soldiers. He yelled a greeting to her and Alysoun's heart lifted. The last few days on her own had sorely tried her spirit. She was not a solitary weasel by nature, not used to being without company, and it had been a miserable trek across Welkin, dragging the eggshell with her.

'Icham!' she cried delightedly. 'Oh, am I glad to see you. Am I glad to be home.'

Icham ran out to meet her. 'Alysoun, you've got the other half of the eggshell. Wonderful! Sylver, Miniver, Mawk and Scirf arrived back last night. They have half. So we've got a complete map of Welkin.'

Alysoun made a face. 'I'm afraid it's not much good to us. For some reason the map has disappeared. It was there when I first found the shell, but now it's gone.'

'You found it at night, right?' said Icham, clicking his teeth in amusement.

'Yes,' she said, 'but I don't see what's so funny. The map's gone.'

'No it hasn't. I'll explain later. Follow me.'

Icham took the eggshell from her paws and led the way along the woodland paths, through beds of celandine with their pretty yellow flowers, past the drooping faded forget-me-not patches, by solitary delicate red campions. In the middle of the wood it was relatively quiet, since birds usually live and work on the edge of woodlands, rarely venturing into their centres. There was the scent of moss and fern, eglantine and elderflowers.

Alysoun breathed deeply in pleasure. 'It's so good to be back,' she said. 'There isn't anywhere on Welkin so beautiful as Halfmoon Wood.'

'You're right there,' replied Icham.

Alysoun asked, 'You told me about some of the others, but what about Wodehed, Luke and Bryony? And Dredless. You haven't mentioned him. What about dear Dredless?'

Icham stopped in his tracks and turned and stared. 'Of course,' he said, 'you were with Mawk and Scirf when they ran away from Hunter's Hall.'

She saw by his expression that something terrible had happened. 'What is it, Icham? Tell me.'

'Well, we got away the next morning, after you had left . . .'

'We couldn't get back,' she told him, 'otherwise I would have returned.'

'I know. Anyway, we decided to go over the lake on rafts and in the fog we got split up. While the raft I was on was wandering around in the mist, we came across a canoe. Can you guess who was in it?'

'No, I can't.'

'Magellan,' Icham said dramatically.

Alysoun's heart skipped a beat. 'The dreaded fox,' she murmured. 'So Poynt's let him come back?'

Icham nodded grimly. 'He's been let loose on us, to bring us to heel. Anyway, he managed to fire one of those deadly arrows of his and wounded Wodehed – then he drifted out of our sight again, thank goodness.'

'Poor Wodehed! Is he badly hurt?'

'He's a lot better now he's in the paws of Lord Haukin. But that's not the end of our troubles, I'm afraid. Things got worse after that. We split into two parties. Luke, Bryony and myself carried Wodehed back here, to get him the treatment he needed. Sylver, Dredless and Miniver went on, up the Yellow Mountains, to try to reach the eggshell.'

Here Icham paused and looked at his feet. 'Unfortunately they ran into Magellan again. The upshot of the encounter was that Dredless was killed by one of Magellan's arrows. Magellan tried to get Sylver and Miniver, but a bridge collapsed and there was no further confrontation.'

'Dredless dead?' cried Alysoun. 'Dear Dredless, gone?'

'I'm afraid so.'

It happened from time to time that a weasel from Halfmoon Wood died or was killed. There had been Logger, and Wistle, and many others who had gone the way of fine weasels. It was a dangerous world and death was never very far away, for any of the band, but Alysoun always felt a part of her died too when one of their number was taken away from them.

She was a sensitive soul, who felt such things more deeply than most, unlike Icham, who saw the need to harden his feelings against such tragedies. To him they occurred so often he felt he would fall apart if he let them affect him the way they did Alysoun. 'I'm sorry, Alysoun. We all liked Dredless.'

'Yes, we did. And now he's gone. Where are his remains?'

'At the bottom of a very deep chasm, where no-one will be able to defile them.'

He hinted at the practice of Prince Poynt, who copied the old human custom of displaying a weasel's corpse on a gibbet, or gallows, out in a field for all to see. Prince Poynt had a great rack, made of wood and wire, on which he stretched the carcasses of those he had dispatched from this life. It was a warning to all who went against his wishes. When you saw the husk of one of your own kind, its pelt blowing in the wind and the rain on a wire rack, you thought twice about treason.

Or so the prince reasoned.

'Well then, at least he's safe there,' said Alysoun. She did not weep. But her heart wept inside her. 'And the others are all safe?'

'Yes, even Wodehed is on the mend, thanks to Lord Haukin and Culver.'

'I'm glad you told me before we went into the camp, Icham,' she said. 'It gives me a little time to get used to the idea. I would have looked for the face of Dredless when I went in, not knowing that he was somewhere else, down a deep shaft in the mountains, at peace with the world.'

They went on through the wood, with Alysoun in quiet contemplation, until finally they reached the camp. Everyone came running out to meet Alysoun, their expressions showing how happy they were that she was safe and well.

Yet even though she knew Dredless was dead, she could not but help looking for his face amongst her living friends, hoping against hope that somehow they had got it wrong and that the renowned marksweasel was still alive.

'Welcome back, Alysoun,' said Sylver. 'I understand you brought the other half of the eggshell. Good for you. Excellent.' He paused. 'Has – has Icham told you . . .?'

'He's told me everything,' said Alysoun, determined not to break down in front of everyone. 'It's – it's very sad.'

Sylver put a foreleg around her shoulders and led her away from the group. 'It is indeed, Alysoun, and I know you probably feel things like this more strongly than most of us. We're having a little memorial service for Dredless tonight. A real weasel send-off – I hope you'll say a few words for us then. Will you do that for me, Alysoun? You have a way with words. We're a little rough and ready, us jacks and jills of Halfmoon Wood, but I know you'll think of something suitable to say of Dredless.'

'A real weasel send-off,' she repeated, with a nod of her head, knowing that it would be a celebration, not a mourning. 'A kalkie?'

'Indeed,' said Sylver. 'A kalkie.'

'Dredless would have liked that,' Alysoun said. 'I know he would.'

And so the weasels got ready for the kalkie, which is a celebration of the departed weasel's life, rather than a lamenting of his death. Weasels see nothing wrong with death, since it is the end of one journey and the beginning of another. The point of death is merely a way station, where a weasel adjusts itself to a spiritual rather than a mortal form.

The *manner* of the death, as in Dredless's case, was something to be angry or sad about. He had been killed unnecessarily, by a creature without a spark of remorse in his body. Magellan was a cold-blooded killer, whose only interest was himself. That much was to be grieved over, but Dredless had had a good life, was well loved by his kind, and deserved to have that life acclaimed with a marvellous send-off.

When the evening arrived, out came the reed flutes, out came the drums, out came the whistles and warblers. A great bonfire was built in the glade, with plenty of dancing room around it. Normally the body of the dead weasel would have had pride of place at the top of the bonfire. It was burned so that it could never be hung on a gibbet.

But since Dredless was not actually there an image of him was put up on the bonfire instead. Along with the figure made of straw and twigs were some darts he had made and stored in a hollow log before setting out on the quest.

When the time came the bonfire was lit and the dancing began – weasels swaying on their hind legs like corn stalks in the wind – weasels leaping and cavorting, shrieking and yelling like mad creatures – weasels crooning at the moon with high shrill voices. The flutes trilled, the drums beat out weasely rhythms, the whistles piped and the warblers ululated.

Even Lord Haukin, old and infirm as he was, came to the fire to pay his respects to the life of Dredless. Since he was a stoat he was not very familiar with the customs of the weasels and their methods of dealing with death, but he knew his presence would be appreciated by them. He was, like Alysoun, a feeling creature, who took on the sorrows of the world.

Just before the flames reached the effigy of Dredless, the substitute for his real body, one by one the weasels stepped forward and cast a stone at him.

And as they did so, each weasel chanted the following words, meant to wipe out any traces of ill-will. 'If in this life you have ever wronged me, Dredless Weasel, for any reason, with or without my knowledge, let this stone strike you for that deed and thus we part even, with no ill-feelings on my part or yours – we are for ever friends.'

The line of weasels went down, one by one, as each stone was pitched, with Alysoun the last to throw.

When Lord Haukin's turn came to cast a stone, he would not. He did not fully understand the reasons behind the ritual, but kept repeating he had nothing against Dredless and therefore had no cause to defile his image. Sylver understood that the old stoat was upset by this part of the ceremony. Lord Haukin did not realize that Dredless, wherever he was, would be very distressed if someone refused to cast a stone at him, for how was he to know he had not wronged that creature accidentally?

Poor Lord Haukin did not understand the reason for all the joy, either, for he, like most stoats, was a traditional mourner, who grieved over the dead because they were missing, because they were missed, because they had gone out of reach.

Alysoun spoke at midnight, when the embers of the fire were still red and warm, and Dredless was still with them, as a glow, as the smoke which drifted through the trees.

'Oh prince of hunters, running through the meadow with your tail high and your ears taut, may you find your place in the new life you now enjoy. Wait for us, for we shall be joining you again, by and by, bringing with us news of this world. Your life was a carnival of creation, which we now celebrate with this kalkie, and thus we send our greetings to you, and say our goodbyes, both at one and the same time.'

The weasels then let out a great cheer, and the music and dancing began again in earnest, while Lord Haukin was assisted back to Thistle Hall, still a little bemused by the air of jollity. 'I shall never fully understand you weasels,' he said to Culver. 'You seem to cling on to life with such firmness, handle it with such serious intent while you have it, yet once it's gone, you treat it like it was a short holiday.'

'Well, that's just our way, Lord Haukin,' said his servant, shouldering most of the weight which did not fall on the hickory stick his master used to get himself along. 'We're a mad lot, you know. We sing to the moon. No point in understanding. There's nothing really to understand.'

'But I like to know all things,' argued the old stoat, as they came to the massive door of Thistle Hall. 'Knowledge is a great and wondrous thing. It is both a weapon and a healer, two in one. It upsets me when my knowledge is incomplete.'

'Begging your pardon, sir – but you can't know *everything*. No creature can do that.'

'I can try.'

'But you mustn't upset yourself when you come up against something which takes more than a lifetime to learn. Weasel customs are in our bones, in our blood, buried deep in the very muscle of our being. You can't expect to learn by attending one celebration . . .'

'Funeral,' muttered Lord Haukin. 'Not celebration, surely?'

'No, we don't have funerals. That's what I mean. We leave that to you gloomy old stoats. Our memorial services are big parties. It's difficult for you, isn't it?'

'Very,' said Lord Haukin, shaking his head sadly. 'But I suppose I'm old-fashioned.'

No, thought Culver, you're simply a stoat.

Chapter Thirty

For one brief morning the black clouds parted over Castle Rayn and the sun shone through. The landscape around the great castle was lit with splendour. All over the rolling downs was a haze of wild flowers, sparkling with raindrops. There were pink campion, blue forget-me-nots with yellow eyes, white ox-eye daisies, mauve herb robert, yellow buttercups. There were tangles of snowy stitchwort along the ditches, dusty miller, violets, tall stately thistles with purple crowns, coltsfoot, clover, cornflowers. Honeysuckle caused havoc in the hedgerows and dog roses burst through the green with passionate petals.

'How beautiful,' murmured Prince Poynt, looking out of one of the castle windows. 'How simply splendid.'

Then he saw Sheriff Falshed's head down amongst the cow parsley, his body nowhere to be seen, and the prince sighed, remembering that he had devised a different punishment for the failure of his sheriff this time, just for a change. 'You must be fed up with hanging from the battlements by your heels,' he had said to Falshed, after the latest attempt to bring in Sylver and his band, 'perhaps you'd prefer to be lower, so that you can see things the right way up, but only at ground level or there would be no punishment, would there?'

Falshed had of course agreed with his prince and so now his head was down amongst the pretty wild flowers.

Prince Poynt decided to go for a little walk, since the sun was shining so brightly, and he ordered the portcullis to be raised and the drawbridge to be lowered. Then he strolled outside the castle, shivering in the warm morning sun. Kicking his way through the wild flowers, he eventually came upon the sheriff's head. 'There's a dew drop on the end of your nose,' he said. 'I hope it's a real one.'

The nose in question wrinkled. A fly, noticing the movement, came and settled on one of the whiskers near by. 'Morning, my prince,' said the head. 'It's a fine day, is it not?'

'For those of us who are not buried up to our necks, yes, I suppose it is. How's that body of yours doing under the turf, Falshed? Anything nibbling?'

The sheriff screwed up his face. 'I think the ants are having a good go, your graciousness. They're coming down the worm holes. I believe my rear left foot is directly in the path of a trade route. The soldier ants have forced a passage between my toes. When I tried to close the pass, they bit me.'

'Well, you can't stop trade, Falshed. That's not good for progress. If the ants have a golden road between your toes, you could probably charge a toll, but you certainly can't block it.'

'No, my prince.' Falshed's head swivelled on his restricted neck. 'Is – is there any chance I might be dug out today, your graciousness?'

Prince Poynt sighed heavily. 'I can't deny you've

disappointed me *deeply*, Falshed. I had hopes you would capture the rebels before Magellan got to work. You know he's killed one of them already? Of course you do! Dredless – quite a sureshot with a dart, I understand. He's also wounded another very seriously . . .'

'And crippled two of your stoat soldiers,' said Falshed, unable to keep the satisfaction out of his tone.

Prince Poynt looked at the swivelling head sharply. 'That was an accident and if you keep that up, I'll tell them to bury the rest of you!'

'I'm sorry, I'm sorry,' said Falshed quickly. 'I didn't mean anything against you, my lord. I just hate that braggart Magellan.'

'Well,' said the prince, softening again, 'I'm not that fond of the fellow myself, but he is a good bounty hunter, you have to give him that. He does earn his crust.'

'He's a cold-blooded maniac,' muttered Falshed, as a fly landed on his eyelid. He blinked rapidly, trying to get rid of the tickling creature, but it seemed stuck fast to him with gluey feet. 'He'd kill anything on four legs.'

'True, true,' murmured the white prince, finding an old conker on the ground. 'Hmmm, hold your head still.'

Prince Poynt placed the conker carefully on top of the sheriff's head, then walked back a few paces and gathered some pebbles.

'You – you haven't got a sling?' Falshed asked anxiously, fighting to keep the conker from falling off his head.

'No, no,' said the reasonable ermine prince, 'I'm just going to throw them – now . . .' He took careful aim and threw. A stone whizzed by Falshed's nose. 'If I manage to knock off the conker, I'll have you dug up. That's fair, isn't it? Hold still . . .'

Another stone whistled by Falshed's ear. The fly was still doing a dance on his eyelid, the ant caravans were still tramping through his toes and a small tic was developing in his left nostril. Under the ground, the clay clung to his fur, cold and clammy, like grave-earth. It was a horrible feeling – worse at night when the blackness came. His whole body screamed at him to be let loose, to run and jump, to *move*.

'Hold – very – still—'

A stone whacked him on the ear, sending the conker spinning off his head.

With his ear ringing, Falshed cried, 'Oh – GOOD shot, your graciousness. Bang on target. Didn't feel a thing . . .'

'I thought it hit you on the side of the head.'

Falshed clicked his teeth in mock amusement. 'Oh, no, no, no, my prince. It clipped the conker off my bonce as clean as a whistle. I'd *know* if a stone struck my head, wouldn't I?'

'Well, what's that lump appearing under your ear then?'

'That? That's – that's a *bee* sting, my prince. I've just been stung by a bee. One of the hazards of being buried up to your neck in dirt. I'm not complaining, mind, because I know I deserved it. I always take my punishment, don't I, my lord, without complaint? I would never presume to question your judgement on these things and I've appreciated the change – my ankles are so much more rested now that I've not been hanging by them over the battlements for the last two days—'

'Shut up, Falshed.'

'My lord?'

'Shut up. You're beginning to sound hysterical. Drat.' Prince Poynt looked up. 'Here comes the rain again. You'd think it might stay dry for a whole day for once, wouldn't you? Ah well, I'll send some soldiers to dig you out – if I remember. In the meantime, *adieu*, sweet Falshed.'

'*Au revoir*, my prince. Say *au revoir*?'

'Oh, if you will.'

An hour later, in the pouring rain, some grumbling soldiers brought spades to dig out the desperate sheriff. He had to direct their digging, or they might puncture him somewhere, but finally he stepped from the hole, the dirt dripping from his fur. He trekked miserably back to the castle and went straight to his room, to climb into a warm tub which Spinfer had thoughtfully made ready for him.

'You're a treasure,' said Falshed, slipping into the suds before a roaring fire, 'did you know that?'

'Thank you, sir, we endeavour to give satisfaction.'

'It was hell out there, Spinfer. Simply hell. It was like being dead, only I was alive. Just about everything that moves under the ground had a go at me – worms, ants, beetles – you name it. It only needed a blasted mole to come along and I would have had a full set.'

'Yes, sir, but calm yourself now, you're home.'

'Thank you, Spinfer,' murmured Falshed, closing his eyes. 'You know my needs.'

When he was cleaned and rested, with a new sash over his shoulder and a bronze-studded belt around his waist, Falshed went to the main hall, where there were games in progress. As he entered, Prince Poynt and the other noblestoats were engaged in a game of cricket. One of the kitchen weasels was acting as the stumps.

Earl Takely was batting and the prince was bowling.

'Take that, Takely,' cried the prince, sending a yorker down the wicket at high speed.

The stumps let out a cry of anguish on seeing the ball hurtle towards his midriff.

Earl Takely was a particularly good cricketer, a fine batstoat, and he struck leather with willow to square leg with a stylish flourish.

The quivering set of stumps let out a sigh of relief and showed his appreciation to the batstoat.

'Stop *hugging* me, blast you,' yelled Earl Takely, shrugging off the kitchen weasel. 'I hate being embraced by the wicket every time I hit the ball.'

'You saved my life, sir,' murmured the stumps. 'That ball would have killed me!'

Prince Poynt was a little piqued. He had tried every trick of his bowling knowledge, from spin to fast ball, and still he could not get the earl out. It was beginning to irk him. 'Let someone else have a go,' he said. 'Stop hogging the bat, Takely.'

'You've got to get me out first,' growled the earl wolfishly. He was possibly one of the only stoats amongst the courtiers who could get away with answering back. A big stoat, with a large army of ferret mercenaries, Earl Takely was almost as powerful as the prince himself. 'Here's Falshed, let *him* have a bowl.'

The prince petulantly stamped away from the bowler's crease, crying, 'Oh, go on, Falshed, but for heaven's sake get the rotter out – he's been in since tea time.'

Falshed was thrown the ball by a noblestoat. He caught it neatly. When it came to cricket, Falshed was no slouch. He knew how to both bat and deliver a good ball. Now his prince had called on him to do a service and for once it did not involve catching weasels. It simply involved hitting one.

'Middle and off,' said Earl Takely, using the opportunity of a change of bowler to line himself up.

Falshed saw his opportunity and stepped in front of the umpire to direct the earl. 'Left a bit, left a bit more – just a teeny bit more – right, that's fine.'

The stupid earl had trusted Falshed to give him an accurate guide to the middle and off position, but typically Falshed had put the batstoat right across his own wicket. The stumps knew what had happened but the kitchen weasel saw the threatening glint in the sheriff's eye and swallowed a warning to the earl. The weasel trembled where he stood, hoping Falshed would be as accurate with his bowling as he was with his cheating.

'Coming down,' said Falshed, taking a long run from the edge of the royal rug. He noted the groove in the floor where the fat ran down when they spit-roasted a joint over the main hall fire. It was towards this groove that Falshed hurled a ball with a particularly wicked spin.

'Go get him, Falshed,' yelled the prince from his throne. 'Knock his blasted block off.'

The ball flew down the hall, struck the edge of the groove, flew up at a googly tangent and smacked the earl on the shin.

'Owzat?' cried Falshed, throwing his forelegs in the air. 'LBW!'

'No ball,' cried the earl, clearly in pain and rubbing his shin. 'Wide.'

The umpire, another noblestoat, murmured, 'Not out, I think.'

'Overruled,' snarled the prince.

'Out!' shouted the umpire loudly, amending his earlier decision with decisive signal. 'Definitely out.'

The earl threw the bat on the floor in a great passion and stamped away from the wicket. 'Bodyline bowling,' he grumbled. 'Should be made illegal. You sure I was middle and off there, Falshed?'

'Ask the umpire,' said Falshed.

'Oh, dead on,' said the umpire.

The ermine-coated prince danced down to the wicket and picked up the cricket bat. The stumps stared around him in terror, knowing the prince was the worst bat in the kingdom. If Falshed kept bowling the stumps would be covered in bruises before the evening was out.

'Me, me, I'm in,' said the prince, placing the handle of the bat on the chalked batter's crease. 'That's enough bowling for you, Falshed. Let someone else have a go. What about Wilisen, let Lord Wilisen have a bowl.'

Lord Wilisen was a weedy-looking stoat who could only bowl under-foreleg at the best of times.

The stumps heaved a sigh of relief.

'Excuse me, my prince, but you've got the bat upside down,' murmured Falshed, going up beside his lord and master. 'Turn it the other way up.'

301

The prince blinked and reversed the bat. 'I knew that,' he said. 'Just testing you. Come on, Wilisen – send down your best ball.'

Wilisen bowled, the ball dribbled over the flagstones of the hall, slipped under the bat and came to rest lightly against the back legs of the stumps.

'NO BALL!' yelled Falshed, picking up the leather sphere quickly and throwing it back hard to Wilisen. 'You put your foot over the bowler's crease, Wilisen.'

The ball struck Wilisen's outstretched paws with a stinging blow, causing that lord's eyes to water profusely. 'Isn't the umpire supposed to say whether it's a "no ball" or not?' he said.

'I am the umpire now,' replied Falshed. 'Lord Elphet's retired – haven't you, Lord Elphet?'

'Definitely retired,' replied the lord, sitting down where he stood. 'Definitely.'

'Now, my prince,' whispered Falshed, 'get ready for an evening's batting. When you get tired, just take a little rest, then carry on when you feel like it. I'm the umpire now.'

'Falshed,' replied the prince, 'why did I leave you out in the meadow for so long? I missed you. I'm glad I was magnanimous enough to let you come back.'

'But that's you all over, your graciousness, nothing if not generous.'

The prince hit two sixes under Falshed's guidance, one of them striking the great shield above the fireplace and denting Prince Poynt's heraldic coat of arms. No-one cared about the dent, least of all the prince.

The prince was ecstatic.

Falshed was back in favour.

Chapter Thirty-one

The weasels of Halfmoon Wood were gathered in the library at Thistle Hall. It was dangerous for Lord Haukin to have them there but he thought the occasion too special. They had brought with them a rare treasure – the great sea eagle's eggshell – and it now sat in its complete form on a bed of satin.

'Wonderful,' said Lord Haukin, his rheumy old eyes filling with tears. 'I have never seen anything so beautiful in all my life. And, er, what's-her-name found it, did she? Jolly good.'

'It's only an eggshell,' muttered Scirf, and you could see he had wanted to add 'silly old stoat', but a warning glare from Bryony stopped the words from leaving his mouth.

'Yes, but such a precious eggshell. The map of the world! What an addition to our knowledge this is.'

The eggshell lay on its bed of satin, struck by rays of moonlight which poured through his one clean window. Culver was not overfond of cleaning windows and he had done this one by special request.

'And you can only see the map by moonlight?' said the old stoat. 'Not in bright daylight? That's why thingamajig thought the map had disappeared for good. The second time she looked at it was in the sunshine. I suppose it's something to do with the chemicals in the shell's surface. You can see the map looks luminous in the moonlight. Fascinating.'

Scirf yawned loudly and was again glared at by Bryony. 'What?' he whispered. 'What did I do now?'

'Now,' said Lord Haukin, 'let's see if we can decipher this map for you.'

The stoat lord then went to a drawer in a desk and took out a piece of glass, thicker in the middle than it was at the edges, and held it over the eggshell. The outlaws were amazed to see that the egg was larger when looked at through the glass. Lord Haukin pored over the map, taking in various points, then finally he gave out a loud 'Aha!'

'What?' cried Scirf, pushing in amongst the outlaws now. 'Whatcha got, Aristoatle?'

Lord Haukin glanced at the ragged weasel with surprise. 'How do you know Aristoatle, the great philosopher of earlier times? He's not generally well known. Aren't you the dung-watcher fellow?'

'I am,' said Scirf, 'but a dung-watcher what can read – taught meself – it's bloomin' boring watching dung, despite the antics of the flies and beetles, so when I found some parchments in a box, I learned to read from 'em.'

'Just like that?' said the sceptical lord, who was rather proud of his ability to read.

Scirf tapped the side of his skull. 'That's not rhubarb in there, m'lud.'

'Funny,' replied the lord with an unusual turn of humour, 'from the amount of soil in your ears I imagined it must be.'

Scirf gave him a nudge, almost knocking over the frail old stoat. 'Quick, eh? No flies on you, is there, m'lud?'

Lord Haukin turned back to the question of the map. 'What I have found here, in the north, right in the middle of the Far Weald, is a symbol which can be nothing but the place you seek – the geographical location of Thunder Oak.'

'Let me see,' said Sylver excitedly, pushing forwards. 'Is that it? That picture of a dark trunk, split in two halves?'

'I would say that could be it and may be used to point us in the direction of the oak,' replied Lord Haukin. 'My eyes may be a little misty, but there's nothing wrong with my rhubarb.'

Scirf gave him another little friendly swipe with his elbow. 'Quick,' said the weasel. 'Very quick.'

Sylver studied the position of Thunder Oak on the map. It did indeed lie in the wind-blasted wastes of Far Weald, beyond the unnamed marshes where the rat hordes were gathered under the stoat Flaggatis. It would be a dangerous journey, to reach such a zone where little grew but stunted dwarf willows, where braided streams ran over stony flatlands and driftwood lay piled as high as foothills. The old oak itself was a thing from times past, when there were forests in the Far Weald, but the last of the great trees in that region had been destroyed by a thunderbolt.

'There's nothing there but desolation and death,' said Alysoun, aghast at the prospect of the mission. 'Is it wise to go, do you think? What if we fail?'

'I don't think we should *all* go,' replied Sylver. 'I believe three of us should try, then if we fail

305

perhaps another party should be sent out. What does everyone think?'

They all believed this to be a better plan than sending out the whole band.

'How do we choose who goes?' asked Icham.

'Since this is an extremely hazardous and dangerous undertaking, I think we should draw straws for it,' Sylver said. 'It's the fairest way to do it. No-one really wants to go on such a terrible journey.'

Culver brought some pieces of straw from the kitchen and cut them into lengths. Then he held them behind his back. Those who drew the two short straws would be going with Sylver.

The first short straw was drawn, rather predictably, by Scirf; the second by Mawk.

'I'm not going,' said Mawk, with a gasp. 'No, put the straw back, let somebody else draw it. I'm not going.'

Sylver, who did not want either Mawk or Scirf with him, said, 'Let's call that a trial run. Put them back in. Draw again.'

The straws went back in, were chosen again, and Scirf and Mawk again drew the short ones.

'We're *meant* to go,' said Scirf. 'It's fate. You and me, Mawk, we'll make a good team. Look how you dealt with the situation at the Black Hostelry! You're a hero, you are, mate. Come on, cheer up.'

'I'm not going,' said Mawk stubbornly. 'I refuse to go.'

Scirf set his jaw. 'You're goin', or I'll knock your block off, you spineless weasel.'

'Perhaps,' said Sylver, 'we should let someone take Mawk-the-doubter's place, if he's that determined—'

'No,' Scirf said, 'he's goin' and that's that. We drew the straws *twice* and they came out the same both times. We're meant to go, and go we will, all three of us. You get a good night's sleep, Mawk, 'cos you're going to need it.'

No-one could argue with that. The straws had come out the same the second time. It was obvious that the god of luck, or whatever, intended Mawk to be in the expedition to Thunder Oak, and it would be tempting fate to let him weasel out of it.

That night, however, something happened to delay the departure of the three weasels. A pack of wolves marauding across the countryside entered Halfmoon Wood. They began to terrorize the place immediately, howling threats at all who resided in the wood. They ravaged any hovels they found, attempted to storm Thistle Hall, but without success, for the manor had thick walls and stout doors. Eventually they were driven away from the hall by Culver and the other servants, who attacked the wolves with irons red-hot from the fire.

Sylver and his band were not so lucky as to have a fortress like Thistle Hall for their protection.

'Come out and fight, weasels,' cried the wolves. 'Let's see the colour of your fur!'

The outlaws were not prepared to commit suicide and so they remained hidden in their various holes. They knew the wolves would not go on to attack Castle Rayn, garrisoned with armoured stoats and ferrets, but were happy to make the lives of the peasants miserable instead. They ate everything in sight, disturbed the woodland with their moon-worshipping howls, and fought amongst themselves with a savagery only

307

matched by the rat hordes of the unnamed marshes.

'We've got to do *something*,' moaned Icham from his secret hollow in an elm tree. 'We'll starve if we stay hidden in these holes for much longer.'

The wolves looked like remaining, however. Halfmoon Wood was rich in game and bandits like these did not intend to abandon such pickings without cleaning the bones. They tore down any structure which looked as if it might contain a creature, dug up any crops that had been planted beyond the wood, and fouled the woodland paths and byways.

'We do as we please,' cried the pack queen, when there were complaints by the rooks, safe in their high nests. 'No-one tells us what to do.'

Wodehed was asked to conjure up some strange monster to rid the wood of the wolves and indeed he did his best. The one creature wolves were afraid of was man. Wodehed knew that there were men who changed into wolves on a full moon and beasts who changed into men. In the end, however, as was usually the case with Wodehed's magic, all he could muster was a 'weremouse'. It was in fact a shrew, rather than a mouse, which changed into a man every full moon. However, even in its human form the weremouse was only a few centimetres tall, and if the wolves ever *saw* it they took no note of the tiny monster.

Help eventually came in the shape of a block. The statue of a woodcutter arrived on the scene. This statue had stood in the market square of Scirf's village, until it had decided to go looking for its birthplace. Now it had crossed County

Elleswhere in search of Scirf, who it believed knew the location of the quarry from whence it had originally been hewn.

The woodcutter's statue came into Halfmoon Wood, bellowing Scirf's name in hollow accents.

'In here,' cried Scirf from a rabbit hole, 'but whoever you are I can't come out until the wolves have gone.'

Woodcutters are an old enemy of wolves from the time when they used to beguile young women in red cloaks. It set to with its axe. It drove the wolves from the wood, promising that, should they ever return, it would cut them to pieces. The pack queen yelled a few insults about the woodcutter's grandmother, but she and her bandits finally quit the county, heading west in search of innocents to plunder.

Grateful weasels crawled from their holes to thank the woodcutter's statue for its intervention.

'I – want – no – thanks,' it said brokenly. 'Just – Scirf – to – tell – me – my – stone – place.'

It meant that it wanted Scirf to tell it the location of the quarry from whence its stone had come, but in fact Scirf had no idea where the granite had been hewn. However, rather than thoroughly disappoint the block he told it that it might accompany the three weasels northwards, and they could question creatures on the way, to see if anyone knew of a granite quarry which might have supplied the village in the past.

The block was a little upset, but agreed to go with Sylver, the reluctant Mawk and Scirf.

These four then said their farewells and set forth in the direction of the river Bronn and the unnamed marshes.

On their way northwards, Scirf questioned every animal they met, asking them about quarries. They were either too busy to answer, not interested enough to answer, or too stupid to know where their own homes were, let alone the birthplace of a searching block. One or two did, it was true, attempt to answer the question, but none with any success.

On the third day the four travellers came to a church which stood on the outer edge of the marshes. This was the chapel of the human warlord who used to rule this part of the kingdom of Welkin. It was a dark, forbidding building, with damp stanchions covered in lichen, gravestones in its yard seemingly planted by a clumsy giant, and broken churchyard walls. Its stones were so ancient they might have come from a place beyond time.

On the gutters around the eaves were gargoyles so ugly they startled you. Black with grime and mossy growths, these creatures stared down at passers-by with hard eyes. Their hind quarters buried deep in the stone walls of the church, they were unable to climb down and search for their own birthplaces, which were lost in the great quagmire of time anyway.

Gargoyles were the oldest statues in the land and their origins were steeped in mystery. The stone from which they had been carved was now so damp, so riven with black rain, so long battered by erosive winds, that not even the gargoyles themselves knew what rock they were made from. They guessed it might be some kind of marble, but they were not sure.

Scirf called up to these creatures, asking them if

they knew of, or could see a quarry from their high position.

'Yes,' cried the gargoyles in chorus. 'We know of a granite quarry not far from here. It's hidden under a network of vines and shrubs. You take the path by the reservoir . . .'

And so the block was given directions to its birthplace.

Before it left, it spoke again to the three weasels. 'You – are – going – to – the – Far – Weald?'

'Yes, we are,' said Sylver.

'Then – beware – of – the – scarecrows.'

With this strange remark the statue then went on its way, leaving deep footprints in the moss.

Chapter Thirty-two

The three weasels decided to spend the night in the church.

There is nothing so gloomy and spooky as an abandoned church and this one was no different to any other. In fact Mawk thought it was probably worse than most. Dark shadows with definite shapes gathered in the corners and cloistered in the rafters. Shades of days past, the shadows were like live things, cold creatures, allies of the stones. They moved in sinister motion with the changing light from the outside world, creeping their way with unseen claws around the walls.

Also inside the church was a host of small creatures, from jumping spiders to death watch beetles.

The whole place was in decay. The altar cloth had begun rotting away and the wooden pews were in a crumbling state. There was a gathering green on the brasswork and a running red about the ironwork. The lectern was beginning to droop like a hot candle and the sagging pulpit looked about to drop.

'What a mess,' said Mawk. 'Wouldn't we be better outside?'

But there was a storm gathering in the heavens above. It was better to be under a roof, even if that roof was not thoroughly waterproof. They made a little camp in the back corner of the church, even managing a small fire.

'Listen to that!' Scirf said, as the wind rose in strength and whistled around the gargoyles outside. 'It's going to be a bad night for voleherds.'

'Who cares?' snapped Mawk, remembering how he had been robbed on the mountainside.

Sylver knew why Mawk was so hostile to voleherds and told him, 'All voleherds aren't like the ones you met. Most of them are honest creatures. You should judge a voleherd by his own character, not by the actions of others.'

'You've met one voleherd, you've met them all,' said the bigoted Mawk.

The three weasels tried to get to sleep, but later on in the night the storm rose to a fury. It hammered on the doors and clattered at the windows, trying to get in. Then the gargoyles started up, wailing and screeching like banshees, competing with the violence of the skies. Finally, Mawk sat up with a start, his eyes wide, his nostrils flaring. 'What's that?' he cried.

'What?' grumbled Scirf. 'I'm tryin' to get to sleep here. Ain't the storm bad enough, without you goin' on?'

'No, *listen*,' Mawk whispered. 'Sylver, can you hear it?'

There was a kind of creaking sound outside, like a set of heavy gates swinging in the wind.

Sylver sat up too. 'Yes. I wonder what's happening out there in the graveyard. Let's take a look.'

'*You* take a look,' Mawk said. 'I'm not.'

So Scirf and Sylver clambered up onto a window sill and tried to look through the stained glass.

There was one small pane missing and it was through this gap that they peered. Outside was a chaos of wind, rain and *stone*. The creaking sound came from stone wings, flapping on stone bodies.

'Look at that, would you?' whispered Scirf in awe. 'Have you ever seen anything like it?'

'What?' cried Mawk from below, feverishly wringing his paws. 'What is it?'

'Never in my life,' Sylver answered Scirf. 'Amazing.'

'Tell me, tell me,' cried Mawk.

But they were too astonished to pay any attention to the third weasel.

They were busy watching a frenzied display by about fifty stone angels, all flying around in the furious wind of the storm, crashing into each other, trying to land on gravestones and yew trees, some blowing stone trumpets, others waving banners on which were carved such phrases as INTO THY HANDS O LORD and NOT LOST BUT GONE BEFORE.

'Look over there,' said Scirf, who could read, 'there's an E missing from the end of that one.'

What the banner actually said now was: LORD SHE WAS THIN.

The angels, some of them only cherubs and seraphs with tiny wings, had strange faces with manic expressions. In the high winds that had helped them to become airborne they flew around like fury, crashing into trees and walls, breaking bits from themselves – an arm here, a leg there, even a head sometimes – then recovering and taking flight again. They were mad with the passion of the storm and their own freedom.

They seemed attracted to the church somehow, like moths flying around a candle flame, as if they could not get away from its influence. No doubt they wanted to be gone, over the countryside, looking for their First and Last Resting Places, but a church is a powerful building. It is especially so for sacred statues, holy relics and hallowed stone carvings. It pulls them to its heart as a magnet attracts iron filings. They find it almost impossible to break away from it.

'It's like a tumblers' ball,' cried Scirf, 'only with the tumblers all drunk on honey dew.'

One of the flying stone angels suddenly spiralled upwards, towards the top of the steeple. Out of their sight it crashed into the iron cross on top of the spire. It went spinning to earth and pinned a stone cherub to the ground between two of its prongs. The cherub struggled madly to find release and only got away when another angel clipped the cross, knocking it flat.

'What is it? What is it?' cried Mawk. 'Tell me.'

The wayward angel which had crashed into the spire's cross afterwards slid down the spire and got its feet hooked on the parapet of the tower underneath. Its momentum swung it over and flipped it through a belfry window. It hit the largest of the six bells with a resounding *clang*. This great bell swung back and forth, hitting others, until the clappers inside were striking demented notes. For many years the bells had been silent. Now they played joyously, ringing the changes. It was a racket, but a cheerful din. They made as much noise as possible.

The church below was filled with the monstrous sound of the bells striking each other.

Mawk's eyes bulged and he put his paws over his ears. 'Stop it, stop it, stop it!' he cried.

Outside, two large stone angels had got caught up in the branches of a cedar and were struggling like frantic beasts to free themselves. They let out high-pitched whines, like creatures caught in a trap, and it penetrated even above the sound of the bells. The angels thrashed and kicked and flailed, until finally one of them was free. The other, unfortunately, had a sharp finger stuck in the trunk. It was doomed to remain anchored to the cedar for the rest of the night.

At that moment the unavoidable happened. A stone angel came crashing through a window, scattering broken glass like hail all over the place. Mawk yelled as he was showered with bits of blue, red and yellow glass, which got in his fur.

He had no time to brush off the pieces, though. The angel began zooming around inside the church, knocking into beams, smashing into standing objects. The lectern was finally snapped in two when the angel struck it with its trumpet. Two of the pews had chunks taken out of them. One of the vestry pillars took a hefty blow from a stone wing.

'Taarrraaaahhh!' blared the stone trumpet. 'Taarrrahh-taraaah!'

The noise was deafening in the close confines of the echoing church.

'Help,' yelled Mawk. 'Stop it!'

The angel began diving down on Mawk, like a giant angry wasp, as if it were attacking him.

'Get it off, get it off,' cried Mawk, folding his paws around his head and running for the safety of a pew. 'It's a mad ticklebrain.'

Scirf said disgustedly, 'It's made of stone, you twerp – it's just gone out of control.'

Other angels came crashing through the

windows now, shattering the glass. Scirf and Sylver jumped down from the window sill. They had seen enough of the dark turbulence of the night outside, with its chaotic angels careering through the swirling gloom. They were in danger of being knocked off their perch as the churchyard angels entered.

Once the angels were inside they began to calm down a little. It was as if this was where they wished to be, within the church which they had stood outside for many, perhaps hundreds of years. They had never been inside before – in this place from whence had once come the music and the singing, the intoned prayers, the priest's warbling voice. They were now seeing what had been withheld from them.

Gradually, one by one, they settled on pews, altar stone, up amongst the rafters, down on the steps. They were clustered like bats, only the right way up. They seemed to find a peace within themselves, as the storm began to wither and die outside, and they had escaped their open places for this haven from the weather. No longer would the elements attack their stone bodies; they were out of the climate's way in here.

'Let's get some more sleep,' said Sylver. 'The tumbling show's over.'

'I can't sleep with that lot peering down on me,' cried Mawk. 'Look how they're staring.'

'In that case,' said Scirf, 'I suggest we go down to the crypt. It's nice and quiet down there amongst the dead bodies. What do you think, Sylver?'

'Sounds like a good idea to me,' replied the weasel leader. 'How do we get down there?'

Scirf looked around him, then pointed with his paw. 'Over there, I think – down those steps. We'll need a candle.'

Scirf led the way down the stone stairs to a dark, damp room below, bearing a lighted candle in his paw. Down here the shadows were colder and damper than ever. There were oblong blocks of stone, which doubtless contained human remains.

Mice scuttled away as the three weasels descended into the utter silence of a room full of death. Here there were small pieces of history lying as aged bones in stone boxes. Scirf breathed deeply. The smell was musty and ugly. Down here the smell had a *shape* and it was that of a rotting carcass.

'Right, then,' Scirf said, settling down on a sarcophagus, 'let's get some sleep.'

'You're not going to sleep *there*?' cried Mawk. 'Not on the grave of a human.'

'Why not? The owner won't mind.'

'How do you know he won't? Maybe he'll haunt you.'

'Listen, if he comes to me at all, I'll simply ask him where the humans went, then the expedition will be over, won't it? We'll be able to go straight home. That'll be nice. So, come on ghost, come and haunt me.'

'Don't say that,' hissed Mawk, looking around with fearful eyes. 'He might hear you.'

Sylver took no part in these discussions, being a little above such silly talk. He simply went into a corner of the crypt and tried to sleep. He felt he ought to leave a guard, but the three of them were so tired it would be impossible for anyone to stay awake.

'I can't sleep down here,' Mawk added. 'It's as cold as sin and the air's too stuffy.'

'Then you'll have to stay awake, won't you?' Scirf said, curling in a loop and settling. 'That's up to you, Mawk.'

But Mawk refused to remain there. He went back up to the pews and settled on one of those. It was not a solution, but the lesser of two evils. The greater evil was spending the night down amongst the smelly dead. Up here there were the angels, but at least they were live stone.

So Mawk spent a very restless night, one eye open and on the perched angels, thinking they were going to swoop on him like predatory birds at any moment.

They didn't. They remained in their roosts. Mawk slept in snatches, from which he would awake every so often with wild eyes, staring about him.

When dawn came he was surprised to find himself still alive. He rose and went to look out of one of the broken windows.

A dusty track led from the church northwards. It was covered in broken branches, leaves and other debris from the storm. Mawk decided that a walk along this country road would be a relief after his ordeal in the church.

He glanced overhead. The angels were still perched up in the rafters, looking down on him with blank eyes. Every so often they would shuffle along their roost like vultures changing their position on a branch. The movement sent a shiver down Mawk's back. These were creatures beyond a weasel's understanding. They were representations of mythical creatures, without brains, without anything except a desire to find the place from whence they had originally come. Who could tell what their instincts would prompt them to do? To attack a weasel might be the whim of a moment.

Mawk hurried across the aisle and down the stone steps to the crypt below. A candle was still guttering in a stone niche, throwing its pale yellow light about the dim interior.

'Come on, wakey, wakey,' cried Mawk in mock levity. 'Let's be up and at 'em!'

Not a weasel stirred in this room of tombs. Only the scratching of beetles and whispering of mice could be heard. Mawk stared at the spot where Scirf had lain. There was nothing there. He then looked to where Sylver had slept. This place too was vacant. It seemed the weasels had gone. Panic welled in Mawk's breast like a stream bubbling from its source.

But gone where? The great church door had remained closed all night, otherwise Mawk would have heard it open. Surely they could not have climbed through one of the high windows. They would have cut themselves on glass in the dark.

This left Mawk with only one conclusion. The two weasels had disappeared from their beds, down here in the crypt. They had either been spirited away, or had found a secret passage.

'Oh Gawd,' groaned Mawk. 'What do I do now?'

Chapter Thirty-three

Despite his misgivings about his own safety, Mawk searched the crypt, rooting around amongst the tombs. It was not a quick business because there were various sections, separated by rusty iron railings, throughout the whole expanse of ground under the church. Finally he came to a spot on the floor where a tombstone had been slid aside and a great black rectangular yawn faced him. 'Oh dear,' he said to himself. 'This must be the place.'

Just as he was leaning over the hole in the floor, the candle finally went out with a soft *phut* and left him in complete darkness. He went into such a dizzying spell of fright he fell forwards into the pit. Yelling, he dropped down and landed on his back with a thud, at the bottom of the tomb.

The smell was atrocious and Mawk gagged. 'Ugh!' he moaned. 'I've got to get out of here.'

The blackness was stifling. He tried to find the walls of the tomb so that he could climb upwards, but his paws met only air. Eventually he found himself walking, feeling his way through the darkness. After a while he came to a cavern where there was some light from tiny holes in the ceiling above. He was disgusted to see that he was surrounded by skeletons and corpses, gathered in heaps, and realized he must be in the graveyard itself, outside the church walls.

'Scirf?' he yelled. 'Sylver?'

There was no answer from either of his companions. If they were near by they were either dead or unconscious. Mawk crossed the cavern, where coffins hung suspended, half-buried above him where they had pushed part-way through the ceiling. Others had crashed completely through and had burst open to reveal their grisly occupants. Grinning corpses watched him as he passed them by, their arms flung wide open in a gesture of embrace with the impact of their landing. Some limbs had detached themselves altogether and were cast about the cavern floor.

This was the hall of the human dead, with a rotten green glow from its surrounds. Here was a feasting area for the worms, who banqueted on such fare. Here the beetles munched on meat and here the gluttonous maggots thrived to dance their massed wriggly dances.

'Sylver? Scirf?'

The miserable Mawk continued on his journey, taking the tunnel on the other side of the cavern. After a while he stopped shouting and simply felt his way along the walls, until he came to a small exit into a place where there was another faint light. Cautious weasel that he was, he poked his nose through for a look round before entering.

On the other side was a cellar or dungeon of some kind and, wonder of wonders, there were Sylver and Scirf, hanging from chains by their forelegs on the far wall. Mawk could not see whether they were alive or dead and was about to call softly to them when a shout went up from another part of the dark room. When he stared in this direction he saw shapes gathered around a table.

As his eyes became better adjusted to the light, Mawk could see that it was a gang of moles. Rough-looking, robust animals, they were playing some kind of gambling game. One of them had a leather cup which rattled when he shook it. Then he cast the contents onto the table top, where they settled into some kind of a pattern. Mawk could see that they were hollyhock seeds.

'Double jeopardy,' growled a big mole, peering short-sightedly at the seeds from two centimetres' distance. 'My count.' He began to laboriously count the seeds on the table, stumbling occasionally over his numbers.

'Seventeen,' cried a second mole. 'I win the next two throws . . .'

'And I get the pot!' said a third.

It was then that Mawk saw what the moles were playing for – not groats or any kind of money – but *worms*. There was a jar full of worms in front of each mole and a dish of them in the middle of the table. The mole who had won the pot reached out and took the dish, emptying the wriggling contents into the jar in front of him.

'How is it that you win two out of every three times, Jaspin?' snarled one of the moles. 'If I didn't know I was in solid company I might suspect that someone was eating a seed or two while my back was turned.'

The biggest mole stood up and put a heavy, hooked digging claw on the table with which he could slash his way through the bark of a hundred-year-old oak, if he so desired.

'Are you accusing me of cheating, Slaker?' he asked softly. 'Because if you are, I hope you can back up your threat.'

The other mole stared down at the huge digging claw and Mawk saw him swallow quickly. 'No, I didn't say you were cheating, did I? I simply mentioned the fact that your luck is – well, extraordinary. I mean, you must admit . . .'

'I admit I'm skilful at rattling the seeds,' growled the big mole called Jaspin. 'That's what *I* admit. I'm a hollyhocker born and bred.'

'Oh, come on, sit down,' snarled another of the moles. 'Let's get on with the game. I'm losing as much as anyone here. Let's not have any slashing of bellies over a few dratted worms. When we ransom those two over there we'll have more worms than we know what to do with. You'll have worms coming out of your ears when Sheriff Falshed gets our note.'

'Yes,' said Slaker, apparently glad of the interruption. 'Big fat round ones.'

Jaspin sat down again. 'Just don't accuse me of anything, that's all,' he said darkly. 'I won't be called a cheat.'

'No-one's calling you a cheat,' Slaker said. 'Just a lucky son of miner's mate.'

Jaspin clicked his teeth in appreciation of the joke. 'Your call,' he said.

Mawk sat in the dark outside the hole and sweated. It was true that he was, in most cases where danger was concerned, what Bryony would have called a 'poltroon' – a coward. Mawk, however, preferred to think of himself as having a 'good instinct for survival', and was never without his wits. He thought things through

324

swiftly and carefully. The situation was this:

He was up-country, deep under a churchyard in turmoil, on his own. If he left Sylver and Scirf to their fate he would have to brave the mad angels *alone*, find his way down-country *alone*, explain the absence of his two companions to the outlaw band – *alone*. Mawk did not like doing anything alone, and certainly not battling his way through demented graven images to make a dangerous journey back to a group of weasels who would be incensed at him for leaving his companions to die.

So, the alternative was to brave the moles – not a wonderful option but clearly the lesser of two evils.

It seemed he had stumbled on a notorious set of subterranean thieves and cutthroats. Bandit mole hideouts were impossible to find. If you did manage to locate one, they moved it within hours, blocking up the passageways behind them. In any case, only a fool or a Jack Russell would go down a hole after a gang of moles, into the world they knew best. They had a network of tunnels which almost covered the area under Welkin. Some of their booby traps, made with springy sharpened willow sticks, were horrible to contemplate.

Mawk told himself he had two choices. He could attempt to save Scirf and Sylver, or he could go back through the hall of death, up into the church where the stony-eyed angels perched like vampire bats. Neither prospect was in any way appealing to him. He would rather the ground swallowed him up. 'Except it already has,' he told himself as a grim joke. 'Oh, I wish I were back in Halfmoon Wood.'

He told himself that the worst that could happen

to him, if he was taken by the moles, was that he would be ransomed along with the other two. 'Oh, well, here goes nothing,' he murmured, his heart beating fast.

He crawled through the hole and stood in the corner of the room. Sylver and Scirf saw him and their eyes opened wide. They tried to indicate that he should go back where he had come from, quickly, before he was seen. However, the next moment Jaspin the big mole looked up. His eyes, too, opened wider, but being narrow mole's eyes, and very blind, they were not made for roundness.

'Who in God's wormery are you?' he said, causing the other mole heads to swivel and stare.

'Hello, my undersoil friends,' said Mawk cheerily. 'I happened to be passing and saw that you subterraneans were playing *hollyhockers*, which just happens to be my favourite game. Never been beaten, as it happens. I'm not *bragging*, you understand – just a fact of life. I'm a natural . . .'

Scirf and Sylver, hanging from their wall chains, looked at each other in astonishment.

'You were *just passing*?' repeated a fat mole, popping a worm into his mouth and crunching hard. 'Where were you going? The antipodes?'

This made the other moles guffaw for a few moments.

'Ha, ha, – no, I wasn't going through the earth to the other side of the world, but I appreciate the joke, sir, I surely do. No, I'm one of those weasels who dislike sunlight and prefer the habitat of more sensible creatures like yourselves. My own kind tell me I've gone native, ha, ha,' continued Mawk, with another double click of his teeth, 'but I pay no mind to such trivial jibing. If someone has more superior natural surroundings to my own kind, well then I see no harm in taking advantage of that.'

'You like it underground, do you?' said Jaspin.

'My dear sir, there's nothing to compare with it,' said Mawk with all seriousness. 'It's the only place to be. The sunless world for me – and all that.'

'And you're not afraid you might run into a gang of rogue moles?' Slaker asked him, with a wink at his companions.

'*Rogue* moles?' cried Mawk in amusement. 'My dear sir, is there any other kind?'

The moles all clicked their teeth at this, finding it enormously funny.

'No, no,' continued Mawk, 'I'm not concerned by that at all. I was raised amongst footpads and cutpurses. Yeggs like yourselves, in fact. I was taught the art of unarmed self-defence by a travelling monk when I was but a kitten and so am well able to take care of myself.'

'Yeggs?' growled a mole. 'Who's this weasel calling a yegg?'

'You,' replied Jaspin. 'You've never been anything else, so why object now?'

Slaker said to Mawk, 'You fancy yourself a hollyhocker, do you, weasel? What's your name?'

'They call me Mawk-the-caster,' replied Mawk, walking to the table. 'Those who know of my reputation. I plough no fields, but I do scatter in brilliant fashion.'

Sylver's eyes rolled up inside his skull and he shook his head slowly.

Jaspin said softly, 'Would you care for a game, Mawk?' and rattled the seeds in the leather cup.

'Why, I'd love one,' replied Mawk, 'but I'm afraid you might find the stakes a little high.'

Slaker said, 'And what stakes might they be?'

'Freedom for those two weasels over there, if I win.'

'And if you lose?'

'I never lose,' Mawk stated, sitting at the table between Slaker and Jaspin.

'In that case,' Jaspin said, putting a moley foreleg around Mawk's shoulders, 'you will be playing for your life. If you win, you and those two hanging around over there can go free. If you lose, you die – horribly.'

Mawk swallowed hard. 'That sounds fair,' he said, trying to keep the catch out of his voice.

Until now Mawk had been quite enjoying himself, playing a valiant part in a play. Now he realized that it was all for real and that he was putting his life on the line. There was no doubt – if he failed to win, the moles would tear off his head and feed it to their worms. What was once Mawk-the-doubter would be a pool of blood and gore, with little unrecognizable bits of weasel floating in it. A mole could rip a weasel from tail to throat with one quick slash.

What was more, he had never played holly-hockers in his life before. He didn't even know what the rules were or how the scoring went.

Jaspin took the leather cup, rattled the seeds, touched his own nose for luck, then threw.

The seeds scattered over the table top, forming a shapeless pattern.

'Oh, *good throw*,' said Slaker, feeding Mawk's panic. 'I always said you were a skilful son of miner's mate.'

'Now you, weasel,' growled the big mole, gathering up the seeds and presenting Mawk with the cup. 'Take your time.'

Mawk swallowed hard again and swirled the seeds around inside the cup. Then he plucked at his whiskers for luck and cast the seeds on the table. The moles pored over his pattern with narrowed eyes. There was a deadly quiet in the underground room. Mawk was ready to faint. Sylver and Scirf were pale-eyed and silent. Jaspin placed his huge heavy hooked digging claw on the table with a clunk. 'Lucky beggar, aren't you?' he said slowly. 'You really *can* play hollyhockers, can't you?'

A soft uniform pair of sighs came from the two weasels hanging on the wall behind him.

Mawk felt elated. A heady rush of blood went to his head. 'Well, you know,' he said modestly, 'some of it's in the paddy-paws and some of it's in the claws of the gods. Now, if you good gentle-moles will excuse me, I'll release my companions and we'll be on our way. If any of you want lessons at any time, I'm available on Mondays and Thursdays in Halfmoon Wood, County Elleswhere . . .'

The claw clamped down over his right foreleg, pinning Mawk to the table. 'Not so fast,' said Jaspin. 'Best of three.'

'Well, hold on a moment,' said Mawk, the panic welling up inside him again. 'We never said that. If you want to change the rules halfway through . . .'

'It's *always* best of three,' replied Slaker. 'I thought you were an expert hollyhocker?'

'Well, yes I am, but in *our* part of the country we

329

play sudden death, you know? I mean, it's much more exciting. One throw and that's it, ha, ha, a kingdom gone and a kingdom gained. Now, if you'll just . . .'

'Best of three,' repeated Jaspin. 'Have a worm.'

He dangled a fat one in front of Mawk's nose and kept it there until Mawk took it in his mouth and swallowed it without crunching. It went down wriggling. Mawk could still feel it moving moments after, when he was shaking the cup again.

'Best of three it is,' he said, belching softly. 'Come *on*, hollyhock seeds!'

Chapter Thirty-four

'Right,' said Jaspin, 'it's your throw first this time.'

Mawk gathered up the seeds and put them in the leather cup. He shook them for so long the rattling was clearly irritating the moles, then cast the seeds onto the table top.

'Oh, *bad luck*,' said Slaker in a delighted voice. 'I thought you never lost at hollyhockers.'

'Wait a minute,' said Mawk. 'Jaspin hasn't thrown yet.'

'If you want me to,' said Jaspin, 'but you've thrown a jabbyknocker – no-one could do a worse throw than *that*.'

He filled the cup and tossed the seeds out again contemptuously, not even bothering to look at them. The other moles murmured in great satisfaction. Mawk knew that he had lost the second throw.

'So,' he said, swallowing hard, 'it's all down to the third throw, is it?'

'Unless one of us throws a widdershins, of course, then the whole game is void and we start again.'

'Of course,' Mawk said, wondering what on earth Jaspin was talking about. 'That goes without saying.'

'Or a hurdy-gurdy,' interrupted Slaker, 'in which case, of course, the thrower gets a second throw.'

'Naturally,' murmured Mawk. 'Hurdy-gurdies are my speciality.'

'Not forgetting,' called Scirf from his position on the wall, 'that if both of you throw a Molly Maguire, the thrower who threw the second Molly Maguire has the choice of whether to rethrow, double his score or halve his opponent's score – unless, of course, he throws a widdershins or hurdy-gurdy on the rethrow, in which case—'

'Somebody shut him up,' growled Jaspin. 'We need to get on with the game.'

Mawk glanced towards Scirf. 'But is he right?' he asked Jaspin.

'Of course he's right, but he doesn't need to go on about it,' snarled the mole bully. 'The rules are simple enough, after all.'

'They are?' gulped Mawk.

'I thought you'd played this before,' said Slaker, his narrow eyes narrowing even further. 'You said you were an expert. You said you never lost.'

Mawk rattled the cup and threw the seeds. 'How's that then?' he cried triumphantly, not knowing what on earth he had thrown. 'Pick the bones out of that lot!'

The moles stared down at the table and nodded slowly.

'Pretty good,' murmured Jaspin, gathering up the seeds into the cup. 'Not bad at all.'

Mawk was elated. He glanced towards Sylver and Scirf, seeking their approval. They were staring at Jaspin, who was now rattling the cup.

The seeds were cast.

'HA!' cried Jaspin, punching the air with his heavy claw. 'YES!'

Mawk didn't like the sound of that. 'Does that mean you've won?' he said. 'Or have you thrown a widdershins, hurdy-gurdy or Molly Maguire?'

'Can't you see, weasel? You're doomed to decorate the wall with your pelt.' Jaspin turned to the delighted Slaker and the other moles. 'Find the weasel some suitable chains.'

Mawk groaned. Two moles came and took him, dragging him towards the wall.

At that moment another mole entered the room. In fact he was so big he seemed to fill it completely. All the other moles stared at this newcomer in silence. Jaspin tried to sneak the cup of seeds under the table but they rattled and drew attention to him. The new big mole let out a long breath. 'What's all this, then? Have you been gambling – AGAINST MY EXPRESS ORDERS?'

Jaspin almost fell over he was shaking so much. 'I'm sorry, Kinger, we – we got bored.'

'I'll give you *bored*, Jaspin. You, Slaker, you let this go on? Who are those three? What are they doing in my secret hideout? I want some answers, NOW!'

Clearly this was not a mole to be trifled with. The prince had arrived back in his kingdom to find it in chaos. His subjects were quaking with fear.

'These? This? Them? Er –' Slaker stumbled over his words – 'they're weasels from Halfmoon Wood. Sylver—'

'Sylver?' repeated Kinger, stepping forward and studying the three weasels. 'The outlaw?'

'The very same,' said Sylver.

Kinger turned to his moles. 'Let them go, you

fools. They're enemies of Prince Poynt. Anyone who's an enemy of Prince Poynt is a friend of the moles. Quickly, get them down. Send them on their way.'

'But – but we've sent a note to Falshed – we could get money for 'em,' said Jaspin.

Kinger tapped Jaspin's skull with his digging claw. 'Do you *ever* think? What's in that great domed head of yours? When has Falshed ever paid a mole for anything? Oh, yes, he'll *promise* payment, but you'll never get a groat out of him in a hundred years. What's more, when he finds out where we are, he'll come down here with a thousand stoats and destroy us.'

'Well,' said Jaspin wildly, 'won't these three tell on us?'

'You have my word,' interrupted Sylver, 'that we will keep your hideout a secret.'

'The word of a weasel?' cried Jaspin.

'There is honour among weasels,' Scirf said. 'If Sylver gives you his word, then – then you've got it . . .'

Kinger stared at the three weasels and then nodded hard. 'I believe them,' he said. 'Set the weasels free.'

'Oh, thank you, sir,' whined Mawk in a silky voice. 'Thank you ever so much.'

'Except that one,' snarled Kinger. 'Cut that one's throat and throw him to the wolves.'

'Erk!' cried Mawk, his heart stopping for a moment.

Kinger added, 'That is, if he speaks to me again, cut his throat and throw him to the wolves. Now get them out of here. I hate the smell of weasels in my den.'

Sylver and Scirf were released from their manacles and the three weasels were then led through a series of mazes up to the surface. There they were sent on their way. They found themselves just half a league from the church where they had spent the night.

'Time to push on,' said Sylver. 'Good try, Mawk. You did well down there. At least you didn't run away. I'm proud of you.'

'You are?' Mawk cried.

'So am I,' Scirf added. 'You didn't do bad at all, but I'm goin' to have to teach you hollyhockers, Mawk. You're a terrible player.'

'Huh, I hope I never have to shake a cup full of seeds again,' replied Mawk. 'So you can forget the teaching. I've got better things to do with my time than gamble for worms.'

By this time the trio had passed through a forest and reached the river Bronn where they looked across at the unnamed marshes on the other side. Somewhere over there the stoat wizard Flaggatis was schooling the rats in their guttural half-language. The three weasels had to get through the rat hordes to reach the Far Weald.

Scirf looked back now and saw they were being pursued. 'Sheriff Falshed's coming,' he cried. 'I can see the shiny helmets.'

'Quickly,' said Sylver, 'we must make a raft and cross the river. He won't dare follow us into the unnamed marshes. The rats would slaughter his stoats.'

'Won't they slaughter us?' Mawk said.

'Yes, if they catch us,' replied his leader, 'but we don't intend to let that happen, do we?'

So the three weasels gathered rushes and

caulking clay and began to make their raft. They finished just as Falshed's troops were coming over the last rise. Mawk jumped on, followed by Scirf, and then finally Sylver stepped on board. Stoats rushed down the slope and flung their darts, which plopped into the water all around the raft. Coots and moorhens immediately swam for cover, godwits and avocets took to the air, ducks paddled screaming for the safety of the far bank.

'Come back!' yelled Falshed. 'You'll be torn to shreds by the rats.'

'If we do come back,' called Sylver, 'will you promise to let us go?'

There was a moment's silence from Falshed, before he cried in response, 'Of course.'

'Yes, I'm sure,' Scirf said sarcastically.

Mawk cried, 'No, perhaps he means it. Maybe we're doing the wrong thing here. I mean – the *rats*.'

It was at that moment that Sylver caught a glimpse of a red coat, further down the bank, half hidden by a flush of reeds. Then the wearer stepped into view and watched contemplatively as the raft went across the river. It was Magellan, his bow and quiver in his paws. He stared at Sylver and even over that distance Sylver could sense the spite, the hatred, being directed at him. Magellan was saying by his presence that he would be waiting, if and when the three weasels returned.

'Mawk,' said Sylver quietly, 'the rats are less of a problem to us than that rusty shape over there.'

Mawk looked in the direction in which Sylver was pointing with his paw. 'Oh, I see what you mean. Yes, well perhaps we will brave the rats.'

Scirf said, 'One day I would like to have a go at that fox, you know.'

'You might get your wish on our return journey,' said Sylver, 'but for the moment we must concentrate on getting to Thunder Oak.'

When they reached the far bank, evening was coming in. The marshes are a spooky place at the best of times, but at night all you can hear is the rustle of adders swimming through the reeds, the murmurings of frogs and birds and, deeper in still, the harsh whisperings of Flaggatis's rats in their rat camps.

There was no time to sleep, even if they did feel brave enough to lie down on the damp rushy islands amongst the snakes. They had to move on through the marshes and be out the other side before the dawn came. Sylver led the way along faint paths in the moonlight.

At times they had to sneak single-file between rat camps, where there were strange ceremonies in progress. Dark shapes with long tails and glittering eyes clustered amongst reed huts, where pieces of rotting meat hung from long lines. The odour of the meat filled the hollows of the marshes. Fires were evident on which it seemed that things were being burned. It was not possible to find out *what* those things were, but they made squealing sounds.

Some of the rats milled around the fires, occasionally letting out insane-sounding shrieks, but whether of joy or fear, of hatred or jealousy, of pain or even death, none of the three pathfinders would ever know.

They did come across raised gibbets made of ghostly white driftwood, bleached branches and roots of trees bound with rags, on which bodies lay open to the elements. Gross carvings and strange drumskins decorated with symbols lined the edges of these platforms, some of which contained only bones.

It was impossible to see, without climbing up to the top of the structures, what types of creature those corpses had been. Indeed, there was no way of knowing whether these corpse-bearers were funeral platforms, or racks to display the remains of tortured victims.

Crows picked at entrails and lights, their weight making the platforms bend, creak and groan, as if the carcass were complaining of its treatment.

The very smell of evil was in the night air. Mawk could not stop trembling as they crept through the marshes, all the while wishing himself back in Halfmoon Wood. At one point they surprised a lone rat, drinking at a brackish puddle in the moonlight, but Scirf stunned the creature with a quick blow to the skull with a piece of driftwood.

'How long before we get out of the marshes?' whispered Mawk, who was going through his worst nightmare. 'Why are we taking this path?'

'Because the more direct route is dangerous,' answered Sylver. 'Do you want to fall into the claws of the rats? Can you imagine what would happen to you?'

'Only too vividly,' groaned Mawk.

At one point they passed a huge hardwood palace, built on stilts. It rose out of the marshes, dominating the scene around it, with dark oily splendour. There were small, mean windows, high curving roofs, and thick-logged towers. At the tops of the towers were rat sentries, their pointed faces clear in the moonlight. Covered walkways ran between towers. Ropes with nooses dangled from outreaching spars, blowing in the night breezes. There were no doors to be seen in the walls.

A single dim light glowed behind one small window in the great wooden fortress with its protective palisade of spikes, while the rest of the place remained in darkness.

'Flaggatis's home,' whispered Sylver as they passed it by. 'The wizard's palace.'

'That light . . . ?' questioned Scirf.

'Him,' replied Sylver.

Rats plopped into the stinking marshwater around the palace, sometimes climbing out onto islands covered in bladderwort to shake themselves. Sylver guessed that the way into the fortress was under the water and that the rats were constantly on their guard against attacks. It would be a brave and perhaps foolish army that tried to take Flaggatis on his own ground.

'I just want to have a quick look through that window,' said Sylver. 'It won't take a minute.'

'Oh Gawd,' murmured Mawk.

Sylver left the other two and swam to the wooden fortress. A weasel's claws are deft at climbing. He found tiny pawholds – small knots of wood, pieces of bark – and climbed upwards, listening for the sentries moving around on the walkways above him. When he reached the window with the light, he peered inside.

Sylver had never seen Flaggatis, but he recognized him instantly. He sat at a table, an old stoat in an open flowing gown of midnight-blue. His pointed face held a mixture of infinite wisdom and ungovernable evil. His whole demeanour glowed

339

with a wickedness which ruled his very life and made him such a miserable creature.

In other respects he could have been Lord Haukin, sitting in his study at Thistle Hall, delighting in the capture of knowledge. Books and parchments littered the floor and table. They were also stacked on the shelves attached to the walls. Flaggatis had various instruments of glass and brass within reach. One, a set of callipers, he held in his paw. He seemed to be checking distances on a chart held down at the corners with heavy badgers' skulls, making calculations, taking notes down laboriously.

Plotting the conquest of Welkin, thought Sylver.

As if the weasel's thoughts had been spoken aloud, Flaggatis suddenly looked up and stared at the window. Sylver ducked out of sight, his heart beating. He had forgotten that Flaggatis was a great if unruly wizard, who would have the power to sense the presence of enemies. Perhaps he could even hear thoughts, when they were spoken like words in a weasel's head.

Sure enough, a hollow moaning note went through the palace, as if someone were blowing through the eyesocket of a skull. Guards began to run from place to place and rat shrieks went up. When Sylver was brave enough to glance in at the window again, Flaggatis was gone, his lamp dimmed.

Sylver climbed back down to the water and swam back to his friends.

The weasels continued through the marshland, running into pockets of rats occasionally, but always managing to stay out of scent and sight. They had not been expected and were a small enough unit to be able to slip through the rat defences. The rats were numerous and savage, but not especially well organized, despite the great efforts of the stoat wizard, who hoped one day to use them to conquer the rest of Welkin.

Finally the three weasels came to harder ground. A great dyke had been built across the country here, an earthen wall several metres high. It was called Ooma's Dyke. On top of the wall ran a live hedge of thorns, which was kept trimmed by the monks of the Far Weald. This earthworks was obviously meant to keep the rat hordes at bay, but Sylver had been told of a narrow tunnel under the dyke, which would take only one weasel at a time.

'It's near a small marsh island covered in lavender,' said Sylver, 'so use your noses to find it.'

Chapter Thirty-five

They found the passage through Ooma's Dyke and ran along it one at a time to emerge beyond.

On the other side the landscape was still mostly flat, with a huge sky around and above it, but the marshes had gone. Instead there were grasslands as far as the eye could see, broken only by the occasional shrub. In the east were some jagged hills, but these were in the distance. Since the air was clear, Sylver could see these tors quite distinctly, and noted the way they rose in coarse, rugged fashion.

Some of the jutting crags had small pine trees clinging to their sparse soil, which dripped their needles upon the plain below. A building perched precariously on a ledge at the top of a difficult and hazardous climb.

This was the Far Weald, a place inhabited by misfits and followers of strange religions.

'Any wolves up here?' asked Mawk, looking round nervously. 'It looks like wolf country.'

'Thousands,' cried Scirf, who had decided he enjoyed teasing Mawk. 'I expect we'll run into a pack of wolves every few leagues.'

Mawk bared his teeth at Scirf. 'No we won't.'

'If you know so much,' sniffed Scirf, 'why did you ask then?'

Sylver led the way across the grasslands, stepping out with a certain urgency. The sooner they found Thunder Oak the better, for Magellan would not allow them to linger long in the Far Weald without attacking them. He was such a devious creature, Magellan. There were good and there were evil foxes, as with any other creature, and Magellan fitted firmly into the second category.

Fortunately the grass was quite tall, so when the weasels were on all fours they were well hidden. When they wanted to get their bearings they simply went briefly up on their hind legs, noted their whereabouts, and then made adjustments to their course accordingly.

Towards evening of that day they came to a place which was eerie in its atmosphere. Sylver could not tell why he believed this part of the weald was any different from the rest, but he felt it deep in his bones. Perhaps it was something to do with the way the light fell obliquely upon the grasslands and lit it with a faint greenish tinge. Or maybe it was the way the brooding sky hung above the place as if it were about to fall any second with a thunderous crash. Or then again, it might have been the silence, which had a heartbeat out here in the wilderness.

But it was only when Scirf gave a shout and pointed that Sylver's fears were confirmed.

Out of the tall grasslands rose hundreds of figures. They were rag-tag creatures, tatterdemalions, things of wispy limbs and bodies draped with shabby, threadbare garments. The great majority of them hopped along on one leg, though here and there were effigies with two. Their faces were for the most part hideous copies of human faces, with saw-tooth mouths, triangular noses and dark circular eyes with no pupils. They wore battered hats, frayed coats, toeless boots. Straw poked from sleeves, from collars, from trouser bottoms. They carried heavy sticks in their skeletal hands.

'Scarecrows,' murmured Scirf. 'I wonder what they want?'

One of the creatures, a tall scarecrow standing higher than a human, towered over the three weasels. Its ragged black tunic was tied with string where its buttons should have been, the chest and arms beneath were a pair of crossed staves sparsely covered with mouldy hay. The sleeves of the coat were worn and showed dirty white at the cuffs. One of the arms had torn away from the shoulder and was hanging limply, threatening to drop to the ground at any moment. Its bruised face peered at them from beneath a yellowish hat with a torn brim. It could have reached down and beaten them with its stick. There was a sort of carved smile on its wooden face, though without any kind of mirth in it. It stared at the weasels with hollow lidless eyes. 'Where – is – the – payment?' it asked.

'Payment?' repeated Sylver. 'I wasn't aware we needed to pay anyone to cross the Far Weald.'

'No – payment, no – pass.'

The scarecrow sounded definite. Behind it the other scarecrows were crowding, nudging each other for a look at the three weasels, who felt distinctly uncomfortable under the glare of so many strange eyes. One scarecrow, like one cockroach, is not a particularly frightening thing. But hundreds of either scarecrows or cockroaches,

344

clustered together, make one's fur crawl in a dozen different ways.

'We have no money to make any payment,' said Sylver carefully. 'If you'll just step aside and let us pass, we'll try to send it to you by messenger later in the year.'

'No – payment, no – pass.'

'We have no *money*, cloth-ears,' cried Scirf. 'Didn't you hear?'

The scarecrow whirled and glared at Scirf with venomous eyes. 'No – want – money. Want – tobacco – pipes.'

'Pipes?' cried Scirf. 'You want pipes?'

'Want – pipes – for – dignity – and – great – presence.'

Mawk muttered, 'You want to look dignified? That'll take more than a pipe, fella-me-lad. I mean, you're a stalwart chap, but I think you need to steer well clear of dinner parties and official functions.'

'What?' cried the scarecrow, rounding on Mawk.

'I said smoking is bad for your health.'

'Me – King – Jumble. Me – great – person,' growled the scarecrow. 'You – ugly – little – weasel. You – give – me – meershaum. You – give – me – briar.'

'No need to get personal, King Jumble or whatever your name is,' sniffed Scirf. 'The fact is, we haven't got any pipes, and that's that. Now if you'll just part your scarecrow ranks, we'll be on our way . . .'

The stick was raised above Sylver's head. 'No – smoking – pipe, no – pass,' cried the scarecrow angrily.

Its words were repeated by the multitude

345

behind it. They crowded forward, waving their sticks. Black, empty eyes regarded the weasels with menace. A sort of low moan rose from the heart of the mob. They hopped and shuffled on their stick-legs, some in kilts, some in leggings. Their puffy, straw-filled arms waved in the air. It was obvious that the scarecrows were serious in their demands for briar and meershaum pipes. And they clearly regarded the north of the Far Weald as their territory, where right of passage could be given only by one of their number.

These creatures were neither human nor statue, but a collection of oddments shuffled haphazardly and thrown together to resemble one or the other of them. They were empty-headed things, it seemed, which spent their time reflecting on their own images as dignified creatures. They had no birthplace, unless it was the corn sheaf, the wood pile and the rag-bag. They had no common image, for each was different from the other. They had no heritage, but what they demanded for themselves and their kind.

Sylver retreated. 'They mean it,' he said. 'We'll never get through that lot with our lives. I'm not sure what to do now.'

Scirf said, 'We've obviously got to lay our paws on some stinking old pipes, somehow. Any ideas, Mawk?'

Mawk considered the problem for a moment, then came up with a possible answer. 'I have heard of a sanctuary near here, where monks who follow a deity they call the Great One reside. Why don't we find this holy place and ask if they've got any pipes?'

Sylver sighed. 'Well, we don't have much

346

choice, do we? Have you any idea in which direction the sanctuary lies?'

'That way, I think,' Mawk said. 'High up on a ledge, in those craggy mountains towards the east.'

So the weasels had to deviate from their direct path and go east, into the jagged hills. It took all night to reach them and by the dawn they were exhausted. They slept in a cave which smelled of bears and then continued climbing a steep goat track, which wound like a whiplash up to a crag, on which was perched a priory of sorts. A bell was ringing as the weasels approached the building by the sheer, dusty path.

Sylver knocked on the wooden door. The sound echoed throughout the stone building within. After a while a small panel in the door slid back, making him jump. The opening framed a fat stoat's face. 'Yes, brother?'

'Er, greetings to the followers of the Great One,' said Sylver. 'We come to seek sustenance.'

'You are weasels of the Faith?'

'No, we are simply weary travellers, who are on our way northwards.'

'The Great One turns no stoat or weasel from His door,' said the monk. 'You may partake of the Wayfarers' Dole. Enter and be thankful.'

'I'm ever so thankful,' Scirf told the monk as they entered a bare courtyard. 'Got any nice stew?'

'Here we eat the grain,' said the monk, carefully closing and locking the door to the courtyard. 'You will receive one cube of bread and a goblet of ale. This is the stipulated Wayfarers' Dole to which travellers are entitled. If you wish to rest, then you may stay half a day. Then you must be on your

347

way. This is a holy place, a place of quiet and meditation.'

A bell was clanging loudly in a tower over the courtyard.

'I see what you mean,' Scirf said. 'Quiet as the grave.'

They were led to a set of stone steps and down to a kitchen, where monks were busy baking bread in the massive oven built for humans. A roaring fire threw out the warmth of a blacksmith's forge and heated the room to a stifling atmosphere.

The stoat bakers managed very well, considering it took three of them to open and close the oven door. It was a bit of a struggle but the job got done. They wore thick gloves of sacking, which had been charred black by the heat. They threw in charcoal and fed a furnace which would have melted pig iron. When they pawdled the bread, it was with platters on long poles, and it came out steaming.

Sylver found the smell of the kitchen wonderful. There is nothing like the odour of newly baked bread to make one's saliva glands run. The three weasels were sat at a table, given a huge cube of bread each and a goblet of ale. They filled their stomachs.

Scirf watched the monks scurrying here, there and everywhere, listened to the matins being intoned in the chapel, and wondered at the simple sparseness of his surroundings. It seemed to him that this was a nice quiet simple life. No concerns about where the next meal was coming from, or how to get a roof over your head for the night. No worries about the outside world. Here was a life without the stresses and strains.

'What 'ave you got to do to be a monk, then?' he asked a passing kitchen friar. 'Be holy, I s'pect.'

'You have to *believe*,' replied the monk, 'and be faithful to that belief.'

Scirf, who had never been faithful to much at all, nodded enthusiastically. 'I s'pect I could do *that* easily enough. You want me to come and stay?'

The monk's eyes opened wider. 'You wish to be a novitiate?'

'Nope, I want to be a monk.'

'First you must humble yourself, become a *learner*, so to speak. You must bring yourself low, cast off all worldly desires, purify your spirit.'

'Oh, yes?'

'Yes. Then, eventually, you may be in a virtuous enough state to receive holy orders. You will become a serving monk, who waits on the more senior monks. Sometimes you may be allowed to go out into the garden to tend the vegetables.'

'Listen, this sounds like a long job – how many weeks before I become a real monk?'

'Some are able to purge themselves and take holy orders within a period of seven years.'

'Seven *years*?' cried Scirf. 'That's a lifetime. Hey, look, friar, I've been a dung-tender for three years. That's a bit like tending vegetables, init? Can I get them knocked off the seven?'

The monk sighed. 'I don't think you quite understand the gravity of the position to which you hope to ascend, brother.'

Scirf nodded. 'I think you're right. I won't be a monk after all. I'll be a night watchman instead. There don't seem to be much difference between the two.'

Once they had eaten, Sylver asked to see the

prior, the most senior of the monks, and they were taken to his cell. The prior was at prayers and the three had to wait outside cooling their heels. Eventually, they were admitted. The prior was now sitting on a high stool at an enormous desk, poring over a pile of parchments. Mawk said he thought the prior looked a bit like Lord Haukin, poring over his books.

'I s'pect they're both very good porers,' observed Scirf, as if he were talking about teapots.

The prior lifted his head slowly, as if the act was very difficult for him to perform. 'What can I do for you, brothers?'

'Everybody's related round here,' muttered Scirf.

Sylver said, 'We're sorry to trouble you with your learning and prayers and everything, but we need some briar pipes to get through that army of scarecrows to the west. Is it possible for you to find us some? You know, the kind humans used to smoke tobacco in. Filthy habit, and dangerous, too, with all that fire and smoke, but we're sure they'll only be used for show, no-one would set light to them . . .'

While Sylver was speaking the prior's expression, even his demeanour, had been undergoing an extraordinary change. His features twisted into an ugly mask; his paws gripped the edge of the desk and went white at the knuckles; his breath came hissing out through his nostrils. 'The scarecrows?' he snarled, his face changing for a moment. 'The scarecrows?'

Then he seemed to be aware that he was in the company of strangers. He set about composing himself again. Gradually he managed to pull him-

350

self together and get himself under control. Finally he smiled sweetly at the three weasels. 'Pipes?' he said. 'Of course not. We don't approve of smoking here, any more than we approve of mirrors.'

Sylver looked at the prior in surprise.

'Mirrors? Who mentioned mirrors?'

'I did,' said the prior. 'Scarecrows hate mirrors – they're terrified of seeing their own image. They're such an ugly, motley crowd of . . . but' – he made a gesture with his forepaws – 'we are not allowed any looking-glasses in this establishment. It was a rule made by our founder. Mirrors encourage vanity. Vanity is the worst of all sins.'

'No pipes then?' said Sylver, disappointed.

The prior shook his head sadly.

'And you're sure you haven't got just one mirror in the place?' asked Scirf. 'I mean, I'd rather give the scarecrows what they want, but failing that we could use mirrors to make 'em let us go through, if that was the only way.'

'No, not a single one,' murmured the prior. 'My order of monks does not allow the use of any reflecting instrument. We have no mirrors, no polished bronze plates, no water tubs – we are not allowed to see our own image.'

'Because of vanity?'

'Just so,' said the prior, putting his claws together. 'Vainglory, brother. The monk who sees his own face and form is lost. The Terrible One will take his soul and mangle it beyond all hope of recognition. You will have to leave, I'm sorry – the mere mention of looking-glasses is a sin. We are modest monks, we do not indulge in such horrific pastimes as studying our own *contemptible* features.'

Sylver said, 'You feel the stoat and weasel form is contemptible?'

'Utterly. Only the spirit is worthy of any recognition, and the spirit cannot be seen in a mirror.'

Sylver stared into the prior's goodly features. They were composed and serene. He could see that they were going to get nowhere with this saintly monk, who saw the use of mirrors as a great evil, to be spurned. When a stoat's soul was set on doing good, there was no turning it with argument. Sylver decided it would be best to leave. 'You have no advice for us, then,' he said, 'regarding the scarecrows – how to get through them, good prior? What shall we do with the scarecrows?'

At the mention of the scarecrows once more, the prior's face again twisted into a demoniacal mask. It was as if the word 'scarecrow' were a trigger which transformed a saint into a devil. Whatever the scarecrows had done to the good prior, it must have been appalling.

'The scarecrows!' he shrieked, with a terrible fanatical gleam in his eyes. 'May they rot where they stand. May they be blown to pieces and the bits scattered by a great wind. May they become homes for woodworms, weevils and moth larvae.'

He writhed in his seat while he spoke the words, as if he had a struggle going on inside him. 'Oh, how I would like to make those scarecrows suffer,' he growled plaintively. 'How I would like to know they grovelled before three lowly serfs, three scruffy woodland weasels, three useless down-and-outs of no apparent worth whatsoever—'

'Here, just a minute . . .' began Mawk indignantly, but Sylver realized something

352

extraordinary was going on and silenced Mawk with a nudge.

'You want to know why I hate them?' the prior said, lifting his pointed face. 'You want to know why I would like them to feel the long foreleg of the priory's law? Because they are runaways! Yes, they were made by humans to protect gardens and fields, and they refused to do the same for us. They pulled up their sticks and just walked away, leaving the gardens and fields at the mercy of the birds. They no longer work for the cause for which they were created – they simply whine for something they call "dignity".'

'Well,' said Scirf, 'I may not speak for my two mates here, but I've got some sympathy with that. Poor old scarecrows was slaves when the humans was here. Now you want 'em to be slaves again? Don't agree with you there, chum.'

'They leave our seeds unprotected,' continued the prior, staring at the wall as if he had not heard. 'We monks rely on our crops to make us ri— to feed the poor. Our corn is stolen by the birds before it is ripe. The birds steal all our raspberries, our strawberries.' He paused to fume, then continued again. 'I do not blame the birds. I blame the scarecrows. Those bundles of useless straw and sticks.'

'Well, we have nothing against scarecrows, as such,' said Sylver.

'You want to pass through their ranks unharmed, don't you?' hissed the prior. 'Those empty turnip heads won't listen to reason, you know. They're as thick as this desk!' He rapped the top of the mahogany desk with his claw. 'You need briar pipes or mirrors to get past the scarecrows, and you haven't got either.'

'No,' said Sylver, sighing. 'Well, we're sorry to have troubled you – we'll be on our way.'

'Wait,' said the prior, his lips tightening over his pointed little fangs. 'Just wait a minute. Let me think.'

Finally he seemed to come to a decision. His brow cleared. A determined look came over his face. 'Why not?' he said eventually. 'But I want your solemn promise that anything I reveal to you here and now will not go beyond this room. I – I may be able to help you.'

Scirf said without hesitation, 'We promise, yer priorship.'

The prior studied his three guests a moment longer, then he pressed a hidden switch under his desk and, to the astonishment of the other three, a stone door swung open in the wall behind him. Even from where they stood the outlaws could behold the glittering treasure secretly hoarded by the prior. It was a cache of mirrors – dozens of them. Some were large and oval, with ornate gilt frames. Others were simple, with wooden edging. Some were hand mirrors, others clearly intended for hanging in great halls. Their silvery surfaces were all highly polished, with not a speck of dust among them. They were clearly loved and cherished objects, items which were in constant use by someone.

The prior turned and reached into the secret store to stroke its contents. 'My lovely mirrors,' he murmured. 'My lovely, lovely mirrors. Who is the fairest of them all?' he added, holding up a hand mirror and peering into it. 'No need to ask.' He wetted his paw and smoothed down the fur on his brow.

The prior then appeared to remember he was not alone and turned to the three astonished weasels. 'We are all miserable sinners,' he whined. 'What can I say to you? The spirit is weak. I am so beautiful I cannot resist adoring myself.'

'You were sayin' about the scarecrows,' reminded Scirf.

The prior's features were again transformed into a hideous visage. 'Take one or two and do as you will with the scarecrows. Make them suffer.'

He then began sorting through the looking-glasses. 'Here, take this one – no, it's one of my favourites – this one, then – no, I can't bear to part with it – this one? Oh, look, I'll turn my back and you choose some, but not the one with the ormolu cherubs around the frame, and not the pretty one with the gold fleur-de-lis on the blue background – oh, oh, just take some and go. Get out of here. And if you ever mention my looking-glasses to another soul, I'll be very unhappy.'

The three weasels went to the cache, took two mirrors each, and hurried out of the presence of this mad monk.

Chapter Thirty-six

The three weasels left the sanctuary and travelled again to the land of the scarecrows.

When the day was bright and the light was good, the three weasels set out to pass through the mob of angry scarecrows. The mirrors had been fixed to the ends of sticks. These they held up and turned, this way and that, so the scarecrows could not approach them without seeing their own faces.

When their reflections were caught, revealing to them their own strange forms, the scarecrows fell back. They cried out plaintively with the agony of souls in great torment. They moaned and clutched at their clothes, plucked the straw from their throats, disfigured themselves. 'Too thin!' they cried, on viewing their limbs and torsos. 'Too thin, too thin!'

It is well known that scarecrows cannot see their own bodies, for having necks made of poles they cannot bend them. They cannot look down at themselves. They can swivel their heads from right to left, even spin them, but they cannot see below the chins they did not own. Having no joints, they cannot lift their arms above their shoulders.

They were in the image of man, yet a grotesque caricature of that image, and they hated themselves not just for being copies, but for being inferior copies, for having no flesh on their stick-bones, for having no soft, rounded parts.

'Effigy!' they cried in despair. 'Effigy!'

The scarecrows obviously knew what the others looked like, but secretly in each straw heart was a hope that they themselves were different, that they did not have bodies and heads like those they saw around them. Each one dreamed that it really had handsome features, a fine complexion, rosy cheeks and bright eyes. Each one was desperate to have sturdy legs with muscles, strong thick arms, a plump waist.

'Is that me?' they would wail, when they glimpsed their faces in the mirrors. 'Oh – is that *me*?'

The weasels felt sorry for the scarecrows and would have taken the time to talk to them. They would have liked to explain to the straw men that looks were not important in this world, only what was in the heart. But of course the scarecrows were so lost in their own desire for beautiful countenances, so frantic to be considered attractive, that they would not pay attention to any weasel trying to advise them.

'You are what you are,' called Sylver. 'You have no need to be ashamed of yourselves. Scarecrows are not supposed to look exactly like humans; they're supposed to look like scarecrows. Stop trying to be something else and be proud of what you were meant to be. In my opinion you have far more worth than the false prior who gave us these mirrors, and he is the vainest creature in the world.'

'But we are hollow useless things,' King Jumble cried. 'We are ugly, empty creatures.'

357

'Only if you *think* you are,' Sylver said. 'It's all in your own minds.'

Unhappily the ragamuffin creatures took no heed of these words, but parted, crying with hollow voices that the weasels were 'crows and seagulls'.

The insults meant nothing to Sylver and his outlaws, of course, for they believed every living thing on the earth was of fine mettle, unless it proved itself otherwise by some malicious act or deed. Crows and seagulls were no better or worse than any other creature. Even amongst the stoats there were those who disagreed with the treatment meted out to weasels.

However, scarecrows had been feuding with certain birds since the beginning of their existence: birds which refused to respect the scarecrow and treated it with disregard and disdain. If there was ever bird lime on a scarecrow's coat you can be sure it would be that of an impertinent seagull or crow. It was little wonder that every member of the crow family, even the beautiful fawn-and-blue jay, and each and every one of the gull community, was considered contemptible by scarecrows. The fact was that the scarecrow, despite its name, did not scare crows – only timid finches, doves and pigeons.

Once out of the land of the scarecrows, the trio had nothing between them and Thunder Oak except a wasteland.

It took half a day to cover this distance, and finally they were in sight of their goal.

'There it is,' breathed Mawk. 'I can't believe it. We've made it.'

Thunder Oak stood in the middle of its own

desert, the last vestige of a once magnificent forest. From the black-and-gold heavens above came shafts of light to illuminate the old oak's husk with celestial splendour. It was a living tree no longer, with stark branches reaching up like human arms, the ends of which clawed at the air like fingers. Down its thick hollow trunk was a mighty split, blackened by fire, where the great tree had been blasted open by a thunderbolt. Ten large men would have fitted easily inside the dark yawning wound.

This, once the heart of the forest, had been torn asunder by a ferocious electrical storm.

'Thunder Oak,' whispered Scirf. 'I never thought I'd see it – I never thought I would. Now I'm here, right at the top of the world, and there's the Thunder Oak.'

'Come on,' said Mawk excitedly, 'let's go and look for the clue.'

However, as they approached the blackened shell of the once mighty oak, something stirred in its bowels.

Mawk whispered, 'I saw something move in there.'

The creature uncurled itself, having been asleep in the dark hollow of the old tree, and emerged to confront the three weasels.

It had the body of a lion and the head, wings and claws of an eagle. The eyes in its feathered head were hooded and unnatural looking. A terrible beak slowly opened and closed in some kind of warning. Massive talons gripped the earth as it walked, crushing stones to powder. The ridged muscles along its leonine back rippled as it walked.

'A griffin,' murmured Sylver. 'Whatever you do,

don't turn and run. Keep facing it. You'll never outrun a griffin. It has wings as well as the fastest legs in Welkin.'

'Oh, Gawd,' whispered Mawk. 'I want to go home.'

'Pull yourself together,' Scirf said, 'it's only a – only a griffin.' He did not seem too convinced himself by the word 'only'.

The griffin paused a few paces from the oak and stood there as if on guard. Now that they were closer they could see that the mythical creature was a statue. It had probably once stood on a building somewhere, but now appeared to have another function – that of protecting Thunder Oak. The weasels were puny beside this stone monster and had to proceed cautiously.

When they approached the oak, the tree's guardian spoke to them in the dull accents of granite. 'Stop! Where are you going?'

'To the oak,' said Sylver without hesitation. 'We seek a clue to the whereabouts of the humans. We are told it can be found in Thunder Oak.'

The griffin seemed to consider this statement very carefully before forming a reply. 'There are those of us,' it said, 'who have no wish to see the humans return.'

'Do you think that's fair on the human race?'

Again, the griffin pondered on this question for a long time before answering. 'Perhaps the humans themselves do not want to be found.'

'I can't believe that they *all* wanted to desert Welkin,' said Sylver. 'Perhaps some of them had their reasons for going, but humans are famous for disagreeing amongst themselves. Maybe those who wish to return are unable to get back. Perhaps they are lost, or trapped in some way. I would like to give them the opportunity of coming home.'

'And if you're wrong?'

'If none of them wish to come back, why then they can stay where they are, can't they?'

The griffin shook its great feathered head and rippled its muscular lion's back. 'You may not approach the oak. I have dedicated my life to guarding its secret. Be on your way.'

Sylver was now at a loss what to do. He knew the three weasels were no match for the griffin, which seemed determined to keep them at bay, whatever the strength of their arguments. The trouble with stone creatures was that you could not reason with them. They had no real reasoning powers, only the pretence of them, just as their bodies were a pretence of real creatures.

'Perhaps if we approach the oak from three different directions,' he told the other two, 'one of us will get through and find the clue.'

Mawk shook his head vigorously. 'I'm not doing that – I'll get killed. You two can do it if you like, but I'm not going any closer than this.' He sounded emphatic.

Scirf said, 'For once I agree with Mawk, Sylver – that there monster would rip all three of us to pieces in as many seconds as there are syllables in "rhubarb". But I think I've got an idea. It might work. Let me give it a try.'

'Anything,' said the desperate Sylver. 'We've come this far – we can't go home empty-pawed.'

Scirf nodded and turned towards the griffin. He then walked deliberately up to the creature, which stood up and bristled as he approached.

Mawk and Sylver had no idea what Scirf was up

to, unless it was to offer himself as a given sacrifice, in order to buy time for the other two to get past the griffin.

Suddenly, Scirf stopped and stood up on his hind legs.

He began swaying from side to side, very gently, like an aspen in a soft breeze. At the same time he began humming softly – the murmur of a satisfied honey bee – while his eyes were fixed on those of the griffin. Sylver watched this extraordinary exhibition with some remnant of a memory crawling out of a hole in his subconscious, though he could not recognize it for the moment, nor say where in his past it had come from.

Gradually, gradually, the griffin's hooded eyes began to close and its body began to wilt. It sank to its knees on the ground. Then after a while it rolled over, its eyes still half open, but now with a glazed look to them. Finally, it lay still, as if stone dead.

Scirf swaggered back to the other two.

'How did you do that?' said Mawk.

'Hypnotism,' said Scirf. 'The old grandweasel used to do it on chickens. He taught me when I was a kitten. It's a forgotten art these days though, init? You see, I thought the griffin, having an eagle's head, wasn't so far off from a chicken. They're both birds, ain't they? And I haven't lost me touch.'

'Well done,' said Sylver. 'Let's get to the oak before the griffin wakes up.'

The three weasels crept past the sleeping monster and swarmed over the oak. They looked in every crevice, every nook and cranny, until finally Mawk reached into a knot-hole and triumphantly extracted something.

It was a small wooden carving.

'This has got to be the clue,' he cried. 'Let's get out of here.'

The griffin was just stirring as they passed it. The trio resumed their old places, well away from the tree. If they tried to run away the creature might chase them. They had to pretend they had not moved.

'Eh? What?' said the griffin, coming round. 'No, you can't approach Thunder Oak – go away.'

'Oh, very well,' said Sylver, 'if you insist.'

The three weasels made off across the waste-land, back towards the land of the scarecrows. When they reached scarecrow territory they did the same as before, using the mirrors to get through the eerie mobs of human effigies. Finally they reached the marshes, where they camped for the night.

'Let's see it then,' said Scirf. 'What is it?'

Mawk produced the carving from his belt pouch. 'It looks like some kind of mouse to me,' he said studying it closely. 'Lying in a pool of water.'

'Dormouse,' confirmed Sylver. 'Look at its bushy tail. It's a dormouse, asleep in the middle of a pond.'

Scirf scratched his head. 'Well, what does that mean?'

'I don't know at the moment,' Sylver replied. 'I expect we'll have to wait until we get back, so that Lord Haukin can have a look at it. He's the most learned creature I know. He'll know what it means.'

'Who's going to carry the carving?' asked Mawk. 'We went through a lot to get it. It's very precious.'

'You can carry it,' replied Sylver. 'You're the best weasel for the job.'

'I am?' Mawk said, surprised. 'Why?'

'No-one has a survival instinct to rival yours, Mawk. You can be sure that if anyone lives to get through this expedition, it will be you. You would send your own grandweasel to the spirit world, if it meant that Mawk survived.'

Mawk frowned. 'I'm not sure I like the way you put that.'

'Whether you like it or not, you're carrying the carving. Scirf and I will protect you all the way. If there's any fighting to be done, we'll do it, so long as you manage to get that carving back to Icham, Bryony and the others at Halfmoon Wood. Is that understood?'

Mawk nodded. 'Yes,' he said simply, putting the carving in his belt pouch.

That night, while Mawk and Scirf were asleep, a stranger entered their camp. Sylver was awake and alert and he challenged the outlander, asking her what she wanted. She told Sylver that she had been sent by Falshed to warn him that Magellan was lying in wait for him in a forest on the other side of the river.

'You're a polecat,' said Sylver suspiciously. 'Why would Falshed send you as a messenger? And why would the sheriff, my sworn enemy, want to warn me against the fox?'

'While Falshed hates you, and wishes to see you dead or captured, he wants to do it himself. He will get no advancement, no praise, from Prince Poynt, when it is Magellan who delivers your dead body up to the castle. He fears Magellan, whose power over the prince will increase if he manages to carry out the prince's wishes.'

'How did you find us? If *you* found us, why couldn't Falshed do the same?'

The polecat stared, then explained, 'I am friend of neither weasel nor stoat, and want no part in your civil war. I am, however, an enemy of Magellan, for who has not suffered because of that fox at one time or another? My family was wiped out in the terrible anarchy after the last king's death – they were killed by one of Magellan's mobs, with him at its head. I told Falshed I would find you myself, but I would not lead him to you. What is between you two must be settled by you yourselves.

'As to how I found you, why, I am the best tracker in all Welkin. Once I'd picked up your spoor just north of Halfmoon Wood, it was simply a matter of time before I found you. I'm no Sheriff Falshed.'

'I see. Well, I appreciate the warning. Have you any idea how Magellan plans to ambush me?'

The polecat shook her head. 'No. Since he waits in the forest I imagine it will be from behind a tree. Magellan is as much at home in the woods as you are yourself, weasel. Unlike our friend the sheriff, who likes four stone walls around him before he can fall asleep at night.'

Sylver nodded. 'You'd best be on your way, polecat – and I wouldn't mention this to anyone else. If Magellan gets to hear of it, your life will not be worth a groat.'

'A half-groat,' said the polecat, clicking her teeth.

Then she was gone into the darkness, only a

trace of her scent remaining behind to linger in the night airs.

Mawk woke suddenly. He sniffed. 'What? Who's that? I thought I heard voices. There's polecat on the breeze.'

'No-one,' said Sylver. 'You must have been dreaming – it was a dream – go back to sleep.'

'Oh, a dream,' murmured Mawk. 'Good night, Sylver.'

'Good night.'

Sylver sat, staring into the blackness across the river, wondering what his destiny was to be. Would he die tomorrow, just as Dredless had died, meeting his end at the paws of the infamous fox? Or would he somehow survive, slip through the trap which had been set for him? Should he go round the wood, avoid it altogether, or should he force a showdown, get it over and done with once and for all?

'It must be done sometime,' he told himself. 'Better tomorrow while I am alert, than some evening when I'm lying in my bed, not expecting any encounter.'

'Yes, tomorrow,' murmured Mawk-the-doubter, in his sleep. 'Good night, Sylver. Good night.'

Good night, thought Sylver, or perhaps, goodbye.

Chapter Thirty-seven

The carving having been entrusted to Mawk, the three weasels made their way back across the dyke. Their journey down through the rat hordes was as fraught as their passage up, but with the fortitude that weasels are apt to display they managed to slip past Flaggatis's swamp palace without incident. They sneaked around the rat camps, where the rats were idle and sluggish during the day, and finally to the river Bronn.

Just as they were approaching its banks, however, they were seen by a rat patrol, which let out a cry of alarm. '*Shtranggis, shtranggis!*' cried the rats, and set off in pursuit of the trio.

Mawk, Scirf and Sylver ran for their lives to the place where they had hidden the reed raft. The whole of the unnamed marshes were up in arms, rats calling to each other that 'strangers' were in the area. The rodents swarmed towards the river, each one of them well armed with crossed bandoleers of darts. So the air was as thick with missiles as the evening swamplands are with mosquitoes. The atmosphere hummed and buzzed with darts, which landed around the running weasels with nasty-sounding plops in water and mud.

'Quickly, quickly,' said Mawk. 'Let's get over

the river – those rats will slowly roast us over a camp fire.'

'Not until they've skinned you,' added a breathless Scirf cheerfully, 'with a blunt kitchen knife.'

This had the effect of adding a great deal of speed to Mawk's already swift retreat.

As they approached their hiding place the air was full of the sounds of screaming rats, all thirsty for the blood of the strangers. Once, Mawk looked back and almost swooned when he saw the savage faces coming up behind him.

The rats had painted their features with dye, circling the eyes, running bars down the nose and cheeks, so that their sharp-toothed mouths appeared more fierce than ever. They warbled with their tongues, setting up such a racket around the weasels it was enough to put a bear into a panic. There seemed to be thousands, *tens* of thousands of rats on the marshes. Mawk could smell their musty coats, hear them splashing through the murky, shallow waters. He was sure he was going to die.

'It was here,' he cried frantically, tearing away at the river bank. 'We left the raft here. Oh Gawd, it's gone. We're going to be killed.'

'Lucky if we do,' gasped Scirf, the dung-watcher not used to such exercise and out of breath. 'More like we'll be tortured until we *beg* to be killed.'

'Into the water,' snapped Sylver. 'Swim for it. Don't look back, Mawk. Just go.'

The three weasels slipped into the river. Mawk was yelling something about the dangers of pike, but the other two took no notice of him. Weasel-paddling, they made for the far bank, darts falling like rain around them. Scirf was hit in the shoulder and rump, but he quickly plucked out the darts, which had inflicted only flesh wounds. Sylver took one at the base of the tail, while Mawk escaped injury completely.

Several rats plunged into the river after the weasels, but when the three reached the far bank, they took out their slingshots. The tables were reversed now and the trio sent pebbles zipping over the water into the swimming rats, who decided almost as one to turn back. Dark bodies thrashed their way to the far shore, where their comrades were dancing wild dances and shouting terrible threats at the weasels.

'That was a close thing,' said Sylver, heaving a sigh. 'You have the carving, Mawk?'

'In my pouch,' Mawk replied, sucking in air.

'Good.'

After making sure the wound at the base of his tail was not deep, Sylver studied the scenery around them. They were outside a large dark forest, through which they would have to pass. This was the place where Magellan was waiting for him. He turned to Scirf and Mawk. 'How are your wounds, Scirf?'

'I'll survive,' muttered Scirf, inspecting the dart punctures. He was bleeding a little, but not badly. 'They didn't hit nothin' vital.'

'Right then, I want you two to remain here,' ordered Sylver, 'while I scout ahead.'

'What's in the forest? Wolves?' asked Scirf.

'Might be,' said Sylver. 'I'd just like to check it out first, before we continue south. You two rest up here, recover your strength. See if you can find something to eat. I'll be back before evening if I can.'

'Before *evening*?' said Mawk.

'Yes, this may take some time.'

Leaving the two weasels looking very puzzled, Sylver entered the forest. His heart was pounding fast, because he knew this was a final showdown between him and Magellan. The bounty hunter wanted his blood and Sylver was going to have to fight to survive. He wished it did not have to be so, but the fox had left him no choice in the matter.

Inside the mixed forest the trees were close together, with sunlight trickling through lacy layers of leaves to a floor covered in dead branches. There its mottled patterns shimmered in a lake of shadow and light. The going was soft underfoot. Within the tightly planted trees it was silent. This forest was no place for birds or animals, there being little cover or things to eat.

Sylver slipped from shadow to shadow, wondering where Magellan would confront him. The odds were almost all on the side of the fox, who merely had to wait and listen for his enemy coming. It was only when Magellan revealed himself that Sylver could attack.

There would probably be booby traps on the path, so Sylver stayed inside the trees. He would not have put it past Magellan to dig pits or make sprung willow catapults which could be triggered by tripping on a stretched cord. He stepped carefully, flowing over suspicious branches and roots as only long supple creatures like weasels can. His eyes were ever watchful, looking for the small sign which meant a fox was in the vicinity. Listening. Sniffing.

Every so often he would stop and try to gauge what was going on around him, if anything. He would just pause and stand there, in the way that animals do, opening all his senses, ready to take in warnings. It was during one of these pauses that he heard the sound.

There was a sharp *crack*, not loud, but unmistakable.

Sylver stayed where he was for the moment, still receptive to any change in the light or sound.

Hearing nothing further, he crept forward, ever so cautiously. He slipped in and out of bars of sunlight, like mist drifting through the dawn's first rays. No human, no matter how alert, would have seen or heard him. He used the grain of the tree bark, the shape of a root, the twists of light and darkness, as backgrounds to hide his approach.

Finally, he came to a spot where the redness of the earth and dead pine needles had an unusual hue.

He stared at this spot, staying perfectly still, for an enormously long time. Again, any human would have lost patience long ago and gone home to dinner. But being a weasel, and being Sylver, he remained. Gradually, he saw the shape of a fox emerge out of the background, even though Magellan was cleverly camouflaged. It had to be Magellan, rather than any other fox, for what would a vulpine creature be doing in a pine forest, simply waiting for something to come along?

Sylver congratulated himself. The fox had surely not seen him approach, or there would have been an attack. So, he had managed to creep up behind Magellan and had surprise on his side. The fox appeared to be watching the path, an arrow ready in his bow, which had only to be drawn and fired. It was true that Magellan was perfectly still, and silent, and his shape kept breaking up with the flickering of the sunlight through the pines, but Sylver was certain he had his enemy at a disadvantage.

What luck, he thought to himself. Either that or my skills as a hunter are better than his.

With infinite patience Sylver unravelled his slingshot, moving a fraction of a centimetre at a time. When the pebble was fitted in the sling's saddle he was ready. He hoped to be able to strike the fox on the temple and stun him long enough to tie him up. Then he could go back and get the other two and they could march Magellan back to Halfmoon Wood, and there decide what to do with the mercenary creature.

However, the distance was just a little too far. Sylver had to get closer if he was to be successful with his sling. A slow, creeping movement would not do now. Magellan would see him coming. He had to use the surprise, make a rush and then sling the stone before Magellan knew what was happening. Sylver prepared himself, then made his swift charge.

Sylver had not gone more than ten paces when he was suddenly jerked off his feet. He flew up in the air and hit the ground with a thump. The slingshot flew from his grasp. There was a searing ring of pain around his throat. His eyes bulged in agony and terror. His breathing was difficult, the air whistling in and out of his throat. All his strength had been torn from him.

He struggled feebly with his forepaws, to tear away the unwelcome collar around his neck, but the wire went too deep. Then his back legs kicked at the iron stake to which he was attached. He loosened it a little, but not enough. With every second he became weaker and less able to escape from the trap. Finally, he lay still, his burst of feverish energy gone.

He could do nothing more.

Magellan came sauntering over from his hiding place. Sylver could see the fox's smug visage through the red mist forming in front of his eyes. Magellan was triumphant. 'I saw you ages ago,' said the fox. 'I set the traps and this one worked perfectly.'

Sylver lay choking on the ground, unable to answer, every ounce of his strength sapped.

'A snare!' cried Magellan. 'Don't you think that was a brilliant stroke on my part? Humans used the snare very effectively. Some of them thought it cruel, but I think it makes a wonderful booby trap. You can't see it, hear it, or even smell it, then – *swack* – it's round your neck and your precious life is gradually choked from you.'

Sylver closed his eyes. The light was beginning to drain away around him. He could hear Magellan's voice as if it were coming from a bad dream.

'. . . such a clever plan,' bragged the fox. 'I thought of it last night. The trouble with you, Sylver, is that you're merely a weasel. You have only a small brain. Foxes are known to be cunning, devious creatures, and the reason they're able to be is because of their superior minds. We are smart animals, sharper than the average creature you find in Welkin, which is why I'm so successful at hunting down you rebels, you outlaws, you scum of Welkin's wild life.

'Now,' Magellan told the dying Sylver, 'I

haven't got enough time to wait until you pass away. I'm going to kill you quickly. Aren't you lucky? I still have to get those other two, you see, camping outside the forest, so I can't afford to indulge myself for too long. You are going to see some sharpshooting here, the like of which you've never seen before. It will be remarkable. However, as you see it, the arrow will pierce you, so you won't be able to appreciate it for long. Are you ready? I'll take it that you are.'

Magellan began to walk back towards a spot he had already decided upon, from whence he would fire the arrow.

Sylver felt the anger well up inside him. He was going to die and there was little he could do about it. Once a snare is embedded in an animal's fur around its neck, and that animal is lying limp and gasping for air, it is almost impossible for the creature to loosen the wire himself.

Impossible.

However, Sylver's rage at the boastful Magellan was so powerful he found himself getting to his feet. The blaze of his fury flared inside him, fuelling his strength. In his demented state, in his folly, Sylver attempted a hopeless act. He rushed at Magellan with his teeth bared.

Sylver wanted nothing more than to get a last bite at the despicable fox. He wanted to show Magellan that weasels did not simply lie down and die, anchored by a wire to an iron stake. He wanted to leave his mark on the creature.

On hearing his approach, Magellan turned in amazement. He stared as Sylver hurtled towards him. Then his face showed that he knew the wire would pull Sylver up short. Perhaps it would even break the weasel's neck. The fox just stood there and watched, an amused expression on his face.

Sylver's charge, however, was more powerful than both creatures had realized. Instead of jerking him up short, Sylver's rush actually wrenched the slim stake from the ground. His momentum catapulted the spike through the air, whipping it towards Magellan. The point pierced the fox like an iron arrow, burying itself deep in his breast.

With a look of utter surprise, Magellan staggered forward, attached to Sylver now by the wire snare.

In jerking the metal stake from the ground, Sylver had further tightened the noose around his neck. He lay there, numb, his senses slipping from him. Magellan staggered forward several paces, fell sideways, and lay on the earth, his nose almost touching that of the weasel. The two dying creatures remained there, staring into one another's eyes, hatred still burning in one, acceptance forming in the other.

'You . . . !' Magellan croaked.

It was the last word Sylver ever heard the fox utter, as the weasel drifted into that unconsciousness which heralds death.

Chapter Thirty-eight

Sylver felt the noose being loosened around his neck and a stick being painfully inserted down his throat. There followed a period when his head was spinning with strange dreams. His limbs seemed detached from his body. He knew he was barely alive, not dead, but it felt as if forces were tugging him both ways, each trying to wrest his spirit from him. Then came a time of peace, when his spirit settled back into his living form, and he gradually emerged into the light.

When he opened his eyes the first thing he saw were the pointed faces of Scirf and Mawk, peering down at him. Scirf clicked his teeth. Mawk stared with a worried expression. Sylver still felt giddy and it was some time before he was able to sit up.

He was still in the forest glade. He looked across at the spot where Magellan had last been standing. There was a lifeless russet shape on the ground. It might have been a pile of autumn leaves, ready to be blown away by the winter winds. Near by was a broken bow, a quiver with its arrows scattered.

Magellan was dead.

The iron stake still pierced the fox's breast. He lay there in the oak mast, the humus already beginning to cover him. The forest would gather him to itself, until Magellan would be part of it, fertilizing the trees, helping the grass to grow. All woodland creatures, good and bad, were eventually taken to the forest's dispassionate heart.

'We thought you was a goner,' said Scirf. 'We thought you was away with the angels.'

'I very nearly was,' croaked Sylver hoarsely, rubbing his throat. 'How – how did you find me?'

'We guessed you were going to some rendezvous or other,' said Mawk, 'so we followed your trail. We found you both – like this. Magellan was stone dead when we arrived. You were just about gasping your last.'

'You disobeyed me,' Sylver croaked.

'Yep, an' a good job we did, eh?' cried Scirf. 'Otherwise you'd be worm meat by now. We only just saved you. Your windpipe was crimped. I stuck a hollow straw down there, so you could breathe a bit. You're lucky to be alive, let alone complainin' about weasels disobeying you.'

'I suppose I am. Thank you, both of you.'

'Are you well enough to travel?' asked Mawk.

'I think so,' replied Sylver. 'Let me try.'

They helped him to his feet. Indeed, he still felt very dizzy, but Scirf supported him on one side, and Mawk on the other, and in this way they were able to proceed south towards County Elleswhere.

At night they camped by the running stream. Sylver ate a little grass and drank plenty of fresh water. By the morning he was feeling more refreshed and was able to walk on his own. He was necessarily slow, but that was not of any consequence, since they had achieved their goal in obtaining the clue. Sylver was happy to dawdle back to Halfmoon Wood.

Finally, they did reach their home. Bryony came

running from the trees to greet them. She spoke bashfully to Sylver, having a soft spot for him. It was always the way when he went on an expedition on his own. When he came back she felt a little shy in the newness of his company. He responded cheerfully and was a little shy himself when the other two mentioned he had almost died.

'What?' cried Bryony. 'Oh, no. . .'

'But I'm alive and well,' he said firmly. 'It's Magellan who's dead.'

'You fought a duel with Magellan,' said Bryony breathlessly, 'and you won?'

'Thanks to God and good fortune, yes – but not, I can assure you, due to my skill as a warrior.'

'Fiddlesticks,' cried Miniver, the finger-weasel, hearing this part of the conversation. 'You are Sylver, the greatest leader of any outlaw band that ever roamed Welkin.'

There were cheers as the others came running up, to add to the praises of Bryony and Miniver. Mawk found himself in the unusual role of hero, swallowing praise with relish. Scirf, too, did not go without being lauded by one and all.

'You may have fleas,' said Icham, 'but you're a stout-hearted weasel.'

'You leave my fleas alone,' Scirf said. 'They went into battle with me – not a single flea deserting in the face of the enemy – they deserve as much praise as I do.'

When the joyful reunion was done, and the stories told, the band all went to pay a visit on Lord Haukin. They had the clue to the whereabouts of the humans. They wanted Lord Haukin to tell them what it meant.

'Ah, how-do-they-call-you?' beamed Lord

Haukin, on seeing Sylver enter his library. 'Come to see my bottles?'

The old stoat was genuinely pleased to see Sylver safely returned to Halfmoon Wood, but it would have been beneath his dignity as a thane and noblestoat to show anything but mild, polite pleasure. He had to disguise the fact that he had been desperately waiting for news from Thunder Oak. Aristocrats have to maintain an air of indifference when dealing with animals of lower status than themselves. Even Lord Haukin was guilty of this rather snobbish behaviour.

'Yes, my lord,' said Sylver. 'I'd love to see your glass bottles, but I've also brought a little carving from Thunder Oak. I wondered if you might look at it?'

The others crowded into the library now, as Lord Haukin scrutinized the dormouse. Even Culver was interested, though he tried not to show it. Lord Haukin studied the piece for a short while, before telling them what he thought. 'It's not a difficult clue to unravel,' he said, 'which is not surprising since it was left by a child. The dormouse is on its own in a pool of water. The water represents the *sea* and the sleeping dormouse is an island. The humans have gone to a small island somewhere in the Cobalt Sea. There they have gone into hibernation, perhaps for ever.

'Wherever the humans are, then, they are surrounded by water and fast asleep.'

The outlaws listened in silence to Lord Haukin's explanation of their find. Then they all began talking at once.

'I think this is a significant discovery,' said Wodehed.

But Icham said, 'Is that all? We're no nearer to finding out where they are than we were before—'

'Oh, yes we are,' Miniver interrupted him. 'How many small islands are there in the Cobalt Sea?'

'Quite a few,' muttered Mawk. 'An awful lot.'

'Not that many, actually,' said Bryony. 'Only a few hundred.'

Sylver said, 'Look – we only got *one* of the clues. You can't expect to find out a great deal from just one clue. We probably need several more before we're even close. Isn't that so, Lord Haukin?'

'Yes, yes,' said the venerable thane. 'Several more – two more at the very least.'

Alysoun remarked, 'Well, we'll have a short holiday, won't we? Before we go looking for the second clue?'

'A *dance*!' cried Scirf. 'We got to have a dance, to celebrate.'

Now there is nothing that weasels like more than an excuse to dance.

That evening in Halfmoon Wood the strange piping music of the weasels filled the air. Other animals were drawn from their nests, from their drays, from their setts, from their forms, lairs and dens, from their dark midnight businesses of hunting and gathering. They came to the glade in the wood, from whence drifted the music, to watch from the fringes. No other creature, save perhaps the brown hare, is as deft at dancing as the weasel and the stoat. The squirrels are good at performing antics, but that is not true dancing, not rhythmic.

The strange reedy music flowed through the glade. Willowy forms quivered, swayed and gyrated in an eerie dance, as if they could hear the pulsing of the heart of the world, and were rippling to its beat. The firelight caught the weasel shapes, as they swirled around each other in ghostly undulating movement, the patterns both unearthly yet strangely familiar. Watching them awakened early primitive feelings in the spirits of the other woodland creatures: ancient blood rhythms, old forgotten songs, chants in an unremembered language.

Not one weasel touched another, as they wove in and out, drawing a figure passed on by racial memory from weasel to weasel, from deep ancestral roots, from the beginning of weasel time. Yet they swept by each other so closely as to make it difficult for a leaf to be passed between their snaking shapes.

The archaic tunes were catching. The watchers began to sway too, to hum, to trill and whistle. The moon began to shimmer, jostling the surrounding stars. Insects filled the moonlit glade like murmuring, glimmering jewels. Crickets played rasping rhythms on their back legs, and jumped and leapt between the dancers' paws. Frogs filled their throats with air and added their bass voices to the gathering choirs.

Even the trees rustled and quivered from their roots to the very tips of their tops.

A weasel dance is a very special event – even the haughty Culver came to take part.

'Magellan is dead, my prince,' reported Sheriff Falshed. 'Killed by an iron stake through the heart.'

Prince Poynt shivered and moved closer to the fire, endangering his precious white ermine fur.

'Was it Sylver who killed him?'

'We believe so, my prince. They met in single combat in a dark forest. We found the fox's corpse, but there was nothing to be seen of the weasel.'

Prince Poynt did not take his moody eyes from the flames. He stared for a long time without answering. Finally he spoke in a very quiet and steady tone. 'Just so, Falshed. Just so. You may leave me now.'

'Yes, my prince. Any further orders? It is your birthday tomorrow. Do you wish for celebrations? Shall I rouse the castle thanes, the noblestoats, to a gathering in the gardens, on the lawns?'

The prince glanced at the nearest arrowloop window. 'I think not, Falshed. It is raining. Besides' – the prince let out a heavy sigh – 'my birth time is also my brother's birth time, give or take a few seconds. Bad memories pursue me on such days. I think we'll forget the celebrations this year.'

'Yes, my prince. Good night.'
'Good night, Falshed.'

THE END

ABOUT THE AUTHOR

Garry Kilworth was born in York but, as the son of an Air Force family, was educated at more than twenty schools. He himself joined the RAF at the age of fifteen and was stationed all over the world, from Singapore to Cyprus, before leaving to continue his education and begin a career in business, which also enabled him to travel widely.

He became a full-time writer when his two children left home and has written many novels for both adults and younger readers – mostly on science fiction, fantasy and historical themes. He has won several awards for his work, including the World Fantasy Award in 1992, and the Lancashire Book Award in 1995 for *The Electric Kid*.

His previous titles for Transworld Publishers include *The Electric Kid* and *Cybercats* for the Bantam Action list; and *House of Tribes* and *A Midsummer's Nightmare* for Bantam Press / Corgi Books. *Thunder Oak* is the first title in a trilogy; two further titles, *Castle Storm* and *Windjammer Run* are also published by Corgi Books.

Garry Kilworth lives in a country cottage in Essex which has a large woodland garden teeming with wildlife, including foxes, doves, squirrels and grass snakes.

THE WELKIN WEASELS
Book 2: Castle Storm

by Garry Kilworth

Rats! Hundreds and thousands of rats are pouring down from the northern marshes in Welkin to seize power from the stoat rulers. Sylver – the leader of a band of outlaw weasels – has no love for the vicious stoats but, with Welkin itself under threat, must offer a helping paw.

But stoat treachery serves only to speed him on his real quest: to find the humans who mysteriously abandoned Welkin many years ago. With his small company of jacks and jills, he journeys south, through myriad adventures, to the dreys of the squirrel knights who live beneath the shadow of an ancient castle – *Castle Storm*.

The second title in a dramatic and marvellously inventive trilogy, *The Welkin Weasels*.

ISBN 0 552 54547 3